Herbert Kastle was born and brought up in Brooklyn. He has been an English teacher, an editor, and an advertising copywriter, but he now devotes all his time to writing. Mr Kastle is the author of many successful novels including *The Movie Maker*, *Cross-Country*, *Hit Squad*, *Dirty Movies* and *Sunset People*.

By the same author

HERBERT KASTLE

David's War

WILDSIDE PRESS

David's War

Published by Wildside Press LLC
www.wildsidepress.com

*In memory of my mother and father.
Eva and Meyer Kastle*

'While I was musing,
The fire burned.'
*Old Testament
Psalms*

'*Dum tacent, clamant.*'
(Though silent, they cry aloud.)
Cemetery Monument Inscription

PROLOGUE: *Wednesday, 12 December, p.m.*

It was eight o'clock, dark and wet, and people were just beginning to emerge from shelter after the sudden rainstorm. The truck came down Fairfax Avenue, street of kosher butchers, restaurants, delicatessens; spinal column of Los Angeles' one true Jewish neighbourhood, the California equivalent of Brooklyn's old Pitkin Avenue and Manhattan's Delancey Street.

It was an open flat-bed truck with waist-high wooden slat sides, and two men stood in the back, in what was now a fine drizzle, scattering leaflets into the street. It moved slowly, music blaring from somewhere under the frame – 'God Bless America', Kate Smith's recording.

At first the still-sparse flow of pedestrians paid it no attention; then there were shouts and three young men burst from a doorway where they'd sought shelter. They were raging, pointing at the truck, and it was then that other people realized Fairfax Avenue was being desecrated. It was then they saw the large swastika banners hanging on the slat sides; realized the men in back were ski-masked, uniformed Nazis with swastika armbands. And when one old woman picked up a leaflet, she turned white with shock at the blatant message of hatred aimed at Fairfax and its people.

The three young men chasing the truck were also part of an organization, though their only items of uniform were black berets. One managed a gasped 'Never again!'; then they were running too hard for slogans.

The fastest, a wiry youth, reached for the open end of the truck. Before he could grasp the edge, he was struck across the shoulders with a bat wielded by the larger of two very large masked Nazis. The way he went down, in an agonized heap, indicated there was more than wood in the end of that bat.

The other two pursuers split up, each taking a different side of the slow-moving truck, sprinting to get to the cab and the driver.

As Kate Smith's powerful soprano sang *Stand beside her, and guide her*, the huge Nazi with the bat leapt to the street, running around to the left, chasing the short youth coming up on the driver. The short youth began to turn, but didn't make it. The bat described a clean up and over arc, striking the black beret dead centre. There was a splatting sound, a melon-bursting-on-pavement sound, and the youth crumpled straight down, his legs no longer motivated by brain impulses.

Meantime, the third youth had managed to grasp the door-handle on the other side of the cab, the passenger's side. He was a muscular, thick-bodied man and his round face lighted with savage delight as he prepared to enter the cab and get at the uniformed Nazi behind the wheel. But the truck suddenly swerved, first towards him, jamming his arm, face and shoulder against the metal door, then violently away, breaking his grip and sending him sprawling in the wet gutter.

The youth struggled to his feet, in time to face the huge Nazi coming past the receding back of the truck, bat already swinging. The youth managed to twist aside, catching only a glancing blow on the right arm. Still, he went to his knees, and the bat came up for the finishing blow.

The truck skidded to a stop, its lights and music going off. There was a shout from the cab. The huge Nazi aborted his swing, ran to the truck and leapt in beside the driver. Before he could close the door, the truck jerked forward, tyres spinning and screeching on the wet pavement. The Nazi in the back held to the slat siding with one hand and flung a bound packet of leaflets at someone on the sidewalk, shouting, 'Jew bastards!' An old man fell and a woman screamed, *'Hitler leibt!'* Hitler lives! The truck was speeding now, swinging around cars. It turned off Fairfax and was gone, leaving four men prostrate. Leaving others stunned, outraged, humiliated, fearful.

Leaving one man determined to wage war.

This was the catalyst for that one man, but not quite the beginning. The beginning could be said to have taken place in 1943 . . . or just two days ago.

ONE: *Monday, 10 December*

The dream was remarkably constant all these years, varying only in length. Sometimes it ended with the woman and child walking away from him, the train rocking through the Pennsylvania countryside, the smell of coal-ash strong in his nostrils, the boy staring back with big eyes at the 'Filthy Jew'.

Sometimes it went on, beyond the true reflection of reality, to the satisfaction he had wanted since 1943, and he followed and caught the hateful young woman between cars and threw her shrieking to her death. In this version the boy had usually disappeared, but not always.

Tonight the boy was there, and the problem of what to do when he screamed his mother's racial epithet, and turned to run and tell, brought David to an excruciating dilemma.

He had never dreamed the boy to a conclusion. He had *begun* to conclude, most often speaking of brotherhood, then realizing it was impossible since he had murdered the mother before the child's eyes . . . at which point he would awaken.

A few times, just a handful over the years, he had begun to throw the seven- or eight-year-old after his mother. And awakened, horrified.

As he awoke now, sitting bolt upright in bed, choking on his own voice: '*Wait!*'

He was shaking.

That woman had been a good Pennsylvania German

parent; the boy had been pink-cheeked and well dressed, and smiling before her voice turned hard and she pointed to the thin, uniformed, eighteen-year-old David as they passed his seat and stunned him by saying, ". . . like that filthy Jew there.' She had gone on, pulling her child to the next car as David sat frozen, as he then looked around to see if anyone else had heard or noticed, as his heart flared with rage as much at her daring to guess at his race that way (because she couldn't *know*, could she?) as at what she had said.

He had considered following and confronting her, but had done nothing because two stops away was Reading and the Army Air Corps pre flight training school at Albright College, and he'd wanted a clean record in order to become a bomber pilot and drop fire and death on Germany. So he had allowed the woman and her child to remain unexorcized, to drift into the memory banks, the recesses of his brain, and fester there.

He sighed, losing the sense of immediacy and pain. It was growing light. He had an early meeting – that dragged-out Canadian deal. He got up and walked to the bathroom and turned on the wall heater, then the shower.

He scrubbed his body, thickening around the middle, especially since he had given up the sit-ups and winter swimming. He washed his dark hair, thinning gradually in front and more perceptibly at the crown.

Vanessa had suggested a gym and transplants. He had considered it because he had wanted to please Vanessa. That was a year ago, and he was no longer sure he wanted to please her.

He was beginning to fail sexually with her, that Ten, that epitome of sexuality – which should have frightened him, and didn't. *That* frightened him, and he had begun reading the personal columns of the *New York Review*, checking ads that had West Coast or Los Angeles in the text, telling himself it was more or less a joke because who could take those pathetic paragraphs seriously?

'L.A. slim mature lady with Masters in Lit. desires intellectual non-smoking male for enrichment of both life styles . . .' He had answered that one before feeling pathetic himself.

When he came into the kitchen, Mrs Gomez had arrived and was making one of her great cheese and tomato omelettes. So he would cut back on lunch.

A half-hour later he was in his office, reading the *L.A. Times*. And was reminded of his dream by a sudden pounding in chest and temples. Page four held a story about American Nazis in California, and included a picture of six men in uniform giving the stiff-armed Nazi salute to a swastika flag. This small group, the caption said, was in San Francisco. Another even smaller group was located near Vargas, and a family-sized group was in the tiny farming community of Bethills in the San Joaquin Valley. Bethills, the text stated, was approximatley six hours by automobile from Los Angeles.

Storm-troopers, swastikas and *Heil Hitlers* six hours from David Howars.

He closed the paper and stood up from his desk.

His secretary Carrie came in just then, but hesitated before speaking. Because Mr Howars looked strangely different.

Trying to think of what it was, Carrie had the feeling that he had grown larger somehow, had been flexing his muscles . . . like Bruce Lee getting ready to chop down an opponent. Or maybe like Arnold Schwartzenegger in *Pumping Iron*, straining to lift hundreds of pounds.

That made her smile. Mr Howars with his conservative suits, shirts and ties from Mr Guy on Rodeo Drive, his greying hair and soft voice, his kind, fatherly face and gentle personality, breaking heads or straining to lift hundreds of pounds? Not likely!

Besides, he seemed normal again.

She told him that Mr Jitzler and the three men he called 'the Canadians' were here.

Jitzler was Swiss, old and fat, but he had the quickest pinch this side of Rome and she had learned never to turn her back on him. She had even complained to Mr Howars, who'd said, 'Slap him . . . after we make the deal. He's guaranteeing foreign distribution.'

She sent them in. Jitzler said, 'Call me Johan, darl-*inggg*. I could do wonders for you!'

Maybe five minutes later Carrie heard shouting in Mr Howars's office. She couldn't believe it – had heard nothing like it in her two years here. The door flew open and Jitzler came out, fast. He was so red in the face, he was almost purple. Carrie gasped as she saw that it was Mr Howars who was shoving him out with a hand at the back of his neck and another at the seat of his pants.

'. . . mine lawyer!' Jitzler was shouting.

'Fine,' Mr Howars said, panting, white-faced, and *threw* him toward the hall door. Jitzler bounced against the door, got it open and ran out, still shouting about 'mine' lawyer and bringing suit.

Carrie stared at Mr Howars, wondering at his being strong enough to handle a blimp like Jitzler so easily. He looked bigger again, as he had beside his desk. And then he didn't. Then he rubbed his face, which was oily, and said, 'I'm sorry,' to no one in particular. And walked out.

When one of the Canadians, a tall, thin man named Bevins, came to the doorway, she said, 'Mr Howars had to see someone down the hall for a moment.'

'Incredible,' Bevins muttered. 'Jitzler's a boor, yes, but still an incredible reaction.'

She had caught him looking her over a few times when Jitzler had been making passes, knew he was shy and uncertain with women, and so was emboldened to ask, 'Just what happened?'

'Jitzler told a joke. How do you get twenty Jews into a Volkswagon?'

She said she didn't know.

'Four in the seats and sixteen in the ashtray.'

11

She frowned. She didn't get it. 'I've got a Volkswagon,' she said.

'You're too young. And not Jewish. The Nazi ovens . . .'

'Oh,' she said, and began to smile; then heard footsteps in the hall and put a finger to her lips. Bevins disappeared back into the office.

Mr Howars came in, looking embarrassed. He went into his office, head down, and closed the door. She wondered if he had blown the deal on *Coast to Coast*, the movie based on the novel he had under option. She hoped not. She planned to ask for a small part – that girl in the motel, maybe. She had been attending Estelle Harmon's school of acting and felt she could handle it.

At seven that evening, after eating far more of the chicken and rice dinner Mrs Gomez had prepared than he should have, David went to the study where the housekeeper left his mail. He put on his glasses. Three letters lay on the desk. One was from home, as he still thought of the big old apartment on lower Park Avenue, just south of the Pan Am Building. Arlene continued to live there with their son, Mark, because New York's rent control law made it not only affordable but the best deal she could find by far.

The second envelope held an advertisement pitching high-priced hair-pieces.

The last envelope had a name and return address unfamiliar to him: Miss Rita Goran in Santa Monica. It was hand-written, or rather printed, in small, very neat letters in deep blue ink. Inside, the hand-printing continued on a book-folded sheet of fine, off-white linen stationery with the letter G embossed at the top. There was a faint scent of perfume, very faint, as if passed on by chance from Miss Goran's fingertips.

He re-examined the thick envelope and matching sheet of stationery. 'Nice,' he said conversationally. 'Some actress has a good background, or is studying it.'

He heard his voice. It didn't bother him. He'd been

talking to himself for quite a while now; generally evenings, as he grew tired; sometimes in the car. He watched himself in the office.

He sat down in the swivel chair, tilted the goose-neck lamp, and read:

Dear Mr Howars

Thank you for answering my advertisement in the New York Review so promptly and courteously. I apologize for being less prompt, and plead an attack of embarrassment. You did not give a phone number. I suppose it is up to the initiator of the project to do that, so you will find mine at the bottom of this letter.

While your note was terse, it was the only one among the four answers I received that seemed honest, that did not suggest a headlong gallop toward intimacies, that did not make me wince at gaucheries and excesses. So even if we go no further, I thank you for that.

Sincerely,
Rita Goran

The signature was thin, spidery, far less attractive than the printing, and perhaps explained the printing. But on the evidence of her letter, he felt he would like Miss Goran.

He read the phone number and glanced at his watch. Eight thirty. A good time to call.

He decided to read his ex-wife's letter first; then felt he was avoiding that call, was afraid of that call, he who dealt with beautiful women every working day.

'That's just it,' he said. 'She may not be beautiful. She may be older than "mature" implies. She may be worn and lost and pitiful. What will you do then? How will you get through your date without hurting her?'

And even that wasn't it, wasn't the bottom line.

'What if she finds *you* worn and pitiful?'

He opened Arlene's letter. Mark was doing well at Columbia after a rather shaky freshman year.

Arlene's wealthy older brother was suffering from high blood pressure caused, he claimed, by the approach of the tax season. Her younger brother was considering divorce . . .

He put aside the letter, lifted the phone and dialled, his palms sweating.

The woman's voice was high and tremulous. For a moment he thought it an aged voice. 'Hello?' When he didn't answer, she said, 'Now who *is* this?' crisply, losing the old-woman tremor.

'David Howars, Miss Goran. In reply to your letter.'

It was her turn to be silent.

'The *New York Review*, you know?'

'Yes, of course. I was . . . taken aback.'

'You gave me the number. Didn't you expect my call?'

'I . . . I find myself surprised at everything that happens in relation to that foolish ad.'

He chuckled. 'I've forgotten which ad was yours. Was it "Slim mature lady with masters . . ."?'

'Please don't repeat it! I wrote it as quickly as I could. The slim . . . that's a Freudian response of some sort. I *am* slim, or relatively slim, now, but I wasn't always. So I tend to overemphasize the quality. As for the rest . . . I based it on what the other ads said. Silly, wasn't it?' She laughed painfully.

'Good enough to get me to answer.'

'I didn't mean to link you to the silliness . . .'

'Look, Miss Goran, would you like to have lunch?'

'Lunch is a fine idea. Lunch doesn't commit us . . .'

'Tomorrow?'

'I can't on a weekday. I teach elementary school.' She paused. 'Aren't you available on weekends?'

Which was a way of asking if he was married. 'Saturday or Sunday?' he asked.

'Saturday.' And then, 'We could meet half-way. From your zip code, I gather you're in the Hollywood Hills or thereabouts. It's a long drive to the shore.'

Which could have been consideration, or fear that he would end up in her apartment making a 'headlong gallop toward intimacies'.

'Whatever you'd like. But as long as you're willing to

14

drive in . . . Scandia, Ma Maison, Bistro Gardens, the Polo Lounge, just about all the fine restaurants are in my area. Pick one and we'll meet there.'

'I've never been to the Polo Lounge. It's in the Beverly Hills Hotel, isn't it?'

'Yes. Saturday noon, the Polo Lounge.'

'I didn't expect to be so royally treated . . . David!'

'That's all right, Rita.' The excitement in her voice was the reason he had offered the well-known restaurants. She would see the way he dressed, the way the captains and waiters recognized and treated him; would learn his occupation, his position; would see the car he drove and the house in which he lived, if it went that far. So that there would be no chance of her finding *him* worn and pitiful.

'Could I have your telephone number, David? In case I have to cancel at the last minute?'

'Home or office?' he asked, thinking she was still questioning his marital status. He supposed married men answered those ads often enough.

'Well . . . home, unless you're at the office on Saturdays.'

He gave it to her.

She said, 'Thank you! I'm looking forward to meeting you!'

He said, 'The same here,' and, 'Goodbye.'

He was no longer nervous . . . until he considered what could happen if Miss Goran turned out to be less frightened and shy than she seemed, and herself made 'a headlong gallop toward intimacies'.

Then again, that was one of the reasons he had read the *New York Review* personals – wanting to try an intellectual, non-showbiz woman in a complete relationship.

It was time to shower, then relax with one of the novels he read in his continuing search for movie properties. After which he would watch the late news and go to sleep.

Dreamless sleep, he hoped.

15

Rita Goran also had occasional nightmares. They concerned William Goran, her late husband, and he would be beating her, as he had in real life, though real life was twelve years in the past.

An over-reaction, she felt, the dreams being far worse than the actual beatings.

Even labelling them 'beatings' was an over-reaction, an exaggeration. Only that once, during the February blizzard, when she had suggested he sell the business before it ruined them, had he done more than shout obscenities and slap her a few times. During the blizzard he had 'experienced a breakdown', as he termed it. He had punched her in the face with his fist, three times, so that she'd had to call Dr Giles. Giles rather than their regular doctor for two reasons: he was within walking distance that stormy winter's day, and he didn't know many of the people she and Will knew.

She was ashamed, terribly, that Rita Goran who had been brought up in a loving home, who had received a fine Hunter College education, who had thought she knew the man she had married, should have cuts and bruises and broken teeth.

Will had been *so* contrite, so sorry afterwards, weeping, kissing her hand, pleading for her forgiveness. Of course she forgave him, and of course she understood the terrible pressure under which he had been living since Goran's Electrical Supply Depot had begun failing.

But he had continued to throw good money after bad, as Daddy used to say, some of it money Daddy had left her and which she had put aside for his grandson's education. Her only child, Roger, who to this day couldn't believe his father had actually done what he had seen on his mother's face. Roger, who nevertheless suspected his mother in his father's death.

The inheritance, as she called Daddy's money, was in her name and couldn't be withdrawn without her signature. Will had talked and talked, mostly at night in bed, wheedling it out of her a thousand or two at a

16

time (and, yes, *frightening* it out of her by clenching his fists as he talked, by bending his face over hers, eyes bulging, neck muscles protruding, coming close to another 'breakdown') until nine thousand was gone and only eleven thousand remained of what was to send her brilliant son through medical school.

It was spring, a fragrant afternoon in May, and such days were magnificent in New York's Hudson Valley; such days had helped Will convince her to move, from her beloved Manhattan with all its cultural advantages, sixty miles north to the outskirts of Fishkill. At three o'clock he came home in a frenzy and said she had to give him the entire eleven thousand 'or the business is lost'.

She said she would put a second mortgage on their jointly owned home before robbing their son. He laughed wildly, clenching his fists (and she watched those fists, fighting the fear, the need to give him whatever he asked for). He said he had already put a second on the house, forging her signature on the bank papers; said he would forge her signature on a withdrawal slip the next morning if she didn't 'come to her senses and save the business'.

'The business is beyond saving,' she said. 'I spoke to Mr Lowell at the bank . . .'

He slapped her, swiftly, before she could see it coming. He slapped her again, and though she anticipated this second slap she didn't move, held by the strange lethargy his violence produced in her.

He pushed his face into hers, whispering, 'If you make trouble, I'll kill us both, I swear it. That business is my life. My *life*, understand, you stupid, selfish bitch?'

He would apologize later. He would cry and kiss her hand. But right now he was clenching his fists, and she said, 'Yes, all right. In the morning we'll save the business.' When she knew the business was finished. When she knew he was a weakling unable to face a new start.

17

When she knew she hated him for what he was doing to their son; and even more for what he was doing to her.

She made dinner. Roger came home and they ate together and he went to his room to study, her brilliant son who, all the teachers said, was destined for medicine.

He had changed after his father's death. He had lowered his goals, his dreams. He'd become an instructor in the New York State college system. He was now an associate professor . . . but what he *could* have been!

She hadn't seen him since coming to California three years ago. She never heard from him unless she phoned. And those calls had become too unpleasant because of his long silences.

Just before she had flown from Kennedy Airport to Los Angeles, he had asked her, 'Did you kill my father?'

She had laughed shrilly and burst into tears. He had muttered an apology, saying it was a 'paranoid delusion' of his. At the last moment, boarding pass in hand, she had kissed him, clung to him, feeling she would never see him again; that she didn't deserve to see him again. Because the answer to his question was yes, she had killed his father.

That beautiful spring day of the slapping, that mild May evening and later, during the cool black-morning hours, she had searched desperately for a way to avoid handing over her son's inheritance. And there was no way, unless she went to the police. Even that might not do any good because Will wouldn't let her out of his sight until *after* they went to the bank and she gave him the money and he took it from the cashier's window to the loan department, so that he would have a few more months in which to lose everything.

Would she get the eleven thousand back if she went to the police *after* he made the loan payment?

Could she go to the police; tolerate the shame of accusing her own husband of forcing her to hand over money?

Would anyone believe her after all the years of model marriage?

She didn't know what she was going to do until she did it. He was in the shower. She was at the sink, staring at her face with the little white scar at the left eye, at her mouth with the new caps on the front uppers. She saw the back of the counter-top heater reflected in the full wall mirror. She wondered if it could shock him into unconsciousness and so give her time to talk to the police.

She didn't allow herself to think it could kill him.

She went to the bedroom and found the extension cord in the dresser. She returned and plugged in the heater, and now it reached the shower tub. She hoped he had the water running full blast, because then it would form two or three inches at the bottom of the tub, coming up over his ankles, the sluggish drain needing replacement, not Draino. She pulled the curtain aside at the back end, just a little, and remembered at the last moment to throw on the heater's switch. There was a soft whirring sound as the fan started. He must have heard it over the shower's hissing because he began to turn.

She dropped the heater, coils downward, into the few inches of water. There was a sizzling sound, a little flash, and he screamed and fell backward. He hit his head with a fleshy thump on the tub's rim, and almost immediately began to bleed from the mouth and nose. The bathroom lights had gone out and the heater had stopped sizzling in the water, lying half under his left arm.

She wanted to run, but forced herself to disconnect the extension cord and take the heater out of the tub. She put the heater back on the counter and the extension cord back in the drawer, drying both with a towel. She went downstairs where the remains of Roger's breakfast were on the table. She went into the little service area where the washer and dryer stood, and opened the circuit-breaker box. She found the lever Will

19

had sticker-marked *Bth*. It was tripped. She reset it, and when she walked upstairs, the bathroom lights were on and the heater was working away with just a little sizzling. She waited until it stopped sizzling and turned it off.

She went downstairs and had coffee and a cold piece of toast Roger had left on his plate. She cleaned up the kitchen and swallowed two aspirins for the very nasty headache that had crept in behind her eyes. Then she returned to the bathroom and took a good look at her husband. He was a big, fleshy man and now he seemed enormous, filling the tub. He lay with one leg twisted under him, the other straight out, his eyes wide open, his lips slightly parted, looking very naked and very surprised. She couldn't be certain, but she felt he was dead – his penis had never been *that* shrunken before.

She walked slowly to the bedroom and lifted the phone. By the time she reached Dr Levin, she was hysterical, begging for help. The hysteria was real, as she feared they would find signs of the electrocution – but they didn't.

Dr Levin later explained that Will could have died of two separate causes. 'He either had a heart attack and fell backward, striking his head and dying of a subdural haematoma caused by a depressed fracture of the skull. Or he slipped in the tub and fell, striking his head, and died of a resultant myocardial infarction – heart attack – brought on by shock. *Or* he died of more or less equal portions of both. If it's any consolation, he couldn't have had more than a few seconds of pain.'

In bed Monday night, a few hours after having spoken to David Howars, she asked herself how she could have been so wrong about Will; how she could have loved him; how she could have married him. Which, with variations, were questions she'd asked herself about several men since Will.

Time was running out. She was almost fifty. She prayed she wasn't wrong about David Howars.

TWO: *Tuesday, 11 December*

Carrie smiled broadly when Mr Howars' girlfriend, Vanessa Brooks, walked into the office.

Vanessa said, 'Hey, howya doing?' and complimented Carrie on her new nail polish and her bulky sweater. They talked cosmetics and clothes for a while, Vanessa rapping just like a schoolgirl with her 'swell' and 'you're putting me on!', but Carrie knew how *smooth* she could talk when she wanted to, how well she did lines of all kinds in movies and TV shows.

Carrie really dug Vanessa, who was a knock-out for an older woman – over thirty – and wore the greatest clothes, like the pale brown, tweedy skirt-suit she was wearing now with pink-striped, man-style shirt and slouchy-brimmed, dark brown hat. Her shoes were always spikes (snakeskin today) and helped her look real tall, as did her long legs, though she was only five five, she'd confessed. She had reddish-brown hair, naturally curly, which Carrie admired. She had a wasp waist, which Carrie *envied*, and which made her breasts look even bigger than they were. She had great posture, a great walk, and Mr Howars's black friend Teddy, bartender at Thomasine's, said she could be elected the Girl Most Men Want To Walk Behind.

She was also a good actress with a hot career. Carrie would settle for where Vanessa was at, professionally, when she reached her thirties. And while Mr Howars was no John Travolta, Carrie might consider settling for where Vanessa was at romantically, too, because, if you

21

could forget his age, Mr Howars wasn't bad in the looks department. And he was loaded in the bread department. Most important of all was what he could do for an actress he dated.

He must have done plenty for Vanessa, at least before she got rolling. Now she was independent of any man's help; she'd been in two TV shows this year that Carrie knew of. She was bound to land a continuing part, a lead part, in a new series sooner or later.

'Where's your Christmas tree?' Vanessa asked, looking around the office. 'It's the eleventh. You should have one up and decorated by now. What will Mr Howars's clients think?'

'I asked him and he said he'd order one. That was a week ago. He must've forgotten.'

'I'll remind him. Tell him I'm here, will you?'

Carrie said, 'Sure thing,' and lifted the phone.

Vanessa always spent a few minutes with Dave's secretary, a nice kid with ideas of getting into acting. But Carrie didn't have a clue as to where it was at. Of course she could learn, just as Vanessa had. Learn to use the looks God had given her . . . or God and the plastic surgeon. Learn to act by going to a good school; Vanessa had suggested Estelle Harmon's.

But first, Carrie had to learn to walk the tightrope between poverty and prostitution that most women serious about acting knew instinctively. Working as a secretary for two years here was death on an acting career. Eight hours a day, five days a week? How could she find the time necessary to hound the agents, the casting directors, the producers and directors and men who backed the films? How could she find time to go to the parties where these people gathered; to display herself and pitch and scramble and claw for whatever advantage might offer itself? How could she go on the time-consuming and nearly hopeless cattle calls where dozens of women gathered for one or two jobs; to whatever auditions the trade papers listed; to wherever the possibility of employment might be? How could she spend as much time with a man who had the power to employ her, or get her employed, as it took? To do whatever she thought necessary to reach the single most important goal of her life – the chance to use the skills she'd developed, the spark she just might have been born with?

Carrie put down the phone. 'He's on a long distance call. He'll buzz when he's off.'

Vanessa nodded, and Carrie looked at her as if something were wrong. Vanessa said, 'What is it, hon?'

'Uh . . . is Mr Howars okay? I mean, is he feeling all right?'

Vanessa played a little game with these secretaries. In all the offices she visited, and Dave's was no exception, she cultivated friendships, invested a little time, and the pay-off was having a sympathetic – at least, not an antagonistic – contact and source of information.

Now she used her relationship with Carrie to draw her out. And with sinking heart heard the story of Dave manhandling Johan Jitzler because of a stupid joke. Jitzler was, as Dave himself had said, critical to the packaging of his latest film, *Coast to Coast*, and Vanessa had a stake in that film. Dave said she stood a good chance of landing the main supporting role of the worn-out go-go dancer. Vanessa thought the part had been written for her – maybe at Dave's directions to the scriptwriter – though she hadn't asked for favours for several years.

Not that she didn't need favours. Kids like Carrie thought she had it made because they'd seen her on the tube doing the female lead in a 'Quincy' and a guest-star role in a 'Mash'. But that was over a period of nine months and there'd been nothing but promises, promises otherwise. She'd never earned more than ten thousand at her acting in any one year, which was where walking that tightrope between poverty and prostitution came in; Dave's picking up the big repair bill on her ageing Jaguar, for example.

23

She listened to Carrie express amazement that Dave could have become violent. She agreed it was 'unbelievable' . . . but it wasn't. Dave had been having bad moments lately – bursts of temper, and more importantly to their relationship, a lack of desire. He'd been a bull for six years, and now he was fading fast.

She said, 'He's just a little overworked. Doctor Brooks will give him some of her special medication.' They giggled together, and the phone buzzed.

Carrie said, 'You can go in now.'

Vanessa opened the door. 'Dave bunny! Three interminable days and nights apart!' She came to the desk, smiling. The smile was natural, unplanned, sprang from the true affection she felt for this protective lover, this helpful friend, this good man whom she trusted beyond any man she had ever known. She glanced playfully at his black leather couch. 'Is it illegal for the *woman* to use the casting couch?'

He smiled, but it wasn't convincing. 'I'm starving. Let's not go home. Let's go right across the street to Thomasine's.'

She said, 'Of course, I wouldn't want you suffering from malnutrition,' but now she was forcing the lines and the smile. Because home was where the bed was. 'We can get together tonight, can't we?'

When he hesitated, she turned away, waving an arm. *'No importante, querida.* Some other time.' Force-feeding a man your love was disaster.

He cleared his throat in a nervous way. 'Maybe we need a few weeks' vacation from each other. Maybe until after New Year's.'

She said, 'We might as well be married,' laughed heartily, and walked out the door. She felt like a fool for feeling like crying.

In David's opinion, Thomasine's was a mediocre restaurant with a great bar. What made the bar great was his old friend Teddy Bear, actually Teddy Brown. Teddy was in the tradition of the mythic film bartender who dispensed alcohol and wisdom at the same time. Teddy also dispensed charm to the ladies and landed a goodly percentage of them.

A black Adonis, he called himself, except that he was sixty-one and no Harry Belafonte. His upper front teeth, lost while protecting a dancer from a drunk when he'd tended bar in a nude club, came out for 'cleaning, spare-rib gummin', and cunnilingus.' He seemed short at five eight because of a strong, stocky build, was just a shade off deep black in complexion, and had receding bushy hair and an evil-looking, drooping, Fu Manchu moustache.

He had told David that his father and brothers were 'still in the pimping trade, back home.' In his cups, he'd also said that his mother had been 'the best little whore who ever rolled a redneck hot for black ass.' She'd died in her late forties 'in bed with a teenaged black dude. The doctor said heart attack. The black dude said too many orgasms.'

The restaurant named for her belonged to Teddy and a silent partner, who David guessed was Mafia. Teddy simply said the purchase price had been offered for favours owed him, which he'd finally called in after the beating in the nude club convinced him he was 'too old to be independent'.

Teddy didn't work his daily shift at the bar just for the money; his cut of the successful restaurant's profits was considerable. His reasons were mainly social and psychological. 'All those white chicks wanting to try what Momma and Poppa would *die* if they knew baby had tried. All those chicks itching for the most forbid-den of all fruit. Which is why I score more with cracker chicks than with the Easterners and hip native locals. Gives hope for the world, don't it?' And there would sound a very evil cackle of laughter.

It sounded now as David helped Vanessa onto a bar stool and seated himself between her and a very heavy woman who had raised her enormous rump to lean over the bar and whisper in Teddy's ear.

25

'Well, maybe,' Teddy said, rocking back on his alligator-boot heels, cackling again. His establishment may have been in the Valley, but it was among Studio City's best, drew a large showbiz clientele, and matched anything in the Basin for style and decor . . . as did Teddy himself. Like David, he wore Beverly Hills' finest, but from hipper shops like Dernier Cri and Le Fancy Pants. (The Lebanese woman who owned Le Fancy Pants was addicted to cocaine and Teddy Bear, and gave him whatever he wanted.) Even behind the bar, as befit a top-grade *restaurateur*, Teddy wore the best: an exquisitely tailored double-breasted black jacket, pleated grey trousers, pale grey silk shirt and matching handkerchief, and those five-hundred-dollar Gucci boots. The only concession he made to his job was going tieless. 'Maybe, maybe,' he repeated, still cackling, 'if you promise not to hurt me.'

The heavy woman smiled uncertainly. She was in her late thirties and had silver-blonde hair fluffed about a round, pretty face. She kept her eyes glued to Teddy, and he said, 'Let me work now, lady, and I'll get back to you.' His voice had changed, thickened subtly in a way that David recognized. The fat woman had kindled a flame.

David became aware that Vanessa had moved her stool closer to his and was climbing back on again. He glanced past her. A large, florid man in expensive cowboy attire, including feathered J.R. hat, jerked his eyes away from her and began examining his glass. Teddy then stepped over and murmured to the man. Vanessa was looking in the opposite direction, down the crowded bar past David and the other bartender, smiling brightly, waving to a woman at the far end. Which, David knew, was her way of detaching herself from an unpleasant situation. Happened all the time to her.

The florid man said to Teddy, voice rising, 'See here, fellow, I don't have to take that kind of . . .'

Teddy interrupted, voice steely thin. 'We all appreciate a knock-out chick. No one blames you for looking,

26

even trying for a phone number when her escort's in the john. But you're a grabber and I want you out of here.'

'Do you know who you're talking to?' The man's ruddy face was turning pale, his hands were clenching into big fists.

Vanessa began to say something placating to Teddy. Teddy reached under the bar. The man got off his stool and hurried out the street door.

Teddy grinned and came up with a stuffed animal – one of the teddy bears that were his trade mark; that he gave to women who caught his fancy. He said, 'You want the usual brandy, Duvid'l? Or would you like to try Teddy Bear's Holiday Spirits? Would you believe hot mulled wine? Electric Egg Nog – no, not acid but a blend of rum, brandy and vodka for a real kick in the head. And my own St Louis Special – a Christmas Zombie with lots of red liqueurs and a small wreath.'

Vanessa said, 'You always make such a fuss about Christmas, Teddy! I'll try the mulled wine.'

David said, 'Martell.' And with more passion than he'd planned, 'How the hell do you stay so cheerful?'

Teddy replied blandly, 'Try killing someone you hate.'

Vanessa laughed, accepting it as a joke.

But David was chilled as if his friend had looked directly into his soul.

Teddy went away. Vanessa said, 'You forgot to get a Christmas tree for the office.'

David nodded, wanting to talk to Teddy, to question him about that last remark. His dream . . . the woman on the train . . . throwing her to death . . .

Teddy was back with their order. David said, 'Let's get together for dinner.'

Teddy was looking at him, appraising him. They had often served each other as listeners and advisers during the ten years of their friendship. They had served each other in more practical ways as well, David as banker during Teddy's lean and occasionally dangerous times

27

before the opening of Thomasine's four years ago; Teddy as contact to the *demi-mondes* of the Sunset Strip who had filled David's needs during his own lean (emotionally) and dangerous times.

Teddy said, 'You got it.' He began to turn away, then stopped. 'Vanessa, you taking care of my main man here?'

She flushed and looked into her pewter mug. 'When he lets me.'

The fat woman said, 'Excuse me for interrupting, but could I have another Rob Roy?'

Teddy said, 'You can have anything you want, lady.'

She'd obviously been drinking for a while. 'I want a Teddy Bear to cuddle. A live one.'

Teddy leaned close. 'Be nice. Write your name, your phone number, on the napkin.' He drew a ballpoint pen from his breast pocket. 'Then either go into the restaurant or leave.'

'Don't be angry . . .'

He leaned closer. 'I'm not angry, big momma. I'm sizzling for you.' He gave her the teddy bear.

She was smiling, biting her lip, flushed with pleasure when she finished writing on the napkin and handed it to him. 'Forget the fresh drink,' she said, opening her purse.

Teddy said, 'Forget the tab,' and watched as she clutched the bear and walked to the door, her huge rump rolling. 'Must be jelly,' he sang softly, and went to serve his customers.

'He can do better than *that*,' Vanessa said, 'even if she is white.'

David didn't bother explaining. It should have been obvious that Teddy sipped from many cups. He said, 'Let's take our drinks to the dining room.'

She touched his arm. 'Hon, you didn't mean that about not seeing each other until after New Year's? What about our plans? The parties?'

He got off the stool. He remembered Teddy quoting an African writer: *To be happy, one must live easy inside*

28

his own skin. His skin felt tight as a drum's. He didn't think he had ever lived easy inside it.

'We'll see,' he said. 'Maybe New Year's Eve. Colleen does expect us.'

She got off her stool and walked with him. 'What about Christmas? We have the studio party on the twenty-second. And Christmas Eve, Dave!'

His head hurt. He had to get home early tonight; had to sleep a peaceful eight hours.

'We've never been apart on Christmas . . .'

'Fuck Christmas!' he exploded. 'I'm a Jew, dammit!'

The maître de at the dining room archway turned to stare. A couple waiting for a table also turned. David didn't know whether they'd heard his words or simply his raging tone, but he decided this lunch was over.

He walked to the street door, pausing at the bar to drain his glass. Vanessa followed him outside, face pale. 'I know you're a Jew. What I didn't know was that it meant anything to you. You never spoke about going to temple or, you know, about *feeling* Jewish.'

'You're right,' he said, and took her hand. It was icy cold despite the warm afternoon sun. 'Forgive me.' They had always treated each other with kindness, with consideration and affection. Six years of such civility and physical closeness counted for something. 'Come to the house tonight.'

She nodded. Tears trickled from her eyes, and he felt terrible.

He also felt worried about tonight.

Teddy phoned Roberta Alden, the big momma, at three thirty. Her voice shook as she gave him directions. Twenty minutes later, at her North Hollywood home, everything else she had shook as he plunged wildly between her thick white thighs.

Afterwards, he put his head on her bulging belly and closed his eyes. And thought of Montecassino. Not that he'd had a fat woman there and not that anything here reminded him of that place of explosions, shrieks, cordite stench, human cowardice and inhuman courage. It was just that he'd been thinking of it for years now, more and more often lately. Thinking not only of the corpse-covered slopes leading to the German stronghold, but of Lieutenant Borden, ex-highschool athlete, freshman enlistee from Texas A & M, who had come to the portable kitchen where li'l black Teddy was working and said he was empowered to 'raise a few fightin' men from this miserable mongrel ratpack'; said it grinning as if in jest, and said it with contempt and hatred. Later, he had humiliated Teddy in a brief weapons refresher course behind the field kitchen, using some of the Southern racist shit of the day: 'C'mon boy, let a little light into that African bone head of yourn,' and on and on. And at last Teddy had answered back, saying that if Borden hadn't been wearing bars he'd have been chewing on a *'boy's* African fist.' So Borden took off the bars and beat the hell out of l'il black Teddy.

Teddy had planned to kill him with a hand grenade on the slopes before the ancient Italian monastery . . . though it was more fantasy than hard plan. Whether he could actually have done the job became academic when the Germans did it for him, in the first few moments of the reserve company's assault.

But instead of gratification he had felt anguish on learning his enemy had escaped him. As he felt anguish now, lying on the warm pillow of flesh, a fine mist of sweat between his cheek and Roberta's stomach, mouth twisting in self-contempt. Because anguish or not, he suspected he would never have fragged his man.

Driving back to Thomasine's, he wondered at his pain. All right, so he hadn't killed his enemy. So he could *never* kill his enemy.

But Montecassino and Borden were thirty-seven years ago. No one suffers over something that far back. And he hadn't begun tormenting himself until four, maybe five years ago, about the time he'd opened Thomasine's.

30

Had anything happened then; anything that had torn open that old wound?

His mind closed down on the subject, causing him to concentrate on the traffic and on a cute chicana waiting at a bus stop. Because there was something very ugly waiting to wound Teddy Bear; wound him more deeply than he could tolerate.

Vincent said he'd brought her to his apartment because he was a gourmet cook. 'Wait, Rita, you'll see.'

She knew what she would see, but last night had been so long, so empty, and there were four more such nights to fill before she met David and could revive her hope, that she hadn't insisted they go to a restaurant as he had promised. Besides, his voice was good; almost as soft and strong as David Howars' and Daddy's.

His meal was basic: broiled steak, baked potatoes, and California burgundy, but she was hungry and ate well. And he sat close beside her and touched her hand as often as he could and she liked hand touching and holding.

They moved to the living-room couch for coffee. He smoked, which she didn't like.

Still, she had decided before coming here she would spend the night with him. This was their third date and he was nice enough looking, vigorous enough for a man of sixty, she estimated, perhaps a year or two older. What he wasn't, she now discovered, was very clever about seducing her.

She tried several times to stop his talk. His talk disturbed her, it was so blatantly a device to get her into bed. She was always amazed at how men of mature years, who should have learned better, continued to say the same stupid things, the same obvious lies, as the men of her youth.

'I've been looking for a serious romance,' he said, leaning forward to stub out his cigarette in an ashtray on the coffee table. He straightened, turning so as to come around facing her, and took her in his arms. When

31

he kissed her, she was repelled by the taste and smell of tobacco. Then he squeezed her breast and pushed his tongue into her mouth.

She began to feel a little heat. His hand went to her knee, then under her skirt. Good, good, because he had stopped talking.

He reached her crotch and she wanted to place her hand on the bulge in his trousers. But she had never been able to do that without the man moving her hand for her.

He began talking again. 'When a man and a woman feel for each other, sweetheart, they don't have to wait a long time to . . . consummate, you understand?'

What sort of an idiot did he think she was? What sort of idiot species did he think women were?

'Your intelligence, your beauty . . .' He was rising, drawing her up with him, babbling on. '. . . will turn my bedroom into a flowery bridal chamber . . .'

They were in a short hallway when she pulled free and turned back. 'Would you drive me home?'

He stood there, staring, as she opened the front closet and got into her lightweight-wool short coat. 'What's wrong?' he asked.

'I have to get up very early for a pre-class tennis game.'

'The hell you do!' It was a shout, and she shrank within herself.

'Rita . . .' He waved his hands. 'I'm sorry. Don't just rush away.'

His voice was calmer, and he had waved hands, not fists. She said, carefully, 'I wasn't rushing away, Vincent. I was asking you to drive me home. Though it's close enough to walk . . .'

'Nonsense.' He had her arm and was drawing her to the kitchen. 'We'll have a liqueur. Or a cream sherry. Then I'll drive you.'

'Well, perhaps a sherry.'

But in the kitchen he suddenly grabbed her, one hand

32

clutching her bottom, and panted in her ear, 'It could be love . . . a lifetime . . . we're both so alone . . .'

She shoved him hard and sent him stumbling backward. 'Act your age,' she said and turned to leave. She would walk or take a cab.

He was grabbing her again, from the back this time, fumbling for her breasts, saying things, ugly things about her being a 'cock-teasing bitch' and he would act his age, all right, 'and so will you!' His voice raged and she tried to conquer fear by telling herself that if she simply persisted in going toward the door, this small stout man with almost no hair would give up. After all, how many sixty-year-old rapists were there?

The thought and her extreme nervousness made her laugh shrilly, even as she fought to free herself from the arms encircling her body.

The laugh was a mistake. 'Cunt!' he shouted, and spun her around and flung her back toward the sink.

And now his hands *were* fists and he was raging and advancing on her, and she choked on her terror and was unable to say she would stay the night if only he wouldn't rage at her, wouldn't hit her. And why did men act this way with her anyway? Why did these things happen to her, she who had loved Daddy and Will?

She turned her back on him and bent over the sink, unable to face the fearsome sight. And saw the dishes where he had hurriedly placed them, the scraps of meat still there and the forks and the steak knives . . .

The terror was too much. He would begin hitting her soon.

She turned, raising the knife, and hacked down at his chest. She felt the blade scrape bone before sliding in up to the haft. She also felt hot liquid spray her knuckles.

She cried out.

He also cried out, a strangling, choking sound.

He was staring down at the knife sticking into the lower centre of his chest and at the brilliant red stain

33

spreading rapidly over his white shirt. He shook his head and stumbled backward. She jerked the knife out and followed, stabbing and sobbing, feeling the hot liquid spray her face. She slashed too high once and sliced open his cheek and said, 'No, no!'

But it was always that way with knives and, while she was sickened, she wasn't surprised as she had been the first time. It was a butcher's shop with knives and if she'd had a choice, if it didn't always happen so fast, if she had been able to plan it, she would have used something else, *anything* else. How the TV shows irritated her with their bloodless stabbings, shootings, beatings! Bad for the children to think it was so neat, so easy . . .

She almost tripped over him when he collapsed, first into a sitting position, then onto his left side. His arms and legs moved convulsively, briefly, and were still.

There was a puddle of blood on the floor, growing larger by the second. She turned to the sink and ran the water until it was hot. She washed her hands and face; washed the knife thoroughly; washed the other dishes and utensils.

She dried everything, found where they belonged and put them away, holding them with the towel. She remembered the coffee cups in the living room, and soon they too were washed and put away.

She stepped carefully up to Vincent, avoiding the puddle of blood, and bent and fingered his neck, trying to find a pulse in the carotid artery as she taught her first-aid class; then tried the right wrist. Nothing.

She went to the little toilet off the entry hall and checked herself in the mirror. Her cheek was faintly stained, as if with rouge. She washed thoroughly and returned to the kitchen and dried herself with the dish towel, which she planned to take with her.

She thought about what she might have touched. She wiped everything she could think of with the dish towel, including doorknobs. She tried to remember what else she should worry about, from the Agatha

Christie mysteries she had once been addicted to. But that was when she'd been married. Since then she had not enjoyed murder mysteries. On the other hand, since then she had become far more experienced in murder than Miss Marple . . . which brought a wan smile to her lips.

She went to the living room and fluffed up the couch cushions and wiped the coffee table with the dish towel. Still holding the towel, she went to the front door, opened it a crack and looked out. She stepped into the hall, closed the door, wiped the knob and put the towel in her coat pocket.

Later, at home, she felt that the long walk had done her good, had relaxed her. She piled her clothes, including pantyhose and shoes, in the centre of the kitchen so as not to forget to take them to a trash bin behind a shopping centre far from the one she used. She hated to lose the coat, and the shoes were almost new, but traces of blood could have splattered onto them. For that same reason she showered, scrubbing herself, soaping her hair three times.

In bed at last, she was amazed that she was so calm, so free of guilt or fear. It was increasingly this way, each time it happened.

Vanessa felt his penis going soft in her mouth, and told herself it didn't mean that he felt less for *her*. Personal problems. Business problems. Perhaps health problems. He'd lashed out at Jitzler, hadn't he? He'd even lashed out at Christmas! So this was just another symptom of a general problem.

He said, 'I'm sorry.'

She began to lie down beside him, but he got up and went to the chair for his robe.

'Can't we talk about it?' she asked.

He walked to the bathroom. 'What's there to say?'

He didn't even sound upset, as he had when it happened the first time, four or five months ago.

She put on her shoes and followed him. He enjoyed

35

seeing her naked in high heels; used to make her walk and dance round the house that way.

He was urinating and said, 'A little privacy, please.' He had never been shy with her before, nor she with him.

But now she reddened as if she had walked in on a stranger, and went to the bathroom off the study. When she returned to the master bedroom, he was almost dressed.

She couldn't believe he had turned off so completely! She walked toward him, seeing herself in the mirrored closet doors, big breasts bouncing, rear end rolling, pubic hair trimmed close in a neat dark triangle . . . and knowing how men reacted and how *he* had reacted, she was excited by her own image.

His voice weary, he said, 'What is this? Show time?'

She began dressing quickly, not looking at herself, feeling nothing for herself because the man in the room felt nothing for her. And the man in the room had been the man in her *life*.

He left the room.

She fought back the tears. She checked the digital clock on the nightstand. Not quite eight. Still time to call Rob Cerjak and ask if his invitation was open. He was going into production with a mystery pilot for NBC and had offered to let her read for a 'strong supporting role that could develop into a continuing part'. But there was a definite string attached.

She used the phone on the nightstand, spoke to him, and they were on for nine. She went down the hallway to the front door, and saw that the kitchen light was on. She hesitated, then walked in. Dave was sitting at the table in his suit, shirt and tie, as if waiting for the party to begin. Just sitting there, hands folded in his lap.

She was suddenly filled with pity. Why, she didn't know. He had everything this town could give, including his pick of women. He had simply tired of her.

But looking at him, she felt it went much deeper than that and was afraid for him.

'Dave, I'm going now.'

'Drive carefully,' he said, as always.

'Why don't you relax? Have a few drinks? Get out of that suit?'

He was looking down at himself. 'I didn't realize I'd put it on again.' He leaned back, unfolding his hands, crossing his legs. He was wearing highly shined black dress shoes. 'I believe it's a classic childhood tie-in. When I was a kid in Brooklyn, my clothes were worn hand-me-downs. I did have a dress suit, blue serge, stiff and heavy, for funerals, weddings, bar mitzvahs. I'd gotten it for my own bar mitzvah, and then was forced to wear it for years, altered, growing as I grew. I hated it. So now I wear suits, good ones, whenever . . .'

He stopped and she realized she'd glanced at her watch. 'I have an appointment,' she muttered guiltily.

'Yes. Don't keep Rob waiting.'

She said, 'Oh Dave, bunny,' voice breaking.

He again folded his hands in his lap. 'Let's not be dramatic. I can't get it up for you. The end.'

She turned and walked out of the house. *The end.*

She got in her car and drove down the winding canyon road towards the city. She was crying. She wanted to turn around and go back to him and say, 'Forget the sex' and 'I'll stay with you forever.'

She reached Sunset Boulevard and turned west. Rob was waiting. A good guy, ethical in his way. He would help her forget her hurt.

She came into the quiet, the order, the lushness and richness of Beverly Hills. She came into the town that epitomized showbiz success. She turned onto Elevado and pulled up before Rob Cerjak's home and told herself that he had more projects, more money, was more important in the industry than Dave.

But her career didn't help her this time.

The first thing she did when Rob let her in was to ask if she could use a phone. 'A private phone, please.'

He showed her to a little powder room. She shut the door and dialled Dave's number. It rang and rang, but he didn't answer.

So he'd gone out. So she was worrying about nothing.

She and Rob had a drink, then went to bed. He was a powerfully built man, a good ten years younger than Dave, and he made up for all the action she'd missed in the past months. Not that it worked for her, but it almost did, and she knew it eventually would.

He didn't feed her any bullshit, but he did hold her afterwards, did say, 'I enjoyed the hell out of you,' did want her to spend the night. 'Just to sleep together, babe.' She felt his liking for her and was comforted by it. But it wasn't time for that yet.

She dressed and went downstairs, leaving him dozing in bed. She used the phone in the powder room to call Dave.

Still no answer and she wondered if he was out with a new woman, one for whom he could 'get it up'.

She asked herself what difference it could possibly make. *The end.*

It *did* make a difference. It hurt like hell. She wanted to find him, scream at him, threaten him, beg him on her knees. She wanted to tell him what she called 'the Impossible Secret' and make him pity her (though she didn't pity herself, didn't accept the doctors' diagnosis), and make him love her again. 'Please, please . . .'

She heard her voice wailing in the car and couldn't believe it.

She raged at his giving her that bullshit about childhood hardship to explain why he was wearing his suit and sitting there as if waiting for the party to begin.

Because he *was* waiting for the party to begin, the bastard! Waiting for her to leave so he could go to one of the young whores who called themselves starlets and would do anything to get next to a producer.

38

As she had done.

But logic and fairness couldn't help her now. She was raging and hurting in a way she had thought never to experience again. Like Billy had raged and hurt when she'd said she was going to divorce him and work full time at an acting career. Like Drew had wept and threatened when she'd dumped him and his coke-snorting and vodka-belting and fast slide from reasonably good TV director to simply awful derelict. As other men would have suffered over her had she allowed it to go that far.

Six years with Dave had allowed it to go that far . . . for her.

And Vanessa Brooks was Mary Bjorn again, back in San Diego and fifteen, and madly in love with Steve Franklin, who read so much and knew so much and looked so fantastic on the basketball court even though he was only second string. Mary Bjorn, who had been so hurt at sixteen when he stopped seeing her that by seventeen she was married to Bill Dinunzio, the mechanic who worked on her father's car – and divorced at not quite nineteen. And in Hollywood to become Vanessa Brooks and never allow herself the folly of romantic hurt again, telling herself it was stardom and money and fame that counted, nothing else . . . including 'the Impossible Secret', which she kept secret even from her own mind and which couldn't be true because it was a full year now and she was still fine, wasn't she?

She drove over Laurel Canyon to Studio City and her apartment in the complex near the Hollywood Freeway. She showered and brushed her teeth and opened the convertible couch and lay down. But she was still thinking of Dave, raging at Dave.

He couldn't get away with it!

David sat at the kitchen table. It was late and the phone had rung four times in the past few hours. He hadn't bothered answering. He was reading yesterday's *Times*, the story about the California Nazi groups. He had kept the paper in his case and read it twice tonight. He wished there had been more information about the group so near, in the San Joaquin town of Bethills, a father and two sons, 'the nucleus,' they claimed, 'of a state-wide organization.' But the reporter said he hadn't seen more than a few neighbours at the meeting.

No pictures, no descriptions, just a sparse paragraph about what the reporter obviously considered a curiosity, a near-joke. And David wanted to know *everything* about them, felt it was vital he know everything about these people who were only five or six hours away and who admitted – no, *proclaimed* – that they wanted to destroy him.

He had called Teddy at Thomasine's and asked him what he knew about American Nazi publications. Teddy had said, 'I have a friend who collects such shit, just to know who's out to get him.' David had wanted to say, 'Exactly,' but Teddy had sounded sarcastic and amused, so instead David asked him to bring along whatever he could borrow from his friend 'to dinner tomorrow, Canter's, for kosher deli, all you can eat'. Teddy had said, 'Oy vay, baby,' and it was set for seven.

THREE: *Wednesday, 12 December*

Adolf Schleisser had been born Frank Shell, but twenty-eight years ago, at the age of twenty-six, he had retrieved the family name his grandfather had seen fit to Americanize on emigrating from Germany. The Adolf was in honour of the immortal who had changed his life and he didn't take it lightly, struggling to live so as to reflect honour of the Führer.

Yet in memory he remained Frankie, living in the farmhouse as it had looked when his father was alive, before Adolf had managed to buy the abandoned vineyards around it, before San Joaquin grapes had become valuable to major wine producers. And riveted to those memories were the four men his father had hired to help him build the little barn that was now a garage, this after his Jew boss at the Bethills Hardware fired him. Sold the store and the building, the bastard, and moved to San Francisco.

It broke the old man, losing a lifetime job, clerking being all he knew. He decided to try farming and had the barn built, and he was no more a farmer than he was a door-to-door salesman, which he'd also tried. After a while he settled for his wife working at the local five-and-dime, and later his social security.

It ripped Frankie apart to see his father sitting on the sofa day after day listening to the radio, and later, when Mom bought the RCA, watching television. So that when he fell over dead from a stroke during 'As The World Turns' it was almost a blessing.

Tonight was another sleepless memory night for Adolf, and he got up, careful not to wake Eva (she'd resisted the name change, but he'd made it a condition of their marriage), and walked barefoot into the living room.

It was 3.00 a.m. by the kitchen clock when he got a beer and sat down at the table. He drank and rubbed his face and tried to think of tomorrow. But the sense and, yes, *smell* of that bygone day stuck with him.

Why the hell did he have to think of such meaningless trash?

It had been a Friday in September. He'd come home after completing his first week of highschool, worried because he'd never been much of a student and Bethills High was full of smart, studious kids, including a few sharp Jews. He was only fourteen, but he already hated them, and not only because of Levinson firing Dad. That goddam kike girl yelling when he kidded round last term in junior high. And Dad talking about Hitler being right and finishing off the Jews and English before the year, 1940, was over.

He came into the yard, riding his bike up from the dirt road that ran about half a mile from the two-lane blacktop, which ran about three miles from Bethills High. He heard laughter and left his bike and walked around behind the house where the barn was to be built. And there were these four men off in the scrub grass, squatting in a rough circle, pants around their ankles. For a moment he couldn't understand what they were doing; then he realized they were defecating. Talking and smoking and shitting.

The smell reached him and he couldn't understand how men, even drifter farmhands, could do such a thing. (Later, his father said his mother had told them to 'do their business' outdoors and not in her neat bathroom. So they had.)

When one of the men looked up at him and laughed, Frankie retreated to the house.

Now he gulped beer and crushed the can in his big hand, angry at himself, at his enemy brain, for going

42

on with the memory . . . the filthy, dangerous memory. And tonight of all nights!

In just a few hours, he and the boys were going to Los Angeles to bait the Yid in his stinking lair. The first such showing of the swastika in a Jew neighbourhood since Skokie, Illinois, when the American National Socialist party had rammed it down their throats and received nation-wide media attention.

By tomorrow night Adolf Schleisser and his National Resurrection party would be on their way, too. So he should be thinking of marching storm-troops, of massed swastikas, of his fondest fantasies: leading another Kristalnacht; herding niggers by the thousands onto ships for Africa; standing before the White House taking the salute of an Aryan army, knowing he could now cleanse his country of racial garbage and prepare for a world cleansing.

Instead, he remembered the rest of that childhood day.

Late in the afternoon, Frankie had been riding his bike and met the man who had laughed at him walking toward the two-lane blacktop. The man was young and stocky and had extremely large hands. He blocked Frankie's path, and as Frankie straddled his bike, grabbed him by the crotch. 'How much you got there? See what I got?' As Frankie froze in shock, he opened his fly and forced the boy's hand inside.

Frankie finally jerked free and ran into the field, leaving his bike behind. The stocky man called out, 'Hey, just a joke,' and continued on his way. When he was gone, Frankie retrieved his bike and rode home. He was shaking so badly he fell off twice, scraping his knees.

The stocky man wasn't there the next day and Frankie never told his father about it, never told anyone, because of the shame. And because – deeply hidden, especially from himself – there had been a quick, undeniable surge of desire when his fingers were forced to touch hot flesh.

Adolf got another beer and went to the window. He

looked out at the yard and beyond it to the fields where the grapes, eighty acres of the small green sweet called Thompson's Seedless, would be growing come the summer. Now the vines stretched in long even rows under a bright winter sky. They were his success, his income, but not his career. His career was to save white civilization.

Tilting his head back to drink, he caught a reflection of himself in the glass and was comforted. How could he be anything but a total man, an Aryan breeder of superb white offspring, with his tall, big-boned frame, his deep hard muscle, his shock of pale brown hair greying only slightly at the sides? His father had looked much the same earlier in his life, but had deteriorated because of failure, because he'd allowed a Jew boss to drain away his courage and ambition.

No sub-human of any trash species would do that to Adolf!

He finished the beer, returned to the bedroom and slipped in carefully beside Eva. She sighed, turning toward him, the bed creaking under her weight. A big *Frau*, heavier than the American ideal, but just fine for him. Yet he inched away as she moved again, not wanting any contact tonight.

Which, he immediately told himself, was perfectly natural, was what a warrior felt before taking the field: the need to keep himself pure and whole with every ounce of energy intact.

Tomorrow would be the true beginning of the Resurrection party. The years of frustration, of inability to gain more than a handful of supporters, would be forgotten. Tomorrow the door to public acceptance would begin to open. And where Rockwell had failed, where Koehl and Collins and Vincent and Mason and Kalemba and Lauck and others hadn't been able to move any meaningful number of people into accepting the truth, he, Adolf Schleisser would.

He slept. He dreamed he was riding his old bike, naked, over a road of writhing male buttocks, bellies, organs. Thick arms and big hands reached up to drag him down. He both dreaded that fall and longed for it. And the organs touched his bare feet and gushed hotly against them and the hands reached his own organ and he began to slip from the bike, groaning in fear and ectasy.

He awoke trembling, sweating, with an erection. There was daylight in the window. He was alone in bed and smelled coffee brewing. Then he heard music on the stereo, the Horst Wessel song:

Raise high the flag! Close up the rank'd formation!
The storm-troops march with quiet, steady tread.

Eva stuck her head in the doorway. 'Time to get up. Your uniform is pressed and ready. The boys called; they'll be here for breakfast.' She paused, tilting her head, listening to the stereo, a smile warming her heavy face. 'I never get tired of it.'

He nodded, and she withdrew. But he preferred the German version, even though he neither spoke nor understood much German; just some military terms, some Nazi political designations. In English, Horst Wessel was melodramatic. But in German, in the exciting, gutteral words . . .

Those comrades who've been killed by Red Front
and reaction
March in our ranks, arisen from the dead.

He wondered if there would be reaction tonight, wondered if there would be blood on Jew street tonight, and if some of it might not be his own. He had nothing but contempt for the Jewish Defence League, but if one of the bastards was there and armed . . .

Hadn't Horst Wessel died on such a street?

It had begun clouding up during the day and the radio said the weather forecast had been revised from 'sunny with high clouds' to 'a rapidly developing storm front – 20 per cent chance of rain tonight; 80 per cent by morning'. Which fit the southern California pattern of an early and heavy rainy season, at least during the past three years. Before then there had been three desperately dry years.

A state of extremes, California. In its weather, its topography, its people. A sunshine paradise most of the time; then floods, mud-slides and drought-induced fires ruining and devouring homes and roads and thousands of acres. An enormous fruit and vegetable garden, this California, with a deadly geological fault that ran under much of it, causing many small earthquakes and promising one hell of a big one. Icy mountains and roasting valleys within driving distance of each other. Jews and Nazis just as close.

It was six thirty and growing dark. David was driving to Canter's delicatessen to meet Teddy and didn't want to think of Nazis. They belonged in history books, not in the town of Bethills in the San Joaquin Valley. He wanted to think of the good day's work he had completed.

He had found a replacement for Jitzler: Bill Cooper, a young Englishman with an excellent record in the sale of foreign rights, with strong personal contacts at Home Box Office and CBS, which would make sale of TV rights easier. And so the Canadians were assured of at least recouping their investment and were ready to go with the financing. It only remained to decide on the numbers, the percentages.

He turned onto Fairfax Avenue and drove south past the corner synagogue and the nursing home and the shops with Stars of David somewhere in their signs or windows; the closest thing LA had to the Brooklyn Jewish ghetto of his youth. He planned to eat chicken soup and *knadles,* a thick corned beef on rye, a hot kasha knish. And thought of how those Bethills Nazis would mock this neighbourhood and this food.

He turned his mind back to work. He was satisfied with his performance on *Coast to Coast.* He had found the novel and optioned it for film development. He had found the young scriptwriter, just a year out of UCLA, and worked with him for four months. He had found

46

the director, Lyle Bratigan, and got him to read and criticize the script without a contract, no mean accomplishment in this paranoid business. Today he had met with Bill Cooper and the Canadians. His work was almost finished. As soon as the Canadians and their bank made interim financing available, he would get his $150,000 guaranteed minimum and move on to the next project.

He might have to step in between the director and screen-writer if relationships became acrimonious during the polish, which was when the director would impose his view of the script and the film.

He might have to visit the Canadian sets and locations if problems developed between the cast and director, but that was unlikely as he had chosen his lead actor in part for his even temperament and highly professional approach.

Another reason for having to go to Canada would be if a hitch developed in the timing; if the film didn't finish within a reasonable six to eight weeks, correct for its three-million-dollar budget. As executive producer, he would get the panic telegrams and phone calls about ballooning production costs. But again, with the people he had chosen, it was highly unlikely.

So he could look for the next novel . . . and he believed he had already found it. Could look for another young writer (the one he'd used on *Coast to Coast* now had a major credit, a high-powered agent, and an inflated view of his worth). Could begin to attend the Hollywood parties where actors and actresses considered bankable – i.e. able to draw financing on their box-office strength – and directors of skill but not yet astronomical salaries, were to be met and talked to. Another modest deal would begin to shape up, and in a year to eighteeen months would be completed, and he would go on to the next. And then the next. Which tonight seemed an empty and pointless way to spend a life.

As he pulled into Canter's corner parking lot, he saw

Teddy step from his blue Cadillac. They exchanged waves.

There was a distant rumble of thunder as they entered the big old deli. Teddy said, 'Why here and not a class act like Nate and Al's? You tired of Beverly Hills, Duvid'l?'

David shrugged. 'Feels more authentic here.' They walked past the take-out counter to the rope. A cheerful blonde woman showed them to a booth in the over-lighted, noisy main room, and a stout, hennaed wait-ress took their order.

Teddy put a plastic zipper case on the table. 'You want this before or after dinner?'

'What is it?'

'Nazi newspapers, magazines, the shit you asked for.'

David suddenly wanted a cigarette, and he hadn't smoked in three years.

'I'd skip it if I were you, Dave. One glance at that garbage made me sick.'

'Can I take it home?'

Teddy shoved the case across to him, and he put it on the bench.

Their food came. Teddy said, 'You split Thomasine's in a funky way. My captain said you were yelling some-thing about being a Jew. That why we're here on Fairfax?'

David chewed a crisp slice of half-sour pickle and tried to think of an answer.

'That why *I'm* here, Dave?'

It was, but now that they were facing each other, David couldn't see what Teddy could offer him. He bit into warm corned beef and sour rye bread. 'It was easier to help me, Theodore, when I was hungry for girls.'

'Maybe you still are and don't know it.' Teddy attacked his food, eating quickly, aggressively. He had a plate of beef flanken and potato pancakes, and David wanted some. And wanted the smoked salmon on the plates of a young couple across the aisle. Wanted to cram himself full of food and somehow save himself from disaster.

He stopped eating. 'My mother used to tell me I was a lousy eater and a lousy student. If I ate she was happy and if I studied she was happy. Eventually I studied my way through college and continued the process at a typewriter, first in an editorial office, then in an ad agency, finally in Hollywood as a scriptwriter. Now I'm no longer writing so I'm eating.'

Teddy looked at him, that evil disbelieving smile curling the ends of his Fu Manchu moustache. 'The Sigmund Freud Show will be followed by a rendition of Gershwin's "It Ain't Necessarily So". Bet you were heavy on Freud in your scripts.'

David chuckled because it was true.

Thunder crashed directly overhead, shaking the old building.

'Your cock still working?' Teddy asked.

'Not too well.'

'Have you tried a new girl?'

'It's about to happen.'

'This Jew business – you want to go back to your roots? Want to sit in *shool* and *dovin*?'

'No such yearning.'

'You want to run with other Jews?'

David began to feel irritated. 'Do you want to run with other blacks?'

'Never. But I'm me. What were you yelling at Vanessa about being a Jew?'

'She was bugging me about Christmas and I took a cheap shot.'

'If that's all it is, why the sudden need to read Nazi garbage?'

David lowered his fork. 'Because I decided to take your advice and kill an enemy.' He had snapped the words; now he forced a smile to take the curse off.

Teddy answered the smile. 'That would do it. That would really help you change girls. Your next one would be a cell-mate at San Quentin.'

David cut into his knish and ate steaming buckwheat groats. Teddy said, 'I don't think you're that crazy. Still, I gotta say I wish *I'd* been that crazy some years ago.'

'Tell me about it.'

Teddy's smile turned evil again. 'No you don't. The spotlight stays on Mr Howars. How about going back to New York? Back to the wife and kid?'

'The wife's got a boyfriend and the kid is in college. And before you ask, Mommy and Daddy are dead.'

'For a visit. To see old friends. The kind of Jews *you* are. To touch base with reality, which maybe isn't here in LA for you.'

Teddy was giving it a good shot, but David realized talk wasn't going to settle his guts, his gloom, the deep disquiet which had invaded his life.

Teddy said, 'I think you've reached a time when you've got to become a Jew. What kind I don't know, and neither do you. But *some* kind, Duvid'l, so you can get back to living with Christmas and shiksas and a few Nazi nuts and the general shit the world throws at Jews. So your insides can simmer down.'

'Like your insides, Theodore?'

Teddy picked up his fork. 'We'll talk about that if I ask you to meet me in darkest Hollywood at the Soul Food House. Tonight we're on Fairfax in Canter's kosher deli.'

The waitress came by and they ordered coffee and nut cake.

Adolf was at the wheel, keeping the unfamiliar GM flat-bed to an average sixty as he had through Delhi, Livingston, Merced, Madera, Fresno, Visalia and Bakersfield, the fertile belt of the San Joaquin stretching in all directions. Carl and Horst sat beside him. All were in uniform: Africa-Korps-style cap, brown shirt, Sam Browne belt across the chest and around the waist, brown pants tucked into black jackboots.

Not exactly what the Old Fighters had worn on the

50

streets of Munich, but a crisp and attractive uniform and close enough.

On the floorboards were their weapons; not the pistols and rifles he would have preferred, because that would have been risking police interference. Even the three Little League baseball bats, drilled and lead-filled at the fat ends, were carefully tucked under the seat. And in the back, on a neck-high storage area, were five bundles of literature wrapped in plain brown paper. Also, a suitcase with their civilian clothing.

They weren't wearing their swastika armbands, nor were the two large black-and-red swastika banners up on the flat-bed's removable wood-slat sides. The sides themselves were stacked and tied.

This was a worked-out operation, meant to cover them against all contingencies – to hide their identities in case it was necessary, and to take full advantage of all possible publicity if things went smoothly. The planning had actually begun a month ago when Adolf consulted two of the party's staunchest supporters, Harv Clory of Clory's diner and his cousin Duke who worked in Cross's junk yard.

Nothing had been left to chance. For example, not until just before they were ready for the demonstration would they pull into an already selected side-street and put up the slat-siding and the big banners, and slip on their armbands and ski-masks. The whole thing would take place after dark so as to cut down the risk of counterattack. As for their being traced by vehicle or licence plates, the truck had been stolen from the diner's parking lot last Friday after Clory called Duke to say the right vehicle had appeared. Duke had driven it to the junk yard where it was easily hidden. The highway patrol had come and talked to the truck's owner, who'd made a delivery from near the Oregon border and wasn't known to anyone in Bethills. They'd given him a lift to the bus depot and that was the last anyone in Bethills had heard of it. Or expected to. Vehicles were stolen at the rate of one a minute in California.

Clory had also given Adolf several credit cards left by various out-of-towners in his diner. One was for an independent service-station chain, which would come in handy and serve to confuse any police investigation that might later develop. The more confusion created the better since, ski-masks or not, they would be seen closely by people on Fairfax.

They had reconnoitred the entire area a week ago, the three of them, driving around in Adolf's new station wagon, with Horst stopping Carl from shouting insults out the window at several disgusting orthodox Jews, saying, 'Why risk the entire project with a possible police confrontation? If they see us now, next week is impossible.'

He'd been right, though Adolf suspected his real motives. Still, Horst was with them now and they would soon be riding down Fairfax Avenue, Carl's cassette player hooked into the big speakers wired to the overlapping sides of the flat-bed, playing 'God Bless America'. Two of them would be in the back scattering leaflets as the driver moved the truck not too quickly down the street, their bats close by, ready to break skull-capped heads in case they were attacked.

Adolf hadn't told his sons yet, but he intended to give up the wheel and get into the flat-bed with one of them, probably Carl. Horst, the younger and smaller, would drive. He was good at driving, as he'd proved during his wild adolescence when he'd been chased by police through Bethills and along miles of back roads and escaped . . . not once but three separate times. The fourth time he'd finally been caught, jailed overnight, and fined a hundred dollars for each reckless driving conviction. 'Just kidding around,' he'd said, grinning even as Adolf had begun whipping him with his thick leather belt.

Adolf glanced past Carl to Horst, thinking his youngest had finally straightened out. Though it was hard to be sure with that one, so unlike his father and brother.

About twenty-five miles past Bakersfield, after traversing the knot of roads called the Grapevine and leaving 99 for 5, Adolf pulled into a service station. A black attendant came over, staring at the caps and what he could see of the shirts and Sam Brownes. 'National Guard having some sort . . .?'

Adolf cut him short. 'Fill it. Premium.'

The black said, 'Sure, general,' and got the gas going. He came back to the window. 'Oil and water?'

Adolf shook his head. Beside him, Carl stirred from a heavy chin-on-chest sleep. 'Where are we?' he muttered.

Horst, sitting against the opposite door, told him, and said, 'You want me to drive a while, Pop?'

Adolf glared at him. 'Okay,' Horst said, smiling a little. Horst had been told a dozen times that Adolf wanted to be called either Father or Sir, *not* Pop. Adolf wondered whether the occasional 'slip' wasn't, in fact, a remnant of his earlier rebellion, when he had refused to take part in the Resurrection party meetings, mocked the swastikas and actually fought his father with fists one time. But he'd been too small to take Adolf, and still was.

Later, when he'd turned twenty, when he'd needed a job and money to achieve independence, he'd come to his father and asked to be allowed to work for his share of the grapes as Carl did. Carl was married and had two young daughters. Still, once Horst proved he could work the fields as well as Carl, he was given his equal share. After that he had joined to form the party's triumvirate.

Not that he was as enthusiastic about the movement as he should be. Certainly not as sufficiently hopeful about the future, and this worried Adolf. A Nazi couldn't be half-hearted about the movement. A Republican or Democrat, yes, but never a Nazi.

Recently, however, he'd begun showing the proper spirit. He'd made the mistake of buying a synthetic suede sports jacket from a Jew shopkeeper in Merced. Naturally, the jacket had proved inferior, despite the

53

Jew's claiming that the label indicating special dry-cleaning instructions had been ignored.

That was the first time Horst had called a kike a kike to his face. It wouldn't be the last, Adolf was certain. Horst was beginning to read the newspapers and watch television in the correct Nazi manner, noting the Jewish names, the references to criminal blacks and illegal Hispanics, seeing the hand of the International Jew behind all that was sapping the nation's strength.

The attendant was speaking: 'That'll be thirteen dollars even.'

Adolf held out the credit card Clory had given him. The black said, 'See the signs on the pumps? We take only cash now.'

'That's what I got,' Adolf said coldly not bothering to look.

The black shook his head. 'Boss's orders . . .'

'Tell him that's what he gets – his own company's card.'

'Or he gets nothing,' Carl said, leaning around Adolf.

The black hesitated, then went around the front of the truck and into the office.

Horst began to say that they didn't want trouble, but Adolf's blood was up.

'You watch,' Adolf said, 'the boss'll be a Yid, or a Chicano stooge for a Yid. Just watch.'

The man who came out was short and heavy and balding. 'A Yid for sure,' Carl said, chuckling. 'We'll make him piss his pants.'

'Howdy,' the short man said, smiling. 'I'd appreciate your paying in cash if you've got it. The company sent out notices in the mail three months ago cancelling credit cards. We're a low-profit discount . . .'

'What's your name?' Adolf asked.

The man paused at Adolf's tone. 'Blake.' Another pause. 'Why do you ask?'

'Ikie Blake,' Carl muttered.

'What's that?' the short man said, and his face flushed. 'What's that you said?'

'We're paying with the company credit card,' Adolf said, 'if you want to be paid at all. And we're in a hurry.'

The black was in the office, looking through the plate glass. The manager turned and nodded. The black bent and got something from a desk drawer.

Horst, who was closest to the office, looking down from the truck's high seat, suddenly said, 'Pay the man, Father.' He dropped his voice to a whisper. 'We don't want trouble before we get to the objective, do we? We don't want to be remembered and recognized in this truck in case of trouble tonight. And that attendant stuck something under his jacket.'

Adolf realized he was right. He took out his wallet, found a ten and three ones, and held them out the window. The manager didn't move.

Carl made a choking sound and lunged past Adolf at the door. Adolf was proud of his son, but with Horst's help restrained him.

The black came from the office, something bulging under his jacket. 'I told you,' he said to the manager, 'they're Klan or like that.' Then, to Adolf, 'Why not let the big one go?'

'Some other time,' Adolf said.

The black smiled and took the thirteen dollars. 'Thanks, General. Come back real soon.'

Adolf started up the engine. The manager stepped back and onto the gas-pump island, as did the black. Adolf drove out, thinking they were right to worry about his running them down because he sure as hell felt like it! Felt, also, the loss of face.

But not as strongly as Carl did. Carl was almost weeping with rage. 'Sons of bitches,' he gasped. 'Oh God, I can't wait any more to begin cleaning up that scum!' He turned to Adolf, his voice whining the way it had when he was a boy and wanted something and couldn't get it. 'Is it ever gonna happen, Father?'

'Just remember how long the Führer had to wait,' Adolf said, the blood pounding in his temples, full of

55

the true feeling, the only real feeling for a Nazi – *hate*.
'Just remember how much he suffered from the Jews
and Communists and their puppets.' He turned his face
to both his sons, smiling fiercely. 'Then remember how
he paid them back! I don't believe those death-camp
stories and the myth of the six million dead for a minute
– Professor Butz proved it's a lie – but Hitler punished
the real criminals. He burned a few hundred thousand
and made the rest work like decent Christians until they
ran from Germany. The rats ran, and even though Germany lost the war it was purified. And so was most of
Europe. Not a handful of Jews left in the Fatherland,
boys, and not many in Poland or Hungary or anyplace
else except England and France. And France is starting
to put the screws to the Yids.'

'And you see what's happened to England,' Carl said,
showing he'd learned his history lessons. 'A third-rate
nation.'

'That manager was a reasonable man,' Horst said
quietly. 'We didn't have to go through all that crap.
He'd have taken our card if we'd simply said we didn't
have cash. Another thing, he might be able to identify
us in a stolen truck if he's ever asked.'

Adolf and Carl looked at him. Adolf was big and
wide, and Carl was bigger, wider, but Horst was a
different type of Schleisser: four inches shorter than his
brother; slim and dark of hair and eyes; lean-faced and
moody with a stubborn streak, a rebellious streak, a
streak which never failed to enrage Adolf . . . except
he'd thought it was gone by now.

'What kind of Nazi are you!' Carl snapped. 'Afraid of
every goddam thing!'

Usually, when these arguments erupted Horst turned
away and made a joke and later some sort of conciliatory
gesture. But this time he got angry, the way he had as
a kid when he'd shouted that they were wasting their
time, were making fools of themselves, he was ashamed
to death of them.

'The only kind of Nazi that has a snowball's chance

56

in hell of surviving, of maybe turning things around our way! If we waste our time, our energies, on gas stations, on everyone who *might* be Jewish, even on all the real Jews we meet, we're going to end up in the slammer, or dead, without accomplishing a thing! If we start fighting with blacks and Mexes, we'll never make it past next week!'

'You Jew-loving bastard!' Carl shouted, grabbing Horst's shirt. 'Ever since you went with the slut Jewess from the ski lodge . . .'

'Let him alone,' Adolf said. 'Let him talk.'

Carl turned and stared. 'Let him talk?'

Adolf nodded.

Horst straightened his shirt. 'Every political party has to have patience. More than patience, *sanity*, at least until it gets power. We're nowhere near getting power . . .'

'Maybe nearer than you think,' Adolf interrupted. 'The economy – that's our hope.'

'Only if it gets worse,' Horst said. 'A *lot* worse and makes Americans begin to hate each other, poor against rich . . .'

'But that's Communist,' Carl said.

'Only if they exploit the issue first,' Adolf said, glancing past Carl at his younger son, hoping Horst wasn't using reason as camouflage for cowardice.

'Communists haven't a chance in the United States,' Horst said, 'just as they didn't in Germany after World War I. They thought they did, but the current of conservatism ran too deep in the German people. And it runs at least as deep in the American people, as Mr Carter found out.'

Adolf was pleased. Horst had been thinking. Which was more than could be said for his beloved *dummkopf*, Carl.

Adolf said, 'But we have millions of blacks and growing millions of Hispanics. Blacks and Hispanics and orientals are tools the Jews didn't have in Germany.

57

They're have-nots, so they'll go left, go Communist, if the economy crumbles.'

Horst was nodding. 'Exactly. And that's the time, the only time, American Nazis will have a chance to gain power. Because Democrats and Republicans don't have a programme extreme enough to handle an economic collapse with the have-nots going radical, going Communist.'

'And we do?' Adolf prodded.

Which was when Horst's enthusiasm seemed to flag, even as he nodded, even as he answered. 'The Nazi programme is to eliminate the opposition, first the Communists, then any other. To *kill* the opposition. It might be the only solution if have-nots take to the streets in a major depression with out-of-control inflation. As it was in Germany.'

'And don't forget the Jew. The enemy. Always the devil behind the scenes. Never forget the Jew, Horst. As long as he thrives, we won't.'

Horst said nothing, turning to look out the window.

Adolf nodded to himself. The cancer spot in his younger son's will to succeed – he had never hated the Jew sufficiently. He didn't understand the holy mission. 'The damned Christ-killers,' he said softly. 'The creators of Communism with their Marx and Trotsky. Chosen by God, yes, for destruction.'

Horst said, 'Did you ever think of this, Father? That if Hitler hadn't hated the Jews, Einstein and other Jewish brains would have been on Germany's side? That the atom bomb would have been on Germany's side? That the Third Reich would have won the war?'

Adolf answered without hesitation. 'There would have been no Third Reich, no Nazi Germany, without hating the Jews. No Hitler. You have to read his own words to realize how deep that hatred, that instinct to destroy them went. Hitler without anti-Semitism?' He smiled. 'Not possible.'

'Then maybe it isn't possible for Nazism to succeed.'

'Count on the world's hatred for the Jew, Horst. Wait

for it to show itself. It'll sweep away more of them the next time, and Israel too. Wait . . . wait . . . even now the nations talk about oil and Palestinian rights and the Jews will be swept away.'

Horst didn't answer, and Adolf knew he wasn't convinced. Had a mind of his own did Horst Schleisser. But that mind needed honing, refining, and the first step was education, even if in the Jew-tainted, debased American system.

'Would you like to take courses in college, Horst?'

Horst chuckled. 'Little late for that.'

'Would you like to take history courses, religion courses, economic courses? Would you like to train yourself?'

'For what?'

'For whatever may come.'

He felt Horst staring at him. He heard Carl's steady breathing; he'd fallen asleep again, as he always did in a moving vehicle. Then Horst answered in a near whisper. 'It's a dream, Father. We don't have half a dozen real members. Just Clory, his cousin, maybe Jim and Verner, maybe two more truckers from Clory's diner. You must know how far from reality . . .?'

'The trick is to *stop* knowing. Then it can happen. Can you stop knowing? Can you train yourself not to know and to become more than any American Nazi ever was, including Rockwell?'

Horst wet his lips, and Adolf felt he was being reached, convinced in spite of himself.

'What we're doing now,' Horst said, 'going to scatter leaflets in a Jewish neighbourhood that say they're dogs and have to be put to sleep, does that make any sense? Can it do any good?'

'Yes, because it's part of being a Nazi. There's the theory . . . and there's the action. The impossible action. The unbelievable action. The two together: the speeches and the slaughter. This little action tonight is a prelude to slaughter.' He smiled, suddenly very happy. 'As a child, Horst, you were beautiful, loveable.

59

Then I stopped loving you . . . you became a Jew-tool like most Americans. Today I love you again.'

'Where did you learn to say such things?' Horst muttered.

'In my German mother's womb,' Adolf said, happy and proud, watching shadows lengthen over the freeway. After a while he put on his headlights and glanced past the sleeping Carl at Horst. Horst also appeared to be sleeping, head resting against the door window.

Horst wasn't sleeping. Horst was thinking: 'You learned to say those things from "Bonanza", from "The Streets of San Francisco", from "All In The Family" and "Mash" and "Happy Days" and the rest of Jew television, Pop, turning the words around to suit yourself. You learned from the movies and the radio and the few books you read before you gave up on reality and turned nut. And the jacket *was* incorrectly cleaned, and the storekeeper *was* right, and I called him names because you were there and needed convincing, and now I get twenty-five thousand a year as my share of the cash crop. Love of money, Pop. A Jewish-Zionist trait, right?

'It was easy to go along with you, Pop, once I understood I wasn't going to become a major league baseball player, a grand prix auto racer, not even a ski instructor. And I still see Janet, the slut Jewess from the ski lodge. I love her, Pop, and have for three years. She wants marriage, but I can't give her that because then I'll lose the cash crop. Then I'll have to take a shit job like those I had in Merced in the paint store and the supermarket; jobs that befit one of my education, ability and Aryan blood.

'Janet doesn't know about the Resurrection party, Pop. She doesn't even know my real name. And if she found out, I don't know if I'd change. It's just too easy to go along with you. And maybe it'll be easy to slaughter along with you too if your impossible dream ever comes true. Others must have done it in Nazi Germany, going along with their Pops and their friends and their neighbours because it was easy. Maybe I'll even slaughter the slut Jewess from the ski lodge. And become what you want, your son, the new Hitler.'

Vanessa had never followed anyone before, but following Dave was rather simple, what with rush-hour traffic to hide in and early winter dusk hastened by thickening clouds. She had simply waited down the street from where he'd parked his car; then followed him onto Ventura Boulevard, heading west, staying back three or four cars and watching the silver Mercedes' tail-lights for signals.

When he passed Vineland, she nodded bitterly. He wasn't going home. So she would catch him with whoever the bitch was; catch him in the act and . . .

And what else she didn't know.

His left blinker was flashing. She just managed to make the turn south onto Laurel Canyon two cars behind him before the traffic light changed. Or, judging by a blare of horns, just *after* the light had changed.

Her old green Jaguar – a classic Jag, she called it, but 1970 wasn't a classic year and two accidents had put the rattles into it – bucked a little as traffic slowed to a crawl during the climb towards Mulholland. Then they were over the crest and heading down into Los Angeles County, into the Basin – Hollywood and Beverly Hills and Bel Air. The real LA. Once she got her career together she would leave the San Fernando Valley. Or once she found the right man.

The right man was in that silver Mercedes. The right man had betrayed her, discarded her, and would have to pay.

She didn't know what the hell she was thinking, what the hell she was doing! *How* could she make him pay? Make shame-shame when she found him screwing another woman? Commit suicide or murder? The whole thing was ridiculous!

They were on Sunset and he was turning left and she should turn right and go to Bob Cerjak's place and forget this stupidity. Cerjak had left two messages on her service. Cerjak could become a serious affair.

She turned left, following the Mercedes, consumed by the need to catch him with another woman, to confront him in this betrayal and to make sure, somehow, that he never forgot Vanessa Brooks.

She wiped at her eyes, surprised that she was crying.

She was also surprised at how much she had suffered since last night. Wasn't it supposed to be the older man who suffered over the young woman?

He turned down Fairfax, picking up speed, putting distance between them. He made the light at Fountain while she had to stop for traffic. She was going to jump the light as soon as a panel truck was out of the way, but an old lady – this neighbourhood was full of them – was absolutely *crawling* in the pedestrian crossing lane.

Vanessa bent her head in frustration. The second the old lady was clear, she jumped the light. She heard a screech of rubber on her left and a male voice bellowing, 'Fucking . . .'

She sped down the street. But she didn't see the Mercedes. It was getting dark and she'd lost him, lost him, damn, damn . . .

She heard the blasting horn. It took a minute to realize it was her own and that she was pounding on it, causing heads to turn.

She was passing Canter's when she caught a glimpse of the Mercedes from the corner of her eye, moving through the restaurant's parking lot. She went to the corner and waited for more old ladies to cross, then turned right and went slowly by the entrance to the lot. She'd been here with David no more than half a dozen times; she wasn't a kosher deli freak and he said her preferring fish dinners was good for him.

She went to the alley behind the parking lot, cut her lights and inched up until she could see between cars to where he was angling into a parking spot.

Someone was coming up to his car. Teddy.

62

She watched as the two men walked off together. They were alone, but she seethed, thinking they were meeting their dates inside, or eating before going on to someone's house. Teddy always had plenty of girls, the bastard!

She suddenly hated that black satyr! And got out and hurried across the parking lot.

When she reached the restaurant entrance, she peered through the plate glass window and saw the hostess just leading them into the dining room. Then they were out of sight.

She had two choices: wait near by to see if they came out with women, or go inside after them.

Thunder rumbled. A wind sprang up, blowing a light spray of rain into her face.

She entered the restaurant and turned left, to the bakery counter, to gain a moment's time. Then she crossed the few feet to the deli counter, where a heavy-set young man in white apron asked, 'What'll it be?'

She glanced to the left, towards the dining room, and ambled along the display counter. It ended a few feet before the rope.

The counter man followed her. When she looked up he was checking her out as if she were a prime pastrami. She would have given plenty to transfer that gleam to Dave's eyes!

'Gonna rain,' he said. 'Better stock up on chicken soup for colds.' He chuckled.

She said, 'Yes,' and walked right up to the rope. She saw them, just off the aisle to the left. They were in a big booth, engrossed in conversation.

A waitress came to the booth. Dave looked up. Vanessa realized she was almost on a direct line behind the red-haired woman, and turned quickly away.

Outside, she ran through a light drizzle to her car, satisfied that they were alone . . . for the time being.

She backed out of the alley, drove to Fairfax and turned north. She was now on the opposite side of the street from the delicatessen and pulled to the curb about twenty feet past the plate glass windows. Where she settled down to wait.

The rain increased gradually until it was pounding the car roof; then stopped completely. A moment later an enormous peal of thunder made her jump.

She found a piece of gum in her purse. She regretted not having bought a sandwich for take-out. She'd hardly eaten since leaving Dave last night and was now ravenously hungry.

While waiting for the check, David opened Teddy's plastic zipper case and drew out a tabloid-sized newspaper, *White Power*. His heart thudded as he saw the swastika enclosed in a circle between the two title words. The sub-title was *The Revolutionary Voice of National Socialism*. It wasn't the most recent edition, but the front-page headline was as contemporary as the latest PLO bombing: *Pro-Zionist Policies Endanger Oil Supplies*.

Teddy said, 'I glanced at the shit when my friend brought it over last night. Despite the *White Power* title, they lean more on your *landsman*, Duvid'l, than on the *shvartzes*. In fact, all the Nazi publications do. Now the Klan's something else . . . hates us both equally.' He lit a cigarette and inhaled with pleasure.

David muttered, 'When're you going to give up that poison?' and began flipping the pages.

'Never. It blocks the smog from my lungs.'

David drew out a second, more recent publication, *American Nazi Digest*, the cover being a full-page photograph of Hitler in leather coat, smiling. The caption read *April 20th, Day of Joy*, mystifying him.

He turned the page to *3 years ago this month: Billy Carter Tells Jews to 'Go To Hell'* and *Homosexual Democrat Convicted in Rape Slaying of 32*, which was the way Nazis had seen the John Gacy case.

Teddy said, 'That one *really* wants the ovens back.'

Which David confirmed when he turned to the next

page. The headline read *HOW THE JEWS DO IT!*, and listed organizations like the Jewish War Veterans and the Anti-Defamation League as tools of Jewish subversion.

Below that article was another: *THIS CONGRESS ONE OF THE MOST CORRUPT*. Included was the sentence, 'As might be expected, Jewish, black and Mexican legislators proved to be the most numerous offenders . . .', which in the light of Abscam proved only that Goebbels's big lie theory was alive and well.

There was no let-up when he turned the page and read: *WASHINGTON INFESTED WITH JEWS*, followed by a full-page listing of names, only a few of which had the parenthesized statement *(white)* after them. Sentences such as, 'Yes, the Jews have quietly captured total control of the federal government,' and, 'Whoever they are, wherever they are, Jews will remain what they are: the deadly enemies of America and the White Race,' sent him on to the next page. Here he found a box headlined by the date, *April 20th* in heavy type and the statement that this was the 'most joyous day of the National Socialist Calendar' – Adolf Hitler's birthday, which explained the cover. It offered cards for the occasion.

These cards come in three striking designs. Order yours today!
Card A   *Hitler full-face*
Card B   *Hitler profile*
Card C   *Doorway to His Birthplace*

The waitress came. David quickly shoved the magazine in the case. She left the check, thanked him and walked away. Teddy said, 'Had enough? Want me to give it back to my masochistic friend?'

David had already drawn out another magazine-size publication. The cover had a drawing of a caricatured Jew facing a microphone, reading a script marked with a Star of David. Underneath was the caption, *What is needed is greater control by a small group of 'chosen people'.*

A few pages later was a cartoon of the Statue of

Liberty with an Afro hair-do and grotesquely exaggerated Negroid features holding a copy of *Ebony*.

Another page had yet another cartoon, showing a slender blond man carrying an enormously fat caricatured Jew, captioned *The White Man's Burden*.

Teddy asked, 'That the *NS Mobilizer*?'

David put the magazine back in the case. He had to clear his throat before answering. 'Yes.'

'Gay Nazis, can you believe it?'

David nodded, feeling flushed and slightly nauseated. 'Hitler's Brown Shirts, the SA or Old Fighters, had its share. There were homosexuals on Ernst Roehm's staff; one of high rank was caught in bed with a known gay the night Hitler had them arrested. They were executed. The need to repress homosexuality creates violent . . .'

'Hey, you going to charge for this lecture? I gave up on college after a co-ed said no thanks.'

David paid the check, picked up the case, and they walked to the door. Where Teddy said, 'You don't want to read that stuff,' and reached for the case.

David drew away . . . then nodded and handed it over. It was dangerous for him, did something to his mind, unhinged it to a certain extent. That feverish feeling, that nauseous feeling . . .

They were leaving the restaurant, stepping into a fine mist, when David heard music. And almost immediately saw the truck approaching, then passing. Saw the swastika banner. Saw the ski-masked uniformed men, the uniformed *Nazis*, throwing leaflets off the truck. And it was early evening and the people still walked on Fairfax, the Jewish people.

'It's a joke,' he said and laughed shrilly and began to walk into the street toward the truck. He was just breaking into a run when his arm was grabbed.

Teddy said, 'What the hell you doing? It's no joke and those bastards will have guns or knives or something.'

'Let go,' he said, panting, and Teddy said, 'Don't,

man!', and David realized he had his fist back and was about to throw it at his friend.

He struggled. 'I've got to *do* something!'

'Someone else is doing it,' Teddy said, holding tight. David turned his head to see three men running behind the truck, gaining on it. 'JDL, most likely, and they're a lot younger and tougher than we are.'

'What's the licence?' David gasped, feeling his heart constructing, feeling his chest would explode. Because those Nazis were here, and they'd been in Germany, and the millions had died, and his mother had wept at the letters stamped in German and translated by the Red Cross lady as 'Address Unknown', which the Jews of Brooklyn with relatives in Germany, Austria, Poland, the Balkans, and just recently France, already knew meant concentration camp and probably death.

Those Nazis had reduced whole peoples to garbage; to piles of clothing, gold fillings, soap and stinking ashes. Now Nazis were flaunting themselves *here*.

'At least the licence,' he said, his eyes blurred, useless, unable to see numbers in the dark, in the falling mist. He sagged, watching the first of the three young men reach the truck and jump for the open end. And fall as he was struck by a bat. The next young man shouted at his friend and they ran past their fallen comrade and split, each going around a side, heading for the front and the driver.

One masked Nazi, the bigger one, jumped down with his bat and ran quickly around to the driver's side, where he struck down the second young man from behind. The young man fell heavily and lay very still, unlike the first who was on his knees in the gutter.

The third young man was trying to open the door on the passenger's side. The truck swerved violently, throwing him off. As he struggled to his feet, the big Nazi came around, clubbed him down and raised the bat to club him again.

There was a shout from inside the truck, and the big Nazi ran and jumped into the front seat. There were also shouts now from pedestrians, especially one shrill old man on the other side of the street.

'Someone's calling the police, *momsers*! We'll see you in jail!'

The Nazi remaining in back of the truck threw a bound bundle of leaflets at him as the truck began speeding away. The old man fell, and a woman with him screamed, and David said, voice thick, 'We have to get the licence.'

Now the truck was really moving, swerving around a car stopped at the corner traffic signal, and the Nazi in the back was shouting and flinging out clumps of papers. David heard, 'Jew bastards . . .' and saw the sheet of paper in the street near by. He turned to Teddy, finally ready to move, and said, 'My car!' because the truck was almost out of sight and the only hope was to get in a car and try to follow.

Teddy said, 'Paper, quick, if you want that licence.' He was holding a pen and moving his lips.

David picked up the Nazi leaflet and gave it to him. Teddy walked back to Canter's and put the sheet of paper on the window. He wrote, but very slowly. 'Wet,' he muttered, and went over his writing a second time, even more slowly. Then he came back to David, who was watching people cluster around the three young men and the one old man; David, who was no longer in a hurry because it was too late to follow the truck.

'We can leave now,' Teddy said. 'I'll find out who owns that truck, unless they used hot plates, which they did if they're not total idiots.'

David walked over to one of the groups in the middle of Fairfax Avenue, a group illuminated by the headlights of two cars forced to stop. He looked over a kneeling woman and saw the man, a teenaged boy, actually, who had first fallen under the bats. He was holding his shoulder, almost crying. 'It's broken, I know it. And no one helped us.'

Teddy was walking to the one who had tried to get at the driver. When David came up, Teddy said, 'Hey,

I think he's had it. Look at his head.' And indeed, the man lay still and blood covered his face and the people around him told his rolled-back eyes, his unhearing ears, that an ambulance was on the way.

The third young man was on his feet, shouting that the police were never around when you needed them, saying that this is what came of Jews like those in the American Civil Liberties Union fighting for the rights of American Nazis, of Jews going unarmed, unprepared, when Nazis were always armed, always prepared to kill Jews.

The old man was walking around rather proudly, speaking Yiddish, saying he'd caused the Nazis to waste a whole package of *dreck* on one *alta Yeed*.

'C'mon, we'll read about it tomorrow,' Teddy said, holding that plastic folder of Nazi publications tight under his arm, wetting his lips, wanting away from here.

But David stood still, feeling he had been made a coward, made inept, made the Wandering Jew, the Victim Jew, when all his life he had been the successful American, from teenaged soldier to Hollywood producer. In a few moments they had reduced him to a caricature Jew like the cartoons in their publications.

But that was being as unrealistic as they were.

He took the sheet of hate literature from Teddy's hand. He walked back to the restaurant where people stood outside, where others were moving towards the groups around the wounded. He looked at the crude mimeographed drawing of the fat Jew, at the swastika-marked first striking the huge hook nose. He read the caption, *Justice is coming from the combined American Nazi parties. Jew oppressors beware!* He looked for a name, an address, but the scum had been prudent.

There was a block of text in smaller print, but he folded the paper without reading and put it in the breast pocket of his jacket. His beautiful grey jacket with the matching vest and trousers. From Rodeo Drive, Beverly

Hills, as were most of his suits. The too rich, too well-dressed, growing-fat Oppressor Jew.

Teddy said, 'I'm gonna leave if you don't come right now.'

'Are you sure you got the correct licence number?'

Teddy hesitated. And David understood that his friend wasn't sure. His friend had acted so as to comfort him, to stop him from dangerous action. Teddy said, 'I took a shot at it. I doubt it's right, but you won't want it tomorrow anyway.'

David took the leaflet from his pocket and handed it back to Teddy. Teddy accepted it, saying, 'I'll try anyway, man,' meeting David's eyes with discomfort.

David knew he should actually feel grateful to Teddy for having saved him from the clubs. But he couldn't, because now he had nothing, no way to strike back.

Strike back for what? It was the three young men and the one old man who had reason to strike back. Nothing had happened to David Howars.

Nothing that anyone could see.

As the dream was nothing that anyone could see, though it had torn at him for more than two-thirds of his life.

He walked over to the young man who was walking around rubbing his shoulder, the still-raging young man. He asked him, 'Did you get the licence?'

The young man said, 'Damn it, no!', and walked in circles and harangued the onlookers for 'doing what the German Jews did – waiting like lambs for the slaughter!'

David knew he was being as unrealistic as the handful of American Nazis, and at the same time said, 'You're right!', raging along with him. The rational side of David Howars fought with the side that lusted for blood, and lost.

David asked some onlookers about the licence and received shakes of the head. He walked over to the old man, who seemed so triumphant, who might have had the presence of mind to get the licence. But he shook his head and gave an answer David understood too

70

well. 'I looked and it was far underneath and the truck began going fast. But it's really my eyes. Without my glasses, I can't read numbers.'

They heard the sirens. A moment later the police were there, two patrol cars arriving almost at the same moment from opposite directions. The street was now full of flashing blue and red lights. An ambulance pulled up very close to where David was standing. He stepped onto the sidewalk to get out of the way, just as lightning flared and thunder cracked. A moment later it began pelting rain.

The police would be looking for witnesses; he should help them. But he didn't want to help them. He wanted to help himself. He hurried to the corner and jogged across, threading between cars jammed up by the blocked street. He entered the parking lot, running faster, feeling extra weight jiggling on his stomach, on his breast . . . and was suddenly disgusted with himself.

He had to get in shape. There was a war on.

Vanessa had watched it all, the entire incredible scene, from what amounted to a front-row centre seat. It had happened so fast – taken no more than a minute or two from the time the truck appeared until the three boys were clubbed – that she'd barely moved. Then the bundle of papers had struck the old man in the chest, knocking him down, and she had given a little scream. Because he was on the sidewalk to her right, only a few feet in front of her car.

Outraged, she had opened her door, leaned out into the street, and from her low, sitting position been able to look under the truck's extended bed to the licence plate.

She had written it down, thinking to wait and give it to the police. But Dave had appeared outside Canter's and she'd wanted to drive away and hadn't been able to because of people blocking this section of Fairfax. Then he'd crossed to the east side of the street, almost

71

to where she was parked. She had slumped low and closed her eyes and prepared for humiliation.

But he hadn't seen her. He had talked to the old man, asking him for the truck's licence number, and no one seemed to have it. She remembered how upset he had been at lunch yesterday with his strange, for him, talk about being a Jew. And what his secretary had said about his violence toward Jitzler, an important man in his movie deal, just for telling a dumb joke about Jews. She had lifted her head and seen his face, his quietly agonized face, and despite his rejecting her, despite wanting to hurt him, had been afraid for him again.

The police and ambulance had come, the rain had come and now he was gone. He could still be going to a new lover, he could still be betraying her, but she couldn't move her car, couldn't follow him.

As for this Nazi business, she didn't know what to do. She had the number of the truck. Those animals should be punished. But if she gave it to the police, they would want her name and it might appear in the newspapers . . .

Just then a van pulled up with the CBS eye on its side. A television news crew piled out and their lights flared and they began filming and interviewing. If she spoke to the police right now, those cameras would show her here on Fairfax and David would see it and since she never ate delicatessen on her own and never came to Fairfax he would suspect she had been following him.

Tomorrow she would phone the police anonymously.

The decision made, she returned to important things: Dave, and how to catch him in the act. (And behind it, the desperate need to somehow regain her position in his life. Because the Impossible Secret was there and had changed things, and there might not be time to find another true love.)

It took twenty minutes before the street was cleared and she was able to drive away. The rain now fell in solid sheets and she hoped it wasn't going to be like the last few years with the floods and slides. Not that it had affected *her* home, but it cut down on everyone's mobility and she needed mobility for her career . . . and to catch Dave with his new girlfriend.

It was raining so hard that she decided not to risk Nichols Canyon, which was the quickest way to Dave's place but was also narrow, twisting and cliff-hanging, a real horror in bad weather. Instead she took Laurel, crawling up the long incline at under ten miles an hour with the rest of the traffic. She had just about decided to forget checking Dave's home when the rain let up. By the time she reached Mulholland, it had stopped.

She made the hairpin turn onto Woodrow Wilson which was also a narrow, snaking road, but if the rain held off it would be a short-cut to upper Nichols Canyon where Dave lived.

It began sprinkling a little and she held her breath as she saw the amount of water rushing along the sides of the road. One more torrential downpour and, as in years past, any dip, any little hollow, could turn into a flood area, a lake to trap cars and, as had happened often enough, to drown people.

She reached Nichols, turned left and then right, and entered the cul-de-sac called Del Flora. Her windshield wipers were squealing dry. She turned them off as she came slowly past the big Mediterranean house with the front slopes of ivy and the large blacktop parking area curving right to the garage. Left of the garage was a wrought-iron gate and alongside the gate a pink brick wall with irregularly spaced open sections. Through these openings it was possible to see into a tiled *terraza* and beyond to David's study and a guest bedroom.

The light in his study was just going on. She stopped, backed a few feet to the curb and saw him moving around near his desk. He sat down, holding something in his hand; then looked out the plate glass window. She wondered if he could hear the Jag's engine, and quickly cut ignition and lights.

He turned his eyes to whatever he was holding – a

book, perhaps. Yes, because she could see that he was wearing glasses; the ones with the thick black frames he found so comfortable and she found so ugly.

She watched another few minutes, wanting to be inside watching TV or puttering around the kitchen, knowing they would go to bed soon, happy that he was doing what pleased him most about his work – reading, searching for new material for new movies.

She shrugged. She wasn't inside with him. But at least neither was anyone else.

She drove out of the cul-de-sac and got home without running into more rain. By the time she finished dinner and went down with the garbage, the sky was clearing, large patches luminous with stars. And the air! The air so sweet after rain! She had to tell Dave . . .

Six years of telling Dave when the air was sweet. Six years of being with him when she wanted to; of loving him when she wanted to; of calling him up when she wasn't with him to say the air was sweet.

She went to the phone as soon as she entered the apartment, not giving herself time to think. 'Hi, it's an old friend.'

He was silent a moment. 'I'm reading a Hollywood novel. A bad one.'

'Aren't they all?'

'This one has a saving grace – a reasonably sharp insight into what makes actresses tick. So I thought of you.'

She fought to keep the lightness of tone. 'Didn't think you did that any more.'

'I'll always do that, Vanessa.'

She almost said, 'Want me to come over?' but was afraid of the answer. Instead, she told him about the air. 'So sweet, Dave. Go out near the pool and take a deep breath.'

'I will, before bed.'

'Bed' was an ordinary word, but it tore at her this evening and she had to fight back tears.

'Vanessa?'

'Sorry, the TV's on and they had a bulletin about Nazis on Fairfax Avenue. At least I think that's what they said.'

'Yes, it happened. I was at Canter's . . . and . . . nonsense.' His voice had changed, grown thin and strained. When she tried to speak, he quickly said, 'I'd like to finish this book tonight . . . talk to you again,' and hung up.

She wondered how much that truck's licence plate would mean to him. Would he be grateful?

She watched television, an old movie. She preferred old movies to new ones because they had really great parts for women. Oh, to have been around during the old studio contract years!

But soon Dave crept back into her mind. She shut the television and took a long, hot bath. Before it was over, she was aching for him in a different way. He had been a totally satisfying lover, considerate of her body, of the sensitivity of her breasts and the delicacy of her pelvic area. He had allowed her to ride him more than he rode her, though he'd admitted to preferring the man-on-top position. She had never failed to achieve orgasm with him, finding the thickness of his organ, the rhythm of his upward thrusts . . .

She was fingering her clitoris. She was gasping, thinking of the way he would clutch her bottom and cry out in ecstasy, which never failed to get her off a second or third time.

Now she was alone in her orgasm; was angry at being alone, but unable to resist getting relief.

Afterward, she lay in the cooling water, trembling, still not satisfied. Because what made it so good with Dave was more than his penis, more than his rhythm and clutching and crying out. It was *him*. It was being with him and talking to him and caring for him.

She went right from the tub to the medicine cabinet where she found the plastic jar of Valium (next to the Cytoxin she took each morning). She'd had the Valium

75

almost a year and there were still twenty-one of the original twenty-four tablets left.

But the good times, the calm times, were going fast.

And so would the tranquilizers.

After they'd all changed into civies, Adolf and Carl celebrated with dinner at a trucker's stop off five, well past the LA line. Horst had a sandwich and coffee instead of the steak and beer Adolf and Carl ordered, and there was no way you could call his attitude one of celebration. He didn't finish his food and left quickly, saying he was going to stretch his legs now that the rain had stopped.

Adolf was disappointed in his attitude, but Carl said, 'Little brother drove *fine*! Got us in and out like he was handling a Tiger tank!'

True, and Adolf reasoned that Horst was now experiencing something like battle fatigue; his first action, and even though it had gone well, there was bound to be a little reaction, a little shock.

Adolf too had been excited, even though he'd taken part in many other actions, alone before Carl came of age, and then with Carl before Horst came into the party.

He and Carl had two more beers and talked about the time they'd held a rally alongside a picket line the Commie Caesar Chavez had thrown up on the road where Ham Burton trucked out his lettuce crop. They were in full uniform and the swastika flag flying proudly, daring that spic pack and their red rag to do something about it. They had nine men marching with them that day, a good turn-out, though when the news people came everyone left but Clory's cousin Duke, and he was more than a little drunk.

Duke was packing a small pistol, one of those Lilliputs, and he said the bullets were soft and he'd scored them and dipped them in cyanide. 'Any fuckin' Pancho comes at me, he's dead for sure!' Which was fine with

76

Adolf, except there must have been fifty Mexes marching that picket line. So he told Carl to disarm Duke.

A few of the spics rushed them, trying to take away the swastika flag. Carl belted one of them so hard he broke half the knuckles on his right hand. Adolf belted another, only not with his hand; he used a home-made blackjack, just a leather tube filled with buckshot, but it put that spic into the hospital for three weeks. Then the highway patrol had come and good thing too, though Carl had Duke's little gun and was waving it to make the pickets back up. They wouldn't have backed up for long, they were so mad at seeing those two *compadres* stretched out cold.

Carl laughed and laughed. 'Let's have another beer, Father. Because tonight was the best. I mean, tonight we nailed four stinking Jews!'

Adolf shushed him because two truckers were looking over. One was a big jungle bunny and the other had a nose that could have smelled kosher.

Carl said, 'Fuck 'em. I can take any jigg . . .'

Adolf said sharply, 'Carl! Discipline! Horst was right about not wasting our energies in gas stations. Or in diners.'

Carl came to attention in his chair, but then he giggled. He'd never been able to handle beer, and it was beer that a true Nazi drank at celebrations. Or nothing, like the Führer.

They left the diner, those truckers still giving them a hard eye. So Adolf allowed himself one little pleasure while going out the door: gave them a small Nazi salute, mouthing the word 'Heil'.

The black half rose. Adolf laughed and swaggered out to the truck with his son. He looked back, hoping those truckers would come after him, because it would be such a joy to club them senseless! But no one showed.

Horst at the wheel, they drove back onto the highway for the long trip home. Carl fiddled with the radio until he found the all-news station. When it came, the story was disappointingly brief, but tomorrow there would be more in the newspapers, especially the Commie *Los Angeles Times*. And in the evening there would be television.

What the announcer said now was: 'An incident involving three or four men dressed in Nazi uniform in the Jewish district of Fairfax has led to several injuries, one of which is apparently serious. Warren Gross, eighteen, was admitted to Cedars-Sinai Hospital suffering from what an emergency-doctor termed severe head injuries.

Adolf and Carl exchanged smiles.

Their smiles disappeared when Horst said, 'What if that kid dies?'

'Kid?' Carl said. 'You mean that sheeny scum?'

'What if he dies? You hit him a hell of a lick.'

'Damned right I did! What'd you want me to do, let him climb up here with you?'

'You were going to club that last one a second time. You'd surely have killed him.'

'So what? Killing Jews is the whole idea, isn't it?'

Adolf said, 'Not yet. Not until it's legal.' To Horst he said, 'Save your worries for your father and brother, for your fellow Nazis. If any of those Jews dies, it's their own fault.'

'If any of those Jews dies, it becomes *murder*.'

'Shut up!' Carl shouted. 'They were attacking us! We defended ourselves! Even if the police found us nothing would happen!' He turned to Adolf. 'That's right, isn't it, Father?'

'Yes,' Adolf said firmly. 'It's self-defence, even if some Jew-stooge judge hates the idea. Remember Greensboro.'

'But we were provoking them without legal . . .'

Now it was Adolf who shouted, 'Shut up!'

Horst muttered, 'Sorry. It's Carl I was worried about. You and I didn't club anyone.'

Carl laughed unconvincingly. 'He's wrong, isn't he, Father? Just the usual yellow streak down his back?'

78

'He's wrong,' Adolf said, and patted his *dummkopf's* shoulder. And thought that Horst might be right. And that Carl might also be right, about that yellow streak.

Later, as Carl slept, Adolf said, 'You want to get out of the party, Horst? I won't mind and I won't hold you.'

Horst didn't answer for what seemed like a long time. Adolf tightened inside because he *would* mind, terribly. Carl wasn't bright enough to be a leader and Adolf was fifty-four, and the Führer had been dead at fifty-six, and there was only Horst to take over, to be ready when America finally turned to the white man's single hope.

Horst finally said, 'No, I don't want to get out of the party. But I want the party to stop risking itself – that means the three of us – in senseless actions like tonight's.'

Adolf began to answer, to remind him that the Nazi had to fight as well as reason. Horst said, 'I know your philosophy of street warfare, Father. It's wrong. It won't be right until we can do what Hitler did – put thousands of trained men, in his case ex-soldiers, on the streets.'

'So what do we do, Horst? Stagnate? Just sit and dream?'

'No. We begin building membership. We stop scaring people away. We tone down. We act civilized. Only later do we show our claws.'

Adolf could have replied, but the beer had gotten to him too, and like his son the *dummkopf* he slept.

FOUR: *Thursday, 13 December*

The police came to Rita Goran's apartment at 5.00 p.m. Though, as she realized when she thought how they had rung the bell only moments after she herself had entered, they must have been watching her door from the street. It was easy enough to do in these open courtyard complexes, so common in Southern California. Her one-bedroom flat was on the second floor, which was also the top floor of what they used to call garden apartments back in New York. This one featured a large pool as centrepiece around which the two tiers of apartments were clustered.

'Rita Goran?' the youngish man with faded brown hair and neat matching moustache asked.

She said yes. He said he was Lieutenant Anthony Stone, LAPD, and he wondered if she would mind answering some questions. She said, 'About what?', but of course she knew. What she didn't know was how they had found her or whether they thought she had done it.

She had never been questioned by the police before and was terribly nervous. But she allowed the lieutenant and another plain-clothes officer to enter her home because to stand on her rights and demand a search warrant would be ridiculous . . . if she had actually not known why they were here. Also, Stone seemed like such a nice person, young and quite good-looking. And she liked the way he was dressed – a basic brown suit, single-breasted and simple, but very neat, the trousers sharply creased, and with a clean white shirt and quiet striped tie.

His assistant, whom he introduced as Detective Lowery, wasn't quite as good-looking, his features large and too mobile. (He seemed on the point of swallowing his lower lip several times.) Nor was he as well groomed – he wore a rumpled hound's-tooth jacket, open-necked sports shirt and baggy blue trousers. He was even younger than the lieutenant, who couldn't have been much past thirty, and considerably larger in a gangly way. But he too was soft-spoken and gentlemanly, without a hint of violence in his nature, which never failed to score points with Rita.

She waved the officers to the couch and considered offering them coffee or soft drinks, then decided that that would seem as if she were trying to ingratiate herself. She sat down in the wing-back chair facing them, crossed her legs and murmured, 'Yes?'

Lieutenant Stone reached into his pocket and took out a small black notebook. 'Vincent Rossa's address book,' he began.

'Vincent?' she interrupted, her instincts operating despite her tension. And with the quick understanding that they had found her name in his book and that they were going to question everyone in that book, she was immediately less tense. Of course, if they found out she had been at his apartment Tuesday night . . .

'Vincent?' she repeated, and he nodded. 'Has anything happened to him?' Which was ingenuous and what she would say if she didn't know and wasn't involved and was just somewhat worried about her casual friend.

'I'm afraid so. He was killed Tuesday evening. In his apartment.'

She covered her mouth. 'Oh my God.'

'Were you close with him – an intimate friend?'

'Oh no, we'd only just met two weeks ago, at a movie. I saw him twice, that's all.' (And the third time had been for a drive up into Malibu and past a restaurant at Paradise Cove where he said they would come 'some other time, but tonight I'm cooking you a gourmet dinner'. Which was the cheap cut of steak, followed by the cheaper seduction attempt, and then the assault. And as far as she knew, no one had seen them together Tuesday. But that was the critical point; that could mean her life.) 'I didn't know he had my address or phone number. We hadn't gotten that far.'

'He *didn't* have them. Just your name and the notation "will call me". We got the unlisted phone number and address from Ma Bell's files.'

'Ah. Can I help in any way?'

Detective Lowery had stopped chewing his lip. He now had a cigarette in his mouth and was lighting it.

'Did you see him last Tuesday?'

She said, 'No,' and, 'Detective Lowery, please don't smoke in here.'

Lowery chuckled. 'I swear I didn't even know I was doing it.' He put out the cigarette in Rita's empty nut dish.

Stone said, 'Did he ever speak about enemies, someone he feared, someone you think might have had reason to hurt him?'

She shook her head slowly, thoughtfully. 'But of course we hardly knew each other. He wasn't likely to confide in me, nor I in him.' She was suddenly sorry she hadn't thought to take his wallet, some valuables; to make it look like a robbery.

Stone said, 'We believe it was someone he knew, someone he might have been entertaining, because we found the remains of two steak dinners in the garbage – judging by the bones.'

Now Rita had something else to be sorry for – not having taken out the garbage.

All she could do was nod and wait, looking as if she were distressed, which she was.

Lowery suddenly said, 'Would you allow me to take your fingerprints, Miss Goran?'

She was startled; then fought panic. She had missed

the opportunity to make it look like a robbery and she had forgotten to take out the garbage. Perhaps she had also left a set of her prints?

Her mind worked quickly. 'Of course, though I don't see what good it will do.'

He chuckled, but now he had steel in his eyes. 'A matching set might show up in Rossa's apartment.'

'It might indeed. I was there after our second date.'

Lowery looked at Stone. Stone said, 'You understand that we're questioning everyone in Mr Rossa's book, as well as those in his apartment house.' She waited for him to say, 'Just routine,' but he rose and thanked her and asked her to give Detective Lowery a business number, if any, in case they had to get in touch with her during the day. Then he walked out.

The big detective wrote slowly as she gave him the school address and phone number. She said, 'Please don't call unless it's very important. I don't like to be disturbed while I'm with my class.'

He nodded, and asked if he might have a glass of water. She went to the kitchen . . . and had a sudden flash, a strong intuition that they were playing a game. They were trying to pressure her, to make her do something that would quickly implicate her.

She went back to the living room with the glass of water.

Lowery turned quickly, guiltily from the door to her bedroom.

And the coat closet near the front entrance was open.

He sipped the water and didn't meet her eyes . . . and he was certainly schooled sufficiently in his work to have met her eyes no matter what he'd done. And to have turned from the bedroom as her footsteps approached. And to have closed the closet door if he'd searched inside.

He handed back the glass, almost as full as she'd brought it. Which was supposed to show her that the glass of water had been a ruse to get her out of the room so he could search for evidence. Which in turn

83

was supposed to make her get rid of something that could tie her to Vincent Rossa's murder.

She saw him to the door, thinking their plan wasn't bad if they were dealing with fools, novices.

He left and she closed the door, smiling a little. She was still frightened, but also amused.

She began preparing dinner – a salad and a small can of tuna packed in water. She wasn't going anywhere so she added sliced onion which she dearly loved . . . then began to wonder, to worry, whether the detectives were playing their game with several people in Vincent's address book, or just with her.

Which made her break into a sweat and sink into a chair and tremble. Because jail was unthinkable – she would die first! Because she had killed several times before and they might have found some common clue, some connecting element of *modus operandi* in all the killings.

Just how many *had* there been?

She'd blocked them from her mind, but now she counted, using her fingers and mumbling names, and in California alone she had a full hand – five. And before leaving New York, and not counting Will, and certainly not Daddy . . .

'No!'

Her shouting voice made her jump up. Insane to consider Daddy, who had died in an accident.

'Like Will,' her voice was saying. Then she was crying, the sobs wracking her body. It was a storm, a hurricane of grief, and it swept away numbers and names, leaving her empty, purified.

She began to eat.

Stone was back at the station when Lowery came in, looking tired. 'Five stake-outs and so far nothing. The captain's going to complain about all the manpower this SIT's using.'

'A special investigation team has to investigate, right?' Stone cracked. 'Besides, we don't exactly have *nothing*. Your little cigarette act got a definite response in two instances.'

'You never did explain the reason for that act.'

'Rossa smoked unfiltered Camels. There were six butts in the garbage and two in the bedroom ashtray. All unfiltered Camels. None with lipstick. Which means it's unlikely whoever was with him smoked.'

'That night. And I don't care what they say about his not having men friends. A man *could* have been there, which would blow your no lipstick clue to hell. Which means we need an eye witness or a confession.'

'You'll never make lieutenant with that attitude. You have to play the odds, work on scraps, and then . . .'

'Hope a snitch gives you the killer,' Lowery finished sourly.

Stone chuckled. 'Right. Still, your cigarette act isolated two out of five suspects.'

'Suspects? C'mon, Lieutenant. Names in an address book. Ladies he dated. And can you see that nice-looking schoolteacher slicing a man up the way Rossa got it?'

Stone leaned back in his chair. 'Did you notice her hands, her wrists? Strong, large, and she's in good shape. I'd say she works out. Golf or tennis . . .'

'Or crocheting. She must be forty-five, at least. All of them are.'

'Attitude, Lowery. I don't think those sociology courses at UCLA are doing you any good. At least not as a detective. And forty-five is a young chick, if you're sixty.'

Lowery sighed and nodded. 'Yeah. I can't seem to see murderers in such . . . ordinary women. They're all like my Aunt Maude. Hell, like my mother!'

'I've seen ladies like your mother and mine who knocked off men like your father and mine. Rossa swung pretty good for a man his age, according to the neighbours. One of his ladies might have wanted him to stop seeing the others. Or resented a heavy make on just the second or third date.'

'Miss Goran?'

'Anything's possible. Let's see if one of those five ladies tries to get rid of a knife, an article of clothing, whatever.'

'And if they don't, as they probably won't, what then?'

'Then we go on to another line of investigation.'

'What other line? His business partner was at dinner with four people and had nothing to gain by his death. Rossa was a widower and childless. That's the whole other line. What we've got here is an unknown assailant walking in on Rossa and cutting his heart out for a reason we probably won't ever learn.' He paused. 'Do you know the percentage of murder cases solved in Los Angeles? Solved nation-wide, for that matter?'

Stone leaned back comfortably. 'I'm sure you'll tell me, college boy.'

'Six in ten is the latest official quote . . . though that's not the conviction rate, which is even more dismal. And that's what the *police* say. In less prejudicial circles, figures such as two or three in ten are bandied about. We're talking about roughly 3,000 murders a year, state-wide. Better than eight a day, Lieutenant. Considering that even more aren't reported as murders, we're drowning in maybe 5,000 . . .'

The phone rang. Stone picked it up, listened; then his eyes flicked to Lowery. 'Yeah . . . I wasn't aware he was studying Nazis . . . a masters in sociology.'

Lowery, who was just sitting down, didn't.

'You can ask him yourself, Captain. He's right here.' He handed the phone across the desk.

Lowery took it, slouching to accommodate the short line. He said, 'Yessir,' several times, and slowly a smile stretched across his wide mouth. 'I believe I *can* be of help.' He listened and his smile slid away. 'Is that important, sir?' He nodded to himself, sourly. 'The family's name got changed at Ellis Island, Captain. My grandfather used to tell the story of how Lowerchowsky was transmuted to Lowery by an official with a sense of humour, or a sense of compassion. But I'm sure I can retain my objectivity, even if I am Jewish.'

Stone's eyebrows rose and he murmured, 'Funny, you don't look like a Lowerchowsky.' Which Lowery ignored and Stone found vastly amusing.

'First thing in the morning,' Lowery was saying, his smile back. 'Thanks, Captain. I know it's a real opportunity . . . yes, thanks again.'

He hung up. Stone said, 'Well, are you joining Israeli Intelligence or what?'

'I'm getting an SIT of my own,' Lowery said, pure wonder in his voice.

'What? SITs are headed up by lieutenants or higher, almost never lower ranks.'

'It's the Nazi business on Fairfax last night. The eighteen-year-old JDL member is barely hanging on and they're getting pressure from the city council which is being barraged by complaints from local residents.'

'So they decided to put a Hebe on the case, right?' He smiled sweetly.

Lowery went to the door. 'I guess.'

'But we got plenty of kosher lieutenants. Why a detective two, and a new one at that?'

'Those courses at UCLA, with research on California's lunatic fringe. Plus a thesis on the American Nazi movement. When the department called the university to find out who among several enrolled officers was particularly suited . . .'

'Up popped the Lone Litvak!'

'You know from Litvak's and Galitzianas, born-again Stone?'

'Before I was born again I had a torrid romance with a *zaftig* JAP. In fact, Detective Lowerchowsky, I almost became an anti-Semite because of her. Or rather because of her father who fucked us up, broke us up, and got his daughter married to a *landsman*. But hell, she didn't hide her religion; why did you?'

'I didn't hide it. You never asked.'

'*Zei gesundt*, baby.'

Lowery chuckled. 'I'll miss you, Stone.'

'I won't miss you, Lowery; you and your negative attitude. Tell me, you going to write off that kid with the fractured skull to the percentages, to the odds on unsolveds?'

'Not him, Lieutenant.'

'Because he's a *landsman*, huh?'

'Because it's *my* case, *my* special investigations team.' He paused. 'And because the bastard who clubbed him was wearing a swastika. A *swastika*. Do you know what that means to a Jew, born-again Stone?'

'I know what it should mean to anyone: a crackpot jerk who thinks Americans can forget that this country lost hundreds of thousands of lives fighting that symbol. Which also means that only the *least* dangerous men wear it. They're too ridiculous to be dangerous; in a big way, a political way, that is.'

'It means that six million dead aren't enough for some people, Lieutenant. *That's* what it means.' Lowery left.

Stone took out cigarettes, used his lighter and inhaled deeply. He checked his watch – almost nine. The stake-outs would continue all night and for two more days. Then they'd have to fold.

He needed a break, but didn't count on getting it.

Lowery was right about the odds. Stone hoped they wouldn't stop the Litvak from nailing the Nazis so he could get back to real police work.

Stone went down to the garage and drove his Datsun Z onto Wilshire. He stopped thinking of Lowery and the Fairfax SIT. He had his own case and he had to find a way to break it, to beat those terrible odds. And the only way to do it was to think on it. And think on it. Until something happened, or it was classified Inactive to gather dust with all the other unsolveds, all the other men shot and strangled and stabbed . . .

He pulled to the curb. 'All the other men stabbed,' he muttered, remembering someone else's SIT; an ageing bachelor male cut to death.

And there'd been one before that, about a year ago,

also a bachelor male, also mature – in his fifties, as Stone recalled.

He U-turned and opened the Z wide, heading back the way he'd come. He wanted to check the files; just those cases that fit his own; just those in the Santa Monica North Station.

Later he would check city-wide; Sheriff's department too.

This could be the big one, a female Jack-the-Ripper. This could be the stairway to Parker Centre and a chief's hat.

'Anyway,' he said, 'it couldn't hoit.'

FIVE: *Saturday, 15 December*

Vanessa hadn't followed Dave until 7.00 p.m. on Friday, and even then hadn't done more than run a quick check on his home.

She'd had a 10.00 a.m. audition set up by Rob Cerjak, which had taken her to Paramount and kept her there until twelve twenty. By the time she'd gotten back to the Valley and Ventura Boulevard, it had been a quarter to one. The silver Mercedes four-door had been parked in its alloted spot in the Dale Building lot, so he was either lunching in his office or was across the street at Thomasine's.

He had been at the bar having a sandwich, deep in conversation with Teddy. She'd given him the social wave and begun to walk towards a TV director at the far end, a real schmuck, but he'd been beckoning and smiling, and any port in a storm.

Dave had stopped her, asked her to join him, and her heart had begun a jazz syncopation . . . all for nought. There'd been a little three-way chit-chat and he'd left, instructing Teddy to put her lunch on his tab.

Teddy had leaned on the bar. 'Sweat it out, lady. He's in terrible shape, but I can't see him letting you go. Give him a little time.'

'Him and his new chick.'

'No new chick. I'd know. Be cool.'

She'd wanted to believe him. She'd also wanted to ask him what to do about the Nazis' licence number, but had feared his closeness to Dave.

90

Later that evening she'd checked Dave's home. He'd been pacing around his study. When he'd finally sat down with a book, she'd left. She'd gone on to a party in Holmby Hills thrown by Pearl Leahy, a business manager who just *loved* stacked starlets.

Pearl and Vanessa had come to an agreement some years ago: Pearl didn't try to seduce Vanessa and Vanessa didn't tell her to fuck off. They got along well that way and Pearl would represent Vanessa whenever Vanessa needed the prestige of management as opposed to agency, which wasn't very often.

The party had been fine. Pearl had introduced her to one Rolls Royce, three Mercedes, and a young, horny Ferrari (her way of classifying moneymen). Vanessa had been propositioned with a Vegas trip, a Palm Springs trip, and (from the horny Ferrari) half an ounce of Peruvian Flake, uncut, he swore, which was a real compliment, the current value of the top-grade cocaine being $2,500 to $3,000. She had left alone, despite the Rolls following her outside and suggesting that she accompany him to London.

In younger days she had been shaken by such action, tempted by such action, but had learned soon enough that it was wasteful of one's self-esteem, and even more wasteful of one's reputation as a serious toiler in the field of film.

Driving home, she still hadn't decided what to do about the Nazis' licence plate.

But today, as soon as she awakened, she had the answer.

It was ten and she was meeting Rob Cerjak at noon for brunch. He was beginning to go heavy on her, talking love-talk on the phone, and she didn't want to believe it. He'd seemed a lot smarter than that. Three or four days, really, and love talk!

Sex she could take. Their deal she could take, perhaps even enjoy in time. But love? He had to be kidding! As her old Norwegian grandpa used to say, quoting a Greek shipmate of his youth, 'The time it takes to know another person is the time it takes to eat a hundred pounds of salt.'

As she and Dave had eaten.

She had grapefruit juice and a handful of raisins, saving her appetite for Ma Maison. She showered and dressed and fiddled with her nails.

At eleven, when Teddy usually arrived at Thomasine's, she went to the phone and did one quick rehearsal of her squeaky-high voice with Lulubelle accent; then dialled. Teddy answered and she said, 'Mr Brown?'

'Yes.'

'Ah'm an admirer. Unknown, unseen, but now Ah'll be heard.'

'Yes?'

'Ah just happened to see you-all coming out of Canter's last night. Wasn't it just terrible about those men in the truck? Can you believe Ah took down their licence number?'

'And you want me to give it to Dave,' Teddy said chuckling. 'What were you doing – tailing him? Trying to catch him with a date?'

'Ah never heard of this heah Dave.' Her face was flaming. 'Ah don't know what you-all talkin' about.'

'Sure you do, Vanessa. I'll pass it on, though it won't be doing him any favours. And the licence is bound to be hot, maybe the truck too. But since you went to all this trouble to hide your little shadowing act, I won't snitch.'

She said, 'Ah don't know who this Vanessa is,' and quickly read off the licence number. As long as she didn't admit it, he couldn't be certain.

'One more time, Vanessa. And I promise not to tell Dave about you.'

'*Lulubelle*,' she said, and read the number again and hung up on his growing laughter.

She wondered how he would explain getting the number to Dave . . . but he was a man of his word and she trusted him. Also, she knew he desired her, knew he would make a play if he was ever convinced she and

92

Dave were really finished, and therefore would want to keep her happy.

Anyway, Dave now had something he wanted, and perhaps later on she could tell him who had given it to him.

It was getting late and she had to hurry. She didn't want to keep Cerjak waiting. He was coming through, step by step, with his part of the deal. Yesterday she had landed a small but challenging role in an NBC movie of the week. Based on that he would expect her to spend the day with him, and perhaps the night.

The night she planned to reject because it was Saturday, date night, and Dave might be seeing his new love . . . if one existed.

Teddy had made her doubt that existence yesterday. Teddy had calmed her, comforted her. Maybe she could cool it, let Dave have his two- or three-week vacation from her. Then they could come back together.

By the time she had driven out of the underground garage, she was thinking she would play today by ear. If Cerjak set up an audition for her with another production outfit where he had muscle, she might change her mind and stay over with him.

But – and she began to sing – 'Please don't talk about love tonight!'

Lieutenant Anthony Stone hadn't exactly levelled with Lowery about Clara, his Jewish girlfriend. True, he had loved her, and true, her father had done everything he could to separate his daughter from the goy. But nothing would have been able to separate them if both had been totally committed to marriage, as both said they were. One, obviously, had been lying.

It hadn't been Clara.

Sometimes he missed her, but he recognized that he hadn't been ready for marriage at twenty-seven. And he still wasn't ready for it at thirty-four.

Not that he hadn't been in love with Clara. And not

that he hadn't been in love at least three times since . . . maybe four.

'Maybe five,' he murmured as he drove into the Santa Monica North Station garage. He loved women, yes, but just didn't seem to like them very much. Why? Maybe his job had something to do with it.

Vincent Rossa was a case in point, wasn't he? Of what women did to men?

Or did the Rossa case actually argue for the other view? A man alone, at that age, on the prowl, bed-hopping. A man who should have been involved with wife and children and grandchildren at age sixty, in-volved instead with a homicidal bitch.

But marriage at thirty-four was no guarantee of to-getherness at sixty. Rossa's wife had died on him.

Then there was Rodrick Bedford, another name in the files. Bedford had been fifty-seven with a loving son and one grandchild, and still ended up with a knife in the heart. While his wife was visiting that loving son and grandchild, he'd been glimpsed escorting what a witness termed 'a large female figure' into his apartment and she'd probably cut him to death, much as Vincent Rossa had been cut.

Jerome Rail, the name on the other folder Stone had pulled, had been single all his life, and active with the ladies all his life. But at a time when most men have learned better, he'd gotten into a real hassle with one – the scratches on his face and the shred of pink material in his hand (believed to have come from a woman's panties), proved he'd tried a very heavy make indeed. His last make, at age fifty-three, two and a half years ago.

Stone went up the stairs and along the wide hallway to his office, waving at three men in the bullpen to his right. A fourth, Lowery, was missing, and Stone won-dered where the Lone Litvak would be working. Prob-ably out of Hollywood West.

But he had no time to waste on Lowery and Nazi kooks. He had something big on his hands . . . or he *could* have, if he put it together correctly; if he found the unifying clue. He'd been thinking of that, searching for that, for two solid days and nights, and his guts ached.

What he needed was to relax tonight; enjoy himself with Debbie.

But she was beginning to question his sincerity, his seriousness; beginning to wonder, 'Where is this relationship going?' Which was always the tolling bell, the beginning of the end, and soon he'd have to find a replacement.

He used the phone and got Al Placer in the bullpen. 'Anything on those stake-outs?'

'Not yet, Lieutenant. Anything decent, you'll get it immediately.'

'I'll decide what's decent. Let's see some written reports. Within the hour. And Placer, I want you to clear yourself Monday for special assignment.'

The young detective's voice grew excited. 'Special assignment?'

'You're going to be searching files all over this city for matches with three other files, one of them Rossa's.'

The excitement died. 'Yeah, Lieutenant.'

'That's the spirit,' Stone said, and hung up.

When the call finally came in on the stake-outs, he listened, said, 'Thanks,' and wondered if it was too late to take that course in computer programming he'd considered at eighteen.

None of the five ladies had made a move more suspicious than buying a quart of vodka and holing up with it for two days (a Miss Loewen, who also bought a carton of filtered cigarettes), or taking an evening gown to the cleaners (another smoker, Miss Breen, whose gown showed no more deadly stains when police quickly ran it through the lab than red wine). The others had gone about what the young Placer categorized as 'really quiet old lives, Lieutenant.'

So he would turn his attention to the Grovernor case, in which a socially prominent Beach resident had been

95

mugged by a man he'd described three different ways at three different times from his hospital bed. Part of that was certainly due to his brains being rattled by pounding fists . . . and part was due to a 2.6 percentage of alcohol in his blood, which constituted high legal intoxication. Grovernor was recovering now and screaming through lawyers and Sacramento political friends for an arrest.

He had another stimulating, challenging case – a robbery in Santa Monica Canyon, an area of old houses, many of which had belonged to silent-film stars. Three stone statues had been taken from a back garden. They were described by the outraged owner, the son and heir of one of these stars, as 'a Venus, an Apollo and an Anubis'. Stone had asked about the Anubis, which turned out to be an Egyptian god of tombs and embalming, with the head of a jackal. The owner felt the statues had been stolen by someone who had come to the house previously, probably as a guest, and not for profit but for decoration. He gave Stone three sheets of paper with over two hundred names taken from his guest lists of parties during the past five years, and wanted him to find and search every one of their homes.

'I got a million of 'em,' Stone muttered, doing his Jimmy Durante, but finding no fun in it. Most police work was of the Grovernor and Anubis variety, so that when a real SIT came along, a juicy murder like Rossa's, you damn well wanted to solve it.

He sat thinking, working through one blind alley after another, until he made a decision. He would add five names to Placer's file search: the five women in Rossa's little black book. He would pray for a mention as a witness, a neighbour, a girlfriend – especially as a girlfriend – in another case; any other case.

And he would place a small side bet that if one of those names did turn up, it would be either Rita Goran or Lois Aelia, the non-smokers.

Detective Two Harold Lowery sat in the unfamiliar office – hell, *any* office was unfamiliar; he'd known only bullpens – in the unfamiliar station and read the folder of witness depositions, no less than eight of them. All basically useless in terms of finding those Nazis.

He couldn't believe he didn't have a licence plate!

Even descriptions of the truck failed to give him a make, a truly accurate and agreed-upon picture.

What he had was three, possibly four ski-masked men – two could have been in the front seat before one from the back joined them – in uniform, with swastika armbands, riding in a truck with wood-slat sides, big swastika banners and a loudspeaker system blaring 'God Bless America' . . . written by Irving Berlin, a Jew, but those morons wouldn't know it.

He also had several copies of a crude sheet of hate literature. Almost funny that inept propaganda, but not quite for a Jew . . . and Harold Lowery felt very Jewish indeed today. Yesterday Captain Gensen had given him a pep talk, ending with the stirring give-'em-hell line, 'Nail those bastards, Lowery, and make your people proud of you!'

But Gensen hadn't minded putting the Lone Litvak (as Stone had called him) to work on Saturday, Shabuoth, the day Jehovah rested from his labours of creating Jews and Nazis. Gensen felt he needed every day of the week for this fragile case.

Well, he wasn't entirely without ways to go. He had a copy of last Monday's *LA Times* with the article on California's Nazi groups – all three of them. He would interview a few more of the many Fairfax Avenue witnesses, then head north. He would personally check out those Nazis, and since he had no faces to find, would try to find the truck. Or a bat which might show traces of blood – a possible murder weapon, as this case might yet turn out to be homicide if the victim succumbed.

The victim was Warren Gross, eighteen, Caucasian; member of what the LAPD considered an extremist group, who had reacted in extreme fashion to a pro-vocation. And ended up with a crushed skull.

But he was something more than that to Lowery now; something more than a name and a smiling highschool graduation picture as printed in the *Examiner*. Lowery had visited Gross's California cottage home two blocks west of Fairfax yesterday, doing what was little more than killing time, satisfying his curiosity because he had nothing else to do while waiting for his SIT to shape up.

Gross had been described as short and stocky by witnesses. His brief moment in the limelight was marked by quick running and sudden falling. He'd been the one to shout, 'Never again!' the slogan, the battle-cry referring to the Holocaust. Never again, it said, would Jews go meekly into concentration camps and gas chambers.

But why, Lowery had wanted to know, would an ordinary eighteen-year-old American kid, born and bred in LA, member of the Fairfax High soccer team, who'd taken a job with an uncle as a roofer's assistant . . . why would a boy born twenty-eight years after Adolf Hitler's death and the end of Nazi Germany be so involved in matters relating to Nazis and the Holo-caust? Lowery was eleven years closer to those events than Gross, but, like other Jews he knew, involved in his own life, his job, and women, and the Dodgers and Rams.

Gross lived with his mother in the home of his ma-ternal grandmother, the father having left the state after an early divorce. 'A Shabuoth goy,' the thin, bespec-tacled, old lady said with contempt, describing the miss-ing father. She had whispy white hair and a million wrinkles, but rock-steady hands and voice. Lowery re-alized she'd made her evaluation of him; had decided he was a *landsman* and could be talked to.

The mother, in her early forties and quite pretty, shook her head and muttered, 'Momma, stop, it's not important.'

'Not important?' the old lady asked. She sat on the couch beside her daughter, and Lowery sat facing them in a wicker chair with a cushion seat. The living room was small, cluttered and very clean. 'A father running away is not important? That's why Warren was with those fools. That's why he's dying.'

The mother dropped her head and began to cry. When she stopped, she spoke to Lowery. 'My husband was American-born. He couldn't take what Momma and I put him through.'

'Put him through?' the old lady asked. 'We spoke of what we knew. Auschwitz, where my Yztrohk died. Where you spent two years of your childhood. Where the devils murdered, murdered . . .' She got up and hobbled out of the room.

'She won't cry in front of anyone, not even me,' the mother said. 'A very tough woman. But she can't forget and she can't stop telling people. My husband ran. Maybe I should have run with him, but how could I leave Momma? We're the only family survivors. I talked too . . . what little I could remember. And Warren drank it in with his milk, ate it with his baby food.' She wiped her eyes with a tissue. 'Momma and I, we're the reason Warren's dying.'

Lowery had tried to convince her that the boy would recover, and indeed that morning he had been reported as 'showing improvement'. But an hour ago, when Lowery had last checked, he had lapsed into a coma. If he did die, there would be a lot more pressure than now, and now was enough for Lowery.

'And for my three assistants,' he thought, unable to restrain a sense of pride. He had a real SIT. Twenty-nine years old and with his own Special Investigation Team! He had three detectives under his command. At least he *would* have them, once they reported on Monday.

His eyes fell on the sheet of Nazi literature, and pride gave way to anger. For the third time he examined the cartoon of a fat, caricatured Jew being punched in grotesquely hooked nose by a Nazi fist and read the hate-drivel. And while he had read racist, anti-Semitic material before – during his studies; in the Liberty Lobby's *Spotlight*, KKK publications and similar trash – this one was flat out. This one bore the obscene swastika.

He got up, restless, anxious to move, to drive north and begin working.

But he had to be here for the shape-up on Monday, to cue the others in on their tasks: search state-wide hot-sheets for the truck, the files for similar violent demonstrations, and the good old snitch lists.

Though whether informers existed within the miniscule California Nazi organizations was questionable.

Still, he wanted to do something and there was little to be done in Los Angeles this weekend.

He could reach Bethills by night, stay over in a motel, and question members of the Nazi group on Sunday. But first he had to ask the highway patrol for a local contact, an officer who knew the area and its people . . .

He was already on the phone, dialling Gensen at home, hoping the captain would remember his offer to 'help no matter when'.

The captain said he would call a friend on the CHP. 'Go pack a bag, Lowery. By the time you're ready, I'll have an officer assigned to help you and a motel where you'll meet.'

Lowery was in his Chevy moments later, starting the drive from West Los Angeles to Sherman Oaks where he had a studio flat in an apartment complex two blocks north of Ventura. It was overpriced, as was all rental housing in Los Angeles, but at least they hadn't turned condo . . . yet.

He tried to remember to call Maria and cancel their dance date, but his mind was on other things. On his paternal grandfather's tales of the *shtetls* – the Jewish towns that had existed in Europe, mainly in Poland and Russia, before Hitler obliterated them and their people – and of the charm of life there, despite Poles who had been no joke to the Jews who suffered their persecution.

100

His grandfather, Mendel Meyer, who had come to New York in steerage and to the West Coast in a box car, an adventurer as daring as any pioneer, considering the timid insularity of Orthodox Jews of his day.

And his grandmother, who had survived her 78-year-old husband by only three months because their's was a marriage made not in heaven but in *earth*, sealed not by words but by emotions and flesh, by seven children, five of whom had survived; a marriage built on knowledge of the special joy and pain of being Jewish in an era that had made the very word an insult.

And he, the Lone Litvak, the joke Jew, had played at Bar Mitzvah and far more seriously at basketball, holding his own at six-one with a team composed mainly of giant blacks who called him Stumpy and grudgingly admitted he had pretty good moves and passable rhythm on the dance floor.

He had forgotten who he really was, except on the High Holy Days and sometimes Passover and rarely Chanukah and never on those lesser known holidays his grandfather had asked him to honour: like Sukkoth and Purim and the one he remembered only from Henny Youngman's old gag-song, 'I met my love on T'ishibov.'

Gag song for the joke Jew.

Now he was full of the need to show his dead grandfather that it was no joke to mess with the tears, the grief of an entire people. And he almost wished he was *not* a police officer so that he could go about it in a different way, a more personal and deadly way.

David was increasingly more nervous as it grew closer to noon and his date with Rita Goran. He had changed suits and was considering switching to a Cardin blazer and grey flannel trousers, perhaps more befitting an afternoon at the Polo Lounge where, the weather having turned clear and mild again, they might sit outdoors.

He left the bedroom, walking down the hallway past

101

the study and guest room to the living room, trying to escape the adolescent pre-date hysteria. Besides, his suit was informal enough for the occasion: a single-breasted lightweight tweed of rustic brown with just a hint of quiet green in the weave. 'This season's most respected fabric,' he'd been told by the salesman, in explanation of the indecent price tag. He also wore a delicate part-wool shirt of pale gold with rounded, button-down collar and a dark brown silk tie. Thick-soled Johnston & Murphy shoes completed an ensemble he felt suited any luncheon date . . . and still he was compelled to go to the guest bathroom and examine himself in the full-length mirror.

The phone rang and he took the call in the kitchen.

Teddy said, 'Hey man, what you doing?'

'Getting ready to go out.'

'Little tennis?'

'Little date.'

'Ah . . . can I pry?'

'Sure. A blind date through an ad in a literary journal. Probably a disaster. I wish I wasn't going.'

'Then don't. With a chick like Vanessa waiting for a kind word . . .'

'That doesn't work any more. It never did, except in bed.'

'So? Wiser men than both of us have defined love as the projection of an erection. Ask an honest psychologist about love. You'll get friendship and habit and similar crap, but if you don't fuck a woman, you don't love a woman.'

'Right. And I don't fuck Vanessa any more.'

There was a pause. 'Then you won't mind my trying a move?'

David wasn't surprised, but still he was shocked. And upset. 'You must know how dangerous it is to ask a divorced man – even if *he* got the divorce – if you can date his ex-wife.'

Teddy chuckled. 'As long as you're up-front with me,

baby. Now to important things. You still want that Nazi licence plate?'

Again David felt shock. But he said, 'Yes,' unhesitatingly.

'I think I've got it. Just kept thinking of it and wham, last night, a sort of subliminal flash of memory . . . Anyway, I'd bet on this one. Want to write it down?'

'Subliminal flash,' David sighed. 'Wham.'

'You got a pencil?'

'Why should I write it down when I'm going to ask you to use your special friends to trace it for me?'

It was Teddy's turn to sigh. 'You've got friends of your own, Duvid'l. And I hate to ask those cats for favours.'

David said nothing. Teddy said, 'Yeah,' flatly. 'I'll get back to you when they get back to me.'

'Thanks, Teddy. I owe you another dinner at Canter's.'

'Look, let's eat somewhere safe, like Teheran.' He hung up.

David walked to the living room and the glass doors leading to the pool. Beyond was the long redwood deck looking out over the little valley. A modest view, a green view, with Rudy Vallee's pink hacienda across the mile or so to the other side; with the hum of Mulholland filtering through pines and heavy brush . . .

And concentrating on the view couldn't stop him from thinking, 'What will I do if Teddy calls back with a name, an address for the Nazi truck?'

He walked to the garage, reached up to the side shelf and found the wooden box under the old blanket. He carried it into the game room, opened it and was looking at two pistols.

One was a snub-nosed, five-shot Smith and Wesson ·38 called a Detective Special; a fine little revolver that, when loaded with hollow-points, would kill effectively at close range.

The second gun he'd had back in New York, illegally, since the Sullivan Law made it almost impossible for anyone but a criminal to own a handgun in Manhattan. Most of the time he had kept it at his Hillside Lake cottage and fired it at a private range near by. A Colt Trooper, also ·38 calibre, but this one would take magnums, six of them, and stop a bull, and not necessarily at close range. It had a three-inch barrel, long enough for accuracy but not target-range long, and could be carried on the person without bulging like a shotgun.

They probably needed cleaning. He'd sprayed them with WD 40 every so often, but they hadn't been fired in five or six years. The last time had been when he'd gone to the Angelus range with Vanessa, who had learned to fire her father. Californians owned far more handguns than New Yorkers because they could be legally bought here with just a few day's wait.

He checked his watch and it was time to leave. He put the box in the guest-room closet, banishing thoughts of Nazis and guns from his mind.

At the Beverly Hills Hotel, he hurried through the lobby and around the left to the Polo Lounge.

The captain said, 'Mr Howars, good to see you again,' and shook his hand. No obsequiousness here. Each captain was more courted during peak hours than any of his clients.

David looked around. They hadn't arranged a recognition signal, a flower or special piece of clothing. He asked if anyone had used his name.

'Yes, this way.' And before he had time to gather his wits, he was being led to a booth across from the little service bar.

The woman had her hands folded on the table, childlike, and was looking to her right. She didn't see David until the captain moved the table aside so he could slide in beside her.

She said, 'David?'

'Yes.' He was anxious to see her, examine her, but he had rushed from bright sunlight into this dim corner, and so he smiled blindly and asked if she cared for a drink.

'Wine. White, if you please.'

'Do you like Montrachet?'

'Yes. Very much. A '76 isn't too extravagant, but it can be excellent if the pressing . . .' She made a sound of self-impatience. 'I shouldn't instruct a man like you.'

The waiter approached, sent by the captain to give an old customer quick service. Which meant the captain would also get quick service; a substantial tip. David had always tipped afterwards, on the way out, rather than on being seated. It was a trade mark, one he had cultivated when such things had seemed important. 'I know very little about wine,' he said. 'I used to know something about Cognac. Then ten years ago I settled on one brand, so I no longer know anything about that either.' And he smiled, no longer nervous, no longer worried about impressing her. Because he was in his element here.

And because Teddy's call had shown him where his priorities lay.

He ordered the Montrachet and turned to Rita Goran, eyes finally functional. He'd had the impression of a rather large woman, and now saw that it wasn't entirely correct. She was slim enough and obviously not very tall. The impression of size came from the strength inherent in her hands, her arms as she moved them, a pair of good-sized shoulders.

Her face was strong-boned, handsome rather than pretty, framed by medium-length dark hair worn youthfully loose. And her smile, now that she returned his gaze, was very nice indeed – full-lipped, wide and steady, showing large, even teeth.

'Do I pass inspection?' she asked. Her voice proved the exception to the image of strength. It held a tremor, and he remembered her spidery signature.

Her clothing, what he could see of it, indicated a certain amount of taste and an equal amount of don't-give-a-damn. She wore a fine wool jacket over a rumpled sweater.

'Do *I*?' he asked.

105

She looked at him, that smile remaining, and nodded. 'But I must confess that you would have had to be very unphysical indeed to make me feel disappointed. I was prepared to like you from your letter and from your phone call. Once I create a mental image . . .' She shook her head. 'I'm talking too much again. My failing.' She looked away.

He was touched. She was perhaps forty-five, perhaps more, but very fit and increasingly attractive to him.

Her hands separated and moved on the table as she again looked at the booth to their right. Those hands intrigued him. Large for a woman, though not unfeminine with their length and whiteness and neat lacquered nails.

'Could you tell me who's sitting at the next table?' she asked. 'Am I correct in thinking . . .?' She seemed embarrassed to finish and leaned back so he could look by her.

There was no mistaking the tall, white-haired man, still trim and handsome after a lifetime in films. 'Yes, Cesar Romero. Would you like to meet him?'

'You *know* him?'

He began to feel a little of the pride in profession, of the pleasure in being able to impress someone not in the industry, that he'd thought had gone. (He last recalled feeling it when his ex-wife and son had visited three years ago and he'd taken them on sets and introduced them to stars and allowed them to see his expertise in movie-making.) 'We did some business together,' he said. 'A very talented and decent gentleman. I'll introduce you.' He began to rise.

'Please don't!' Her hand grasped his forearm, as strong as he'd expected . . . but the thrill that went through him he couldn't have expected.

'Perhaps another time,' she said, and quickly added, 'if, of course, there is another time. Right now, I just want . . . to sit here . . . to . . .' She moved her lips helplessly.

He felt that empathy again, and finished for her: 'To begin the process of knowing each other.'

Her smile was sudden and beautiful. 'Yes, thank you.'

He found himself taking her hand, threading his fingers with hers. When she helped, when she squeezed, he felt a sudden surge of desire, a definite genital reaction. And this from hand-holding when four days ago fellatio from a beautiful young actress had failed.

She asked about his work, 'Having done business, you said, with Cesar Romero.'

He began to talk. He told her about his profession, placing himself accurately and honestly among the lower order of movie producers, but saw that his self-depreciation had no effect on her, that she was wide-eyed and intent on his descriptions.

He asked about *her* profession. She tried to wave the question away, murmuring, 'Just a teacher.' He told her how he'd thought to be a teacher himself, back in Brooklyn, and how difficult he'd found student-teaching in his senior year at NYU. He praised teachers and pushed her with questions and only after she had answered briefly, without enthusiasm, realized that she wasn't being modest, she just didn't care much for her work.

'I like my eight- to ten-year-olds,' she said. 'I believe I do a good job with them. But I didn't teach when I was married and I wouldn't be teaching now if I hadn't been widowed.'

They drank wine. They ate. He asked if she would like an insider's tour of Beverly Hills, Bel Air and several of the finer canyons. She nodded. He said, 'Ending with my own canyon, my own home?' She nodded again, and raised a hand to cover a childlike smile of delight.

Later, he would remember that he had been short of breath from then until it actually happened.

Teddy's partner in Thomasine's was forthrightly named Ricco Malafortuna. Ricco was a second generation

American and could easily have been forgiven both the desire and the act of changing his name to something a little more in keeping with his lean and personable looks, his West Coast ease of speech and dress, his very considerable and very American charm. But Ricco was also very honest – not in his profession, which was the antithesis of so-called honesty, but in his recognition that his family name, Malafortuna, loosely translating to Bad Luck, truly suited him in soul, in spirit. Not that *his* luck was bad. Far from it. Just the luck of those who crossed him or the Organization.

Some people liked to say Mafia. Others Cosa Nostra. But for Ricco and his Los Angeles branch, Organization was not only more discreet but more accurate. It wasn't purely Siciliano any more, so Mafia and Cosa Nostra were misnomers. There were Anglos with family roots tracing back to the Mayflower on the board of directors. There were soldiers of Mexican descent, as well as blacks and Orientals. There were Jews and Moslems and, unthinkable in the past, a number of gays, especially in San Francisco.

All worked toward the same goal: to bring profit to the Organization and thereby to themselves. Teddy fell into this category, though barely. He never allowed Ricco to gossip about this soldier, this capo, this big man or that. He turned away from stories of laundry operations in which millions from back east were used to buy legitimate businesses here in the clean west, though he damned well understood that Thomasine's was one of many such that Ricco bought or backed in partnership with a front man. The front could be the original owner, failing or owing the Organization in some way, or a new purchaser like Teddy.

Teddy had been owed for past favours in the cat-house trade in St Louis, and for one act of keeping his mouth shut during a drug bust in a nude club on the Sunset Strip. He could have taken a bad fall – almost a kilo of skag had been under his bar, placed there by a courier who spotted a narc tail. But the narc had gotten a good look at the courier, and the law was able to make the bust and conviction without Teddy's testimony . . . which he steadfastly refused to give, insisting he'd never seen whoever dumped the heroin a few feet from his nose.

Ricco had expected the favour to be called right then and there, but Teddy had gone on tending bar, hunting white tail, drinking more or less heavily, until he got into some sort of stupid fight and lost his front teeth. Then a change had come over him – recognition of age, was Ricco's guess; he'd been at least fifty-five – and he'd called in the favour.

Ricco and the Organization had been pleased to pay off. Why not? A debt owed was uncomfortable. The Organization liked it the other way around: people owing them. Also, Teddy was a sharp operator, a spook who knew how to charm the ladies and make it pay off in heavy bar tabs. And a steady businessman who kept a close eye on his employees and watched the restaurant end for quality of food and service. So that Ricco had little to do but collect the Organization's 50 per cent.

Ricco was thinking of opening a branch of Thomasine's on Restaurant Row, the area of LaCienega Boulevard between Sunset and Wilshire. One place had changed hands three times in two years and was failing again. But he didn't expect to have an easy time convincing Teddy to get the new restaurant going. Teddy liked his poon-tang and his friends, and had limited ambition for big bucks.

The Organization, on the other hand, had a voracious appetite for big bucks, especially clean bucks. The whole structure of organized crime was changing. Sure, the cash from gambling, drugs, loan-sharking and prostitution kept coming, but more and more of it had to be laid off in clubs, restaurants, stores, wherever a front could be manoeuvered or trusted. So that Ricco was getting a good deal of pressure to increase his output as a 'finder' – a locator of legitimate investments.

Which was why he was absolutely delighted when Teddy phoned him Saturday morning and said, 'Got a favour to ask, partner.'

Ricco was in the bosom of his family – at late breakfast in his Brentwood home with his wife, Senta, his teen-aged son, Gary, and God's surprise gift, his daughter, Rosemary, born four years ago when he and Senta had just about given up on a second child. He held Rosemary on his lap, feeding her bits of bacon, and spoke to Teddy. 'Anything you want, Teddy Bear.' And he meant it. That new restaurant was worth a minor massacre.

'A very small favour, Ricco.'

Rosemary slid off his lap and ran for the front door. Senta called, 'You can't go out like that!' Ricco turned from the table, murmuring, 'Big or small, Teddy, you know the drill.'

He heard Teddy sigh. 'Shit, man, all I want is a vehicle traced. I mean, anyone at the DMV could do it.'

'Then you don't need me, do you?' But he knew Teddy wouldn't have called if the job were that simple.

'It's that Nazi business on Farifax, Ricco.'

'The kid who got clubbed is a friend of yours?'

'Not exactly. Anyway, the truck must be stolen, at least the plates, unless they're complete psychos. And it's a police case – homicide if the kid dies. So it's a matter of some complexity, some delicacy.'

'Love the way you ghetto blacks talk.'

Teddy gave him a chuckle, followed by a licence number and a nothing description of a flat-bed truck. 'The licence is exclusive, Ricco. The cops don't have it.'

'That'll keep them out of our hair.' He wrote the number on a pad.

Teddy was silent a moment; then said, 'You're not really serious about the LaCienega branch, are you? It'll cost a couple of million.'

'Maybe five before the opening. But you know how wealthy I am, partner.' He enjoyed a hearty laugh.

110

'You'll more than double your income *and* your love life.'

'Don't need the increase in either area, partner. And you left out doubling the chances of the Feds noticing my emergence into the big time.'

'You borrowed the money from one Ricco Malafortuna, baby. You can't be expected to know everything about him.'

'And what if Thomasine Two fails?'

Which was when the fun of this conversation disappeared for Ricco. 'Don't allow yourself to think that way, Teddy.' Because Ricco never allowed himself to think that way. Finders who found losses for the Organization were automatically in trouble. All businesses, he told himself, penalized failures . . . but not, he had to admit, quite as drastically as the Organization. Being assigned to run skag in from Turkey or coke from Peru wasn't beyond possibility. Even having an unfortunate accident . . .

Though the big men weren't inclined to play zero any more; at least not with members who *tried*. Still, failure was a very bad concept, causing him to feel doubt about Teddy's will to succeed. 'Your favour *is* very small, Teddy. Sure you want me to handle it?'

'No, I'm not sure. It's not even for me. And before you ask, there's no pay-off.' He paused. 'Except that of helping a friend settle his guts.' Another pause. 'Maybe I'm wrong to say it's not for me. Maybe it's a way of dumping some lousy memories, of settling an old score.'

Ricco made no comment. This was a man talking to himself; talking himself into something.

Senta came back into the kitchen, carrying their little girl. Both were giggling. 'She was on the street, dancing that tarantella your uncle taught her. Picking up her nightgown and whirling around.'

Ricco was suddenly upset. He cleared his throat, 'I'll get back to you, Teddy, soon as I have anything.'

'And if you don't get anything?'

111

'A try is the same as a favour, Teddy, you know that.'
After hanging up, he began to say something to Senta.
But it was an angry something, based on her allowing
Rosemary to run into the street, and he choked it back
and went to his study.

He got a cigar from the humidor and chewed it sav-
agely. Rosemary out alone, dancing in the street! And
rich area or poor area, the street was where danger
lurked, where crime of the sort he feared and detested
took place every day. Crime that made no sense. Crime
that struck down men, women and children for pen-
nies, for hatred, for no logical reason. Not a sensible
stick-up. Not a swindle. Not anything that made the
criminal richer or more powerful in any way.

Racial crime. Junkie crime. Sex crime. Psychotic
crime. These Rico Malafortuna, a prince of logical,
profitable, civilized crime, feared as he feared nothing
else on earth.

An understandable fear, he assured himself . . .
though he knew Senta would think it excessive, obses-
sive. But he based it on fact, on the local TV news
shows and their nightly horror stories: murdered children; kidnapped children; raped and murdered men
and women and children. *And for no logical reason!*

If the Organization killed, you knew why. There was
purpose, sometimes justice, to it.

His cigar was almost chewed through and he spat out
pieces and threw it in the waste basket. He hated this
fucking city! He hated *all* cities with their minorities
making war on themselves and on whites; with everyone killing for a hard-on, a dollar, a dusted toke, a
sudden senseless urge. For *nothing!* Everyone killing for
nothing! How could a businessman make sense of it?
How could he relax and live his life . . .?

He took several deep breaths. He got a fresh cigar.
Then he picked up the phone and punched out a number, putting Teddy's action in the works.

David's tour of LA's richest, most famous neighbourhoods was reduced to a brief ride up Bellagio Road in Old Bel Air, during which time he realized Rita was looking at him and not at the mansions. Looking at him with meaning, reinforced by her hand, moving as if by itself to touch his thigh.

He said, 'Can we go directly to my home?'

'Yes, please.' Her voice was weak, and terribly exciting.

Rita herself was terribly exciting, this despite her maturity of age, her inability to match the theatrical beauty of women like Vanessa, her quiet, conservative, almost dowdy mode of dress.

When they had walked from the Polo Lounge, the wine making his head spin, he had seen a woman of about five six, with strong legs and body, with a stride like an athlete, with an electricity about her that would take much examination, much thought to define. Because it was almost a worrisome thing, composed perhaps of tension, of fear, of incipient violence. Though as her hand touched his thigh, he felt that all this had to be sexual in nature.

And therein lay the excitement and the promise.

He returned to Laurel Canyon and from there to his home, moving the Mercedes around curves at high speed, making the fine sedan perform as he rarely did, barely slowing for Woodrow Wilson with its narrow hairpins and fenced-in cliffs.

Rita gasped a few times, with laughter following close. When they reached his house she gasped again. 'Oh, how beautiful! And *large*. I thought you lived alone?'

'I do. I just live well.'

They went inside. This was a tour he was determined not to abort. He was suddenly proud of his home, as he had been eight years ago on first moving in. He wanted her to see it room by room, and then the pool area, and then the orange and lemon trees along the sides.

But leaving the game room, coming into the service

113

area, she bent to adjust a seam, or perhaps a shoe, and her rear jutted out at him. And while it wasn't a youthful Playboy-type image, a Hollywood starlet image, while it was a middle-aged woman's rear clothed in creased grey wool instead of libidinous disco or punk fashion, he was violently aroused.

Or perhaps it was *because* of the middle age, the rumpled skirt, the dowdy normality, the obvious desire fighting the weak-voiced, frightened, violent tension – that electricity she gave off – that made him take her by the waist and say, 'Don't stop me, Rita.'

He moved himself into her. He felt the firmness of her flesh. He said, 'I'm sorry,' meaning he would have liked to have treated her with more care, more respect, seeing her for several weeks before attempting anything like this.

At the same time he was delighted with his need, his passion; delighted with her as she remained bent over and began moving her body in an unmistakable way.

He pulled up the dowdy grey skirt . . . and surprise, there were tiny black silk panties underneath. The thought that she had worn them to be seen by him drove him wild! This quiet, strong, literate woman wanted him to pull that black silk off her ass!

And he did, and grasped her naked flesh and clutched her between the legs, and opened his trousers, wanting to do it right there.

She straightened when she felt what he was pushing into her. She turned, stepping out of the panties, her skirt falling back down. She came into his arms for a kiss. She held him more tightly than Vanessa ever had; more tightly than Vanessa ever could. She *was* strong; strong enough to make his breathlessness, with him since the Polo Lounge, something different, something physical as her arms really crushed him.

He laughed, gasping, 'Don't break the lover.'

She let up then, looking upset. He quickly kissed her on that worried mouth. 'Just a joke. Let's go inside. I want more crushing.'

114

Her head went down, her face flamed, but she walked with him as he led her through the kitchen and along the hallway to the master bedroom. He dropped to his knees there and took off the skirt and pressed kisses between her legs where a thick thatch of genital hair grew, untrimmed, unshaven, untinted, in opposition to the nearly universal custom of the actresses, the LA chicks, the women – girls really – he had dealt with since his divorce.

He rose to take off her blouse, her brassière. Her breasts were large and dropped considerably, swinging as he turned her away to slip the harness over her arms.

Vanessa had fixed her breasts some years before he had met her; the job was excellent and almost undetectable. Many Hollywood women had the plastic-bag insets filled with sugar-water that had replaced silicone. And while he agreed that for sexy actresses boob jobs were often necessary to enhance and extend careers that now included considerable nudity, he was delighted that Rita's breasts were what they were.

He kissed them. He stepped back to take off his own clothing. As he was unbuttoning his shirt, she opened his trousers and pulled them down in one brisk, almost fierce motion.

From then on a change took place that surprised and startled him. She became the aggressor, the lover intent upon putting the partner into bed.

And more than that, there was the strength of those hands, those arms, coming into play again. There was the way she moved him to the bed and lay him down and kneeled to bite and suck his genitals. The way she *kept* him down, grasping his rigid member and slowly straddling him.

She put him into her and bent over him, clutching his shoulders with those large, white, powerful hands; holding him down and riding him in a kind of rape that had him struggling at one point to shake her loose.

But God how it worked! How he thrilled as she slid herself up and down the length of his penis. He wanted

115

to thrust, to plunge up into her, but her rhythm was different from his and dominant and he finally lay back and enjoyed it.

At her point of climax, her face twisted and she took her right hand from his shoulder and held him firmly by the throat. If he too hadn't been coming, and coming harder than he could remember in years, he would have torn the hand away.

But then again, as with her mounting him, as with her holding him down, there was definite erotic compensation. And a moment after her orgasm her grip loosened, her hands withdrew, she rolled off him and onto her back.

Looking at her, he felt an immediate revival of need. Her hair was wild now. Her legs, powerfully muscled in calf and thick and hard in thigh, were parted. Her wide, flat stomach heaved as did her chest and the large breasts hanging off to each side.

He raised himself on an elbow, intending to kiss her, to start things over again . . . and realized she was asleep.

He tried to sleep too, but checking the bedside clock saw that it was only two o'clock. He rose quietly, went to the bathroom and showered.

When he came out, the bed was empty and her clothing was no longer on the floor. Neither was his. He found his suit neatly hung in the closet, the sliding door back so he could see it.

He began to take it out, then changed his mind and found a pair of tailored jeans he'd bought at Le Fancy Pants and never worn. And a sports shirt and an old blue blazer. Slipping into loafers, he felt relaxed and happy, and wondered how long it would take to get her back into bed.

At least a few days, he discovered, when he found her outside near the pool. She wanted to be taken back to her car. She wanted to go home.

As he stared, dismayed by her sombre tone, her averted eyes, she suddenly kissed him on the cheek. 'I'm

116

really shocked at what I did, what I felt, David. To use the vernacular, you turn me on more than I'm accustomed to.'

But when he tried to take her in his arms for a real kiss, she pushed him away and moved to the door. 'Let's leave now.'

He didn't drive as quickly this time. She kept looking out the window, obviously avoiding conversation. He allowed it to stay that way until they pulled up at the Beverly Hills Hotel. 'When can we get together?' he asked.

'Please don't push me, David.'

He said, 'Fine,' voice hardening, staring straight ahead, waiting for her to get out.

When she did, he began to move the car, but she bent to the window. 'Can't you understand? It happened too quickly for me. I have to get it under control. You don't want me proposing marriage tomorrow, do you?'

He looked at her, and was shocked to see tears on her cheeks. 'All right,' he said quietly, and smiled. He waited until she returned the smile before driving away.

Vanessa stayed with Rob Cerjak until five o'clock, and the man was insatiable! When he began talking about 'commitments' and 'meaningful relationships', she said she had to go. 'My mother's visiting . . .'

He shrugged, reading the look in her eyes. 'Still need time to make the break with Howars permanent, right?'

She got dressed, promising they would have dinner on Monday, and she sprung for that only because he was setting up an audition at Universal. Leaving his house she felt worn and – surprise, surprise – *guilty*. Sex without love was one thing. But sex without passion?

She drove directly home; then went to the phone and dialled Dave's number. Definitely not cool, she knew. Teddy would disapprove.

'Dave!' she said, acting surprised. 'Hey . . . sorry. I

guess I dialled the wrong number.' She laughed a little. 'Force of habit.'

'That's all right.' His remote, disinterested tone chilled her. 'How're things going? Get any work through Cerjak?'

'As a matter of fact, yes,' she said, upset and wanting to upset him. 'But the guy must live on Vitamin E . . .' She cut herself short and laughed again.

He was silent. She suddenly regretted the crudity. 'I only meant . . .'

'I know exactly what you meant. We started the same way, didn't we?'

He was angry, which was some satisfaction to her. 'I guess so,' she said, her voice small, sorry she just hadn't hung up when he'd answered and satisfied her need to know where he was.

Not that his being home at five thirty didn't mean he wouldn't be out with a date at eight or nine. Or, come to think of it, that the date wasn't in his bed right now.

That thought revived her anger and she said, 'But we sure as hell didn't end that way, did we, tiger?'

'I think we should say goodbye, Vanessa.'

'Goodbye!' She hung up, then felt awful. She wanted to call again and apologize. But she decided to wait until nine or ten . . . and check on him at the same time.

She had a long, hot bath. She ate a salad and watched television. She checked her watch for at least the fifth time, and it still wasn't late enough to make that call.

She finally gave in and took a tranquillizer.

She made the call at eight thirty. He took a while to answer and his voice was thick with sleep. She felt she'd wakened him and wanted to hang up . . . but she also wanted to know if he could speak without restraint, without worrying about a woman lying beside him.

'Dave, it's Vanessa again. I'm sorry I was so nasty before. Forgive me?'

'Oh . . . Vanessa.' He cleared his throat. 'I must've dozed off. Sexy novels always put me to sleep.'

118

She laughed. 'Some sexy women too, I guess.' And quickly added, 'Just a joke, hon.'

'It's all right, Vanessa. I don't blame you. I blame me.'

'Damn right you're to blame!' she wanted to shout, reacting again to his casual tone, to his obvious I-don't-give-a-shit-what-you-do attitude. But instead she managed to say, 'Goodnight, Dave. Call sometime.'

He said, 'Yes,' with about as much enthusiasm as a corpse, and she hung up so as not to be tempted to rage.

She found herself pacing the apartment. She wanted to feel calm, *tranquil* as the word tranquillizer promised. She gulped another Valium, got the script for the Paramount TV movie, and took it to bed. She wouldn't begin to memorize her part for another few weeks yet, not wanting to peak too soon. Besides, she would use a dramatic coach to sharpen up for the part.

After about half an hour, her eyes began closing. She shut the light, relieved that she was finally falling asleep. But she couldn't keep fooling around with mild tranquillizers during this period of extreme stress. In order to stay cool, to stay off Dave's back and retain a chance of getting together with him again, she had to be able to fall asleep the moment she began to feel uptight.

She would call Blair Gordon tomorrow morning. She would ask him to phone in a prescription for Quaalude to the Waldon Pharmacy down the street. After all, he was her doctor, in charge of the Impossible Secret . . . which was why she hated seeing him.

Another reason for staying out of his office was to keep him from being a hypocrite about his Hippocratic oath and trying to hit on her. And trying to talk her into what he called a 'staging operation', which would take out a part of her and scar her and answer questions she didn't even want asked.

He would press her to come in for an examination.

He might insist on it as the price of that Quaalude pre-scription.

Well, she would do whatever was necessary to get the Quaaludes. The one time she had tried the powerful drug, it had knocked her *cold*.

David had fallen asleep after lying down fully dressed. The action with Rita had drained him. And Vanessa's calls had distressed him. She obviously wasn't going to drop out of his life with just a cheery smile.

Not that he was sure he wanted her to. If he hadn't begun to feel guilty with her – which led to impatience and a degree of anger – he might have enjoyed her obvious need to speak to him, to keep their lines of communication open.

What he needed was time. Time to explore what Rita Goran could mean to him. Time to learn whether or not he would begin to miss Vanessa's stunning looks, the warmth and ease of their previous relationship.

Still, as long as he had no lust for her, as long as he was impotent with her, beauty and warmth meant nothing.

Yet he knew that lust could return. It had failed him in his second year of marriage when career problems had eaten into his soul. He had played around with a secretary then, totally different in looks and personality from Arlene, and in four months had settled his career problems by beginning to write. And returned to Arlene's arms for many more years of conjugal satisfaction.

He turned on the bedside lamp and picked up the sexy novel. He read until he felt hungry; then went to the kitchen and got the beef casserole Mrs Gomez had left in the refrigerator. He put it into the microwave oven along with a bowl of spiced rice and some quick-heat rolls. But he remembered feeling the excess flesh, jiggling on his body as he'd run through Canter's parking lot. Remembered thinking he had to lose weight, because there was a war on.

He didn't want to think of that war; didn't want to remember the truck and the masked men and the swastikas. Especially not the swastikas, which he hated, which caused the saliva to dry in his mouth and the hunger to flee his stomach. Which made him remove the rice and rolls and go to the counter-top television to find entertainment, to find release from thoughts of Americans who would wear swastikas. 'Filth who would wear swastikas!'

He heard his voice shouting then, saw his hands trembling then, realized the war was indeed very much on for him.

Whatever happened between him and Rita, him and Vanessa, the war wouldn't end. As no war ended because of men and women and sex and love. As his war, World War II, hadn't ended for him until he'd crashed the PT 19 in the field near Bennington, South Carolina, leading to eleven months in Northington General Hospital. Which finished his dream of dropping flaming death on the people who were destroying his people.

He had healed and his life had gone on, and there had been more wars. But they hadn't been his wars. Now his war was starting up again.

He used the remote channel selector, trying to find something interesting, something amusing. And the hour changed; it became ten o'clock; a local news programme came on.

His oven chimed; the casserole was ready.

As he ate, the newscaster began the LA stories. Third among them, after a series of mud-slides, was 'the death of Warren Gross, eighteen-year-old member of the Jewish Defence League, struck down by a club-wielding Nazi last Wednesday on Farifax Avenue.'

David changed channels and found a situation-comedy rerun.

He ate. He laughed a few times. But he remembered Warren Gross, eighteen, struck down by a club-wielding Nazi last Wednesday. As he remembered Seymour Skolar and Harold Nash and the other casualties of his

121

war. As he would always remember and love them. As he would always despise the others who had found ways out of fighting his war, including a cousin, who had become a non-person to him and remained so to this day.

He finished dinner and went to bed. He hoped he would hear from Rita, but it was no longer as important as it had been an hour ago, before the first casualty of his war had been posted.

Teddy hadn't been on what people called a 'date' in years. Even then, he had rarely taken a woman to the movies, to dinner, out in public. Because the whore's son knew how to get to the nitty-gritty, down to brass tacks, 'into the jam and out again'. As he'd done tonight with Roberta Alden, the big momma, who slept the good sleep of sexual exhaustion beside him while he lay smoking a fine Columbian joint.

There *had* been a time when he had tried to break the quickmake pattern of his past, but it had lasted no more than a few months. Later, he had joked about it, characterizing it as a campaign to seduce the lovely and square Miss Florence Adler, but it had been something far more complex than that. It had actually been a last fling at fantasy, at living the Great White American Dream before he gave in to his middle age and removable bridge and the recognition that if Teddy Brown was to enjoy any of honky society's goodies, he would have to go outside society to get it.

Between the time he'd lost his teeth, also his guts for the nude clubs and their rough action, and the time he'd called in the favour owed him by the mob and become half-owner of Thomasine's, he had tried to find a dentist who could give him a seven-piece permanent. Which took him finally to Camden Drive in Beverly Hills and Logan Harris, DDS, the very best there was, according to Dave.

'It's not possible in your case, Mr Brown,' Harris said, tapping Teddy's upper-left four-piece permanent.

'There's no anchor for such a large bridge because you already have a bridge here. However, I can make you a very attractive removable . . .'

Teeth in a glass at night. That was what threw Teddy. That was what nailed home the fact that he was fifty-seven years old and still playing macho-man, Iceberg Slim, big-time drinker, spender, playboy.

He said okay because there really wasn't any other game in town for him. And within nine days Harris justified his heavy fee with a bridge that clamped on tight and blended in with what was left of Teddy's own pearly whites.

Just so the experience shouldn't be a total loss, he hit on the receptionist, a lovely redheaded chick with freckles across her nose, maybe thirty-five years old, with a great smile and no obvious hang-ups about black dudes. Though he couldn't be sure about this last, since yokking-it-up in the office was one thing and kissing the jigaboo another.

It turned out she was quite willing to 'go out on a date', this delivered with downcast baby blues, shy smile and warm flush rising from that bosomy neckline up over the freckles.

How could he explain the Teddy Bear diet of dinner at home and sex by nine to this obvious straight, square conformist? So he simply said he would pick her up the next night. She said fine and, 'Do you like Japanese food? I'm a Benihana freak.'

The next night he learned that the Benihana restaurant on LaCienga had communal tables only. So that on his first legit date in years he was not only subjected to Friday night crowds, but also to having to sit at a table with eight strangers and try not to notice how they were trying not to notice the black with the freckled redhead. Not that anything dramatic happened; after all, this *was* Beverly Hills. Still, he wouldn't have classified it as fun . . . until they finished and drove out towards the beach. It was a balmy July evening and she said she wanted to breathe some sea air.

It all paid off beautifully after they parked facing the black Pacific at Santa Monica. There were few other cars in the municipal lot, and it was time to find out how she felt about kissing the jigaboo.

He never again used that hard phrase, that angry thought, in relation to Florence Adler. When he put his arms around her, she sighed and turned up her mouth. The kiss he gave was the kiss he got – sweet and steamy. He was dying to grab those swelling tits, reach under that clinging skirt, put his cock in her hand and eventually everywhere else.

But he was afraid and he waited. And later – two months later – realized he'd been wrong to wait. She was a woman and she wasn't with him to discuss the Emancipation Proclamation, right?

Still, she looked happy as a clam with the kisses and hand-holding and the long walk they took along the blacktop path.

The next day was Saturday and she asked if he would care to join her 'for a jog through Beverly Hills'. It seemed she lived south of Wilshire in 'a very nice older-type apartment house that costs far too much, but I love the walking to work, and shopping and jogging in the Beverly Hills Flats.'

The Flats was the area restricted to single-family dwellings between Sunset Boulevard and Wilshire on north and south, between Doheny and the curving Wilshire on east and west; a few square miles of beautiful homes and wide, tree-lined streets, the streets populated by a handful of gardeners and delivery men, the wealthy residents being either at their pools and tennis courts or away for the summer.

He met her at what was for a bartender the ungodly hour of 8.00 a.m. He had a blue jogging outfit given him as a present by some chick or other, which he'd tried on once, then put away.

They jogged three blocks and he had to stop. He bent over, gasping, feeling like a clown, the black Adonis

124

with removable teeth and no stamina. And that damned jogging outfit was too hot for July.

She was patient. They walked a few blocks, then tried again. He did better this time, lasting almost five blocks at a Stepin Fetchit shuffle. He could see she really wanted to run, so he gasped, 'Listen . . . go ahead. I'll walk back . . . wait for you in the car.'

She said he didn't have to wait; she could jog home after finishing here.

He nodded slowly, seeing bug-off-grandpa-time . . . but then she said, 'We could get together tonight, if you haven't anything else to do.'

He had plenty else to do, including a party at a swinger's club, but he said, 'Eight o'clock.'

There was another dinner, more private this time, followed by sitting on the couch in her apartment. More kisses, more hand-holding, and finally a little make-out action – about what he'd had at thirteen back in St Louis. Still, her breasts were beauties and her thighs whipped cream.

When she clamped those thighs together, murmuring, 'Teddy, please,' he did what a man should never do – take the standard, automatic words of refusal as Scripture. Because he was accustomed to strippers, hookers, actresses, cuties, make-out chicks who knew what they wanted and said NO only when they meant it.

Still, it was fun and he was beginning to live the Great White American Dream that had lurked far back in his mind – perhaps lurked in every ghetto kid's mind – and he left with a hard-on and a heartache.

The next morning, he was back in the Flats, jogging along Elevado, trying to ignore the feeling that people were peering out of their windows, watching the jigg run down the street in cut-off jean shorts, striped polo shirt and old ankle-high sneakers (he hadn't had time to buy a new summer jogging outfit yet), then picking up their phones to call the police.

But he persisted because he was going to show Florence Adler what he was made of. He ran two hours that morning, with pauses for nausea and stitches in the side and pure exhaustion. And he ran again at five-thirty, when everyone else was coming home from work.

Teddy Bear didn't have to work for a while. He was easing out of bartending in the nude clubs and hadn't yet decided to ask Ricco Malafortuna to call in the favour owed him. Teddy Bear could concentrate on becoming something he had never been . . . and never could be, he had realized later.

He had run twice a day for seven days, despite the wringing-wet sweats and the near fainting-dead-away exhaustions. By the time he called Florence the following Monday morning at the dentist's office, he was ready. She said yes, she would enjoy a prework run with him tomorrow at seven, 'If you're sure, Teddy.'

Was he ever! He was nicotine-starved, alcohol-free, a good six pounds lighter than a week ago, edgy as hell, and able to jog clear across the Flats from Doheny to the Wilshire curve. Now if she wasn't impressed with *that* for a week's work, he'd quit!

She was, though she set a pace he couldn't maintain for the whole run, causing him to wave her on three blocks from their goal.

She took him home and asked if he wanted to shower. He started to say yes, because he wanted to shower with *her*, but that innocent freckled face smiled at him and he said, 'You first.' And cursed himself for playing at Andy Hardy.

They showered separately and went to dinner. Afterwards she said she had a very early 'wake-up' so goodnight.

He trained another week, and ran with her the first Saturday in August. This time he not only kept pace, but even sprinted out ahead toward the very end. At night they went to dinner, and no early wake-up. On the couch he kept trying to break through – not *her* defences, as he wasn't sure she was putting up any,

126

but his, a mixture of fantasy based on all the white movies about freckled-faced love. If he fucked her, it would be like everything else, like his past. If he didn't, then perhaps he was entering a newer, better, *whiter* life.

She turned him down for a fourth date. He didn't blame her. She'd wanted the thrill of black cock, or at least of a skilled sexual partner, and gotten Henry Aldrich without the 'Coming, Mother!'

He'd seen her one last time. His bridge had needed a minor adjustment and he'd gone to the dentist, then walked her home.

That was more than a month after their last run. That was after a ton of shit came down on him: After he'd called Ricco agreeing to the deal on Thomasine's. It was also about the time he'd begun thinking of Montecassiano, sweating over Lieutenant Borden . . .

Teddy sat up in bed, suddenly unwilling to remember more. He considered walking the big momma, but the memories were already there, moving through his mind. Besides, there was nothing that *terrible* about them. 'Minor shit,' he muttered.

First came the accident, not even a respectable fender-bender, but with elements that stuck in his craw.

It was about a week after Florence Adler had dumped him. He'd gone back to work at the Class Act Nude Club, less to pick up the bread than the chicks, and after three days was about to make his first score. Her name, at least on the marquee, was Danielle Darling. She was a tall, busty blonde who dug his chatter and the promise of cocaine cut only mildly with baby laxative.

At 3.00 a.m. they'd put the club to bed and were on their way up Coldwater to his North Hollywood apartment. Coming around one of the canyon's snaking turns, he saw headlights swinging toward his side of the road . . . and before he could jerk the wheel right, there was a scraping sound.

He pulled over and stopped. Looking back, he saw

that the other car had stalled out in the road. By the time he hurried over there, a third car had stopped and an elderly man was getting out. 'Need any help?' he asked.

Teddy said, 'Don't know yet. Just a little scrape, but I want to see if the driver's all right.'

Together they approached the other car, a Continental Mark IV. A middle-aged woman with an angry face and an even angrier voice said, 'You must be drunk! You drove into my lane!'

Teddy said, 'If you'll look where you are, lady, you'll see you're on *my* side.'

'I swerved after you hit me.' And then, to the man who'd stopped, 'Please call the police. These people don't carry insurance . . .'

At that point, Teddy snapped, 'I'll be in my car,' and walked quickly away.

Danielle Darling was upset when he told her they had to wait for the police. 'I looked at your car, Teddy, and it's just a long scratch. Paint-work, hon.'

The woman had lost a piece of moulding. End of damage. They'd simply brushed against each other.

By the time the police arrived, the woman had gotten her car started and moved it to the side, the Good Samaritan had left, and there was no way for Teddy to back up his story that the woman had been in his lane. Not only that, she was a real bitch, talking a mile a minute and using the word 'drunk' several times . . . until Teddy said, 'Now wait a minute! I'm not drunk and I don't have to listen to this garbage!'

One of the two officers, young, slim, hard-faced, said, 'Yes you do. She tells her side, you tell yours, and we all go home. Unless we decide to test you for alcohol blood-level content.'

'How about testing *her*?' Teddy said, watching the other officer over at his car, examining the damage . . . and Danielle.

'Do you claim this woman is drunk?' the young officer

asked, trying to make it sound ridiculous and succeeding in making it sound threatening.

A lifetime of defensive speech and action when dealing with the law made Teddy shut up then, though he burned inside.

The other officer, bigger and older, returned and murmured in his partner's ear. The young cop said, 'Okay, I'll check it,' and ambled over to Teddy's car. Where he checked Danielle, leaning in the window for what seemed like a hell of a long time.

When he came back, he grinned a shit-eating grin at Teddy. 'Understand why you were in a hurry, man.'

Teddy spoke calmly. 'She stalled out on my side of the road. There was a witness, but he left.'

The older cop said, 'You got a nice bit of witness back there. Now we'll let the insurance companies take over.'

Teddy gave up then because it was 3.00 a.m. and, underneath it all, LA was a redneck town.

He never heard from the woman or her insurance company, but made sure she and her company heard from him. Not that it did any good, and he picked up the hundred-thirty-dollar touch-up tab. And told himself the whole thing was nothing; a very minor irritation in the life of a black American.

And by itself, that's just what it was.

But it didn't stand by itself. He'd just come off the Great White American Dream (another nothing), and before that the attempt to defend a dancer from a drunk (not quite a nothing, since he'd lost all those front teeth and the notion that he could fight it out with the young guys). Even so, he might have gotten by it, if two other 'nothings' hadn't followed in quick succession.

After less than twenty-four hours of relative peace and quiet, he came home from the club to find his door open and his apartment cleaned out. Not just the TV and stereo and some cash tucked into the pocket of an old jacket, but the old jacket itself and the new jackets and every stick of furniture.

He went to the manager's apartment, asking how the

hell he could be wiped out that way with the whole house not seeing who'd done it.

The manager resented being awakened at four in the morning and said so. He also said, 'A moving van came and two of your friends loaded it up, and when I asked, they said you were moving and would come by to get your security money.'

'My friends? You've seen me with them?'

The manager shrugged. 'I don't know. They were black men.'

A detective came over the next day. He was black, which should have been an improvement and wasn't. He ambled about the empty studio flat, shaking his head. 'The manager claims they were friends of yours. You sure you don't owe someone . . .?'

Teddy had been very light on the sauce since Florence Adler and his jogging programme, but that night be began drinking seriously.

Two nights later he worked a party at the Crescent Country Club where Ricco Malafortuna was an officer. In keeping with his recent spate of luck, one of the moneyed and usually sedate members got bombed, grabbed someone else's wife and all hell broke loose. Ricco motioned for Teddy to help him eject the drunk and between them they got him out to the parking lot. Where he shouted, 'Fucking spade bastard!', and swung at Teddy. Not at Ricco, who had also thrown him out, and who was also standing there, but at the 'fucking spade bastard'.

Luckily, his aim wasn't as good as the drunk's in the nude club, so Teddy's removable bridge remained intact. His nose, however, didn't fare as well, gushing blood all over the nice white jacket bartenders wore at the C.C. Club.

Teddy had tried to murder the bastard, and it had taken Ricco and two car-park boys to prevent him from strangling the man he later learned was Roy Cloever of Cloever Food Markets.

Teddy hadn't understood his complete loss of control

130

that night . . . but he did now, sitting in bed, adding up the few weeks of anguish, the four or five incidents, each relatively minor by itself, that had totalled a very serious attack on his stability, perhaps his sanity.

And the punch that had cost him his teeth, the fight that had kicked off the bad few weeks, wasn't as simple as he'd made it out to be; wasn't just a drunk punching a bartender who had come to a dancer-waitress's defence.

The drunk that time had been one of a group of three college football players, members of a team visiting UCLA. A really big kid with shoulders like an ox, trim and fit and well over two hundred pounds. A good-looking kid with dark blond hair and wide grin, who sat with his friends and consumed large quantities of California champagne, while the girls, five on duty that night, stripped down to buff just a few feet away on the raised stage. After the third bottle, the blond kid began to lunge forward, grabbing repeatedly at the dancers.

His friends pulled him back each time, so Teddy wasn't worried . . . until he shoved one friend too hard and that friend said, 'Screw him!', and walked out. The blond kid quieted and shortly afterward was helped up by his remaining friend.

Teddy was glad to see them leaving, except that they weren't. The friend asked for the john. Teddy said, 'Back and to the left.'

'Hey, Clyde,' the blond kid said, showing Teddy lots of teeth without really smiling, 'get us another bottle of champagne. And keep your eyes off the naked girls.'

Teddy nodded, wishing some of his regular customers would come around, just in case the kid got rough. But when a regular did walk in a moment later, he wasn't pleased. Because Mel was blacker than he was. And all five dancers that night were white.

The blond kid was coming from the john, alone. Mel was sitting on a stool, his back to the bar, sipping a Scotch and watching Yolanda, billed as the Pocket-Sized

Venus, who did indeed pack a hell of a lot of woman into four feet eleven. Mel was giving out with the mock wolf-whistles and Yolanda was laughing because every regular knew that she was hooked on Corinne, a dancer at another club. Mel's whistling was a running gag between two hip friends.

The blond kid came to a stop right in front of Mel, staring at him. Mel said, 'Hey, man, down in front.'

The blond kid said, 'I told the bartender to keep his eyes on the champagne. I'm telling you to keep your eyes on your drink.'

Mel laughed and moved two stools to the left.

The blond kid stepped over and again blocked Mel's view. 'You listening to me, Clyde?'

Teddy came quickly around the bar. Mel wasn't known for his patience, and if the opposition was too big he'd cut him down to size with his sticker. 'Mel, take a table. This customer's friend will be along any minute.'

'This customer's friend took off, Clyde.' He looked at Teddy and wet his lips. Then, in the way of drunks, he forgot his point and headed back to his table, where Honey, who had danced earlier, was now working the floor. With no more than a half-dozen customers scattered around the club, she was alone, wearing the bikini panties and high heels waitresses wore at the Class Act.

The big kid came up behind her. Mel said, 'That mother's gonna do something.'

Teddy said, 'Split, Mel, please.'

'A pleasure, but you need me, baby.'

The big kid sat down, looking up at Honey's bare breasts. Teddy said, 'No, it'll be cool. Goodnight.'

Mel walked out. Teddy started back behind the bar, because Honey had cleared the table and was nodding as the big kid ordered more champagne.

And then he was pulling her down on his lap, his hands all over her.

She yelled, and Yolanda stopped dancing, and Teddy

132

had no choice. He ran over, saying, 'That's enough! You'll have to leave!'

The kid laughed and squeezed Honey's breasts. She said, 'Christ! That hurts!' and kicked at his ankles.

Teddy threw an arm around the kid's throat from behind.

The kid let Honey go and she was away like a shot. He rose, twisted, and threw Teddy back against another table.

Teddy said, 'Leave now and there won't be any trouble.'

'And if I don't, you'll call the *pohleece*?'

'That's right. You're creating a disturbance.'

'In a nigger whore-house.'

Teddy stepped in and began a short uppercut to the chin, which should've put the young ox to sleep.

But the kid was a natural brawler. Drunk or not, he had the moves. His shoulders swivelled and Teddy was punching air, stumbling into the stage. When he turned, he was hit flush on the mouth and bade farewell to his pearly whites. Down he went, thinking it was his lousy luck to always be involved with *big* honkies, like Lieutenant Borden.

He did have one bit of luck: the kid decided against beating him to a pulp because the girls were all screaming. He ran out, though Teddy didn't know it until a good five minutes later, the world having gone rather remote on him.

He'd buried the racial implications of that night's action. What was the point in remembering?

As he'd later buried the implications of the minor shit which followed Florence Adler and the end of the Great White American Dream.

Except that it had begun tearing loose inside him the night he'd tried to strangle the supermarket king.

But even then, he'd managed to rebury everything the very next night when he'd contacted Ricco and begun the process of reconstructing his ego, his station in life.

133

And he'd seen Florence Adler again, when his bridge had needed adjustment. He'd been the last patient and waited around to walk her home, even though she didn't seem all that enthusiastic about it. Still, she nodded when he asked if he could come up for a few minutes. She served him a Scotch and began to leave the living room, saying, 'I have to prepare dinner for a few guests.'

She never made it to the kitchen. He reached out and took her wrist. He held her there, finished his Scotch, and drew her onto his lap. He kissed her neck, her lips, then put his hand inside her blouse.

She'd had breast massage from him before, part of their kiddy romance. This time he removed the blouse and brassière, then the skirt and pantyhose. He stood her before him as he remained seated, turning her this way and that, naked in her high heels, and laughed softly. 'I wondered if your ass was freckled too.' He put his hands on that freckled ass. He put his fingers into that fair-haired cunt. She said, 'Teddy, no, please!' squirming away.

He slapped the freckled ass and said, 'The bedroom.'

'My guests,' she whispered, shaking her head.

He slapped her ass again, a good clout this time, and she grunted and led him to the bedroom.

Where he slipped out of his pants and drew her head down. She hesitated, and he put her over his lap and spanked her. He watched the way that freckled ass rose and fell, knowing it was her turn-on, she loved the game.

Well, so did he, he told himself . . . but it wasn't entirely true. Sure, she was prime stuff and he would spank her bottom red and fuck her while her dinner guests knocked at the door and she said her little Teddy-no-please routines.

And that's almost exactly what happened, the guests ringing the bell from downstairs and later phoning from near by. He listened to her speaking on the phone,

134

saying she'd been taken ill and had slept heavily; then he got up to leave.

She begged him to stay the night. He said he couldn't. She said, 'At least another . . . you know.'

He was capable. She turned him on all right. But he wasn't ever going to get what he wanted from Florence Adler. He wasn't going to get the hand-holding and walks along Fraternity Row and 'Let's tell my folks we're going steady' and the wedding with Judge Stone beaming at him, and all the bright, white, blue-eyed people slapping his back and loving him.

Instead, she had drawn him back to bed and her freckled ass had pumped him, milked him, sent him stumbling out into fabled Beverly Hills a drained and pensive man. And he had never called her again and never returned the calls she'd left on his service.

By then his month of 'bad luck' (as he managed to think of it) had begun emerging in thoughts of Lieutenant Borden. All the little shit had added up to something intolerable: that if you live in a society that wants to be rid of you, that would be much happier without your presence, you're like the Jew of the thirties in Nazi Germany, a victim waiting for the crime to take place . . . and therefore he didn't trust his fellow Americans with his life, his well-being.

How could he go on without eventually exploding, without eventually killing someone, if he accepted that consciously; if he thought about it, dwelled on it? How could he continue living the good life?

So he substituted Montecassino, the past, because that pain was built around one man and a dead man at that. Hating one dead man gave him a few bad moments, but he could survive the many hours of his life. While the reality brought home by his month of 'minor shit' was that this whole fucking city, this whole fucking country, was out to get him.

Now he turned to the big momma, shaking her, wanting her awake to help him bury that reality, terrified of that reality. He kissed her, told her he needed her.

135

She put her arms around him and murmured, 'Honey, you're shaking.'

He stopped shaking as they began making love.

But later, after returning to his condo, he felt the tremor beginning again, and poured himself a shot from the first bottle his hand grasped inside the cabinet.

Brandy. Dave's drink.

Dave, perhaps his only real friend.

Racial hatred was grinding down his friend: those scumbags in the truck on Fairfax, twisting his mind, his heart. And racial hatred was. grinding down Teddy Bear.

He didn't give a shit about other Jews and other blacks; it was Dave and Teddy being wrung out by scumbag trash. It was two loners, two non-joiners, being forced to join the ranks of the tormented.

He made a decision which calmed him. He would help his friend punish the scumbags, the common enemy, those emperors of hate, the Nazis.

SIX: *Sunday, 16 December*

The contact from the Highway Patrol was waiting when Lowery arrived at 12.10 a.m. at the Eucalyptus Lodge, named for the two-lane highway which ran off 99 and through the town of Bethills. Eucalyptus Road was lined with the beautiful trees, and while the motel was modest by main-route standards, it was clean and quiet.

'Nice,' Lowery said, putting his suitcase on the floor and looking around the room. 'The town too, from what I saw of it.'

'The people too,' Don Manguson said, a very young officer, stocky in his tan, booted, highway patrol uniform. 'Except for a few fools. And that's all those Nazis are, sir. Fools.'

Lowery sat down on the bed, motioning the officer to the room's one armchair. He nodded, encouraging Manguson to go on, but he didn't agree with this town booster, this local boy so protective of the Bethills image.

'No one will rent them meeting rooms . . . like here, for instance. Van Loughton, the manager, won't even let them in the dining room if they're wearing swastikas. Especially in the summer when he fills up with travellers almost every night.' His grey eyes flickered and his thick, sincere face showed strain. 'People of the Jewish faith come through just like anyone else. We're all Americans, right, sir?'

'Harold,' Lowery said, and nodded, and then added,

'Including those Nazis, only we're going to find out just where they were Wednesday at 8.00 p.m.'

'Okay, Harold. But it's too late to do anything tonight, right?'

'Right. Let's have breakfast here about nine.' He waited for Manguson's nod. 'Unless you know where the Schleissers like to eat?'

'Home, mostly, like everyone from around Bethills.' He paused. 'Sometimes at a diner on Eucalyptus Road. You must've passed it.'

'Back towards town about a mile or two?'

'That's it. Small place; doesn't get the traffic the diners on 99 get, but the owner does enough business to stay open.' Another pause. 'Harv Clory. He's friends with the Schleissers.'

'Clory doesn't mind the uniforms, the swastikas?'

'No, not much.' A shrug. 'Fact is, he's a supporter, along with his cousin Duke and a few others.'

Lowery wanted the names of those 'few others'. He wanted to write them down and have them checked out when he got back to Los Angeles. But he didn't push the home-town boy. He stood up, stretching. 'Beat, Don. We'll get going at breakfast.'

Manguson rose. Lowery walked him to the door; then asked, 'Would you say a dozen supporters at Clory's diner?'

'No way. I know more about the Resurrection party than anyone because I've lived here all my life, and there are four from Clory's and two truckers that come through a few times a month.'

'That's six. Nine with the Schleissers.' He opened the door for the stocky patrolman. 'Not much of a menace, Don, just as you said.'

'Exactly.'

Lowery was in bed a few minutes later. Where, despite his long day and six hours behind the wheel, he had trouble falling asleep. In the morning, the Lone Litvak would be breakfasting with Nazis.

Rita Goran was up at six thirty, though she wasn't due on the courts for her match with Lois Turner until nine. She wished she could begin playing right now; work off the incredible tension which seemed about to blow through the top of her head!

She dressed in her grey sweatsuit and went downstairs to jog along Arbor Road, increasing her pace until she was into a strong, loping run.

It was foggy, chilly, damp, as winter mornings in the Santa Monica area often are. It was also sweet of air and completely quiet due to the absence of traffic this early on a Sunday morning. She kept going, block after block, until she'd unwound; then turned to retrace her steps, dropping back into a comfortable jog.

She began to think of the game with Lois Turner, a strong player in her mid thirties, tall and angular and a classic fireball server. Also a classic lesbian, Rita suspected, because the phys-ed teacher had shown certain signs during their one social evening out together. Such as taking her hand at dinner and holding it for no logical reason. And breaking into harsh laughter when Rita asked if she was married. 'Who can find a tolerable male partner in this day and age!'

Not that the idea of lesbianism repelled her as much as it had during her innocent married years. Living in Los Angeles, one came into almost daily contact with gays of both sexes. Also, she couldn't help wondering what it would be like to engage in lovemaking with a woman.

She picked up the pace as she came within three blocks of home. No point in thinking of lesbians. She had enough trouble with heterosexual relationships . . . including the latest one.

David Howars was everything she could ask for, and yet she was actually considering not seeing him again. Not that he didn't stimulate her physically, emotionally and intellectually (the lack of any one of these having caused her to drop other men), but because the stimu-

139

lation was too intense. Because she feared what would happen if he didn't feel just as strongly as she did.

She had actually fantasized his rejection during their lovemaking, which had led to something new, violence on an *assumption* of mistreatment: that impulse to crush his windpipe, to choke him as she approached orgasm.

Terribly depressing, this last. There had been no violence in David Howars and therefore no reason for her to react with violence.

Terribly dangerous too. The police had watched her for a few days, she was certain of it; that car following her to school on Friday and parked outside the house that night and Saturday; perhaps Sunday also, when another car had been parked in another spot but with the same kind of man sitting inside. Which led to the possibility that they had followed her Saturday to the Polo Lounge and then to David's house. If so, and if something happened to David, she would be connected to him and to Rossa.

But nothing would happen to David. She had never hurt anyone who hadn't hurt or threatened her *physically*.

At which point she began to think of Daddy . . . and laughed aloud, a shrill, piercing sound. Daddy had died in an accident! Naturally she felt some guilt, having been there and not been able to help him.

She broke into the hundred-yard dash to end those thoughts. She looked around as she ran and saw nothing suspicious, nothing to upset her. The police-type men seemed to be gone. She hadn't seen any since Sunday, though they might have grown more skilful at concealing themselves.

She slowed at the house, then decided to jog one complete turn around the block. She kept her eyes moving, crossed the street twice to double-check, but by the time she returned to the front entrance she was convinced their surveillance had ended.

If it had ever begun.

In the shower, she told herself she was the victim of

an overactive imagination. That included her reactions to David and to her tennis partner, Lois Turner.

She would let some time pass before seeing David again.

In the meantime, she would accept the invitations for dinner that Lois pressed on her every time they played tennis; the invitations she had declined since that one social evening three months ago. She wouldn't reject love with David and she wouldn't reject friendship with Lois.

She refused to consider what she would do if 'friendship' included something else.

Don Manguson was in civvies when he came to Lowery's room – neat blue slacks and a V-necked sweater over a sports shirt. He said it might be better that way. 'In case they wonder who you are. So they don't draw a connection between my uniform . . . well, you know.'

Lowery was wearing his old grey suit and striped shirt without tie. He checked his off-duty weapon, a small Belgian automatic that he carried in an armpit holster, and was glad when Manguson showed his own weapon, a Detective Special in a back-pocket sheath. 'Though there's no way, Harold, we're gonna have trouble. Not even if the Schleissers and the three or four others are at the diner. You got the wrong people for that Fairfax problem.'

In Manguson's Pinto, they listened to a newscast and learned that the Fairfax problem had become the Fairfax homicide. Manguson muttered, 'Shit, that complicates things,' as they pulled into the parking lot with the big new sign, *CLORY'S*, over the old, railroad-car diner. 'Anyone connected with Nazis around here is going to *expect* police investigation.'

A man was on a ladder, hanging a line of coloured Christmas lights along the edge of the roof. 'Duke Eiser,' Manguson said, 'Harv Clory's cousin. A hard drinker, hard case all around. Brawler, record for minor felonies, not a particularly good citizen.'

There were three other cars in the lot, and Manguson pointed at one. 'Jim Borst is here, another Resurrection party supporter. But I don't see any of the four Schleisser vehicles.'

They parked and got out. The man on the ladder turned his head. Manguson said, 'Hey, Duke.' Duke Eiser said, 'Hey yourself, junior,' without a trace of humour, and turned back to his work.

Manguson murmured, 'He just loves the law, old Duke does.'

Lowery said, 'Is one of those four Schleisser vehicles you mentioned a truck by any chance?'

'Almost has to be, Harold, seeing they're farmers. Or grape ranchers, as folks here call 'em.' They passed to the left side of the ladder on their way to the diner entrance, and Duke Eiser looked down at them. Manguson said, 'Friend visiting me from Los Angeles.'

Eiser said, 'Don't say?', his eyes fixed on Lowery. He had a dark, sharply angular face with at least two days' growth of pepper-and-salt stubble. His hair was brown with sun-streaked and grey tints. He wore jeans and a navy blue jacket . . . and suddenly zipped down the jacket and opened it wide, saying, 'Warm in the sun,' which it wasn't, there being a touch of frost in the chill December air.

Then Lowery saw the T-shirt underneath: the large black swastika with *Resurrection* printed above it. He froze in shock. Outside of movies and TV, he had never seen anyone wear a swastika.

Manguson said, 'How's Adolf and the boys?'

Eiser was still looking at Lowery, smiling. Lowery felt heat creeping into his face and had to look away.

'Adolf Schleisser, you mean?'

'Any other Adolfs of your acquaintance?' Manguson said, voice tinged with irritation.

'Well, let's see, there's . . . uh, Adolf Zuckor, the Hebe from the movie business. Or is he in Jew heaven now?'

Lowery's eyes snapped up. He felt like a fool for

142

reacting; then figured what the hell, he was here to ask questions, not play undercover Gentile. He looked straight into Eiser's small brown eyes.

'And there's Adolf Hitler, of course,' Eiser said, his smile growing.

'Not any more there isn't,' Lowery said. 'He's worm-shit now.'

Manguson chuckled. Lowery said, 'Of course, he always was.'

Eiser zipped up his jacket. 'Hey, junior, better tell your friend where he is.'

'He's in Bethills,' Manguson said, 'in the San Joaquin Valley, California, USA. Or do you figure somewhere else?'

'I mean this diner.' Eiser wasn't smiling and cool any more. His thin lips were pressed tight, his hands were clenched, his chest heaved under the jacket. He looked like one mean and slightly psychotic forty-year-old; scratch the *slightly*. 'I mean Clory's.'

Manguson opened the door, waving Lowery inside. 'Sure, Duke.'

Lowery would have liked to taunt Eiser a little more; get him down off that ladder and then . . .

He walked on, shaking the violent fantasies, telling himself he was an officer of the law and above such things. He walked through the door, tense, not knowing what to expect inside.

What he found wasn't swastikas, pictures of Hitler, uniformed Nazis. What he found was an ageing diner, standard shabby, with a short counter and seven red-topped stools. With four red booths on either side of the centre door. With a couple in a booth at the far left end, and a big, young, tow-headed man sitting dead centre of the counter. That big man turned to see who had come in and raised his voice: 'Customers, Harv.'

A swinging door behind the counter opened. A man about Eiser's age, but shorter, thicker, came out of the kitchen wearing a white shirt and white apron. 'Or one customer and an eagle scout.'

143

Manguson said, 'Gee, I've missed this gourmet restaurant, Harold.' Then, to Clory, 'A friend of mine from LA. How about some of your famous German pancakes and bacon?'

Clory nodded, running a hand over his nearly bald head. He had a thick reddish moustache, as if to compensate for his loss of hair. He stared hard at Lowery, as did the young man.

Then Manguson drew Lowery to a booth on the right. On the way they passed a glass-topped display counter holding candy bars, ballpoint pens, pocket combs, a whole panoply of fly-specked specialities . . . including a few swastika shoulder patches, the only sign of Nazi involvement.

They sat in the last booth on the right, 'for a little privacy,' Manguson murmured. Lowery faced into the diner. Behind him was a door marked *Men*. At the other end was one marked *Women*.

And that was Clory's diner: a Nazi dump enclosed by toilets.

Manguson said, 'The big blond guy at the counter is Jim Borst, another sympathizer. Except for the Schleissers, Hugo Verner who moved upstate, and the two truck drivers who come through occasionally, the entire Resurrection party is right here.'

'As far as you know.'

'We keep them under spot observation; have for years. They're not breaking any laws, so that's as far as we go. Though during one of the spot checks we learned that two of the Schleissers and Clory went to San Francisco for a rally of several Nazi groups. They managed a grand total of forty-seven people, including wives, so you can see how big a menace they are.'

'I'm not concerned with how big a menace they are,' Lowery said (which wasn't entirely true). 'I'm concerned with three or four men who conducted an illegal demonstration and killed an eighteen-year-old boy.'

'As I said, Harold, it's not like them . . .'

144

'And Bethills is closer to LA than any other location having a Nazi group.'

'That so?'

'And the Schleissers have a truck, which I want to see.'

'No problem. What about questioning Clory?'

Lowery shrugged. He understood now that he hadn't expected any of these people to answer questions. He'd simply wanted to see them for himself; get the feel of Bethills; decide if he should try for an undercover man – someone who would settle in Bethills and eat at Clory's and act like a virulent anti-Semite. Someone who could be recruited into the Resurrection party.

But that cost money and since Prop Thirteen the department – *all* departments – were short of money. Especially for fishing expeditions.

Clory brought the food. 'You want coffee or what?'

'Coffee,' Manguson said, getting Lowery's nod. When Clory walked back behind the counter, Manguson said, 'Want me to handle the interrogation, Harold, or will you?'

'Go ahead.' Lowery tasted the pancakes gingerly. They were excellent, and the bacon was crisp. He began to eat, figuring it was probably his last chance to be fed by a Nazi.

Clory returned with two cups of coffee. Manguson said, 'Harv, listen, I've got a problem and maybe you can help me.'

Clory stood there, smoothing his thick moustache. Which was when Lowery noticed the tattoo on the inside of his right forearm, about where the concentration-camp tattoos had been placed. In a chilling imitation of the infamous blue numbers were the letters H-i-t-l-e-r. Lowery shifted his eyes away, controlling a surge of rage.

Manguson said, 'There's been some trouble, Harv. Three, four men in Nazi uniform beat up on some people in Los Angeles. Now we don't want strangers coming here and bothering *our* people, do we? It'll be

145

better all around if it's handled by a local boy. Think you can tell me who was involved? It's really a minor matter.'

'You mean the Jew who fell down and broke his head?' Clory asked blandly. 'The one who was trying to attack some peacefully demonstrating brothers? The one who went to hell last night? If so, I don't see any problem, Don.'

At that point Lowery gave up on getting anything in this diner, and probably from the Schleissers. It looked like his first SIT was going to end in an Unsolved, unless someone had been incredibly stupid and used his own truck. And, as long as he was dreaming, that truck still held the swastika banners and the bloody bat.

He admired Manguson's chutzpah as the young trooper said, 'The Jewish kid died? Hell, that doesn't change things much.'

'Only a little bit,' Clory said, deadpan. 'From assault to murder, as the queers in LA will see it.' Before Manguson could reply, he turned pale brown eyes on Lowery. 'Isn't that so, *officer*?'

'Not so,' Lowery said, sipping coffee, which was also excellent. This Nazi would be a definite asset to any prison kitchen. 'The dead man was attempting an assault on one of the Nazis. The Nazis were demonstrating – although without a permit – not attacking. They simply defended themselves.'

'And using a lead-filled bat makes no difference?' Clory's lips seemed to twitch a little in an abortive smile.

'How'd you know about lead-filled bats?'

The abortive smile was totally aborted. 'Read it.'

'That's funny. None of our witnesses offered such information. The bats looked normal to them. Where'd you read it?'

Clory turned away. 'I forget.'

'Mr Clory,' Lowery said sharply.

Clory turned to face him. So did Jim Borst at the counter. And so did Duke Eiser, just now entering the diner.

146

'You could be right about those murder charges,' Lowery said. 'If a grand jury returns an open homicide indictment, it's a different ball game. It could mean ten years. Anyone indicated as an accessory could get almost as much . . . but we'll say one to three years. And withholding evidence brings you into the accessory category.'

'Brings *me*?'

'A figure of speech, Mr Clory. Brings anyone.' He looked at Borst and Eiser. 'Is protecting an acquaintance worth one to three years of your lives?'

No one answered.

Lowery said, 'If you decide to save yourselves that kind of trouble, contact Officer Manguson and he'll contact me. It would really be advisable. There are going to be a lot of eyes down here.' He drank more of that excellent coffee as the silence deepened.

Christ, to get a break, some sort of blue-sky clue that would at least prove to *him* that the Resurrection party was guilty! If *he* could be sure, he would never give up; he would find some way, no matter how long it took, to bring those bastards to court!

'I'd help if I could,' Clory finally said, voice bland.

Jim Borst said, 'Hey, me, too.'

Eiser turned to the counter, calling, 'Harv, let's have three eggs. And something kosher on the side. I built one hell of an appetite doing the Lord's work.'

Jim Borst laughed. Eiser sat down beside him and they murmured to each other, glancing at Lowery, faces split by grins.

Clory said, 'Well, if I don't see you two again, Merry Christmas.' Then, as he walked towards the counter, 'To the one who's human, that is,' this last said so softly Lowery barely caught it.

But catch it he did, and rose, saying to Manguson, 'I'll pay you outside. If I stay one more minute, I'll break a few laws myself.' He strode to the door, looking neither left nor right.

He heard Jim Borst laugh again, and Eiser's voice

147

whispering words that all sounded like 'few' and 'true' . . . and 'Jew'. As he opened the door, Clory sang out, 'Come again real soon,' and this time it was Eiser who cackled.

He was outside, and not a moment too soon. He could almost *feel* teeth shattering under his fists.

He walked around until Manguson joined him. 'They're a lot of bullshit, Harold. I still don't believe . . .'

'I *know* you don't believe! Let's get to the Schleissers.'

Manguson was quiet as they drove through town, then off on another blacktop road which ran through fields of grape vines. He slowed at a narrow, climbing dirt road which branched off to the right. 'This is it. You got any sort of plan?'

'No plan. Just take me up there and point out the truck.'

Manguson turned, passing a big mailbox on the left decorated with a red-stencilled swastika. 'Yessir,' he said.

Lowery realized he'd been too curt with the young officer.

'Sorry, Don. Must admit they got to me in that diner. I'm Jewish, you know.'

'I wasn't sure. But hell, they got to me too and I'm Danish.'

They went up the dirt road, entering an earth circle with a white clapboard house to the right, a fenced-in pasture with a dog racing towards them to the left, and straight ahead across a grassy section a shabby faded-red barn. One of the barn's double doors was open and a vehicle could be seen inside.

'That's the truck,' Manguson said. 'Go ahead and look. I'll talk to whoever shows.' He pointed at a shiny Ford station wagon and dusty Ford LTD parked near the house. 'The wagon is Adolf's, the other his son Carl's. I don't see Horst's van.'

Lowery was already out, but before he could begin walking, a very big man – broad as well as tall – came

148

out of the house onto the porch. The dog, a German Shepherd, had reached the pasture fence and was going crazy trying to leap over, barking madly. The big man said, '*Shaddup!*' and the dog slunk away, trembling. Lowery decided it had been beaten by the big man. Looking at the clenched fists, the glaring eyes, he decided more than dogs had been beaten by that man.

'Hey, Carl,' Manguson said. 'Your father home?'

The big man nodded, continuing to glare at Lowery.

'This is a friend of mine . . .' Manguson began, but Lowery was certain that someone from Clory's Diner had already phoned the Schleissers. He interrupted the trooper by flipping open his wallet and showing his badge. 'Detective Two Lowery. Mind if I look at that truck?'

The big man had begun to protest when another man, older and just a little smaller, came out of the house and stood beside him. They both wore swastika T-shirts with the word *Resurrection* and both showed impressive muscular development.

'Go right ahead,' the older man said. 'If you like it, you can buy it.' He chuckled.

Lowery walked across dirt and then some browned-out grass to the barn.

The truck was a small Ford pick-up, bright green, and as different from the flat-bed used on Fairfax as you could get.

He walked further into the barn towards light coming from a back door. He pushed open that door and looked around. He didn't expect to find another truck and so he wasn't disappointed. But he walked behind the house too, playing it by the book; then returned to where Manguson was talking to the men and to a heavy-set woman who stood behind them in the open door.

Manguson said, 'I explained to Adolf,' he indicated the older man, 'and his son Carl, what we're interested in.' He turned to the Schleissers. 'Detective Lowery would be very grateful for any help you could give us.

149

We understand it was self-defence so the sooner someone comes forward to offer information – or to present
himself for the authorities to question – the easier it'll
be.' He spoke to Lowery. 'You don't think there'll be
any charges preferred, do you, Detective Lowery?'

Lowery was having a hard time divorcing himself
from those swastikas, but he did notice that the son,
Carl, was sweating about the face and that he looked
nervous enough to break and run. And wouldn't that
be beautiful! He said a silent prayer for it to happen and
felt the Browning Baby under his left armpit, a tiny ·32
automatic, but loaded with six hollow-points and quite
capable of putting these oxen away.

He snapped out of it, keeping his eyes from slipping
back to the T-shirts. He watched that tense, sweating
man and decided to play a hunch. A hunch that kept
growing stronger as he shifted his eyes from son to
father and saw that the father, despite his apparent
smiling ease, was watching the son more carefully than
he was watching the police.

Maybe he was worried because the son was a violent
fool.

And maybe he was worried because the son had
killed a boy on Fairfax Avenue and seemed about to
break and run.

'I'm afraid charges *would* be preferred, Officer
Manguson.'

Manguson was startled.

'I'm afraid that with feelings running as high as they
are in the Fairfax area, the politicians would pressure
the District Attorney to file on homicide.'

'How could that be?' Carl Schleisser asked, voice
hoarse. 'It was self-defence . . .'

'That's what we heard on television,' Adolf Schleisser
interrupted, still maintaining his easy smile and manner. 'A harmless demonstration attacked by neighbourhood thugs. And one thug ran into medical problems
and died.'

'The Nazis didn't have a permit to demonstrate, Mr

Schleisser. They were deliberately provoking the Jewish population. I know you're sympathetic to their views,' he spread his hands, 'but the best way for anyone concerned to handle this . . .'

'Now hold on,' Adolf Schleisser said, chuckling. 'We're concerned only in that our general philosophy matches that of the people who demonstrated in Los Angeles. But the Resurrection party wasn't involved, wasn't there. I know because I'm the leader. And Nazis obey their leader.'

Carl Schleisser was shaking his head, muttering, 'No, not involved.'

He was so obviously afraid, so perfect a suspect on his reactions alone, that Lowery had to try and get him aside, though he couldn't see Adolf Schleisser allowing it to happen.

'Could I speak to you, Carl? While Officer Manguson speaks to your father.' He casually gestured for the big man to come down from the porch.

Carl Schleisser actually began to move forward, but his father grasped his arm. 'Come on inside, Officers. We'll sit at the table and talk comfortably.'

Lowery nodded, watching as Carl steadied under his father's hand, wiped his forehead and went quickly inside.

Adolf beckoned them, smiling.

Manguson seemed uncomfortable and murmured, 'You sure, Harold?'

But Lowery felt certain he was no longer susceptible to Nazi paraphernalia. He wanted to see if anyone else was inside the house; perhaps that second son Manguson had mentioned. He wanted to speak to Adolf's wife, to any other wives or girlfriends. He wanted to find as many weak links as possible and figure out how to exploit them. Most of all he wanted to get at Carl Schleisser.

And yet, as they entered a large country kitchen, he was immediately aware of the tinted, idealized photopainting of Hitler hanging over an archway leading to another room. And of the satiny-red, gold-fringed banner on the wall to the left – two SS lightning bolts above a skull and crossbones encircled by small black swastikas.

Adolf Schleisser pointed to the banner. 'A labour of love by my wife, Eva. Not historically accurate, but something to honour the SS.' He smiled at her.

She smiled back placidly, and Lowery decided that this stolid Hausfrau would be no help to him.

She was asking if they would have beer. Lowery said, 'Too early for me,' and turned his head as Carl went under Hitler's picture and out of the room.

'He has work to do,' Adolf said. 'Sit down and enjoy something to eat.'

'We just had breakfast,' Manguson said. 'But you know what I'd like, Mr Schleisser? To see your house. I've lived in Bethills all my life, but this is one of the *old* houses and my father said it's a real landmark.'

Lowery understood the officer's ploy. So did Adolf Schleisser, who said, 'I'm sorry. Everything's a mess. My wife wouldn't allow it.'

She shook her head immediately. 'No, I'm sorry.'

Adolf said, 'Unless, of course, you have a search warrant.' He said it in a bantering, just-kidding-around manner and laughed and nodded at the officers, inviting their laughter.

Manguson smiled and shrugged, glancing at Lowery.

Lowery didn't laugh, didn't smile. Lowery wondered if the next room held that bloodstained bat – stained, that is, by the standards of a big-city police lab, a modern forensic department which could raise traces of blood in porous material, including wood, months after a crime was committed. Wondered whether the evidence that could drag this laughing Nazi and his sweating son and his smug accomplices into LA County Jail, that could make all the Resurrection party scum quake and suffer and sweat, was within a few feet of where he stood.

He'd have traded a promotion for that search warrant

Adolf Schleisser had joked about, though he knew the odds favoured the bat having been disposed of immediately after the demonstration. And even if Carl was stuffing it under a bed right now, it would be gone long before he could get a warrant. If he could *ever* get a warrant, considering he had hunches and not evidence.

He walked to the front door. He said, 'I'll be seeing you and your son again, Mr Schleisser,' without smiles, without masking the threat in his face and voice, and turned his back on any possible response.

Manguson joined him in the Pinto. 'That about finished us, Harold.'

'Not quite. Do both of Schleisser's sons work here with him?'

Manguson nodded. 'And a few hired men, in season.'

'The sons have any off-season jobs?'

'The Resurrection party is their off-season job.'

'Those two men in Clory's – Jim Borst and Duke Eiser – where do they work?'

'Jim for his father in a milk delivery company. Duke at Bethills Auto Wrecking, which people around here call Cross's junk yard.'

'Old cars, wrecked cars? They have a crusher, a compacter?'

Manguson nodded, driving down the dirt road to the blacktop. 'Want to go over and look around? It's empty on Sunday, but we can get onto the lot.'

'First I'd like you to run a search through your computer.'

Manguson turned left, driving back between the winter vineyards.

'I want to know about any trucks stolen in the general area before and including Wednesday, December 12th, the date of the Fairfax incident. Say within a month.'

'Sure. Shouldn't take long. We don't have the rate of vehicle theft you people have in LA.'

'Drop me at the motel. If you come up with anything, we'll visit that wrecking yard.'

153

Manguson's young face brightened. 'Hey, Harold, a way to go!'

Lowery nodded glumly. A way to go, no matter how narrow.

'So *Horst* is yellow,' Adolf Schleisser said, voice heavy with sarcasm. He looked at his older son . . . and suddenly couldn't restrain himself, lunging over the table to slap his face. Carl grunted and rocked in the chair, but didn't try to get away. His eyes stayed down and he seemed to shrink inside that big, powerful body.

Eva said, 'Adolf, he didn't do anything!', coming over to stand behind Carl, trying to protect him the way she'd always tried to protect her sons from punishment.

Adolf shifted his glare to her. She backed away. 'Please,' she whispered. 'He tries so hard to be what you want.'

'He's too goddam stupid to be what I want! He's a *dummkopf*, unworthy of the swastika, of the name Nazi, of membership in the Resurrection party!'

Carl sat very still, head drooping.

Quite suddenly, Adolf's rage passed and he sank back into his chair. 'You had no reason to sweat, to show fear to those officers. Especially to that Jew detective.'

Carl's voice was low, submissive, as he said, 'I hope he's not a Jew. If he is, he'll try harder to get us.'

'You're saying you're afraid of a goddam blood-sucking kike?'

'No, no,' Carl said, raising a hand as if to fend off another blow. 'Not afraid. Just worried. About the police. Because it's like Horst said: I killed him and now they're after me and they won't listen to self-defence.'

'*You* know you killed him. Horst and I know you killed him. The police *don't* know it, and there's no way they can find out. Unless you keep acting like a frightened rabbit, shaking in your boots and letting them see your fear.'

Eva brought mugs of coffee and thick slabs of the

154

cornbread she'd made for breakfast. Carl began to eat, taking huge mouthfuls, and Adolf expected to see that cornbread gone, as usual, before he and Eva barely had a chance to get started. But Carl stopped eating. 'Clory also knows. At least that we were the ones in Jewtown. And so does Duke. And you got to figure they told Jim; maybe Hugo if he came around.'

'So? They're all good party members. All loyal Nazis devoted to me and you and Horst. All happy for our victory Wednesday.' He sipped coffee. 'And two of them are involved. Clory and Duke stole the truck and hid it. And Duke destroyed it.'

'Clory's got his wife, Marjory. Duke drinks too much. Jim doesn't really care for politics, just the uniform. Any of them could talk to the wrong person.'

Adolf watched the sweat pop out again on the *dummkopf's* forehead; watched the way he kept blinking, kept wetting his lips. And knew that *this* was the only one who would talk. Was already talking with his sweat, his frightened eyes.

'How about Rose and the girls?' he asked, thinking of what to do.

'Well, I told Rose, before I thought the Jew would die. The girls didn't hear. They're too young anyway at seven and eight, except to come to auxiliary meetings.'

'They don't come *much*,' Adolf said.

'I know. But Rose wants them to make their own decision about being Nazis later, maybe at fifteen.' He paused. 'She wasn't happy when I told her about clubbing the Jew.'

Adolf didn't waste time worrying about Rose. She was a hard-as-nails Irisher who'd fought her father with her fists when he tried to stop her from marrying Carl. Adolf had thought them well matched, until now. Now he understood that his older son was a weakling.

He stood up. 'Go home and pack for a Christmas vacation. You won't tell anyone where you're going, and you'll leave the girls with us. They'll know a little more about the party when you get back.'

155

Carl also stood, nodding eagerly. Eva said, 'But won't we have Christmas dinner together, the whole family?'

Adolf said, 'He needs the rest. We'll have the girls. Maybe Horst.'

'Horst hasn't been home on Christmas for three years. A family should . . .'

Adolf lifted his hand. 'Enough!' He looked at Carl. 'I want you and Rose to stay away until at least the first. I want you to straighten yourself out.' He came around the table, putting his hands on the massive shoulders, looking into the wide blue eyes. 'Do you hear me, Carl? Relax, and understand there is nothing to be afraid of. The truck is gone. The bats are gone. The leaflets are gone. The ski-masks are gone. The uniforms are like anyone else's, especially since we didn't wear the Africa Korps hats. Do you see how safe we are?'

Carl nodded. 'Yes, father.' He smiled a little. 'It'll be good to get away. Rose and I haven't been alone for a long time.'

'Then get going,' Adolf said. 'Bring the girls over on your way out of town.' He stepped back, raising his stiffened right arm. *'Heil Hitler!'*

Carl came to attention, returning the salute, shouting along with him. When they finished, Eva was wiping her eyes, murmuring, *'Seig heil.* If only he was alive to lead us.'

Adolf thought, 'Your son Horst will lead us.'

Horst, who was gone on one of his many visits to San Francisco where he stayed with 'friends'. Adolf knew that meant women; loose women.

Well, his son was young and this was America, not Germany, and a leader grew up differently. What counted was that Horst had intelligence and caution, and Adolf was becoming convinced that a degree of caution was necessary. Hadn't Hitler himself shown considerable restraint before gaining power? Hadn't he backed away from confrontations with Hindenburg, the establishment, before being certain he could win?

Carl was kissing his mother and going out the door. Adolf felt he would be fine; that the situation was under control again. That Jew detective could stay in Bethills till hell froze over and never find a thing, because there was nothing to find.

Actually, now that the *dummkopf* was steadied and on his way out of town, Adolf began to enjoy the fact that the JDL Jew had died, though it meant he couldn't advertise the Fairfax demonstration even among other Nazi groups. He and his sons had *done* something, had killed one of the enemy. And not had to stand trial for it like the hot-headed fools in North Carolina, who were lucky not to have ended in jail.

First blood for the National Resurrection party! First trickle of what would become a *river* before he and Horst were finished!

Horst Schleisser hadn't felt really hungry since Wednesday night. He always experienced tension – hell, it was *fear* – in the gut. But today Janet insisted on lunch at Fisherman's Wharf.

It wasn't the one in San Francisco. They had driven to Monterey for the weekend and explored the scenic beauty of adjoining Carmel. Back at the motel Saturday night, their room overlooking the coast had provided a dramatic view of black boulders and crashing white surf under a superbly clear winter's sky. And the fury of the sea seemed to have triggered a corresponding sexual fury in him. The truth was he'd been trying to wipe out Wednesday night and Fairfax Avenue.

He had never talked about anti-Semitism, about Fascism, certainly not about Nazis to her. But today, sitting in the seafood restaurant at the end of the Monterey wharf, flooded by sunshine and soothed by soft music from the bar, the subject kept pressing at his tongue. Because driving here he'd found the news on the car radio, as he'd found it several times a day since Wednesday. And because today one of the stories was the death of that JDL kid, forcing Horst to consider the

157

possibility that he would soon be facing exposure as a Nazi and trial as an accessory to homicide.

What would his woman think of him then? Would it make any difference if he explained that the reason he was a Nazi was to get the money, the leisure, to allow them to be together? Could she understand he *heiled* Hitler for a living?

'Hank, look!' She was pointing out the window at the bay, face alive with excitement. 'How cute! Like a wet puppy!'

He followed her finger to the choppy, sparkling water, where an otter was swimming by in traditional otter fashion, on its back, munching a fish held between its paws.

'You're a lot cuter,' he said, 'and you don't drive the local fishermen wild by eating half their catch.'

She laughed, leaning over the table to present her lips.

He hesitated, glancing around, never having been able to match her freedom of emotional expression, her confidence in others accepting what was natural to her. But today he needed her as never before.

Their lips met, and it felt so good, was so comforting that he drew her back for a second longer kiss. And ached inside with the need to have her *know* him. Not Hank Jackson, which he'd made up on the spur of the moment, but Horst Schleisser, whose name alone might be an affront to her.

Janet Koen was his age, twenty-five, her birthday in May while his was in July, which allowed him to joke about his 'older woman'. She was small with a fine figure, slender everywhere but in bust and bottom. She had eyes that were green now, grey in different light. She had full lips, especially the lower on which he loved to nibble, a strong, narrow nose, high cheekbones, and shoulder-length auburn hair which she swore she had never touched with dyes. Beneath that crowning glory was a mind that snapped at information and gave quick,

158

intelligent opinions . . . and later reassessed, re-evaluated and gave more detailed and thoughtful opinions.

She commented on everything, was critical of much, and loved him without question. Though there must have been things about which she would have *liked* to question him: such as the divorced parents who 'weren't around long enough to count', and owning a small apartment house and smaller truck farm 'in the least attractive part of the state'.

She had read his unwillingness to go further and accepted him on his own terms. But she had asked him to 'swear you're not married, Hank'. He had sworn, saying the time would come when he would marry *her*.

He meant it. He would marry her, when a third of the grape ranch became legally his. That meant Pop would have to die and his will remain unchanged, leaving Horst, Carl and Mom equal partners. Horst could handle Mom and Carl, ignoring whatever they might feel about his marrying a Jewess, but Pop was something else again. And Pop was only fifty-four years old and strong as an ox.

The waitress brought their food: broiled snapper, brown rice, heaped coleslaw, warm sour-dough rolls, steaming cups of tea with lemon. They almost always ate the same things, just like a family would in its own kitchen. But from choice, not necessity, influencing each other constantly.

She smiled at him as she raised a forkful of fish, and he couldn't help thinking how Pop would see her.

Pop would fit her into his caricature of the slut Jewess. Pop would say she was dark and oily and talky. That her motives were hidden, dangerous, manipulative. That she would reveal herself as evil and grasping some day, part of the world-wide Jewish conspiracy. That she would try to rob him of his Aryan birthright – whatever the hell that was.

Pop would pour out the Nazi poison, saying her nose was big, her eyes shifty, her skin swarthy, her face 'verminously ugly', as he'd called a pretty TV actress with a Jewish-sounding name.

If you looked at a woman that way long enough, she began to change, to *grow* ugly. And he had to drop his eyes from his beloved's face, had to stop thinking of the Nazi poison, even though he'd brought it up only to reject it.

'You're not eating,' she said, voice worried, as if it were critically important. *The Jewish Momma* – the other caricature, the funny one. But Pop laughed in a special way, a hard, hating, dangerous way. And he had tried to figure out how to add arsenic or insecticides to the kosher foods sold in supermarkets, the foods Jewish Mommas bought for their families. He'd studied urban-warfare pamphlets and talked of hypodermic needles inserted into frozen dinners, a high-intensity spray to penetrate cardboard cartons of matzot, even of opening jars and simply dumping poison inside.

Horst had quoted statistics that showed many Gentiles ate kosher foods and Pop had dropped the idea. Not because of those Gentiles whom he called Jew-lovers, but because he'd been unable to find a method allowing him to treat large amounts of food in relative safety.

'Maybe you're not eating because I forgot to say grace,' Janet joked. 'I would, but you know what the Reverend Bailey Smith of the Southern Baptist Convention said, don't you?'

Horst remembered the name from something Pop had told him, but couldn't pin it down. He shook his head.

' "God Almighty does not hear the prayer of a Jew," ' she quoted, smiling. 'And Smith is the *president* of that organization. Poor clown, he's forgotten his God Almighty *is* a Jew.'

He gave her the laugh she wanted, but seized the opportunity to break years of silence on the subject now tormenting him. 'Speaking of clowns,' he said, 'I was reading something about American Nazis.' He busied

160

himself buttering a roll. 'Right here in California – three separate parties. It was an article in the *Los Angeles Times*.'

She continued to eat, watching him, waiting.

'They don't add up to more than a handful of active members, all three of them put together. Of course, they claim to have sympathizers. Do you know anything about them?'

'A little. I've read what's available, which isn't much. Historical Nazis, the Hitler-era variety, are of course well represented in books and periodicals.'

'Meaning American Nazis aren't worth bothering with, right? Even for you, as a Jew.'

'That's not so,' she replied. 'They're bothering with Jews, so Jews have to bother with them. The Anti-Defamation League of B'nai B'rith publishes occasional updates on the various Nazi movements and my boss is on their mailing list. While these Nazis haven't gained many new members, they have the capacity to influence people with their publications. There are always people who will believe the very worst about races and religions different from their own, and the Nazis specialize in printing such poison.' She took a forkful of rice, looking at him, blinking, thinking.

He too ate, though without pleasure.

'Do you know,' she said, 'that one of the largest publishers of anti-Semitic material in the world, George Dietz, came here from Germany in 1957? I wonder what Immigration thinks of Dietz.'

She was on her way, getting into her subject, and said that 'haters' all over the world got their 'fixes' from Dietz and that no one knew how many tragedies this caused.

'Like Frederick Cowan, the American Nazi who killed six people in New Rochelle, New York, including a police officer, and wounded four more officers before committing suicide. Cowan owned many of Dietz's publications. Granted he was a psychotic personality, Hank, there's still the question of whether he'd have

161

done what he did without the stimulation of that hate material.'

When Horst muttered that it had to be against the law, she shook her head. 'Our constitution, our freedom of speech and press, protects Dietz and allows him to turn out his vicious tracts in Reedy, West Virginia, whereas in his native Germany it's against the law. Back there he'd be thrown in jail.'

She mentioned other racist publishers, including Gerald Lauck, who called himself head of the overseas branch of the German Nazi party. 'Sick and dangerous people, Hank.' She sipped water; her voice fell to a whisper. 'And they want to destroy people like me. I never understood it . . .'

Her voice trailed off and she looked out the window. He cursed himself for bringing up the subject. He wished another otter would swim by and bring back her brightness, her happiness.

He said, 'Never heard of those men. And neither have most Americans, I'll bet. So who cares?'

Yet Horst Schleisser *had* heard of them. Pop spoke glowingly of Dietz as the source of many of the books, pamphlets and leaflets he read and handed out at meetings, and of Lauck as a contact to the 'Old Fighters' in Germany. Pop had especially high hopes for the books which 'proved' that six million Jews couldn't have died by Nazi hands. Horst had read two at Pop's insistence and seen the point. If the Jews *hadn't* died, then Jews had manipulated Christian society and gotten reparations and a whole country, Israel, which they didn't deserve. And Pop wouldn't hear of the Nuremberg Trials, calling them 'Jew frame-ups'.

Janet was speaking again, saying that Dietz's Liberty Bell Press published hatred in English, German, French and Spanish. And that the market was still expanding.

'Still,' Horst said desperately, '*we* don't know anyone who reads that crap, or who wears swastikas and says Heil Hitler.' He managed a laugh. 'Who knows any Nazis, right?'

'Who can be sure he *doesn't* know any Nazis?' She jabbed the air with her fork, intense, angry, saying that the Nazis who wore uniforms were only the tip of the iceberg; that underneath were the 'closet Nazis' in the Liberty Lobby, a 'so-called conservative group' which numbered over a hundred thousand anti-Semites and assorted malcontents, run by an admirer of Hitler and Nazi Germany named Willis A. Carto. And those in the various Klans who preferred the American image over the German. 'And there are a great many more people looking for a scapegoat, looking for someone to blame for the economy, for the disintegration of American world prestige and power, for their acid stomachs or zits or haemorrhoids.' These were the kind of people, she said, who had given American Nazi Harold Covington 43 per cent of the vote in the North Carolina Republican primary for the office of district attorney.

Horst laughed sharply, from shock. He knew who Pop would prosecute.

'More than 56,500 Americans voted for a Nazi, Hank. And that's in the one state in the union where they were given the chance. They haven't been given the chance, state-wide, anywhere else, so far.'

Horst hated the way this conversation was going, the way she kept building the Nazis' importance, when he had hoped to get a contemptuous laugh, a 'They're nothing, darling,' and so been able to feel a little less guilty.

'Know what he said after the election?' she asked. ' "If you scratch a conservative, you'll find a Nazi underneath." This country is rushing backwards to racism, Hank! The Moral Majority and New Right make a far more comfortable climate for Nazis than the old liberal consensus.'

Later, however, as they walked along the pier towards his van, she did her usual reassessment. 'As a Jew, I guess I tend to over-react. Covington's dead wrong – I'm a Republican conservative myself. The chances are really slim that Nazis will ever gain any sort

163

of real power in this country. It would take a national débâcle . . .' And so on.

Which didn't offer Horst much comfort. His father agreed with her that it would take a débâcle to bring them to power, but he *counted* on it. He bragged that he and Carl had desecrated a synagogue in a nearby town with swastikas, obscenities and the spray-painted message, 'We'll be back in the depression!'

As soon as they entered their motel room, Horst put on the television. He found a news round-up, but nothing more about the Fairfax mess. He would have to call home tonight. He would use the street phone near Janet's apartment. She had to return to Frisco for her job as a legal secretary, his little Brain, and planned to complete her education and become an attorney herself within a few years.

And he had to return to Bethills on Wednesday for the Resurrection party meeting and his role as Führer-in-training.

God, he wanted to forget the whole Nazi madness, especially that deadly stupidity on Fairfax Avenue! And couldn't forget it, not even for a moment.

He turned to Janet for comfort, grabbing her as she stood looking out the window at the sea. He pressed himself into her swelling rear, caressed her breasts; then picked her up and carried her to the bed.

He didn't allow her time to remove her dress, though she murmured, 'It's brand new, honey.' He pulled down her underclothes and got between her warm thighs.

She forgot her new dress and cried out that she wanted him, loved him, 'Can't live without you, darling!'

Later, she kissed his chin and said, 'To what, I wonder, do I owe this weekend of super-duper sex?'

He rolled over, hiding his unsmiling face, and gave her one of their standard gag lines, delivered in Yiddish dialect as she had taught him:

'Don' esk.'

164

Bethills Auto Wrecking, or Cross's junk yard as it was known to locals, was situated on the easternmost edge of Bethills County, a geographic area far larger than the square mile of homes and businesses which made up the town itself. The yard covered what looked like at least five acres to Lowery, and was surrounded by a rickety wire-mesh fence, half-down in places, and by flat, brown, winter fields in all directions.

Manguson drove his Pinto off the blacktop highway onto a dirt road which followed the wire fence on their left. 'Easier to get in the back, and no one's likely to see and call old man Cross.' He grinned. 'I'm still afraid of him. He used to chase me and my brother when we were kids and sneaked in to play around the old cars. Wicked old bastard would kick us in the ass if he got close enough.' He paused for reflection. 'Guess he isn't doing much of that any more – must be over seventy by now.'

'It looks like anyone could get in here,' Lowery said, seeing more sections of sagging fence-stakes and torn wire. 'How does he protect his equipment? He must have a tow-truck, welding and cutting devices . . .'

'Sure, and a crane with magnetic pick-up and a compacter that can turn a vehicle into a solid metal cube. And sometimes valuable cars – wrecked Rollses, Mercedes, Caddies worth thousands for their parts. So he's got another fence around his office and work area; a good one that's going to give us trouble.'

Lowery didn't worry about it. Manguson wouldn't have driven him here without being able to gain entry.

The young trooper had called him at the motel about four hours after they'd parted, not quite able to hide his excitement. 'Got something might interest you, Harold. No less than five trucks stolen in a ten-mile radius around Bethills within the past month. One of them was an old Chevy Series Sixty, a flat-bed that would fit the general description of the one used on Fairfax Avenue.'

'A Chevy?' Lowery had asked. 'Are they big enough?'

'This one is. And nondescript, which would explain no one being able to give the colour. It was brown, the owner said, *once*. But it saw years of rough service and the paint was faded and when he described it to the responding officers he said colour wouldn't help much in finding it.'

Not bad, Lowery had thought, but still not enough to explain the excitement pushing up through the young officer's voice. 'C'mon, Don. It's two thirty and I'll have to be heading back to LA soon. What else?'

The answer had come in a rush. 'It disappeared from outside Clory's diner while the owner was having dinner, 9.00 p.m. Friday, December 7th. That's the Friday before the Wednesday of the Fairfax demonstration. That's just five days . . .'

'Got it,' Lowery had said. 'So come get me.'

Which Manguson had done in short order. Now he said, 'If they'd intended to use the truck again, they'd have hidden it somewhere in the area. And with Duke working here, we might just find it.'

Lowery nodded. 'The boy didn't die until late yesterday. You say the junk yard is closed down on weekends. The compacter too, I guess.'

'Yeah, but Duke runs it. He could've destroyed the truck yesterday, or early this morning.'

'Or right after the truck returned from Los Angeles. Or not at all. So let's get inside and find out.'

The back gate had a chain wrapped loosely around the posts, which Manguson unwrapped. 'We'll drive around a bit first; see if they hid it with the wrecks, the junk.'

They drove along the aisles used by tow-trucks. They saw very few wrecked trucks and nothing matching what they were looking for. They got out once to search behind a mound of rusting auto frames, engines, assorted heavy parts. And came upon a huge dog, part boxer, ripping and tearing at a bloody lump of dark fur.

'Jesus!' Manguson exclaimed, stepping back and

bumping into Lowery. 'Cross's mutt! Complete forgot about him.'

But while the dog growled menacingly, it didn't move from its meat.

Lowery said, 'I guess he's had his kill for the day. Looks like a cat.'

'*Ugh*! I oughta shoot the bastard! I got a cat of my own.'

They returned to the car. Manguson drove back towards the open gate, turned right and drove down the aisle formed by rickety fence on their left and junk on their right. He turned right again at a massive pile, a veritable hill of assorted fenders.

Directly in front of them was an area enclosed by hurricane wire-fencing, perhaps nine feet high, topped by three feet of barbed wire on outward curving rods. The double gate was bound with heavy chain, secured by a brick-sized padlock.

They got out of the Pinto. Lowery looked at the lock, and Manguson looked at Lowery.

'All right,' Lowery said. 'Impress me. How do we get inside?'

'Couldn't you climb it?'

'Maybe, if that dog was at my ass.'

Manguson chuckled and took a key from his pocket. He got the padlock open, unwrapped the chain and shoved the gate inward.

Lowery walked past him to a metal shack, where he glanced through the window into a small office.

Having played detective and examined what didn't concern him, he turned to look at what might – a sky-high crane with a hanging circular section, a thick disk of raw, shiny metal.

'Where's the claw?' Lowery asked Manguson, who'd come up beside him.

'Cross replaced it with that electromagnet. It can pick up whole cars and drop them right in there.' He pointed behind the crane's massive cab where a giant compacter stood like an open box, its sides painted black. 'Cross's

167

pride and joy. It can crush and press vehicles into two-ton squares. There's a place in San Francisco that sends out trailer-trucks to get such squares. Cross makes good money off them and they make good money off the Japs.'

'Who then make good money off us,' Lowery said, 'selling the scrap back as Toyotas and Datsuns.'

'I always buy American,' Manguson said. 'Always Fords, like my father.'

'You're a dying breed,' Lowery said, but he always bought Chevies, like *his* father. He walked towards a long, one-storey building with a front composed of sliding doors, several of which were open. He stepped inside to gloom and a penetrating metallic odour, a taste-feeling like biting into a piece of foil. There were metal tables, rotary saws, tanks connected to welding equipment, sledges and chisels and tools scattered all over the place.

'They cut up cars here for their parts,' Manguson said. 'Well, another strike-out, Harold. You hungry as I am? There's a great steak house just off 99 . . .'

But Lowery was walking away from him, out the doors and towards the compacter.

This place was perfect for the truck stolen from Clory's diner two Fridays ago. This place could swallow that truck until time for the demonstration – an old vehicle in a lot full of old vehicles. And swallow it again after the demonstration, until Duke Eiser was alone or with a fellow Nazi . . . like any time on Saturday or Sunday when Cross's junk yard was officially closed. Then into the compacter it would go to be pressed into a two-ton metal square to be shipped to Frisco and Japan. And the Nazis could sit in their diner and make fun of the Jew who was dead and the Jew cop who could never find out who had done it; laugh their heads off, because what the hell was one dead Jew to the spiritual descendents of the killers of six million?

Manguson was calling him, but he kept going. He reached the compacter, stepped up onto a foot ledge and looked down at the thick steel base. And saw something.

He stared at a thin strip of metal, perhaps a foot long, no more than three inches wide at its widest, an inch at its thinnest. A fragment of fender, or hood, or door. Dull brown on the painted side.

Manguson was standing beside him. Lowery pointed at the strip of metal. Manguson climbed over and picked up the strip. He examined it, then handed it to Lowery.

'The truck was brown,' Lowery said. 'This kind of dull, faded, worn brown.'

'No way to tell if it came from a truck, car, or van, Harold. Or a motor cycle for that matter. Certainly no way to tell if it came from a Chevy Series Sixty.'

'Maybe the Chevrolet people will know.' And even that wasn't important at this moment, because *he* knew. Together with Harv Clory's slip about leaded bats and Carl Schleisser's sweating face, this strip of metal from the last vehicle to have been placed in Mr Cross's compacter gave him the certainty he needed.

He skipped the steak dinner in favour of a hamburger eaten as he drove back towards LA. Half-way there he ran into a downpour. 'Shit,' he muttered. Rain again, with three hours driving still to go.

He remembered what his grandfather used to say, only half-humourously, when things went wrong: *T'zis shvere tsu zein a Yid*. It's tough to be a Jew.

Harold Lowery muttered the phrase, feeling more Jewish with each hour spent on this case.

SEVEN: *Wednesday, 19 December, a.m.*

It had been raining on and off since Sunday evening, heavily at times. The news media began saying that this rainy season threatened to match last year's and last year's had brought near catastrophe to Los Angeles. But it wasn't until Wednesday morning that the skies really broke open.

Other things also broke open, including a few dams across southern California. And, in a parallel sense, events broke open the life of David Howars, precipitating change for himself and others.

Mrs Gomez, his housekeeper, called to say she was afraid to drive the canyon road to his house. She also apologized for waking him at seven thirty, but he assured her he had been up for hours. She didn't believe him, attributing it to 'how kind and nice a man he is,' as she told her husband, Nacho, after David said she was perfectly right not to risk the trip.

'Kind and nice,' as he might be, David had been up since five fifteen, when the almost solid sheets of water falling upon the roof had awakened him. He had then gone to the living room and the sliding glass doors and thrown on the outdoor lights.

The pool was about to overflow, which would send water rolling up to the glass doors, where it would seep through the bottom to soak the carpeting, as had happened last year. So David put on a hooded windbreaker and went out to get the garden hose. One end in the pool, the other running down the alleyway to the street, and the drain-off began immediately.

That was the circumstance that led to his being wide awake when Mrs Gomez called. And to his sitting at the kitchen table, sipping coffee, when Teddy called at eight.

'How do you like this weather, Duvid'l?'

'You called about the weather? At this hour? I wasn't aware that you got up before ten.'

'*Eleven*. Then I rush to make Thomasine's by noon.'

'So what's this?' And he knew, he knew, and began to breathe quickly.

Teddy was silent a beat. 'I almost hate to pass on what my contact told me about the Nazis' truck. Either you're going to be disappointed and grouse around for a week, or you're going to hook it up with something in your head that's not in mine and begin risking our asses.'

David switched the phone to his left hand and wiped a sweaty palm on his bathrobe. 'Just my ass, Teddy.'

'We'll see. The truck is a GM make, Chevy Series Sixty, whatever that means. It was stolen from a diner parking lot in a town called Bethills. That's north . . .'

'I know where it is. When was the truck stolen and what's the diner called?'

'The night of Friday, December 7th. Clory's diner.'

'Clory's.' David carried the phone to the counter where he kept pad and pencil. 'Thanks.'

'How'd you know where this Bethills is? I never even heard of it.'

'Read about it. And before you ask more questions, I have to get going. My Canadian backers' legal consultant flew into town to enjoy our liquid sunshine. I'm picking him up at the Sportsman's Lodge.'

'Don't do anything rash, Duvid'l.'

'I probably won't do anything at all.' He hung up.

He showered and shaved. He thought of Rita and how she had sounded when he'd phoned her Monday evening. Remote. Though she'd said they would get together 'soon'.

He wished they could get together tonight. He wanted to stop thinking about the Bethills Nazis. Because with decision time near, he was afraid.

He dressed and went to his study and got the *Times* with the article on California's Nazi parties. He skimmed until he reached the part about the Bethills group, a father and two sons.

'Adolf, Carl and Horst,' he said aloud. Taken together, the very essence of unregenerate Nazism was in those names.

How dare he be afraid!

The guns were in the guest-room closet. Would he take them, put them in the car, drive to Clory's diner in Bethills, begin the process which would bring him to the house of Adolf Schleisser and his sons, where the National Resurrection party meetings took place, where the swastikas and pictures of Hitler were to be seen, where the hatred and calumny against Jews spewed forth?

Would he walk in and begin shooting? Would he kill the three of them and whoever else was wearing a swastika and *heiling* Hitler?

Would he then run and hide from the police? Would he shoot at them too when he was caught, as he would almost have to be with such a stupid plan, a non-existent plan?

Would he die in the shoot-out? Or surrender to die in the gas chamber? Or, since his lawyer would certainly plead insanity brought on by history, by the Holocaust, rot to death in prison or a padded cell?

He was back in the kitchen. He sat himself down, forced himself to consider this thing in *real* terms.

He had sweated and raged and hated and told himself he would strike back somehow.

But the guns represented suicide. Only a man willing to die would use the guns. Only a man *wishing* to die would use the guns, as David felt he would if he had

172

a terminal disease. A beautiful way, a useful way to die in such circumstances. A triumph in such circumstances.

But he wasn't in those circumstances and his dying would be the enemy's triumph.

His triumph would be to kill them and get away with it.

He could ask Teddy to ask his partner for a hit man. Whatever it cost, he could have the Schleissers killed professionally. And professional killings were rarely solved.

But there would be no satisfaction in that. One didn't hire mercenaries to fight one's personal vendettas, one's holy wars. He had to kill his enemies himself.

There were other ways to kill than with a gun. More clever ways. Safer ways.

There were poisons. There were bombs. There were cane swords, garrottes, gasses . . .

In his office was a large file of movie scripts, all but a few quite bad, none of which had been produced. Hollywood was innundated with such scripts. Being a member of the Producers Guild guaranteed that you would receive your monthly quota. Being listed in the trades as actively seeking new properties would double the quota.

Some of those scripts had been written in response to hits, to trends, as imitations of popular films, and included a high percentage of action themes.

He had James Bond spin-offs by the gross; almost as many inspired by *The Godfather*, *The Sting*, the TV detective characterizations. And while the level of writing was mainly twenty fathoms deep, the violence was occasionally up there with the best, full of creative murder and mayhem.

He remembered a scene detailing how to electrocute a man through his own stream of urine. In a public toilet. Using a simple metal grille which was often already in the urinal, and a length of insulated wire with a plug at one end. You connected the other end to

173

the grille, used a nearby electrical outlet for the plug, and when the victim began urinating, electricity surged up the perfect conductor of his salty waste and killed him.

He also remembered that the same author, Jackson W. Colfert, had sent him two more awful scripts. He would look up those scripts and others. He would find the best techniques . . .

He stopped then, realizing he was actually considering murder. He grabbed the phone and punched Rita Goran's number. She answered sleepily.

He said, 'Listen, it's idiotic to go on this way. Let me come to your place. About two. I'll bring dinner, including a good Montrachet.'

'*No!*'

Her vehemence shocked him.

'I'm sorry, David. I'm half-asleep. They cancelled school . . .'

'You're going to blow it for both of us,' he interrupted, angry now.

'Not so. If I see you too soon, *then* I'll blow it.' When he didn't respond, she said, 'Perhaps this weekend.'

'Make it definite or forget the whole thing.'

She hesitated. He was ready to slam down the phone when she said, 'All right, Friday at seven.'

'It's a date.' He hung up . . . and nothing had changed. Friday was three days away. And even if they met today, nothing would change, except perhaps his sperm count.

As he had realized the night Warren Gross died, wars didn't end because of love or sex or friendship. Nothing was going to save him from having to fight his war. Time to go to the office and read bad scripts and find good murder techniques.

But in the car, driving slowly through the unceasing downpour, a part of him continued to search for a way out.

Rita Goran lay very still after replacing the phone on

174

the night table. She'd had her back to her bedmate and hoped the sound of even breathing indicated uninterrupted sleep.

Then the hand took her shoulder and the strong voice said, 'It won't work. You're like me, Rita. Last night proved it.' Lois Turner's long, thin face was rising into her view, the blonde hair mannishly short, the brown eyes small and glittering. Lois Turner's lips parted and she smiled. 'Kiss me, darling.'

Rita's response was to jerk free and get out of bed, where she stood naked and shivering, looking for the bathrobe she'd flung down somewhere last night.

Last night . . . she couldn't believe last night! She'd planned to accept friendship from the tennis player who aced the best competition the Grange Club had to offer, and had been aced herself by wine and technique.

Lois also rose, also naked, and came around the bed. 'Men won't satisfy you any more, Rita. Just remember last night. Just remember what we did.' She'd reached Rita; was pressing her tall, angular body into Rita's more voluptuous figure; was beginning to kiss her face, her neck, running her hands over her bottom. When her lips reached Rita's breasts, she sighed. 'Come back to bed.'

Rita didn't want to, but the wet tongue licked her nipples, reminding her, arousing her, and she was drawn slowly along.

Lois Turner was five ten, whipcord lean and whipcord tough. She had small, hard breasts and a small, round butt and long arms and legs that could do more than defeat tennis opponents; that could wrap themselves around a woman and hold her helpless while the mouth drained that woman of resistance.

As it had drained Rita last night, then infused her with fire. First served Rita, then taught Rita to serve.

Rita cleared her throat, said, 'Wait . . . don't . . . I want to shower . . .'

But Lois pulled her down, wrapping those long, lean, hard arms and legs around her. Lois began murmuring

175

her inducements – 'You'll be happier than ever in your life, free at last of men and their brutality' – began moving her mouth down Rita's belly.

Rita lunged upward, jerking out knees and elbows, catching the lean woman by surprise, causing her to cry out and roll away, hugging herself in pain. Rita fled from the bedroom, saying, 'No, not me,' over and over, afraid the dream of love and marriage would die with one more infusion of Lois Turner's fire.

She took her raincoat from the hall closet and got into it, trembling; then went to the kitchen and put up water for coffee. She heard Lois calling. She didn't answer, but watched the short foyer. Reaching for a spoon, she touched the bread knife and jerked her hand away as if it were burning hot. She continued to watch the foyer. And Lois stepped into it, still naked.

'Rita, I understand. It's a new experience.'

'Get dressed,' Rita said, and put her hand back in the drawer.

Lois began to walk towards her. Rita took out the knife.

'You're kidding,' Lois Turner said, stopping.

'Go home.'

'All right, but first coffee and some civilized conversation. Lend me a robe.'

'No coffee. No conversation.' Rita stepped forward, the long knife rising, the threat of the unnatural, the too intensely desired passion, like fists in her face. 'Get out!'

Lois Turner stumbled backward, hands raised, face suddenly drained of blood, mumbling, 'Yes, if you say so.'

Rita mixed decaffeinated coffee and sipped it, still standing, still holding the bread knife.

Lois came down the foyer, dressed in her tan pants suit. She got her raincoat from the closet, opened the front door and turned. 'You're ill. You need help.'

'Get out! I'm not unnatural like you!'

'I've never known anyone more unnatural!' Lois slammed the door behind her.

Rita decided on a hearty breakfast of oatmeal, sliced banana, whole-wheat toast. A hearty, normal, American breakfast for a hearty, normal, American woman. Who would be seeing a man who was crazy about her on a normal, American dinner date. A man with whom she was falling in love, which was nothing if not in the American norm!

She busied herself preparing the food; then sat down to eat with a second cup of coffee.

She was well rid of Lois Turner, though she regretted the loss of a superb opponent on the courts. Only an uncertain backhand had kept Lois from dominating their matches. What she needed was corrective lessons from a top-flight instructor.

Rita remembered her own lessons at the Women's Tennis Society in mid-town Manhattan. Daddy had started her there, telling her it was a 'social sport and very useful for young ladies who want to meet eligible young men'. Which it was, at that time. Now it was a national craze, jamming the courts and necessitating club membership for any serious player.

She'd been thirteen and her instructor had been impressed with her natural strength, saying it was unusual for one of her age and sex. Daddy had come to see her play in her first tournament when she was fourteen, which was also the year Mother had died of stomach cancer. Watching her waste away during three horrible months, hearing her delirious moans towards the end, had destroyed Rita's belief in a compassionate God. It upset Daddy when she said so at the funeral, but after she rejected their minister's little talk about God's will and the Lord moving in mysterious ways, Daddy never again pressed her to attend church.

He himself hadn't attended all that often while Mother was alive, but after her death he never missed a Sunday and rarely the Wednesday night discussion meetings.

He also never missed Rita's tournaments as she began applying herself to the game of tennis in serious fashion. Knowing he was in the stands would make her try harder, play better, and she won a fair share of the ribbons and cups handed out as prizes.

Rita had loved both her mother and father without giving it particular thought. But with her mother gone she concentrated on her father, worried about losing him, demanded more of his time, poured out all of her adolescent affection on him. He began to seem incredibly handsome and she assured herself that loss of hair and a certain fullness of waist were signs of maturity without which a man was green, callow, unfinished as it were.

After a while she began cooking part of the evening meal, cajoling the easy-going black housekeeper into teaching her the art. When the woman was off, she prepared all the meals Daddy was willing to take at home, though he kept pressing her to spend more time with her friends and said he had to spend time with his.

She refused to consider that his friends might include women. She was now fifteen, growing fast, and Daddy was the centre of her existence. She rushed home from school to make sure his evening meal was being properly prepared, and to prepare as much of it herself as she could.

It was at this time that the cook suddenly left, saying she'd landed a better job, though she also told Mr Stanley that his daughter was 'a pest around the kitchen'.

Rita was against Daddy hiring a replacement. He laughed at the idea of her handling all the cooking and housework, saying he earned enough as partner in the small brokerage firm to not only live on Riverside Drive – still a much-preferred residential area in 1947 – but to have full-time domestic help. 'In fact, I've been thinking of a live-in housekeeper, using the guest bedroom that's going to waste.'

178

'But we don't *need* anyone!' Rita wailed, clutching his hand. 'Pay *me* the money and I'll buy you presents!'

Daddy thought it 'cute', laughing her into silence. He patted her head and gave her one of his rare kisses, and the new cook showed up the very next day. Rita wept, wondering that her father could ignore how much she loved him, how much she wanted to do things for him.

The new cook welcomed Rita's desire to help . . . at first. Then she too began to find Rita a pest around the kitchen, and went to George Stanley, asking him to keep the girl from interfering with the housework.

Daddy told Rita he was considering sending her to boarding school.

She was stunned. 'But why? I'm doing well at my studies. I'm happy at home.' He was sitting in his armchair, and she came over and touched his hair, his face. 'I don't want to live apart from you, Daddy!'

He moved impatiently away from her caress. 'You spend too much time at home. You don't go out enough. You're almost sixteen and you never date.'

'Never' was an exaggeration. She'd dated a few times, attending school dances with classmates, but it was true that she hadn't formed the romantic and sexual attachments of many of her friends.

She begged him not to send her away, and her tears, her near hysteria, caused him to back down.

The new cook left. Daddy surprised Rita by not insisting on an immediate replacement. She was overjoyed, and for three weeks she cooked for him, cleaned for him, had him all to herself. At least when he was home, which was less and less often.

The Monday beginning the fourth week he arrived late, ate the dinner she'd prepared, complimented her on it effusively (which wasn't at all like him), and without further preamble said, 'I'm going to get married.'

She stared. He rose from the table, smiling. 'You'll like Edna Rawlins. We'll visit her next Sunday afternoon.'

Stunned, Rita mumbled, 'But Daddy . . . it's so soon after Mother . . .'

He said he'd known Edna for almost a year, 'through church services and discussions'. That Rita would 'grow to love her'. That they would probably move into Edna's place, 'as she has a beautiful brownstone in the upper Fifties'. That he was lonely since Mother had died, Edna was lonely since her husband had died, 'and we both need love'.

Rita tried to say *she* would give him all the love he needed, but he interrupted her, told her to get used to the idea, to be happy for him, 'and for yourself because Edna will make a loving mother'.

That night, Rita had a series of fragmentary dreams. She awoke, remembering her mother's face drifting in limbo, weeping. She rose and went to her father's room. The door, as usual, was closed. She knocked softly. No answer. She entered and went to the large bed he had shared for so many years with Mother. He lay on his back and she stared at his face, his beloved face. She whispered, 'Daddy, please talk to me.' He had changed his mind about sending her away to boarding school and he could change his mind about this.

He continued to sleep. She shivered despite the long flannel nightgown. It was February and 3.00 a.m. and the apartment was cold. Finally, she pulled a corner of the covers aside and slid in beside him. She was still trembling, still cold. So she moved closer to him, put her arms around his body, pressed against him, kissed his pyjama-clad shoulder. 'Please don't get married,' she said, beginning to cry. 'Please, Daddy, I'll love you enough if you'll only let me.'

He awoke, saying, 'What? Rita?' And then, feeling her arms, her body, shoved her away and began to shout at her.

She didn't understand everything he said, but the words 'sick' and 'filthy' sent her running from the room, covering her ears.

She didn't sleep all night. In the morning, hearing

him moving about, she crept from her bed to try and explain to him, to assure him that her feelings weren't *that* at all.

He was in the kitchen, drinking coffee. He didn't let her speak. He said she wasn't going to school today. 'I'm taking you to the office of a psychiatrist, a friend. I haven't told him anything yet because I couldn't say the words.' He kept his eyes away from Rita, never once looking at her. 'Get dressed. He's just three stations downtown on the IRT.'

That was how they had come to be on the subway platform at 10.00 a.m. The rush hour was over and there were few people around. Daddy wouldn't talk to her and she found she could no longer talk to him. How could you talk to someone whose heart was full of revulsion for you, whose eyes couldn't bear the sight of you?

Impatient as always, he leaned out to look down the tracks for the train. Then paced around. Then leaned out again.

She stood beside him. She felt she had to try one last time. 'Daddy, please don't take me to that doctor. Please listen to me. It's not what you think.'

He ignored her. He muttered about the subways 'deteriorating', and, oh, if he had lived to see them with the spray-painted graffiti and the muggers and the degenerates!

But he hadn't lived. He had leaned out again and the train was finally coming and he'd lost his balance and fallen on the tracks, screaming.

Her mother's sister had taken her in. She hadn't had to change schools, had been able to continue her tennis, because Aunt Donna and Uncle Vance were well off and lived just eight blocks away. In fact, her life hadn't changed much at all . . . except for having lost her father in what everyone called 'that tragic accident'.

Only Rita had known she'd actually lost him hours before the accident, at 3.00 a.m. in his bedroom. And knowing that had carried her through the funeral and

181

the months afterward in stony silence, without tears, worrying her aunt and uncle.

One night the following summer she'd awakened screaming 'Daddy! Daddy!', and on being comforted by her aunt had wept heavily. This satisfied conventional wisdom on the nature of grief, and her aunt said, 'The dam has broken. You'll feel better now.'

Actually, she'd felt worse, having remembered something she'd successfully buried since the moment of the accident. As her father had leaned out to look for the train, she'd bumped into him, nudged him, by chance of course.

She'd had a few more nights of screaming, of weeping, and then she'd buried the memory again, more deeply, more successfully.

Now, sitting at the kitchen table, the spoon frozen half-way to her mouth, the oatmeal cold in the bowl, she whispered, 'Daddy'. She heard his soft, strong voice, so much like David's. Experienced again the anguish of his rejecting her love, his misunderstanding her love. Saw that subway platform and felt her side bumping his rear, felt her body *pushing* his body, heard his scream.

She left everything on the table and went back to bed, curling into a foetal position, shutting her eyes tightly, shutting her mind against the past. She prayed that David would not reject, would understand, would save her, and himself.

Vanessa dressed carefully: snug skirt and blouse setting off her full-breasted, wasp-waisted figure; white rainhat highlighting her long reddish-brown hair and small delicate features. Dressed as if for a date.

But this was no date and she would have cancelled if she hadn't wanted those Quaaludes so badly. A perfect excuse the ongoing storm, right? But Dr Blair Gordon had refused again to phone in the prescription, just as he'd done Monday. Had insisted she come in for an examination. 'Long overdue, Vanessa, for one with your potentially dangerous illness.'

She'd tried to argue him out of it, laugh him out of it, flirt him out of it, and he'd finally exploded with 'Potentially dangerous is a euphemism I use with you, lady, for potentially *fatal*! I like you, I'd like you to like me, but I'm speaking as your doctor now and I tell you to either begin treating this disease seriously or get another doctor! I won't officiate at your burial!'

And that's why she was driving from the garage into a pause in the storm, which was still a heavy downpour. Cars that had pulled to the side during the really bad part were just pulling out again, and she watched traffic carefully, drove slowly, tried not to think of the Impossible Secret.

Which wasn't easy when she came into Blair Gordon's outer office. It was nitty-gritty time.

She checked in with the receptionist behind the sliding frosted-glass panel and sat down in the pink-and-brown waiting room. There was another person there, a youngish man, small and neat-looking, with a hesitant smile which he flashed in her direction, nodding. She looked away.

But then she found herself looking back at him, nodding in response. And crossing her legs and opening her raincoat to show her salient features, as David jokingly called her breasts.

He came up in his brown plastic seat like a bird-dog scenting quail. His smile returned and his lips moved a little. With her long experience in the game, she could see him beginning to shape words, approaches, make-out pitches.

The receptionist opened the door and said, 'Miss Brooks? Room three. The doctor will be with you shortly.'

Vanessa followed her inside, knowing that she had been trying to block the Impossible Secret, to fight off death. And what better way was there than with a man?

Any man, if the fear was at your throat. Even a stranger in a doctor's waiting room.

The receptionist said, 'Remove your blouse and any necklaces or ear-rings.' She left the narrow little room, closing the door.

Vanessa hated these rooms. All successful doctors had them now, stalls in which you awaited the great man, who was usually part of 'a medical corporation', as was Blair Gordon.

The corporation was doing well. Gordon was a Rolls, as Pearl the lezzie artists' manager would say. His office was in prestigious Encino. His home was in more prestigious Royal Oaks, where he lived with his young son and a housekeeper, his wife having opted for alimony and total freedom in Chicago.

'She's a compulsive swinger, a nymphomaniac,' Gordon had said. 'All she really needs is a room, a bed, the Pill. She's certainly got the looks . . .'

So had Blair Gordon, Vanessa thought, when the dark, strong-looking man in grey pants and white medical jacket opened the door. About thirty-eight, maybe forty, and a real hunk. Played tennis and golf, and skiied in winter, and had done his share of surfing as a youth. And smart enough to have made it through medical school while living the good life. And to have become one of LA's top haematologists.

She had her blouse off, had worn no necklaces or ear-rings, was sitting on the paper-sheeted table.

He smiled his white-toothed smile and she had to admit it warmed a part of her, not necessarily her heart. (More running from fear?) 'You're looking great,' she said.

'You too,' he said, but his eyes didn't do the male trick, the sliding up and down. He had business on his mind, did this particular Rolls. And his business was her life.

Without further pleasantries he stepped over and began to feel her neck, murmuring his explanations, part of his bedside manner, meant to reassure the patient

184

with knowledge. But in her case it was hardly reassuring.

'Hodgkin's disease is a form of leukaemia. I'm checking for enlargement of the lymph nodes in your neck where we last found inflammation. Ah . . . not much change . . . not any that I can see. Raise your right arm, please. No enlargement in the armpit. Left arm . . . fine, fine. I wouldn't say spontaneous remission, but no measurable deterioration. Let's check the thoracic cavity.'

His strong fingers probed, his head bent and swivelled, his eyes peered . . . and she wanted to pull him to her breast, kiss his mouth, grab him between the legs, anything to stop him! Hodgkin's was a form of leukaemia, and leukaemia, which she'd looked up in the dictionary, was 'an almost uniformly fatal cancerous disease, categorized by excessive production of white blood cells and often accompanied by severe anaemia'.

Her form of Hodgkins's disease *could* be mild, he'd said. 'Uniformly fatal' didn't apply if the spleen remained free of infection. They had to perform a 'staging operation', which meant removing her spleen to see what stage the infection was at.

Now he said it again, finishing his examination, telling her they simply had to find out. 'If the spleen is unaffected, then your prognosis is excellent for full recovery and cure!'

She was in a sick daze, as whenever the Impossible Secret emerged. And yet she had practically none of the symptoms, except for 'a slight imbalance in the white cell count' as the studio physician had told her after the examination, including blood test, for that week of work on foreign location – Lima and nearby Indian ruins. He was puzzled and suggested she see a haematologist. Which in turn had led her to Dr Blair Gordon and the Impossible Secret.

'And if my spleen isn't free?' she asked Gordon, voice hoarse.

He waved a hand, an attempt at reassuring unconcern. 'Chemotherapy and X-ray treatment, if called for, will still give you many years . . .'

She got off the table, pushing him back, and reached for her blouse. She didn't believe this, as she hadn't a year ago when it all began. She *wouldn't* believe this! She felt fine . . . or almost fine. She wouldn't think of it for another year and what he called spontaneous remission would occur and she would never again have to feel death at her throat, where the lymph nodes that had swelled, slightly, were located. Never again have to come here and feel her life slipping away.

'We're not finished yet,' he said.

'I am,' she whispered, having trouble buttoning the blouse with weak, icy-cold fingers. 'Can I have my prescription?'

'Quaalude? You don't need it. You need to take your Chlorambucil, your Cytoxin. *Are* you taking them?'

'Yes.' She finished the buttoning. 'Well, the Chlorambucil ran out.'

'Did you renew?' he asked, growing angry. 'You didn't, did you?'

'I forgot,' she said, stepping towards the door. 'I've been taking the Cytoxin.'

'You forgot,' he said, shaking his head. 'What's wrong with you? You're supposed to be examined regularly, at least once every three months, and I haven't seen you in almost a year!'

'I'll get the medication today. I'll come back for examinations whenever you want.' Tears were entering her eyes, her voice. 'Please, Blair, let me go now.'

'You know you have to face this,' Gordon said. 'Eventually you'll have to undergo that staging operation.'

She nodded. She knew. Which was the real reason, she supposed, she'd finally come to him. To find out if it had grown worse. But it hadn't and she could leave.

She said so, wanting reaffirmation of what he'd murmured during his examination.

'True, but the examination isn't over. We need a

186

blood test and X-rays . . . a complete lab work-up. I have to ask you questions.'

She sank back against the table. 'Ask.'

'Any weakness, increased fatigability, haemorrhaging?'

She hesitated. She'd been extremely tired at times, especially when working. That third day on 'Mash' she'd felt faint.

But she'd skipped breakfast and they'd kept shooting past noon and it was natural, normal.

'No, none of that.'

'You hesitated. Tell the truth.' He suddenly shouted, 'You're the worst fucking patient I've ever had!'

She found herself laughing. He grinned a little and put his hands on her arms. 'If you were my girlfriend I'd be able to treat you properly.'

'Yes, but in office or bedroom?'

'Both, Vanessa.' His eyes finally did the man-thing, travelling over her body. And she was relieved because he wouldn't turn on for a dying woman, would he?

But he didn't have a chance. Simply looking at him was a reminder of the Impossible Secret, which had to become a real secret once again.

'Blood test, you said?' She stepped around him to the door.

She would allow all the tests and treatments he wanted for today. And tell him about the weakness at the studio that time, and about the lack of energy at other times, mainly at night. She would promise to refill her chemotherapy prescriptions, and would indeed take both as she was supposed to. She would promise to return in three months, but this promise she wouldn't keep. Once out of here she would stay out!

She wasn't sick. Not with anything like *cancer*!

An hour later she was back in her car. She would go directly to the Waldon Pharmacy and fill her prescriptions, including the one for Quaalude she'd wheedled out of Gordon. She would sleep like a stone tonight, would sleep without thoughts of Dave, but she wouldn't give up her dream of love.

Having the Impossible Secret out in the open, even if only for a few hours, made her more determined than ever to keep the man with whom she had eaten the hundred pounds of salt.

Detective One Al Placer had a choirboy's face and a satyr's mind. But maybe every healthy man in his early twenties thought that way, Tony Stone mused, watching Placer talk and grin and pitch like crazy at the policewoman delivering a folder to his desk.

Hell, he himself wasn't that different at thirty-four. And he had a file full of men who were dead because they weren't different enough in their fifties and sixties!

Stone was standing in the wide entry to the bull pen. 'Al, how's the file search going?'

Placer stood up, holding a large Manila envelope. 'Got something, Lieutenant. Not sure what, but it's in the area you discussed.'

Stone turned and led the way to his office, where he sat down behind his desk and motioned Placer to the chair.

Placer opened the Manila envelope and took out a single sheet of paper. 'This is a photostat I made of a page in a homicide report. Two and a half years old, unsolved, from the Hollywood Station. Man named Andrew Kolett, fifty-eight, widower, stabbed six times, twice to the heart. In his own kitchen in an apartment on Cherokee.' He leaned over the desk to hand Stone the page. 'From an officer's report of interrogation of neighbours. He didn't get anything pertinent to the case, but maybe we did. I've circled the interesting part.'

Stone read: 'Mrs Amelia Grober said she'd seen the victim enter his second-floor apartment about 12.30 a.m. the night before discovery of the body. He was with a woman. She said it was dark and she didn't get a good look. When asked to attempt a description, Mrs

Grober said, "She looked as big as Mr Kolett and she walked up the stairs a lot faster than he did. Athletic, I'd say. Maybe she wasn't really as big as Kolett, but strong-looking. And one more thing, Kolett smoked a lot and I heard her ask him to put out his cigarette before they went inside." '.

Stone waited. Placer said, 'Well, you asked for MOs like Rossa's – knifing of an elderly male still hitting on the girls, right?'

'Right.'

'And the non-smoker,' Placer said. 'That fit.'

Stone nodded.

'I didn't come across any of the five names in Rossa's book, so we bombed there.'

'Any initials, say on purse or handkerchiefs? Anything at all that could fit those names, especially two of them?'

Placer knew he was being tested. 'Rita Goran and Lois Aelia. Nothing at all, Lieutenant. But what about the description given by that witness, Amelia Grober? I didn't see Rossa's women.'

Which was why Stone missed Lowery, who *had* seen them. Then again, so had he, and Lois Aelia was small and slight. She wouldn't fit.

Rita Goran, on the other hand, would.

'Al, I want you to visit Rita Goran's apartment about five today, just to get a look at her. Say we forgot to ask her if Rossa drank heavily. You're going to keep looking for MOs like Rossa's and women like Goran. And read this folder.' He gave him the one he'd pulled from the files on Rodrick Bedford, stabbed to death about a year ago, seen with a 'large woman' the night before the discovery of his body.

Placer said, 'Yessir,' and rose.

'One more thing. I want a quick residential rundown on Goran. Where she lived before.'

Placer nodded and left.

Stone closed his eyes. The Great Detective at work. 'You see, Watson, the manner in which I apprehended the mass-murderer Goran was by applying the astounding hunch, the incredible guess.'

Nevertheless, he was going to set up a part-time surveillance of Rita Goran. A floating surveillance, as an instructor at the Academy had called it. A few days on, a week or two off. Dating days – Fridays and Saturdays, mainly. A loose net, a long-shot try, a wish and a prayer.

He would put in some free-time hours himself. He had a great personal incentive for solving these killings. The way it looked, Tony Stone would still be trying for weekend shack jobs when he was sixty. Had to make the world safe for dirty old men, right?

EIGHT: *Wednesday, 19 December, p.m.*

On returning to work Monday morning, Lowery had sent Forensic the piece of metal he'd found in the compacter. The lab would do what it could, then ship it to the FBI lab in Washington. They in turn would route it to the proper General Motors metallurgists, who might be able to tell what sort of vehicle it had come from.

Even if he got a definite make on a Chevy Series Sixty, he'd have nothing to take to the DA. The Nazis' truck had not been so identified.

He himself didn't need that identification. He was already certain that the Schleisser family, with the help of the scum at Clory's diner, had driven that truck down Fairfax Avenue and clubbed a boy to death.

Warren Gross had been buried Tuesday. Several hundred people had attended and there'd been emotional statements made before the TV cameras: people calling for quick arrests, for crack-downs on all California Nazis, for retaliation by bombing and burning of the Nazi meeting places mentioned in the *Times* article.

It would die down. Jewish groups, even activist ones like the JDL, were rarely involved in violence utilizing guns, bombs, arson. Though he wondered if that wasn't the only way any sort of parity could be gained in this particular case.

He had assigned his three-man SIT to question every possible witness, including the staff at Canter's delicatessen, and learned nothing new. He'd had them search the files for similar demonstrations and they hadn't been able to find anything even faintly like it. The fact was, Nazis in this state were usually circumspect about obeying the law, at least in public matters like demonstrations. They knew how fast the police would come down on them, unlike police in some Southern communities who tended to move slowly when Nazis and Klansmen were reacting against leftist demonstrators. Which had led to the slaughter of eight Communists in Greensboro, North Carolina, and the depressing acquittal of all the accused.

He had attended Warren Gross's funeral yesterday, watching for anyone from Bethills, anyone who might look as if he was enjoying himself.

Later, he had gone out with his girl and found himself talking about the case, though Maria obviously wasn't Jewish and was surprised to learn that he was. Then it was her turn to surprise him: her mother was Jewish, her father Greek. The 'I'm of French descent' was some sort of protective device, though why anyone so knock-out needed one was beyond him.

They'd spent last night together, closer somehow than they'd ever been. And she'd explained the protective device, telling him how cruel children could be in a good private school where upper-class Anglos predominated, where 'young ladies' giggled about everything that differed from their own experience and even a French background could leave one out in the cold and open to amused contempt. 'Imagine what half Greek half Jew would do,' she'd said. 'Anyway, I didn't have the courage for public pronouncements and grew comfortable with the lie.'

He understood. He'd never actually lied about who and what he was, but as with Tony Stone, a man he'd worked with for over a year, he hadn't ever brought up the subject. Nor had he brought it up with Maria until last night.

They'd held to each other in a new way, a deeper and closer way. Maybe she wasn't exactly the *Yiddishe maidelah* his grandfather had wanted for him, but Lowery felt the old man would eventually have approved. He also felt he owed the Schleissers and their fellow Nazis a vote of thanks. He and Maria had taken a giant step forward in transforming a disco-and-bed relationship into something that held promise for the future.

This morning he'd called Captain Genson. Genson's secretary had said the captain would return his call as soon as possible . . . which was now, twelve noon. Lowery hadn't been sorry for the wait. He'd feared what Genson's response would be to his request, and his fear was justified.

'Undercover man?' Genson said, and chuckled. 'To infiltrate the Nazi group?' Another chuckle. 'How are we going to justify that, Lowery? You haven't presented me with a single piece of hard evidence implicating the Bethills family or their supporters.'

'I know they did it, Captain.'

'Prove it. Convince the DA and I'll find you an undercover man.' Lowery was silent. Genson said, 'Just do your best. That piece of metal is promising. The furor is dying down, so you have time.' *Click.*

The key phrase was, 'The furor is dying down.' Soon the case would be allowed to slip into the Unsolved files.

He decided to ask Lieutenant Stone for advice and picked up the phone.

Stone gave him the big greeting. They chatted a while, then Lowery said, 'Why don't we meet for a drink later? Five thirty, the Hammock.'

He hit lucky. Must be an off-night with the chicks for Handsome Tony.

David had found the three scripts authored by Jackson W. Colfert, an impossible writer and an inspired creator of murder and mayhem. He asked his secretary to get him a sandwich and to hold all calls until further notice.

'Including Mr Walton?' Carrie asked.

Burn Walton was the Canadians' legal consultant on *Coast to Coast*. They'd met in his suite at the Sportsman's

193

Lodge to go over the contracts, and at eleven thirty David had fled. If he was going to Bethills to kill people, why quibble over a turn of phrase, a small-print attempt to gain another quarter point: *in the event executive producer does not distribute among star and featured actors . . .*

The points were a long shot to produce income above his guarantee anyway, so to hell with it. And to hell with the insidious thought that it was somehow a 'Jewish trait' to fight for every last percentage; that thought had been stimulated by the Bethills Nazis. The thoroughly Anglo Walton had no such hang-ups about fighting for a quarter of a point with him, and would be calling about it.

'Including Walton,' he said, and began to read.

She didn't leave. 'Mr Howars, what about a tree? It's only five days till Christmas.'

He'd always had a tree in his office. After all, this was an American industry with American traditions.

'Want me to buy it?' she asked.

'Not this year, Carrie.'

'Oh?' She waited for an explanation.

He gave none, and she finally left.

It was twelve ten when he settled down to read. It was twelve thirty when Carrie brought him his lunch. It was a quarter to two when he rose, hoping that J. W. Colfert had thoroughly researched his perfect crimes because David Howars was going to try a few of them.

He stopped at Carrie's desk. 'I won't be back today. I could be gone all of tomorrow too. I expect to be back Friday, but if not I'll see you Monday.'

She showed surprise. He realized he wasn't thinking ahead; that unlike the Christmas tree this required an explanation.

'I'm taking a little time off. My nerves . . .'

She nodded emphatically. 'Good idea, Mr Howars. I'll hold down the fort. Have a good time.'

When he walked onto Ventura Boulevard, it was raining lightly. When he entered the parking lot and approached his car, it stopped. He nodded to himself,

194

thinking it was a long ride to Bethills and if Jehovah was aware of it, stopping the rain made sense. Time to help one of the Chosen People. 'Right, Big Buddy?' he said, trying to smile.

Driving towards the hardware store west of Laurel Canyon, he thought of a brief novel by Elie Wiesel, *The Trial of God*, that he would have given anything to put on the screen, but that he couldn't have raised a dime on. The book, which dealt with a pogrom in the late 1600s and a resultant trial of God arranged by the only two survivors, was based on an actual trial of God that Wiesel had witnessed while a prisoner in Auschwitz. God could not be exonerated in either trial, fiction or fact.

David remembered his mother, head down on the kitchen table, weeping over the letters returned from Poland and France, the Address Unknowns that meant death for her two sisters and brother and their children; for her aunts and uncles and cousins. He looked through the windshield at a heavy grey sky and felt a terrible pain, a terrible anger.

And was surprised at himself because he hadn't believed in anything being up there since childhood.

He parked the Mercedes and went into the big store. Where he walked around, picking out items but not asking any salesperson for help. It wouldn't do for someone to remember him and his purchases, though they were normal enough, innocuous enough.

Just before bringing his items to the check-out counter, he heard himself speaking. He glanced around and was relieved to see that no one was close by.

What he'd said was, 'Thou shalt not kill, huh?', with rage for the Great Killer.

Back in the car, driving to the sporting goods store on Vineland, he tried to reason with himself. 'Forget God. Concentrate on the job.'

And yet he couldn't help it; like Tevya, Sholem Aleichem's milkman character who talked constantly to God, and to mass audiences via *Fiddler on the Roof*.

195

But Aleichem and Tevya had lived in a time of relatively small pogroms, finite agonies, before the advent of swastikas and victims by the millions, when there'd still been hope all would end well.

After buying the air-pistol, he drove back past Ventura into the snaking canyon short cut. And still felt words pressing at his tongue, felt the need to continue attacking God. Because *someone* had to be responsible; *someone* had to take the blame for this mad-house world!

At the kitchen table, he worked on his purchases, and was done within the hour.

He had transformed a white extension cord into a murder weapon (according to J. W. Colfert) by cutting off the end with the multiple outlets, stripping off the insulation a quarter of an inch, attaching the raw wire to a small wire-mesh cover which fit over a cake of urinal deodorant, and insulating the exposed wire with white waterproof tape.

He had filled a kitchen syringe, normally used to inject butter and oils into roasts, with a strong solution of rat poison and kerosene. The arsenic content was sufficient to kill alone, and the kerosene made it certain . . . if he got the opportunity to jab it into a brown-shirted belly.

He had three empty 20cc hypodermic syringes, used as props in demonstrating the critical drug scene in *Coast to Coast* to his then as-yet-unconvinced director, and they would remain empty so as to inject deadly air bubbles into Nazi veins.

He had the high-powered air-pistol and box of soft-lead pellets. He'd scored the pellets deeply with a knife so they would fragment on impact, then dipped them into his rat-poison solution so as to increase their deadliness. They would be fired into a Nazi's eye where they would bring death, according to J. W. Colfert.

He had a can of Mace given him as a gag gift by Teddy two birthdays ago ("so the starlets won't rape you, Duvid'l"), and a beautiful Bowie knife, and an ice-pick, and his two pistols.

He packed an overnight case and changed into casual clothing. He tried to think of what else he could take. He remembered the jar of sleeping pills, which could be a deadly poison in quantity.

He was sure he would find more death-dealing material here at home, if he looked. Was sure he could get deadlier poisons if he waited and used friends like Teddy. Cyanide, for example, which would guarantee quick death even if adminsitered by pellet gun. Or Rycin, which could be poked into a man's thigh with the tip of an umbrella, as had been done to Communist defector Georgi Markov by Soviet agents in London.

But it was after three and the freeways were dangerously slick, and no matter how fast he drove he couldn't get to Bethills before nine. And he didn't want to wait; had waited all his life; wanted to do something *tonight*!

He put the small suitcase and the airline bag with his weaponry into the trunk of the car. He thought a moment, and returned to the game room and called Mrs Gomez. He told her he was going away for three days and she was to consider the time a paid vacation. She was still bubbling happily when he said, '*Por nada*', and 'Goodbye.'

He put two apples in his pockets and turned to the garage; then hesitated, thinking of Rita and Vanessa and whether he shouldn't call them. Then of his son. And of Teddy who wanted to help him.

He understood immediately that it was a final attempt to put off this trip and what it entailed.

'You still on their side?' he asked the skies as he drove towards the Ventura Freeway. 'Still trying to make us stand still for it?'

He ate an apple and found classical music on the radio. He fantasized about tomorrow, his quest accomplished (and didn't define it further), returning home ready for Rita and their date. And also, perhaps, for Vanessa, healing the hurt in her voice.

Teddy stood behind the bar, the phone to his ear, his

197

back to the customers thronging Thomasine's for the popular Christmas Week (December 17th to 24th) brunch buffet, which could be eaten in the dining room, at the bar, or moving about, plate in hand, cocktail-party style. It was so crowded today people were standing not because they preferred to but because there wasn't a vacant seat in the house.

Great. The bread was pouring in. He should be relaxed and happy. But he was worried. He'd expected to hear from Dave by now; had been sure his friend would want to discuss how to approach the Bethills Nazis. Because, man, who could just go up there alone and take on a gang of crazy bastards whose goal in life was to kill you and yours!

Yet the fear was growing in him that this was exactly what Dave had done. Dave's secretary had just told Teddy he'd split for a 'short vacation', yet Dave hadn't mentioned a word about vacations when they'd been at Canter's, when Dave had eaten at the bar last week, or during their subsequent telephone conversations.

'Did he make plans in advance?' he'd asked Carrie, and she'd said, 'Not that I know of. I think it was spur of the moment, made right at his desk this afternoon.'

Made right at his desk after thinking of those Nazis and blowing his cool. Grab a piece and a handful of slugs and go to Bethills to commit suicide.

He had dialled Dave's home number and was now listening to the ring hit number ten. He hung up and looked around, hoping Dave had walked in.

An older chick, still prime, was calling to him from the far end. With a young AD/DC friend who liked swing sessions. They were ready to go, and Christ, how he wanted them when he thought of the alternative.

Yet he had to locate Duvid'l. Had to assure himself his friend wasn't on his way to destruction.

He dialled Vanessa, hoping she and Dave had made up and that he'd be there.

She answered groggy-voiced, which surprised him.

Sounded like a booze or drug hangover and that wasn't Vanessa. 'Can Dave make it to the phone?' he asked.

'Dave? My Dave? Where is he?'

Yeah, where. He said, 'Sorry to bother you,' but before he could hang up she came awake. 'Teddy, is there anything wrong? Why isn't he at work or someplace where Carrie can reach him?'

'Hey, we all disappear for a few hours. I just needed him to settle a bet. You know that great brain of his.' He pressed the disconnect before she could dig further.

Dave had mentioned a blind date when they'd talked Saturday. Could he have split town with her?

But wouldn't he have given Carrie a number where he could be reached?

Not if he was planning a two- or three-day shack job.

That had to be it. Dave and his new chick were spending a few days together in bed – Palm Springs or La Costa or anywhere they could find a little luxury and a lot of privacy.

Had to be.

Teddy sighed and walked towards Ahearn, his main man behind the bar. Dave had never split that way, shacked that way before. It wasn't his style. The odds favoured his using the information Teddy had given him this a.m. to risk his life this p.m.

Clory's diner was six or more hours away. Dave had left his office about two, Carrie said. He'd have to go home for a few things. At least for the guns he'd once showed Teddy. Which meant he couldn't have left for Bethills much before two thirty, three.

He'd get there at nine, nine thirty.

If Teddy left right now, from Thomasine's, and pushed the Caddy hard, he might get there about the same time. Or just a little later. Because it was only three thirty.

He turned abruptly to the register and unlocked the cabinet underneath with his key. He crouched there, with music and laughter inundating him, with people calling him for drinks, for talk, for action. And using his body to block the view from all of them, removed a ·45 automatic. He jammed it in his waistband a little behind the left hip and rose carefully, buttoning the pigskin jacket, grateful for the Cardin-style flare that would hide the big handgun.

He spoke to Ahearn, telling him to call one of the alternate bartenders. He walked to the front end, flipped up the hinged section of bar, and, waving and smiling and not stopping for anyone, got out on the street. People walking from the parking lot tried to stop him, to chat with him, but he said, 'Later,' like some TV jig, which they really dug.

He had never played roles with Duvid'l.

He pulled out of the parking lot and hit the street doing sixty. He skidded around the corner, heading for the Ventura Freeway. If he lost that man, he would lose a critical element in his life – his only friend.

The last Wednesday of each month was meeting time for the National Resurrection party, but because this month it came out the day after Christmas, Pop had moved it up to the third Wednesday; today.

Horst had driven over from his Bethills apartment, a one-bedroom place in a six-apartment set-up; the largest, the newest, the only decent apartment rentals in town. It had started as a condo, but no one had been willing to put down the twenty thousand plus, so Lew Banyon had rented. Not that he'd wanted Horst as a tenant, saying, 'I don't hold with your Nazi crap and I tell you straight out I don't want to see or hear any of it around my apartments. I spent four years of my life killing those bastards.'

Horst had given his word not to wear his uniform where anyone could see. He wouldn't have anyway, no matter where he'd lived. He always brought it with him to the grape ranch, changing there.

He'd driven his van in from Frisco at three this afternoon, showered, picked up his uniform and driven over to the house. He already knew that an LA detective Pop

200

called 'a beanpole Jew' had been there, along with a local highway patrolman, and that both officers had been to Clory's and asked for help in solving 'the Fairfax killing'.

Pop said everything was destroyed – truck, bats, banners, masks and literature – and that nothing could implicate them. 'Except we ourselves, Horst. Your brother Carl . . . he's fine in action, but he's got no head, no heart for afterwards, for hiding his feelings.'

That's why Carl and Rose were gone 'on vacation'.

Pop also had a surprise for Horst. 'You're going to speak at the meeting.'

Horst had tried to beg off, but Pop was insistent. 'It's time, Horst. Little by little, you've got to take over. I want them to hear your ideas about using restraint, building membership, all the things you said in the truck last week. I'll handle the subject of Jews until you develop your own approach. Try thinking of it as the International Zionist menace, not the kike girl you laid.'

Horst had fought down sudden rage, telling himself today would be the worst; then he would be able to stay away from Pop until Christmas dinner. After that he could leave and be with Janet until New Year.

Tonight's meeting would start at seven and end about nine, when everyone would go to Clory's for pie and coffee. That rarely broke up before eleven and the Schleissers stayed until the very last. Sometimes strangers came in off the road, and Horst flushed hot just remembering startled faces and quick exits.

Other times, however, the strangers stayed around, smiling their approval, joining in with their own hatred for Jews and blacks. Lately there was widespread anger about Hispanics, which Resurrection and other Nazi parties were able to tap: the Cubans who'd emigrated through Florida, and the continuing flow of illegals from Mexico, Central and South America. The detested 'spic' who was going to 'dilute the white Christian Aryan,' as Pop put it.

Horst went to the small back bedroom that had once

201

been his and began changing clothes. It was only five, but Pop wanted full uniforms at dinner tonight. Carl's kids would be there and Horst hated the thought of their seeing the swastikas and listening to Pop's ideas, Pop's hatreds . . . though they got it at home too, he guessed. They came into contact with Jewish kids in school, and those kids would eventually suffer for what Pop and Carl said; for what other parents who attended NRP meetings said.

It was when he thought of his pretty, red-headed nieces, of someone else's nieces and daughters and sons, of the children who had to pay the tab for Pop's ideas, that he truly hated his father and was least able to justify his life in this family.

But then he finished dressing and examined himself in the mirror, adjusting the swastika armband. A good-looking uniform, if you didn't associate it with corpses being shovelled into ovens. If you didn't think how the love of your life would feel if she saw you in it.

He went into dinner, holding out his arms for the two girls who had been playing in the fields when he'd arrived, kissing them and thinking how much like their mother they looked, and Rose was a beautiful woman.

But his beautiful nieces already had poison in their minds. They got into an argument about who would sit between Grandpa and Horst, and the older said, 'You got a nose like a Jew!', and the younger said, 'You stink like a nigger!'

Grandma and Grandpa chuckled, but the beauty of his nieces was gone for Horst and the hunger for his mother's cooking dried up in him, and he sat quietly, covering his pain with a smile.

Later, bringing in folding chairs from the barn, hanging the World War II German flag on the wall, he was suddenly afraid that he wouldn't be able to continue this double life. That in order to keep his sanity, he would have to give up Pop and the money, or Janet and love.

Pop came in from the living room carrying Grandpa's worn copy of *Mein Kampf*, which he set on the table beside the New Testament.

Horst quickly placed pamphlets entitled 'World Jewry and the Oil Crisis' on the chairs and asked his mother for two aspirin. He swallowed them and walked outside.

It was dark now, a chill evening with fine mist falling, the air sharp and sweet. Country air, which in the spring would change texture, growing dry, rich, pungent as the vines awakened. Then the heavy work would begin.

He wished he had some heavy work, soul-cleansing farmer's work, to do right now.

'Horst, come inside,' Pop called. 'I want you to hear my introduction to your speech.'

Reluctantly he left the sweet air, the shadowed view of winter vineyards, and entered the house where the uniformed, jackbooted Nazi stood waiting. Where the mirror-image of himself stood waiting.

They'd had one round of drinks, sitting in a back booth of the quiet little pub called the Hammock.

Stone ordered a second round, lit a cigarette and said, 'Okay, Harold, what's happening on your SIT?'

Lowery gave him a quick rundown, concluding with, 'It's a dead end, right?'

'It's no more a dead end than the Rossa case. I've got a hunch my perpetrator's Rita Goran, and you feel the same about Carl Schleisser.'

Lowery drank bourbon neat, and nodded.

'Then you've got to find a way of applying pressure. Something like my floating surveillance of Goran.'

'Your case and suspect are here in LA, Tony. My case may have taken place in LA, but everything that can solve it is in the San Joaquin Valley. And Captain Gensen won't help.'

'You say the Nazis are six hours away? Six hours isn't impossible, Litvak. You feel the son might crack if you got him alone? Then get him alone. Gensen won't help you with an undercover man and he can't authorize your assigning Los Angeles detectives to another county. But he won't say anything if you're up there yourself.'

'He might.'

'He won't say anything because he doesn't have to know. Just *go*, Harold. Again and again. Apply pressure to that weak link. Use the good offices of that highway patrolman.'

'What if the Schleissers complain of harrassment?'

'There's only one good thing about having to deal with Nazis, Harold. No one in California government or politics gives a shit what they think. Their complaints won't move anyone, at least for a while. Take the media, for example, which would jump on your ass if you were hassling illegals, or blacks, or anyone else with a base in ethnic politics; with an audience and voting public rooting for them.'

Lowery finished his bourbon.

'Take my word for it, Harold. You have time to try a few tricks. Of course, if instead of just bending the rules you break them – like using your gun barrel on the son's head, or worse yet shooting a hole in his Nazi hide – you'll catch it. So forget you're a Lone Litvak and remember you're a cop.'

Perceptive, Lowery thought, even as he answered, 'I never forget I'm a cop,' and hoped it was the truth.

The meeting would start at exactly seven, Pop believing that punctuality was an Aryan trait. The attendance wasn't bad for the week before the holidays, seven men and two women, all of them in the first two rows, the back two remaining empty. Horst kept his eyes on those empty rows, and on the door, and saw that Pop did too.

If strangers showed up, it could be the police. Even so, Pop was wearing his automatic, a 9mm Walther Heeres Pistole made in 1931 for the German army; a

204

savage-looking weapon in the Luger tradition. He walked around, shaking hands with the regulars – Clory, Duke and Jim, all in uniform; nodding at the two truckers, Bo Haskell and the big man, bigger than Carl, who called himself Poison and obviously didn't want to be named on the party's membership and mailing lists.

There was a salesman and his wife who showed up at irregular intervals, plump, sleek, middle-aged people who always had jokes about Abie and Rosie, the rabbi and the nun, the black preacher and his lady parishioners. They'd brought another couple, about their own age, whom they introduced as friends from Oakland 'who've had their fill of Yids helping the scum of the world immigrate to our country. We've gotta stop them, Adolf!'

Horst took mental notes, sweating about his speech, forcing himself to think Nazi, *gut* Nazi, because he had to satisfy Pop, this audience. And while Pop had a page of speech written out, Horst would have to play it by ear.

'Extemporaneous speaking,' Pop had said when Horst tried one last time to get out of facing the audience, 'was the Führer's strongest point. Lincoln wrote the Gettysburg Address on the back of an envelope, but the Führer made better speeches at the beginning of his career with just a few minutes' notice. In beer halls, on streets, whipping crowds into a *frenzy!*' His voice quieted. 'You don't have to do that much, Horst, but show them you can lead.'

Which meant show *Pop* Horst could lead. Which meant tough times ahead, threats of losing his income, if he gave it a half-hearted effort, or flat-out fought against a leadership role.

As Pop was moving around the audience, the door opened. Horst tensed, but it was Hugo Verner, who'd moved and wasn't expected to show. He said, 'Sorry I'm late, Adolf. It's a long drive from San Antone.' He wasn't in uniform, which Pop asked about.

'Hell, Adolf, I didn't want to be explaining to service station jockeys and what not.'

Pop turned away, unsmiling, and glanced at his grandchildren, who were running in and out of the kitchen. He spoke to Mom, who quickly got them and brought them to the last row of seats.

Pop stepped to the table and motioned Horst to take the chair beside it. Horst sat down, knowing he would only have to stand again in a moment. It was part of the tradition, Nazis jumping up to sing and shout and *heil*.

He quickly wiped away the cynicism, the contempt creeping into his mind. He thought of what he would say, and while his hands were still sweaty, while the headache still lurked behind his eyes, he began working something out.

What Janet had said in Monterey he would say . . . only he would make it a boast; bend it into a Nazi triumph.

Looking at his audience, he wondered what the hell he was sweating about. Just shout 'Kill the Jews!' and these idiots would cheer.

But Pop . . . Pop was something else again. Pop expected more from him. He had to surprise Pop.

He began shaping ideas, muttering phrases under his breath. And Pop said, 'Rise and face the Führer's picture!'

No 'please'. No 'ladies and gentlemen'. An *order*.

The audience rose, including Mom and the girls, and faced the picture over the archway to their right.

The younger girl giggled. Pop said, 'Be quiet or you will be taken outside and left alone in the rain!'

Mom whispered to her and the child nodded, frightened.

Pop said, 'Adolf Hitler lives forever. Adolf Hitler will be redeemed. Adolf Hitler, *Seig Heil!*'

On their feet, right arms saluting stiffly, they all shouted, 'Adolf Hitler, *Seig Heil!*'

Pop repeated it twice more, and they repeated it after

him. Then he turned, arm coming down slowly, hand hooking in the belly section of his Sam Browne belt.

An impressive figure, Horst had to admit, and wondered would the audience think *him* impressive, so much smaller than Carl and his father? Though Hitler hadn't been a big man; no bigger than Horst Schleisser. It was the aura, the charisma that had made him big. The mad perception of a goal and the mad pursuit of that goal.

Pop said, 'Sit,' and took out his page of notes. Horst watched and listened, but he also worked on his own speech; on a method of imposing his own aura, his own charisma on this tiny Reich tonight. For Pop's benefit, of course.

Only for Pop's benefit? Or was there something else going on inside him? Wasn't there a challenge? Wasn't there a thrill that occasionally seized him when his father *ordered* and people, no matter how few, obeyed as Americans never obeyed? Didn't he wonder if they would obey him too?

Pop said, 'For the benefit of newcomers, I'll state what the membership already knows. We have no NRP pledge, no song, no oath, no nonsense. We have only the Führer, Adolf Hitler, and the hope that his time will come again through people like us. The National Resurrection party gets its name in part from the obvious need to bring this nation back from its mongrelized sleep to full Aryan life. But also, Resurrection applies to the Führer, Adolf Hitler himself. For only by his rebirth can we be made free and strong. Not rebirth in a mystic, religious sense, for he never died in that sense. But in a solid, realistic manner. By a new leader rising to whip this nation into shape! A leader following in the Führer's footsteps, and so resurrecting Adolf Hitler in the only manner the Führer would want!'

Duke Eiser, who'd weaved a little on the way in, jumped up and shouted, '*Heil*, Adolf Schleisser! Show us the way, Adolf!'

Pop nodded briefly and waved Duke back in his seat.

This time his hand came to rest on his holstered automatic, and he stood as the warrior revealed. 'I've tried for many years to warn our people here in our community and on trips to the larger cities, about the International Jewish Conspiracy, the Zionist lies and plots, the things the Führer knew and helped his people to know. He almost succeeded in bringing Aryan society to a *Judenfrei* – a Jew-free – state, expelling them and making Germany a Garden of Eden. But they plotted, they blackmailed, they brought the Devil himself up from Hell . . .' He sighed, waving his arms. 'And our world is the result. America, once land of the free, is now land of the Jew, the nigger, the mixed-breed Hispanic, the Oriental, and the degenerate.'

He paused, and Horst cleared his mind to examine the audience. They had heard all of this before, from this same man. That they agreed, that they liked hearing it, was evident in their nods.

Also evident, in their too relaxed air, was the fact that they weren't excited, moved, whipped into 'a *frenzy*.'

'We've made enemies of the people who want to give us their oil and their friendship, the Arabs, by letting our Jews support the Israeli-Zionist Jews. Arabs, who are among the few people who don't want to come here in great numbers like the increasing waves of racial garbage, penniless, ignorant, not even aware that it is Jewish brains and Jewish money manipulating them, shipping them here. For only in a mongrelized America can the Jew rest easy.'

Clory said softly, 'We won't let him rest, Adolf. Our time is coming.'

Adolf looked at his friend, nodded, and his hand gripped his holstered automatic. Then he smiled, broadly and triumphantly. 'You're right! We won't! There are other Nazi parties. There are the Klans and the Liberty Lobby and hundreds of thousands of concerned citizens. They're still disbanded, disorganized, waiting for something they know not what. But *we* know, don't we?'

'For the Führer,' Clory said, clenching both fists in his lap. 'For the new Hitler.'

'Adolf Schleisser!' Duke shouted, jumping up again. 'Adolf . . .'

'Not me,' Adolf said, his voice overpowering Duke's. He waited until Duke sank back down, frowning, puzzled. As were the other regulars. This was something new. Adolf had never rejected the cloak of leadership before, though he'd said things like, 'We' (meaning he) 'have a long way to go,' and 'If someone else comes along, I'll know it.'

Now Horst stiffened, embarrassed even before Pop spoke the words, fighting the embarrassment because a Nazi, especially a leader, came on with what Janet called, 'super-chutzpah'. Because a Hitler flinched from nothing, and tonight *he* had to be a Hitler.

'Not me,' Adolf repeated, 'and not any other leader in the various Nazi parties, Klans, associated aware groups. But one of us; one of the NRP.' He paused while the audience stared. 'Some of you have known him from childhood. But no one knows him like I do. No one has heard him like I have.' He turned, pointing at Horst, saying, 'My son, Horst Schleisser, who will begin his crusade tonight!'

And there he was, rising to stand before these ten people plus his mother and his nieces. There he was, a two-bit Caesar waiting to sweep a sleezy band of malcontents, plus family, into 'a *frenzy*'. While attempting to camouflage the usual sad racial garbage so as not to be a carbon copy of his father and the other Nazi leaders. Leaders whose speeches they read in the various tracts, newspapers, periodicals that flowed from the sick and frightened men who ran America's hate presses.

'I'm speaking to you because my father has ordered it. And a son obeys his father and a Nazi obeys his leader.' He looked at Pop, now sitting down, now fighting back a smile of pleasure. ' "I obey" are the only words a Nazi needs to know, unless he is the leader.

209

Until now, "I obey" was all I needed, all I wanted,' he turned to the audience, 'as it must be all you need, all you want. The NRP and Adolf Schleisser keep us sane in this insane, mongrelized society. The NRP and Adolf Schleisser lie behind our awareness, our often painful, foolish daily lives and jobs. They nourish us, comfort us, give us purpose, make existence worth while. We're blessed in a way the ordinary Christian can't possibly understand.'

He didn't allow himself to focus on his audience; not yet. His eyes were turned inward, shaping thoughts into words. But he heard the assenting and excited murmur, and Pop along with them: 'Yes.'

'Now I'm leaving that blessed security and comfort. My father has told me I'm to lead . . . at least to learn to lead. And a son obeys his father and a Nazi obeys his leader.'

He was getting the rhythm now, remembering Martin Luther King's great speeches, the repeat phrases helping whip the audience to 'a *frenzy*'. And this audience was murmuring, 'Yes,' and his father beside him was murmuring, 'Yes.'

'We're not as rich a country as we once were, but don't be troubled by it. We're not as mighty a country as we once were, but don't be frightened by it. Because while rich and mighty we were tools, we were fools, we were humiliated by Vietnamese and Cubans, by snickering Communists who knew we were being betrayed, who knew they couldn't lose, who had their Jew friends whispering in presidents' ears. So our *not* being as rich, as powerful, means our people will begin to awaken. Our being in and out of recessions and depressions, our being humiliated by Russian sub-humans, means our people will begin to look for reasons. *Why*, they'll ask. And you will be here to answer. And I will be here to help you answer.'

He paused, finally looking at them, seeing their rapt attention, their parted lips, their bodies crouching in the chairs. He was giving them something old and comforting packaged in a new and exciting way. 'I will be here to help you answer because my father has ordered it.' He looked at Clory, at Duke, nodding slightly, willing them to know what came next, to say it along with him. And while they didn't speak up, they did move their lips, did murmur along as he said, 'And a son obeys his father and a Nazi obeys his leader.'

'Yes!' Adolf said.

'Harold Covington, you'll remember, ran in the Republican Primary for district attorney of North Carolina. He got over 56,000 votes. A uniformed Nazi wearing the sacred swastika got over 56,000 votes in an American state. People were surprised. I wasn't. It was the first time an entire state was given the *opportunity* to vote for a Nazi. No other state has done it since. But they will.

'Here in California, a Klansman, Paul Metzger, received 32,000 votes for US Congressman in a San Diego County Democratic primary. And the recessions and depressions will come one after the other, the mongrels will continue to drown our white heritage from all the black and brown and yellow cesspools of the earth, the American people will hear what we have to say, what *I* have to say about who is behind it, who is to blame, and what must be done to save our nation and white civilization. I will say it now that it isn't yet popular. I will say it later when it will begin to be popular. I will say it in the near future when it will be the will of the entire American people!

'And why will I do this?' Long pause, seeing the expectation come into his audience's faces. 'Because my father has ordered it. And a son obeys a father . . .' They were saying it with him now, softly but saying it . . . 'and a Nazi obeys his leader.' Glancing to the right, he saw Pop's lips moving too, heard Pop's voice saying it too.

He had them, this handful of clowns! And he could have all the clowns in the American Nazi movements! He could have more than Nazis, have the sweaty, explosive people in the Klans and the Liberty Lobby, what Janet called the closet Nazis.

Though he wasn't thinking of Janet now; he was thinking of how good it felt to move people, bend people to his will.

'Robert Ardrey was a writer who examined the inherited animal nature of man, the violent nature of man. He was accepted by many, and rejected by many more. Those who rejected him rejected the brute side of man, the genetic claw-and-fang side of man. But the NRP not only accepts, it *celebrates* this violence, this warrior drive that no amount of Jew-inspired psychology and philosophy can eradicate. Because we know, as did our Führer, that it is the blood, the genes, the *race* that makes the man.

'In a book called *The Social Contract*, Ardrey spoke to America's citizens: the politicians, the police, the criminals, the various races. He warned them that in their conflicts with each other they would lose their freedom. But we in the NRP *long* to lose the freedom to rob, to murder, to be victimized! Ardrey's thinking was chained by mongrelized educators and publishers. What he said was something like: "We'd better examine our social contract while we still have the right to do so, before it dies on us because of inter-racial warfare, crime, loss of ethics, loss of belief in democracy, near anarchy. Then thieves and victims, anarchists and conservatives, saints and sinners, the whole society will have to bow to one strong will. Then *order* will be all." '
He looked at Pop. 'You've been saying the same thing, teaching me the same thing, since childhood.'

'And Adolf Hitler taught it to me,' Pop said.

Horst faced his audience again. 'Ardrey didn't want that, but we do. Because we will be the ones giving the orders!' He took the quantum leap, raising his voice, embarrassment a forgotten emotion. '*I* will be the one giving the orders. Because my father has ordered it.' He lifted both arms towards the men and women sitting

212

there, leading them in the bellowed chorus, 'And a son obeys his father and a Nazi obeys his leader!'

He faced the picture of Hitler. He led them in the salute and *Seig Heil* three times, turned and walked from the kitchen into the darkened living room as if overcome by emotion.

He heard the outburst of applause and shouts of, '*Heil* Horst! *Heil* Horst!'

He sank to the couch, laughing, shaking his head, thinking he was absolute leader of a nation of twelve adults and two children.

But his heart pounded; he listened as they kept shouting.

His father spoke from the doorway, saying, 'Horst,' and the way he said it, voice trembling, ended Horst's laughter.

They met half-way in the darkened room, and his father hugged him. 'Horst, Horst,' he said, and Horst was shocked because Pop was crying.

Crying! Adolf Schleisser!

'Horst, I knew it. You're what we've needed. You can speak to big audiences, soon. We'll rent halls and raise money for the Party. In Los Angeles. In San Diego. In San Francisco.'

Not San Francisco! Janet . . .

His father hugged him and drew him back to the kitchen, where small group or not, clowns or not, these people cheered and *heil*ed him.

Finally they began going outside to their cars, calling, 'See you at Clory's.' Duke Eiser, who'd never been overly friendly, shook his hand and said, 'Terrific! I mean . . . terrific, Horst!' He seemed cold sober and stared at Horst as if he'd never seen him before.

Pop was hugging him again. 'Remember what I said about going to college, preparing yourself? That's going to be my next order.' He smiled. 'And a son obeys his father and a Nazi obeys his leader.'

Horst said, 'Yes, Father. But what about my work on the ranch?'

213

'You'll get your share while you go to college. You'll pay one third of your expenses, and Carl and I will pay the other two thirds. It will be for the party, for the cause, and we'll all pay equally.'

A hell of a deal! Horst thought. He would keep the old man happy and also get an education. He wouldn't have to be around for the meetings too often, and could arrange to live with Janet if he went to school up north.

But as Mom waved him and Pop off in the station wagon, he knew it was more than that. It was a chance to see how far he could actually go with this leadership thing.

Pop was saying Horst should start wearing a pistol at meetings. 'You still have the Smith and Wesson I bought you for your twenty-first birthday, don't you?'

Horst said yes, at his apartment, and he'd wear it next time. Horst asked Pop if it was legal to wear a handgun outside the home, seeing the Walther automatic still on his right hip. Pop went into a harangue about freedom to bear arms.

Horst tried to think of Janet, and couldn't. But no sweat; he'd be with her the evening of the twenty-fifth.

Or, if Pop made an issue of it, a day or two later.

Certainly by New Year.

Christmas with the family wouldn't be all that bad. He had to talk this college plan through with Pop.

When they got to Clory's, everyone came over to their booth. Jim slapped him on the shoulder, but the others didn't touch him, treated him differently from the way they had before the speech. 'Respectfully' was the word that came to mind.

Jim was nudged aside by Clory and whispered to. He spread his hands apologetically; then just stood back, listening.

No one else slapped Horst on the shoulder. Everyone spoke of big meetings and getting new members. Finally Clory began serving pie and coffee, and Pop and Horst were left alone.

'I only wish Carl were here to see,' Pop said.

214

Horst smiled to himself. He didn't think big brother would be too happy about the new Führer.

David made excellent time, the Mercedes holding the slick roads at high speeds.

He saw the sign reading, 'Bethills 9 miles'. He was almost there and should be thinking of how to find Clory's diner, and what he would do when he did find it. Sit outside and watch for Nazis? Go inside and look for Nazis? Walk up to a Nazi and say, 'Pardon me, may I inject rat poison into your stomach?' Open up with both pistols, saying, 'This world's not big enough for the two of us, pardner?'

He covered another two quick, smooth miles. He loved his car; had loved the 450 SL he'd had before this sedan. He'd owned an old Porsche SC before that which had given him excellent service. Three German cars after a lifetime of Plymouths, Fords and one knock-out Studebaker Hawk.

He was a Jew who had hated Germans before, during and for some time after World War II; who had thought never to give anything to rebuild their bloody nation, certainly not his custom, his money. But their cars had been great and time had passed and their people had worked and prospered and who could hate forever except Nazis?

Which had him looking up into the black sky and saying, 'All that Your people want is not to be hated, dammit!'

He made a lousy Tevya. No sense of humour about persecution. No real love for the mute Being up there.

Actually, he made a lousy Jew.

He thought of Teddy then. Because Teddy made a lousy black. Which had him smiling as he covered another mile and was six miles from Bethills.

He and Teddy, and a few hundred thousand others, he guessed, made lousy Jews and blacks and whatever because they longed for the American Melting Pot.

215

No more Melting Pot, according to the academicians. It never worked, they said. A myth, they said.

It had been no myth for David Howars. He had hungered to become American. He waved not flags nor did he join, but he assimilated like crazy.

'Let's hear it for the Melting Pot,' he said, and was closing fast on target. At a quarter to nine. Despite many heavy rain showers.

The gas station swung into view around a long, gentle curve in the highway, as did the sign reading *Bethills*. And David Howars was suddenly filled with his nightmare: the woman looking at him, labelling him a 'filthy Jew' without knowing him.

Could he pass in the eagle's nest, in Clory's diner? Had the thin, eighteen-year-old face been more Semitic than the full, middle-aged face he swivelled into sight with his hand on the rear-view mirror?

'Funny, I never thought I looked Jewish,' he said; and on impulse swung off the highway into the gas station.

The attendant wore a yellow slicker that fit him like a tent; a thin old man with a prune-wrinkled face and a shy smile. 'Fill 'er,' David said, and got out to stretch his legs. 'Do you know Clory's diner?'

The old man's smile died. He fit the hose into the tank-opening and gave David a long look. 'Nutsies,' he finally said. 'Take a right at the second traffic light. That's Eucalyptus Road. Straight through town about two miles along. On your left, big sign, small joint. Nutsies.'

'*Nazis?*' David asked, taking out his wallet.

'You want to call them that, call them that. It's not what I call them.'

David paid and got his change.

'*Nutsies,*' the old man said angrily, and went back inside the little office, slamming the door.

So there was one person who didn't classify him as a Jew; one person who thought David Howars might be a 'nutsie' himself. Which was comforting.

He reached Eucalyptus Road and turned right. The rain began again. He drove through a cluster of buildings and out into darkness, and saw the diner on his left. He pulled into a large parking lot that had a bunched group of cars facing the diner. He decided to find parking space around the back, somewhere more secluded. He had used his own car and his own plates, not as clever as the Nazis on Fairfax. He could be traced.

If he had it to do over again . . .

He stopped himself there because he would probably do the same thing. It was now or never. If he waited days and got a hot car and planned to the last detail, he would see how ridiculous the whole thing was and go home and screw Rita Goran and set up the next movie and grow fat and happy.

He drove slowly to the left of the parked cars, around the west end of the diner. The blacktop continued and he entered darkness and a service loading area where delivery trucks and garbage trucks could do their business.

He shut his lights in case someone looked out a grimy window, the only lighted one facing the back. He inched his car to the far north-east edge of the blacktop, a good twenty feet from that window, and parked. When he got out and walked to the diner's west end, he was unable to make out the Mercedes.

He could now go in and massacre Nazis and his car would never be seen.

Of course, *he* would be seen.

Besides, he'd forgotten to select anything with which to accomplish his massacre, and went back to the car, thinking he made a lousy warrior. He opened the trunk, glad the drizzle had stopped as his hair was matting uncomfortably.

Decision time.

He put the Detective Special in his right-hand raincoat pocket; it wasn't any bigger than a hairbrush.

He knew immediately that he'd wasted his time with knives, pellet guns, rat poison and hypodermics of

217

kitchen and medical variety. The same with sleeping pills . . . unless he decided to swallow a dozen after being trapped.

A frightened grin stretched his lips as he took out the modified extension cord connected to the urinal-deodorant cover. It was in a plastic bag and he stuffed it into his left pocket. He closed the trunk softly and began walking around the diner to the front entrance.

'Whatever happens,' he said to the black, forbidding sky, 'it's Your fault.'

Clory kept a half-gallon of California brandy under the counter for special occasions. Everyone had a shot or two in his coffee, and Horst had three more straight in his water glass, responding to toasts. Clory wasn't licensed to serve hard liquor, but he wasn't worried about anyone reporting him to the Alcoholic Beverage Commission. The only people here were people who'd been at the NRP meeting.

Twenty minutes later, the sleek salesman couple and their friends announced they were leaving. They shook hands with everyone, but when they came over to the booth where Horst and Pop sat, they grew quieter, murmuring congratulations to Horst on his speech. Finally, the salesman stiffened inside his blue suit and raised his arm. '*Seig Heil!*'

Pop gave a little flip-up salute in return, murmuring, '*Heil*,' and Horst simply nodded. As the foursome walked to the door, Horst rose from his seat. Pop asked where he was going, and he said to play the jukebox.

'Not your usual garbage, I hope.'

He meant rock and roll. Clory didn't have many such numbers. He had mostly country music, and at least two German Army marching songs.

Horst said, 'One of the marching songs,' and walked to the door where the jukebox stood. Where the salesman group also stood. They began to leave, but the salesman's friend's wife – a big, good-looking blonde of about forty with a juicy body – turned back. She stepped

218

over to Horst, speaking softly and in a rush: 'You made my heart stop; you were wonderful; could I call you some evening to help me understand the history and traditions of American Nazis? I'd be so grateful.' Then, in a whisper, '*Heil* Horst,' leaning into him for an instant, body pressing his for an instant, before she was gone.

He stepped over to the jukebox, glancing around to see if anyone had noticed. Clory was facing him from behind the counter and gave him a little smile. The others were on stools, their backs to him, getting refills of spiked coffee, talking and laughing.

Horst chose to ignore what could have been a bid by Clory for manly confidences. He turned back to the jukebox, examining the selections, still smelling the woman's perfume.

He was excited. He had felt manly, felt sexually powerful in his uniform as she'd stood before him. He wondered if she would want him to wear the uniform, at least the boots and swastika, when he made love to her.

The truckers were there, Poison towering over him but standing almost at attention, saying, 'A great speech, Horst. I'm gonna come to all the meetings now. I'm . . .' He swallowed. 'I'm gonna buy a uniform and try to get more guys to meetings.'

Bo Haskell, who had a uniform but rarely wore it, said, 'I'll wear mine next time, Horst. We'll get some members for you.'

'Hey, Horst'll get the members. All we got to do is bring them to hear him speak!'

He said, 'Thank you,' and shook their hands. Then Poison, looking embarrassed, gave a small Nazi salute and murmured, '*Heil* Horst.' Bo Haskell did the same, much louder.

That set off a general round of *heils* and toasts and Horst had to drink another stiff brandy. As the truckers left, Horst found a fresh drink pressed into his hand. And though, unlike Carl, he'd always been able to hold his liquor, his head was beginning to spin. But not just from alcohol.

Hitler had been a sexual ascetic, some said a sexual cripple. Either way, he hadn't reached out for the women he might have had. Horst Schleisser knew how differently he would act in similar circumstances, and smothered a laugh, and wanted to hear a little cool rock music. But a son obeyed his father, and he dropped in two coins and selected the record hand-marked *Deutsche Märsche 1*. There was another German march, and he pressed that one next. Clory changed them every so often from his home collection purchased through *New Order*, *White Power*, or other Nazi publications.

In time, the NRP would begin to distribute a similar publication. In time, Horst would begin printing his own books, pamphlets, wholesaling his own records. And the profits would help the party reach out for new members. And soon there would be hundreds, then thousands *heil*ing him . . .

The thunderous mix of drums, brass, marching feet, and male voices bellowing out in German stirred his blood. He breathed heavily, and tried to tell himself he was being a fool. A Reich of twelve adults and two children. A party of six regulars and a handful of sympathizers, and he was standing here, bombed on brandy, dreaming of ultimate power. The German Army marched, and their rousing voices swallowed his mind, and he understood his father as never before.

But what of his love, his Janet?

He didn't want to think of her. She was reality and he wanted to let this crazy dream take him for tonight. He had rejected it all his life and would probably reject it again tomorrow. But tonight he had hypnotized his father, the NRP regulars, and a sensual woman. It was fun! It made him forget Fairfax Avenue and police. Made him forget the tension of his double life.

And there were other women beside Janet; women who would not only accept what he was but would love him for it. Women who would worship him . . .

The door opened. A man looming large in a tan rain-coat stepped inside, looked at him and seemed to freeze.

Instantly, Horst was aware he wore a Nazi uniform; was jolted from his pleasurable dream; was made uncomfortable and put on the defensive. Because of this, he stared back at the man, saying with his eyes, 'Well? What of it? This is my turf.'

The man smiled. 'No night to be driving to San Francisco.'

Horst nodded, released by that smile from discomfort and anger. 'You're right. Try some of Clory's coffee, the best.'

'I'll do that.' He walked to the counter, where Jim Borst and Hugo Verner were getting ready to leave. Jim was also in uniform, and the stranger nodded at him and took a stool two removed from Duke Eiser. He brushed at his wet hair and picked a menu from between the Heinz and A1 sauces. Horst watched as Clory, who had drunk as much as anyone, ambled up to him in full uniform with an apron around his middle.

The stranger said, 'If I'm interrupting a private party, just tell me. But I like the atmosphere, the music, and I'd really like some of your famous coffee.'

'Famous where?' Clory asked, none too friendly.

Horst knew he was looking at the stranger's face, at the thinning hair and whatever features might fit into his obsession with Jew noses and Jew lips and Jew heads. Just like Pop. No one was safe from their suspicion, unless he joined the NRP.

Horst walked over, no longer gripped by the music and Führer dreams. One stranger, one example of the real world, and the nonsense began to slip.

'Famous with me,' Horst said, and sat down beside the stranger. 'I just invited him to have a cup, on the NRP.'

Clory nodded and said, 'Anything else?', unfreezing, but only because the Führer designate had pushed him.

'Perhaps in a few minutes.' He turned to Horst. 'Local political group?'

Horst nodded. Clory poured from a silex and said, 'National Resurrection party.'

'I'd like to attend a meeting next time I come through.'

Horst was wondering what this man really felt about walking in on uniformed Nazis and swastikas and German marches. Had to be a shock.

He tried to imagine what it would be like if he and Janet came upon a place like this. And shuddered and stood up. The stranger was probably unwilling to look for another eatery on such a lousy night. So he was being pleasant. But imagine if he was Jewish, a man his age with memories of the war and the Holocaust!

He didn't want to think of that either, not of Janet and not of the real world and not of Jewish men with memories of mass murder seeing Horst Schleisser in this uniform.

He walked back towards the booth and Pop. Duke stumbled after him, touched his arm, said, 'You'll be famous . . . you'll shee . . .' He shook his head, really drunk now. 'Sorry. Want you to know . . . great leader.' He raised his arm, and Horst knew he was going to shout '*Heil* Horst!', and the stranger would hear, and it was impossible!'

He grabbed Duke and spoke softly. 'A good Nazi obeys his leader, right, Duke?'

'Right.'

'A good Nazi isn't drunk in public. Go home.'

And just like that, Duke Eiser, who would jump anyone, even a friend, for a lot less, turned and shambled out the door.

Now there was just Clory, Pop and Horst. And the stranger who was sipping his coffee and saying something complimentary to Clory.

Clory leaned on the counter, warming to him, explaining where and when the meetings were held. Relieved of responsibility, Horst went on to the booth.

The brandy was on the floor beside Pop, because of the stranger. 'You want one, Horst?'

Horst said no, he'd had enough, and Pop said, 'Me too. A leader must know when to stop. Duke won't last once the party begins to grow. Too loose in his ways. With drink. With women.' He paused. 'But now he's useful. We'll need other trucks and cars disposed of before we're through. We'll draw more blood . . .' He glanced around at the counter, and at the stranger who couldn't possibly hear him.

'He's all right,' Horst said, trying to head off what he knew was coming.

'That man's a Jew. Or part Jew.'

'Would he stay? Would he like the people and the music? Would he talk to Clory with the uniform and swastika?'

Pop blinked at Horst's sharpness of tone. 'Sometimes a person's face is a mystery to him. Jews who were adopted by Christian families. Jews of converted parents who don't tell them, out of shame. Half Jews and part Jews, but always the blood shows.'

Horst wanted to remind him of Kirk Douglas, whom he and Mom had loved, especially in *Spartacus*, until someone had told them he was Jewish. Before then Pop had talked of his Aryan blue eyes and cleft chin and 'strong German features'.

The stranger had risen and was walking towards them. Horst nodded at him. The stranger smiled, including Pop with his eyes, and went on to the men's room.

'Maybe not that one,' Pop said, 'though it could be. Family and race must be carefully traced back through at least three generations.'

Horst was suddenly very tired. It was only nine thirty, but this evening had been endless with its emotional ups and downs. He wanted to go home. In order to do that, he had to get back to the ranch and his car.

Clory called, 'Pour yourselves a drink while that guy can't see.'

223

Adolf said, 'Not me, thanks. What I want is the john. All that coffee and brandy.' He chuckled.

Horst realized he had the same need.

Clory came from behind the counter. 'Think I'll close early. Poison's always crapping about sending truckers over, and they never show.'

Horst got out of the booth before Clory could sit down.

He went to the men's room, emptied of Führer frenzy and energy and soon to be emptied of coffee and brandy. Which put it all into perspective, and he decided to call Janet.

David had prayed that the men's room would be empty. This place was more of a shock than he'd been prepared for. Storm-troop uniforms and swastika armbands and German war music! And coming face to face with that young Nazi as soon as he'd stepped in the door! He'd had to fight a wild impulse to pull his gun and simply shoot as many of them as he could.

Then having to smile and chat with the filth! The sweat had been pouring down his sides and it had been heaven entering the privacy of the men's room, being alone, having those detestable symbols removed from his sight.

There'd been three men left when he'd come in here, and he had wondered if the two in the booth were Schleissers. But no matter; all three were in Nazi uniform and all three could die.

He'd had to splash cold water on his face before calming down and being able to look around.

The room was small, windowless, shabbily white, with a sink and fluorescent-lighted mirror. With a urinal to the left of, and close beside, the sink. With a booth three or four feet away from the urinal, an air-vent grille in the wall high above it.

The horizontal fluorescent tube over the mirror wasn't lighted. The small round ceiling fixture was.

Now he was ready, though his hands trembled as he

reached into the raincoat pocket and drew out the plastic bag. *Hughes Market*, it said, and he wondered if Mrs Gomez had bought fresh fish as he'd instructed, in line with his new diet. And shook his head, muttering, 'Stop it!' Yet he couldn't empty his mind of trivialities; was thinking of the men's room at Thomasine's and how much larger and cleaner it was.

'You'll miss your chance!' he said, and stepped to the sink. He examined the wall beside it and below it and there was no electrical outlet. 'God help me,' he said. '*Quick!*' If one of them walked in it would be too late for anything but the gun and the gun was suicide, and yet he felt he would have to attack some way because of those uniforms and swastikas.

He saw it then, the black plastic outlet at the left side of the chrome fluorescent fixture; a double outlet for electrical shavers and toothbrushes and water piks. And murder mechanisms, because according to J. W. Colfert it was the amperage which killed, not the standard 110 voltage.

Now he moved frantically fast, tearing the extension cord from the plastic bag, cursing as the metal half-cup grille-screen caught, raising the possibility that the wire he'd attached to it might have torn loose.

He got it out and it hadn't torn loose and he said, 'Thank You'. And wished he had time to consider who the hell he was thanking. He began to plug the cord into the outlet, then stopped, because if there was juice in the outlet *he* would be the one to get the jolt of electricity when he placed the metal grille in the urinal.

Which reminded him: was there already a grille there?

He dropped everything in the sink and looked in the urinal. There was a round, white block of deodorant, but no grille-screen.

He took the grille from the sink, its white extension cord trailing, and placed it over the block of deodorant. The cord hung over the edge of the urinal, blatantly noticeable.

He took the plug end and raised it to the fixture, and

225

the wire lifted and its white blended with the urinal's porcelain white and it was less noticeable. But anyone urinating, looking down, might still see it.

He should have brought tape. Clear Scotch tape would have allowed him to fasten the extension cord . . .

The door opened. David leaned forward as if examining himself in the mirror and saw the reflection of the young Nazi pass behind him. David ran his right hand over his face, and in his left held the plug attached to the electrical cord attached to the metal grille in the urinal. He waited for the Nazi to enter the booth, which would finish this idiotic plan.

The Nazi stepped to the urinal. His zipper made a sharp, whining sound.

David brought his left hand up to his face, clenched around the plug, the cord trailing down and to the urinal. He brought that hand to his head as if arranging his hair, afraid to glance at the Nazi and see that he had noticed the electrical cord; that he was looking at the man touching his face and head with a clenched fist trailing an electrical cord.

The unmistakable sound of urination began.

David brought the plug to the outlet. The outlet was stiff, unyielding, as if never before used. He shoved hard, and in it went.

Nothing happened.

He stared at the plug, firmly inserted in the outlet, and suddenly understood. The fluorescent wasn't on. There was no current entering the fixture.

He saw the little black button at the right end of the fixture, and jerked his hand up to it. He first tried to turn it; then pressed it in. It clicked.

Things happened quickly then. With his finger still on the switch, David heard a gulping sound and saw the young Nazi execute a shocking bit of gymnastics; leaping upward, head thrown sharply back, face distorted by a violent, straining rictus, penis still streaming

226

yellow. And along the yellow flow seemed to pass the shadow of a shadow, the jolt of electrical current.

The Nazi fell stiff and unyielding, straight back, thumping heavily on the tile floor. His penis (circumsized, it appeared) hung through the fly, trickling urine onto the brown trouser leg. His shiny black jackboots stuck straight out; his arms lay at his sides; he didn't move in the slightest.

There was a smell something like singed hair, and David looked for the vent-fan switch. Such a smell could be a clue.

He found it beside the light switch near the door. He threw it on and the hum began in the vent above the booth. By the time he had pulled the cord from the socket and shoved it along with the urine-wet metal grille into the plastic bag, and the bag into his left pocket, the smell was gone.

But another smell was seeping from the body; faeces or intestinal gas.

David gagged, as much from sight of the corpse he'd created as from the odour, and reached for the door. Then he remembered the fluorescent fixture, pressed the switch, and the light over the mirror went off.

He stepped to the door and looked back at the body. The young man's face was free of its rictus grimace, smoothed out and relaxed, the eyes closed peacefully. Nazis didn't deserve such easy deaths.

David opened the door. His hand slipped on the metal knob and he realized his fingers were wet with the Nazi's urine. He shuddered and stepped out into the diner, where the Nazi counterman was talking to the Nazi customer, both sitting in the booth near the men's room. The German chorus continued to roar out their German march and he recognized the words *Deutchland und Führer*, and welcomed them because he didn't want to feel sorry for that young man who would never live to be an old man.

The two Nazis looked at him. The counterman said, 'Want anything more?' David said, 'Next time, when I come to the NRP meeting,' thinking they couldn't know he had done anything to the young Nazi; would believe the man had died of a heart attack or stroke, because what evidence of foul play was there? Even an autopsy, according to J. W. Colfert, would fail to produce anything incriminating.

He could even return and kill another one. But as he offered to pay, and as the counterman said, 'NRP's treat' and as he went on towards the door, he knew he wouldn't be back.

Outside, the rain was coming down again and he broke into a run. He reached the back and the Mercedes, and without lights drove around to the front and the road. He looked at the diner and through the window saw the two Nazis in the booth. Then he was speeding back towards 99, feeling sudden and overwhelming exhaustion.

There had been signs for motels all along the freeway, and his eyes grew heavy at the thought of a bed.

He shook himself and unbuttoned his raincoat. He opened both front windows, allowing chill, wet air to whip into the car, reviving him.

He was reaching for the radio when blinding bright lights bounced into his eyes from the rear-view mirror; headlights coming up behind him incredibly fast. He was doing better than sixty and they were overtaking him as if he were crawling.

Pursuit?

He drew the ·38 from his pocket as he watched those headlights coming closer; tensed as they began to swing out to his left; gasped and crouched as they came alongside.

A Japanese compact raced by; a fool applying for a place on the highway fatality roles by doing ninety or better on a slick road.

He was sweating and felt cold and closed the window. He made himself think of the Nazi; of having killed a young man who had spoken to him and sat beside him and seemed reasonably agreeable. Except for his uniform and swastika. Except for the strong possibility of his having helped kill Warren Gross.

He remembered the way the figure had leaped and fallen and lain there. He remembered the smell. He looked into himself and decided he felt very little – very little regret and about as much triumph.

What he did feel was relief. That it was over. That he had finally struck back for thirty-five years of nightmares.

Then, with a sudden jolt of joy, he knew that he was free of the train, the despicable woman, the little boy staring at him. Free of the lifelong, pain-infested dream.

'Well,' he said to the drenching skies, 'a break at last.'

When Adolf saw Horst lying there, his first instinct was to kneel and beg his son to live. But his next instinct was even stronger and he lunged out the door, shouting at Clory to get a doctor, an ambulance, 'Help Horst!' While he went after the stranger in the raincoat, because he was the only one who'd been in there and Horst was lying deathly still and it had to be the Enemy, the Devil, the Eternal Jew. He drew his Walther and went into the rain to hunt as his heroes had done in the Old Country in the thirties and forties.

He stopped because there was no car in the lot and because he realized now that the Jew had left a good five minutes ago. But he couldn't accept it, shouting, 'Bastard!', and ran around back where he might have hidden. Where he might have accomplices, more vermin waiting to ambush Adolf and Clory and other Aryan fighters; to shoot them in the back; to perform ritual Hebrew murder as could have been done to Horst.

There was no one to be seen, front or back, but he couldn't believe the Jew would have come here by himself. They didn't have that kind of courage. They ran in packs, as in the famous Nazi movie which showed first Jews rushing about and then rats scurrying in their stinking passageways and you could understand that the Jews were the rats and the rats were the Jews.

He heard a car in front and turned there, thinking it had to be the Jew, an accomplice, someone to punish for robbing him of his son on the very night he'd begun to climb towards the heights.

He ran, and the hate and pain and brandy surged through his mind, and he panted, '*Has* to be!', because there was no way he could survive this night without vengeance, without an enemy to kill.

The Cadillac had stopped some distance from the diner. Its engine was still running, its lights still on as the man stepped out, looking at the lighted windows. Then he heard Adolf and turned to face him.

And Adolf saw with fierce joy that the face was black. *Black*! The Jew tool! The nigger in the Cadillac! The joke that was no joke but a terrible menace, threatening this country with bastardization.

He screamed the word, '*Nigger!*', and stopped and aimed with both hands on the Walther, the Aryan swift sword, the answer to books and newspapers and movies and television and everything the enemy controlled.

From the diner's doorway, Clory shouted, 'Adolf, wait!'

And Adolf might have. Despite the rage and pain and brandy. Despite the overwhelming need for blood. Might have waited if the nigger had raised his hands and pleaded, begged.

But he had jerked at the sound of Adolf's voice; at the word 'nigger'. He reached under his jacket and came out with a gun.

Adolf laughed like a child.

Teddy had reached Bethills at nine thirty and stopped at a gas station for directions. The place had been closing down, the pumps already off, so he hadn't filled up for the trip back to LA, which he'd figured he'd be making shortly. Having six hours to think had put everything in proper perspective.

He'd gone off half-cocked and that's all there was to it. Dave was in a motel with his blind date. Teddy only wished *he* had someone to take to a motel, 'So it shouldn't be a total loss.'

The blond kid turning off the lights in the office had said, 'Clory's diner? We got better eating places, Mister.'

'I'm meeting someone there.'

'I wouldn't if I was you,' the kid had muttered; then nailed home the point. 'If I was black, I mean.'

'I'm hip, man. But how do I get there?'

The kid had finally told him, and he'd driven the Seville through rain and darkness until the sign appeared on the left. He'd pulled into the lot and checked out the two cars parked nose-first against the diner. Neither had been Dave's Mercedes, and a deep-gut feeling had told him to move out.

But hell, he'd come all this way and what could they do to him for going in and looking around? Bethills was still in the United States, right?

Still, he'd decided to walk very lightly here, so far off his own turf, and stopped about twenty-five feet from the other cars, leaving the engine running in case he decided to split fast.

He'd just stepped out into a driving rain when he'd heard something from the left side of the diner.

He'd turned his head, and felt as if he'd been punched in the solar plexis. The big man had been running, but that wasn't the shock. The big man was a big Nazi: uniform and boots and swastika. And a big fucking pistol in his hand.

Teddy had shifted weight, preparing to jump back inside the Caddy and burn rubber, because that's what a wise man did at a time like this. No questions and no heroics.

But then the situation had changed. The bastard had yelled, 'Nigger!', and Teddy had frozen, hadn't seemed able to get his eyes off that uniform, to end the echo of that word which he'd heard plenty of times before, mostly in jest from other blacks or old friends, but not for a long time in a context like this.

231

Make that *never* in a context like this with a Nazi pointing a gun at him and expecting him to do Mantan Moreland, Stepin Fetchit, Rochester Anderson saying, 'Feets, do yo stuff!', and running so fast he overtook a car on the highway while the Nazi fuck chuckled at the cowardly darkie.

He had ceased being a wise man, even a rational one. He had forgotten the odds of trying to beat an already aimed gun and gone for his own gun under his jacket and back on his left hip – a cross draw with his right hand and no way to beat the Nazi if the Nazi really meant it. And the Nazi had better really mean it because Teddy Bear certainly did.

The shots came fast and close together, but for Teddy there seemed to be an eternity between the first, which ripped the air past his right ear, and the second, which struck him in the lower left side of the chest.

That eternity was filled with fear, and also some satisfaction because he knew there had to be a reason this Nazi was running around wild-eyed and ready to kill, and that reason must be what Dave had already done up here. So let's hear it for Duvid'l, and for Teddy who'd been on target figuring out where his friend had gone.

The shot that hit his chest missed the heart but smashed ribs and tore through the left lung, and he was going to die and knew it. But another slow-motion eternity was upon him as he began to fall backward.

He wasn't surprised to be dying this way. It was as if he had been waiting for it to happen all his life; waiting for the hatred of the land of his birth to catch up with him. Only he'd thought there would be a woman, white of course, at his side and a few crackers turning red in the neck at the miscegenation of it all.

He never had time to feel pain because the slow motion was only in his mind. His body had just reacted with nerve-deadening shock to that bullet passing through chest and lung when another bullet tore through his neck, creating pain beyond pain which was again shock, and death by massive and instant heart failure. His last thought was, 'Hey, you had it all, while this poor shit . . .'

Adolf stopped after firing three shots only because the black had fallen. He wanted more enemies, more blacks and Jews to kill!

Clory said, 'Christ Almighty! Horst's sitting inside! He thinks the booze and excitement . . .' He reached the black. 'Jesus, Adolf! He's dead!'

Just like that, everything ran out of Adolf and he knew what he had done and was terrified. Voice beginning to crack, he said, 'So what do we do, cry about the nigger?'

'It's not the nigger, Adolf, it's you. How do we get *you* out of this?'

Adolf's brain was fogging. He was unable to think. He was unable to lead. He was Frankie again and afraid of the man with big hands who'd been crapping in the circle of men; also attracted to that man and lustful for the dream penises spurting against his bare feet.

He slammed a hand to his head to drive away the senseless thoughts. 'Get Horst!'

Clory said first to help him put the black into the Caddy and the Caddy around back. 'I'll close down and we'll figure something out.'

Adolf said, 'Yes,' thickly, trustingly, as Frankie had done. Adolf thought how his father had crumbled and died because of a Jew, and he was afraid that now it was his turn.

The bloodline. The bloodline always showed in the end. And his blood and Carl's blood was Father's blood. And Father's blood was sick with failure.

But Horst. Horst looked like no Schleisser . . .

'Adolf, for Christ's sake, give me a hand!'

They got the black in the front seat where he lay against the passenger's door and bled from the neck and chest. Clory threw the man's gun on the floor and said, 'Go inside. I'll be there in a minute. *Go on!*'

233

Adolf stumbled up the steps to the diner. He reached for the knob, then realized he'd kept the Walther clutched in his hand the whole time. He put it back in the holster and went inside. Horst was slumped in the booth. Adolf said, 'You're not my blood. You're the Führer's blood.'

Horst looked up.

'Help me,' Adolf said, and Frankie took over and he began to shake and cry.

Carl Schleisser had called at eight o'clock to speak to his father, but Mom said he and Horst had left for Clory's.

He'd get Father tomorrow. He'd tell him he was fine and in full control again, and apologize for the way he'd acted when the cop had come around. He flushed just thinking of it.

Mom wouldn't let him say goodbye; she kept asking where he was. He told her Father had said not to tell anyone, but it was a nice hotel in an expensive vacation area and they were enjoying themselves.

Actually, it was a small motel in San Diego and it was raining so hard they hadn't been able to do any sightseeing. Rose wasn't in the best of moods and neither was he, no matter what he told Mom and planned to tell Father.

On Monday he'd almost belted a greasy little spic waiter who hadn't brought them the right potatoes with their steaks. He'd wanted French fries and Rose mashed, and they both got baked. When the spic apologized, saying the potatoes belonged at the next table, Carl said, 'Sure, Pedro.' That got him a hot look and a long wait for their dishes to be returned. By then the steaks were cold and he called for the manager. The waiter spoke in Spanish and the manager turned to Carl and said stiffly, 'His name is Albert, not Pedro. Mine is Francisco, not Pedro.'

Rose had to hold him down, and by then two more waiters were there. They left without paying for their soup and salad, which gave them the best of it. Still, Rose wasn't interested in anything romantic that night.

That's how it had been going, with a Jew, or something damned close to it, smoking a cigar in a bar where they stopped for a few drinks yesterday and refusing to put it out when Carl said, 'That rope is bothering everyone around.'

The bartender was a big spade and came over and said, 'Everything all right, Mr Graymore?' to the Jew-or-close. They stuck together, that garbage, and Ikie said, 'He comes in here and sits down next to me and my cigar, and the whole joint's empty.' So then Carl said that the cigar was bothering his wife, and Rose said, 'Who, me?', and walked out. The bartender gave him the tab, one hand under the bar, and Carl, who'd figured to walk away, had to pay up.

He and Rose quarrelled bitterly about a wife being supposed to stick up for her husband, especially a Nazi wife who had to follow the Führer's guidelines for women. She snapped back with, 'Hitler said, "The goal of female education has invariably to be the future mother." He didn't say we had to back up scaredy-cats taking their fear out on everyone around them!'

He'd slapped her and the bitch had come at him clawing and kicking. So now he had a bruise on his right shin and one hell of a scratch on his right cheek. And they weren't talking. Some vacation!

Mom put the icing on the cake by saying, 'Carl, you would have been so proud of your brother tonight! He spoke to the meeting, and *how* he spoke! I know you and your father haven't always been pleased with Horst, but now! They were shouting "*Heil* Horst". Can you imagine? Your father hugged him and cried. Actually cried! I never thought I'd see the day! Horst is going to college just like I always wanted for him. Later he'll take over some of the burden your father has been carrying.'

Carl almost choked on his rage. Horst wasn't even a

real Nazi, the little prick. Father always said it was *Carl* who was his strong right arm.

But Father had never believed in Carl's ability to take over leadership of the NRP. *Dummkopf* he said when he got mad. Well, school was a long time ago and Hitler himself had never gone further than what was high-school here and failed at everything except being a soldier and a Nazi.

Mom was saying that his elder daughter was still up and wanted to speak to him. Then Bunny was on the line, babbling away, and what she said gave him a splitting headache.

'. . . all the people clapped and yelled, '*Heil* Horst!', even Grandpa who was happy like you've never seen him, Daddy! Then they went to have a party because Uncle Horst's the new Führer and he likes me better than he likes Else . . .'

He gave the phone to Rose, who was lying on the bed and not looking at him and not talking to him. He went into the bathroom and found the tin of headache tablets in his toilet kit. When he returned to the bedroom, he found out he'd made a mistake giving Rose the phone. She was smiling one of her hard little smiles and said, 'Horst makes one ten-minute speech and everyone is charmed to death. Two years ago your father gave *you* a chance to speak. You worked on it a month and it took an hour to read and your father said, "Never again, the audience can get its sleep at home." '

He leaned towards her, clenching his fists, and she quickly rolled across the bed and got to her feet. 'Not again, you don't,' she said, a big, hard, beautiful woman who looked like death to him tonight. 'Hit me once more and you can move back with your parents.' She walked out the door, even though rain was beating against the picture window.

He shrugged. She'd be back in a few minutes, when she'd cooled down. He turned on the TV. He watched the end of a half-hour comedy and laughed a little and sneered a lot and nodded to himself at the credits with all the Jew names.

And he became aware that ten minutes had passed and Rose hadn't come back. Where could she be, walking out that way in just her skirt and blouse and not even a kerchief over her head?

He thought of it then, and ran out and along the covered ground-floor walk to where their car had been parked near the ice machine. No sign of the brown LTD, the beautiful Ford sedan Father had helped him pick out along with his own station wagon last May when Horst had been off in San Francisco with one of his sluts.

A beautiful day that, he and Father buying the cars together, not only family but fellow Nazis. He and Father so close and no Horst around to get in the way and spoil things the way he always did.

Now he turned and walked back to the room, the rain splashing him, chilling him. He walked slouched, hands in his pockets, as he had from school when the subjects had eluded him and the kids had mocked him. Before he'd grown too big to be mocked. Before he'd proved he could beat hell out of anyone, big or little, who mocked, or disagreed with him, or even irritated him. As the Führer had said, 'The one means that wins the easiest victory over reason: terror and force.' Hell, he'd known that without Hitler!

In the room he lay down again, tried to watch the tube again. Would Rose abandon him here? And Father – would he make Carl *heil* Horst, honour Horst, obey Horst as the head of the NRP? Was Horst the one who would finally turn things around for the party; for all American Nazi parties? Would he become famous, powerful . . .

He slept. He dreamt. He'd had dreams before, of course, but nothing that had bothered him very much since childhood. Back then he would come awake crying about falling from cliffs, or, after that cramp while swimming in the pond, about sinking and drown-

237

ing. Father had slapped him, saying no young Nazi 'weeps like a woman', and in truth he hadn't had many after that.

Not even the Fairfax killing had led to nightmares. To fear, yes. He was afraid of the police and of going to jail, but somehow he didn't dream about it. Maybe because the boy who'd died was a Jew and therefore not quite human to him. So the deeper fear, the fear of being a murderer in the eyes of God, was missing, and no guilt touched his soul.

But now he had something that not only touched but *burned* his soul. Now he feared and hated, and the object was *very* human to him: Horst, his brother. Now he saw an amalgam from the old newsreels of Hitler's rise to power: the massed thousands of Brown Shirts; the swastika flags and standards; the thundering kettledrums; the broad stone steps rising to the wide stone podium on which stood the group of leaders.

And above that group, on a height alone, stood the Führer, one hand on hip, the other gesturing imperiously. Only it wasn't Adolf Hitler. It was Horst Schleisser.

Horst had grown the little black moustache and combed his hair over one side of his brow and he spoke in the hysterical German outpouring just like Hitler. But Carl was somewhere close by and he knew it was his kid brother. Recognized the face and the voice, then recognized the cynical little smile as Horst the Führer turned his head and winked at him.

Carl was stunned. Horst was faking the whole thing! Horst had control of all these thousands of Nazis, had all this power, and he was laughing at it, at them, at himself!

He said, 'You can't do that, Horst. What will Father say?'

Horst the Führer pointed down at the next level, where Father stood with Göring and Goebbels and Himmler and Lincoln Rockwell and Mussolini and some Japs too. Father was smiling proudly, adoringly at

Horst. Then he looked at Carl and said, 'Get down there with the troops, *dummkopf!*'

Horst's voice rose shrill and hysterical: 'With the troops, *dummkopf*! Or into concentration camp!'

Carl was afraid, but not of Horst. He was afraid of Father and the famous Nazis. He was afraid of the thousands of storm-troops . . .

They were gone! Father and the rest were gone! It was much later and he'd somehow missed seeing everyone go.

Horst hadn't gone. Horst still stood there, one hand on his hip and the other outstretched. His strident German poured out and he stamped his booted foot and he lowered his head . . . and smiled cynically, mockingly at Carl. 'Didn't I tell you down with the troops, *dummkopf*? Haven't you learned to obey when the Führer commands?'

That's when the hatred, the jealousy, the blocked rage at the unfairness of it all broke free, and Carl lunged at Horst. And bellowed that foul song he'd heard in school when one of the kids had brought his father's Spike Jones record to history class because the teacher wanted 'artifacts from the actual time of World War II'.

'When the Führer says,
We are the Master Race,
We *heil* (raspberry)
Heil (raspberry)
Right in the Führer's face.'

He grabbed Horst and punched him in the face, the sides, the stomach, and kept punching, punching, hearing him scream, feeling teeth and ribs break under his fists, seeing blood gush from the nose, the mouth, the battered eyes and ears. Kept beating with his big fists and kept singing the foul song that Father had said never even to mention.

'Not to love the Führer
It is a great disgrace,
So we *heil* (raspberry)

239

Heil (raspberry)
Right in the Führer's face.'
Horst's screams began growing weaker, bubbling through the bloody mouth. And still Carl kept beating and singing, killing Horst with his fists.

After a while there was no face to punch, only a pulpy red mass. He let go and the uniform collapsed, a bag of blood and splintered bone.

'Are ve not de Master Race?
Ya ve are de Master Race . . .'
He turned to leave, satisfied, cleansed of hate and jealousy . . . and shrieked and covered his eyes. Father and the famous Nazis and the thousands of Brown Shirts were back, coming up the steps at him, clubs and guns and ritual daggers in their hands. He tried to run, but he was on the top step with what was left of Horst and there was nothing beyond but a sickening drop into the terror-filled void of childhood nightmare.

They were almost on him now, Father and the thousands of Nazis, all screaming, 'You killed the Führer!' He screamed back at them that it wasn't the Führer, it was his kid brother, Horst, the phoney Nazi, the Jew-lover, the wise-guy lech.

But they had him, the thousand hands and weapons. First among them was Father, who jammed the muzzle of his Walther into Carl's mouth. And Carl found he was still singing the foul song:

'So we *heil* (raspberry)
Heil (raspberry)
Right in the Führer's face.'
Father began pulling the trigger. Carl jerked backward, tottered, and fell into the bottomless pit, a child again, kicking and shrieking in terror, and knew that when he landed Father would slap him for daring to 'weep like a woman'.

It was Rose who was slapping. No, not slapping, rubbing his face, saying, 'Carl, stop it!'

'I was dreaming,' he said, voice hollow.

'Let's go for a ride. We're getting cabin fever.'

'All right. I'll wash my face. I'm sorry about before; you know.'

He went into the bathroom and splashed cold water on his face. And thought that if Adolf Hitler had had an older brother, he'd never have lived to be Führer!

Horst said he was sick and couldn't think of what to do about the black; and he was more than sick, he was horrified, terrified. He couldn't be sure, but he felt that the stranger in the raincoat had done something to him. He had caught a glimpse of a white cord and seen the man's hand moving near the fluorescent fixture.

He thought about it, and the feeling grew that he'd been attacked in some novel, clever way.

And why not? If the stranger was Jewish and connected with Warren Gross, he had every right to strike back at the people who preached death to his race. Death to *him*.

Horst Schleisser had never thought of it directly before, but this uniform was a death threat to an entire people. Wearing it was not only an attack, it was an invitation to *be* attacked.

He wanted to take it off forever, no matter what it meant in terms of the cash crop. His life meant more than money.

And now that reality had struck, so did Janet.

But Pop was begging him for solutions, and Clory was waiting expectantly.

He finally said, 'What did you do with the truck?'

Clory said, 'Duke compacted it at Cross's junk yard.'

'Then do the same with the Cadillac.'

Pop said, 'Yes! The Führer's brain!'

Clory nodded, not at all excited, and Horst was certain he'd thought of it himself. Clory said, 'And we'll leave the black inside to be compacted along with it, right?'

Horst shook his head. 'Don't know about that. Might be an odour in a few days. Then they'd trace it back to Cross's and we could have trouble.'

'Yeah. We could bury him somewhere.'

Horst said, 'In Cross's. Move some junk from the bottom of one of those huge piles. Bury him. Move the junk back. Tonight.'

Clory muttered, 'Tonight, Jesus. I'll call Duke. We'll all pitch in.'

Horst said, 'I can't go with you. I'm weak as a baby.' He turned to his father. 'Give me the car keys. I've got to lie down.'

Pop said, 'Yes, here,' and handed them over like a trusting child. Tomorrow he wouldn't be as trusting. Tomorrow he would begin to understand he had been abandoned by his son the Führer.

Clory got on the phone. Adolf sank into the booth and looked at Horst, eyes blinking, seeking. Horst said, 'It'll be all right.' Adolf smiled a little.

But it would never be all right. Pop was a murderer. The Nazi mania that had been building all his life had finally led to his killing a man simply because that man was black.

Horst stood up. His father followed him with his eyes. Horst felt sick at the way his father had disintegrated, and sick at the way an innocent man had been killed. 'In the morning,' he said, 'you and Clory find the Walther's shell casings out in the parking lot.'

His father nodded eagerly.

Horst didn't know if they could get away with it, but he hoped so. Destroying Pop and Carl wouldn't bring anyone back, neither Warren Gross nor the black. And more selfishly, destroying Pop and Carl might mean destroying Horst. He hadn't killed anyone, but he'd been around both times, in Nazi uniform, and how would a jury feel about that?

Definitely an accessory in the death of Warren Gross, by reason of his driving the truck. Maybe tied in to the death of the black if they failed to believe he'd been unconscious in the men's room.

He repeated, 'It'll be all right.'

Clory, hanging up the phone, said, 'I hope so, Horst.

242

Get some sleep now. We thought sure you were dead for a while.'

Horst had thought so too.

He drove out of the lot and onto the road, almost flooring the gas pedal. The further he got from Clory's, the better he felt.

When he reached the ranch and the house, he went straight from the station wagon to his van and started the engine.

His mother came out on the porch and called to him, but he merely waved and took off.

At his apartment, he began packing. Everything. The sparse furniture he would give to Goodwill or the Salvation Army. He was through here.

Emptying the medicine chest, he caught a glimpse of himself in the bathroom mirror. He tore off the uniform and shoved everything into the trash; then cut up the swastika with scissors and flushed the pieces down the toilet.

It was almost midnight when he began carrying out bags, suitcases and loose clothing. He loaded the van quickly rather than neatly, thinking that tomorrow Janet would help him get settled . . . with her.

His heart lifted.

But two deaths lay between Horst Schleisser and any real sense of joy.

NINE: *Friday, 21 December*

At six thirty, David called Thomasine's one last time before leaving for Alberto's Ristorante where he was meeting Rita Goran. He had been trying to reach Teddy since Thursday noon and couldn't understand his friend taking off this way.

Nor could Ahearn, the senior bartender, who said, 'Still nothing, Mr Howars. He never said a word to me about leaving town or not coming in. And he said nothing to his partner, who's been calling more than you.'

Neither Teddy nor Ahearn had ever brought up the mysterious partner on their own before, though Teddy had blocked a few of David's questions with bad God-father jokes.

'Look, Mr Howars, Mr Malafortuna, the partner, would like to speak to you. He thinks that maybe together you can figure out where Teddy went. He left his number.'

'I'll get a pencil,' David said, truly upset for the first time. Because if *those* people were in the dark, Teddy had covered his tracks a little too well . . . or had had them covered for him.

He copied the name and number. Ahearn began to say goodbye. David said, 'Mike, one question. You say the last time you saw Teddy he asked you to call one of the alternate bartenders. Did he say how long you'd need the alternate?'

'No.' He hesitated. 'Look, I already told Mr Malafortuna everything.'

'Tell me, please.'

Another pause. 'Well, we were real busy. Holiday Brunch you know, and the place was stacked up like you wouldn't believe. He never walks out at times like that. So that's one thing.'

But it wasn't the main thing, David knew, from the way Ahearn paused yet again.

'Before he walked over to me, he was kneeling at the cabinet under the first register.' Sigh. 'Where we keep the ledgers and where Teddy keeps his gun. The ledgers are still there. The gun isn't.'

David thanked him, broke the connection with his finger on the button, and dialled immediately. A woman with a heavy Spanish accent – the ubiquitous Southern California Mexican maid – answered with the number he had just dialled, plus, 'I help you, please?'

He asked for Mr Ricco Malafortuna, was told the Malafortuna family was away for the weekend, and left his name and number.

He returned to the master bath to splash on cologne. Because he was sweating with sudden fear for his friend.

He didn't want to fear. Especially tonight. He wanted to enjoy Rita and have her enjoy him so that they could move towards some sort of regular relationship, even if only on irregular occasions.

He also had plans to call Vanessa soon; to see her again. He felt a stirring of loss there, in addition to guilt at the sudden way in which he had dropped her: his choice of words, the 'can't get a hard-on so goodbye' kind of kiss-off, this after six civilized years. Reprehensible, no matter what the psychological pressures, the inner tensions. Behaviour suiting a Nazi.

And it was the Nazis who had brought about much of this healing thought, this positive feeling. Having struck back at them, having cleansed his soul of rage and hate – 'And let us not forget fear, Duvid'l' – he was

245

free to have some warmth, some sensitivity again. He'd even had Carrie buy a tree . . .

He'd heard himself say, 'Duvid'l.'

Only Teddy called him that since his mother had died. And Teddy was missing.

Foolishness. Teddy was a big boy. In terms of violence, a far bigger boy than Duvid'l. No one had done anything to him.

He left for Alberto's, succeeding for the moment in allaying worry for his friend. On Monday he would talk to Malafortuna – what a significant name! – if Teddy hadn't returned by then. Together they would learn the reason for Teddy's decision to take a Christmas vacation without notice.

But Teddy *would* return this weekend. Or phone to explain.

In the car, he got the all-news radio station, but the California rundown still had nothing on the young Nazi he now realized from re-reading the *Times* article was Horst Schleisser. Not a word in the papers or on television either.

Of course, it was a small story, since no one would consider it murder. A man dropping dead at a urinal. He would probably never hear of it.

But he also had to consider the possibility that the other Nazis, one of whom was the Schleisser father, *did* consider it murder. That while they might not know exactly how he had done it, they were looking for him to avenge their comrade, their child. That one of the diner's employees bringing garbage out back had noticed the Mercedes. That his licence, or part of it, was known.

Which had him glancing into his rear-view mirror, wondering if he was being followed through the on-and-off drizzle that had been LA's weather for two days.

He reached Sunset, where the heavy traffic was comforting, and he was able to continue on towards his dinner date in reasonably good spirits. Now if only

Teddy had just returned to Thomasine's and was safely back behind the bar.

But he would resist calling until tomorrow morning.

Rita Goran drove slowly, though the rain wasn't much more than a heavy mist at the moment. She was watching her rear-view mirror for a particular pair of headlights, the right (showing left in her mirror) tilted visibly downward. She wasn't certain, but thought they might have been behind her since she'd left the Thrifty's in Westwood, where she'd bought chewing gum, and that they were a few cars back in traffic right now.

She wouldn't have noticed them – wouldn't have been watching for them – if it hadn't been for something that had happened yesterday late in the afternoon. A young man had come to her door and flashed his credentials, introducing himself as 'Detective One Albert Placer'. He'd said Lieutenant Stone had asked him to check on something they'd forgotten to ask her about Vincent Rossa. 'Did he drink heavily?'

She had looked directly into the cherubic detective's brown eyes and said, 'They really waste your time and our tax money, don't they, sending you here to ask me something like that? When the lieutenant could pick up the phone and call me.'

'Routine,' Placer had muttered, and thanked her and left. But not before his eyes had checked her up and down and every which way; and not because he was attracted to older women, she would wager.

He'd been sent to see her, to know what she looked like. Which meant he was looking for her description in records of past criminal cases, past murders.

Her breath was coming fast, she was beginning to perspire, and she wanted to remain fresh and relaxed and attractive for David Howars. And sweet of breath, which was why she'd stopped to buy chlorophyl gum.

She could be mistaken, she told herself. The police weren't any different from other government agencies in their waste and duplication of effort. Placer's eyes hadn't shifted, blinked, or shown any other signs of unease when she'd kept looking into them yesterday. She could be reacting with her long-time suspicion of people's motives, especially when it came to men.

The headlights swung out some three cars back, passing two of them, and settled in behind the car directly behind her.

She was on a main route, Wilshire Boulevard. When she turned north, towards Melrose and Alberto's restaurant, she would see.

Ten minutes later, she did see. The lights turned too, and were now directly behind her.

A moment after that, the lights stopped at an intersection she'd just passed, directional signal blinking a right turn. She slowed, and a car came up behind her and sounded its horn.

She pulled to the right to allow it to pass, watching in the rear-view mirror as the car with the titled headlight made its turn, leaving Doheny.

So much for her suspicions!

She drove on, passed the Japanese sports car that had given her the horn a moment ago, and realized she was going to arrive early for her date.

She didn't want that. She watched for a gas station, saw one on next block, and pulled into it. She still had half a tank left, and in her little Toyota that meant better than two hundred and fifty miles of driving, but filling up would kill some time.

Asking the attendant to check the oil and tyre pressure stretched her stop to fifteen minutes; then she drove out and concentrated on following David's directions, turning east on Melrose and watching the south side of the street for what he called his 'comfortable, relaxing hang-out'.

She would get comfortable and relaxed too. She would drink Montrachet and eat the Italian fish dish he'd recommended. She would lose her fear of the police and lingering desire for the hateful Lois Turner and suspicion of David's feelings for her. She would show him such affection, such passion, that he would begin to love her. And remembering last time with him, she felt there was a possibility he already did.

It was Christmas vacation, and perhaps she and David would go somewhere together. Palm Springs or another of the glamorous places she'd read movie people frequented.

By the time she swung to the curb in front of the restaurant, where a red-jacketed parking attendant opened her door, she was full of hope for this evening and for a new start in life.

Tony Stone had been monitoring the surveillance on Rita Goran, which had started at noon today at her apartment. While at the station he had checked by radio with Al Pacer, who had drawn the duty. Nothing had happened, the subject remaining inside her home, until a quarter after six. Then Placer reported she was driving west on Wilshire and he was following.

Ten minutes later Placer said traffic was such that if she had any suspicions she was under investigation, she might have spotted the tail. That's when Tony Stone decided a pick-up and switch was necessary, and that he was going to take over himself. He had a two-way radio in his own car, as did most ranking officers, and the Datsun Z's comfort and hi-fi equipment would make a long, lonely Friday night bearable.

He had the radio room set up direct communication between his car and Placer's, and ran for the garage, pausing to pick up an empty quart bottle from the desk sergeant's supply, the only 'portable john' available for LA officers on stake-out. By the time he pulled into traffic, Placer was reporting the subject stopping at a Thrifty Drug.

Stone drove east on Santa Monica, hoping Rita Goran would eventually turn north, as she had the time she'd met a date at the Beverly Hills Hotel. And that date lived even further north, up in a canyon. So staying on

Santa Monica could eventually save Stone ten or fifteen minutes.

Of course, she might be cruising, stopping at stores here and there. Debbie liked to shop that way. Down to a Broadway, over to a May, then to Ohrbach's.

Whatever Goran was doing, he would stick with her. And continue the floating surveillance indefinitely. Because Placer had checked the DMV, the DWP, and the phone company for address changes, and bingo! She had lived in Hollywood, on Cherokee Avenue, which was where Andrew Kolett had lived until he was murdered on a spring night two and a half years ago. Not only that, they had lived in the very same apartment house on that very same last spring day of Mr Kolett's life!

It was beyond him why the witness who described a woman who 'looked as big as Mr Kolett . . . athletic, I'd say' couldn't also say it was Rita Goran, a fellow tenant.

And would have to remain beyond him since the witness, Mrs Amelia Grober, had gone to her reward nine months ago, this coming to light when Placer tried to interview her earlier today.

Placer said she had been eighty-three when she'd died, eighty-one at the time of the crime, which might have explained why she hadn't recognized Rita Goran in the dark. Another explanation: while the victim was a long-time tenant, almost four years, Rita Goran had lived there a total of five months; only two, the management stated, when Kolett died.

So no identification. So not nearly enough for the DA to put before a grand jury.

Just enough, perhaps, to convince someone at Parker Centre to okay a search warrant and heavy questioning, but that would be worse than nothing. That would give Rita Goran warning and she would become even more cautious, more composed and close-mouthed than she'd been at her apartment.

If he had been dealing with a hysterical type, he

might have tried to break her. But Lowery said she hadn't even blinked at the generally successful routine of sending a suspect out of the room for a glass of water, then leaving signs of an illegal search. And Placer said she hadn't bought the story of his interviewing her to find out if Rossa drank heavily: 'Practically called me a liar while looking me right in the eye.'

Too tough for games, Miss Goran. And small wonder. Tony Stone was now convinced she had killed Rossa, Kolett, and if the pattern of mass murderers held, quite a few others.

Placer's voice crackled over the radio. 'She's coming out, Lieutenant.' And five minutes later, 'Still continuing east on Wilshire, approaching Beverly Hills.'

Since Tony Stone was also approaching Beverly Hills, he decided he couldn't wait this far north any longer, no matter what Goran's eventual destination. She might suspect that she was being followed. She might abort her plans.

'She's signalling to turn north on Doheny, Lieutenant. The last stretch she was jockeying to the sides and slowing, maybe to get a look at me. Can you get here?'

Stone said he could; he was just about at Doheny himself. But the Friday night traffic had thickened. He decided he had to take a chance, and swung out left, blowing his horn and passing half in the east lane, half in the west, straddling the double yellow line. If a black-and-white appeared, he'd lose whatever time he'd gained by having to stop and show his credentials.

But his luck held and he made the two blocks to Doheny, bumping over the roadway's reflector studs, then cutting back in at the red light, squeezing between the left-turning lane and the inside lane of eastbound traffic, then cutting hard right across both eastbound lanes, horn blasting steadily, earning shouts and fingers from enraged drivers heading in all four directions, as well as on the two feed-in obliques which met at this congested intersection.

He was racing south on Doheny now, and took time to call Placer. 'Where are you?'

'North on Doheny, coming up on traffic . . .'

Stone stopped listening. He was approaching an intersection and a traffic light, red again. He leaned on his horn and swung to the right, passing in an empty stretch of parking lane, then slowed for a car going east with the light, and shot across the intersection in front of yet another car. And cut back into the driving lane as a parked car loomed up ahead.

'Where now, Placer?'

'Just leaving the traffic light at Third.'

'I'm approaching Third,' Stone said, surprised, seeing the green sign up ahead. He did just manage to cut left and make the U-turn in front of traffic. More shouts and horns and fingers, and he didn't blame them. Only a cop was allowed to drive this badly.

He looked for the two-door sedan Placer was driving, licence plate beginning 004, and saw it as a panel truck pulled left into the turning lane. Placer was now directly ahead of him. And two cars ahead of Placer, Goran's white Toyota sedan was creeping along.

He tapped his horn lightly, said into the mike, 'Al, I'm here.'

Placer immediately used his blinker to signal a right turn, pulling over at the next corner. This left Stone behind a Caddy, which was behind Goran.

When the Caddy turned into a garage-way, Stone was directly behind the Toyota. But Goran didn't know his car, so he could stay put, at least for a while.

She was barely moving, obviously watching Placer make his turn back at the intersection. To play it very cool, he tapped his horn and passed her.

He watched her in his rear-view, and saw her pick up speed as soon as Placer completed his turn. He was approaching the traffic light at Beverly Boulevard, keeping right. He was travelling slow-normal and she was travelling fast-normal, and she passed him. Which allowed him to drop back two cars and resume his tail more comfortably, so that when she suddenly pulled into a gas station mid next block, he was able to park and wait without being obvious.

On leaving the gas station, Goran continued north past Beverly and slowed as if watching for a particular street.

That street was Melrose, where she signalled a right turn. He waited behind her and made the turn as she did.

A few blocks east on Melrose, she pulled up before a restaurant and a stand-sign reading: *Minimum Valet Parking Fee $1.00.*

Stone went on to the next corner, watching in his rear-view. By the time he U-turned and headed back, she'd gone inside the restaurant and her car was being driven further east, to be parked on the street.

He went to the west corner, U-turned again, and parked at a meter where he could just see the restaurant entrance. He waited ten minutes before calling in to give his location; then lit a cigarette, got some tapes from the glove compartment, and settled back to wait with Credence Clearwater and Arthur Rubenstein.

'What's the point?' Highway Patrolman Don Manguson asked. 'It's getting dark and raining again and what would we be looking for?'

Harold Lowery leaned over to the armchair and poured another inch of Old Granddad into Manguson's glass. He didn't have a specific answer to the young patrolman's questions, but there *were* reasons in his mind. Just had to work around until he could make Manguson see them for himself. 'Well, Carl Schleisser seems to be away for the holidays, and his father . . .'

Manguson sipped, covering a wince. 'Yeah, really boozed out, old Adolf. Funny, I don't recall ever hearing he put it away like that. But of course, it's coming up Christmas.'

'Sure I can't get you some ice?' Lowery asked, half-rising from the bed. 'Machine's just down the hall.'

253

'No, that's all right.' Manguson sipped again, determinedly.

Lowery fought back a smile. He'd been the same as a youth, hating the warm bourbon but unwilling to drink it in any less manly a way than his father. Now he took a good pull, enjoying the warmth flooding his stomach. 'We're not going to get a crack at Carl until he comes back. And we're blocked from Adolf by his condition, especially since he's no longer playing 'What, me worry?' and wouldn't even let us in the door. As for Clory's, it was a morgue.'

'That's funny too, like Adolf's boozing. Clory's should be hopping this time of the year, all the Nazis and their friends hanging around the one place they're welcome. Instead, Clory puts an old wino on the counter and splits, which kills his Nazi get-together trade. Something a little off there.'

Lowery nodded. He had arrived at three o'clock from LA to meet Manguson at the Eucalyptus Lodge. They'd been driving around Bethills for almost four hours, trying to question Nazis, giving up a half-hour ago. 'Then there's Horst Schleisser,' Lowery said, 'seen on Wednesday but gone away again. And Duke Eiser taking a week off, according to Mr Cross at the junk yard.'

Manguson sipped steadily now, obviously getting used to the warm liquor. 'You can trust old Cross. He's no Nazi or sympathizer. He hired Duke years ago and stuck with him, but he doesn't allow any swastikas or crap at the yard.'

'Jim Borst,' Lowery continued, leaning back on an elbow, 'telling us we should have heard the great speech Horst Schleisser made Wednesday night and that he's a new Hitler. And surprised as hell to hear he's gone away again. The two truck drivers . . .'

'Bo Haskell and an ape known as Poison.'

'They're gone, as usual. And Hugo someone . . .'

'Verner.'

'. . . gone back to Texas. That foursome of salesmen and wives Borst told us about – split back to Merced,

254

and Borst doesn't know their names and no one else to question.'

'My point exactly, Harold. So what good will it do to go to the junk yard in the dark and rain?'

Lowery sighed. He'd hoped Manguson would pick up the nuances, the signposts. 'I'm not sure, Don. But I drove six hours to get here and I'm not about to waste it lying on my ass.'

'Wouldn't mind a few hours on my ass,' Manguson muttered. He finished his drink, and shook his head emphatically when Lowery reached out with the bottle.

'I know you gave me your time off, Don, and I appreciate it. And I appreciate your offer of spending tomorrow . . .'

'Only if there's good sense to it,' Manguson interrupted. 'Your lieutenant made good sense when he said to follow your hunch, put pressure on Carl and whoever else might crack. But now there's just no one to put pressure on, and going to Cross's isn't going to change things.'

'Tell you what. We'll go in separate cars. Let me into the work area and leave.' He got off the bed. 'I'll meet you for dinner at the steak house in a few hours, on me.'

Manguson also rose. 'We can go in one car, Harold. But give me a *reason* for this. I can't believe you're just killing time.'

Lowery got his raincoat from the closet. He wanted to be honest with Manguson; the man was invaluable up here. But giving his reasons wasn't going to be easy; required specifying what until now had been random and unspecific thought.

'You said it yourself, Don: about Adolf's drinking, and Clory's giving up holiday business, and Carl, Horst and Duke all gone at the same time. Something's funny.'

'Carl was gone before.'

'Because Carl, I believe, was the one who clubbed Warren Gross to death. And his father saw how he

255

acted when we came around last Sunday and got him away from any possible interrogation.'

'Let's say you're right. No one's been killed since, so why should *other* Nazis split town?'

Lowery buttoned his coat. He looked at Manguson, who still wore his tan patrolman's jacket. Manguson looked back at him, and Lowery nodded slightly, and Manguson gave a little laugh. 'C'mon now, Harold, we don't have any reason to believe the Nazis slugged someone else into the next world.'

'Don't we? The word you used was "funny" and I agree. *Something* happened around here a day or two ago. I'd say Wednesday, the night of the Nazi meeting, because that seems to be the break-point – the time after which everyone flew away like little fairies into the night, or drank so much magic potion they became immune to police officers.'

Manguson chuckled, zippered up his jacket and followed Lowery to the door. 'Fancy guesswork.'

'Based on circumstantial evidence and deductive reasoning.'

'But why are we going to Cross's?'

'Because there's no place left to go.'

Later, in Manguson's Pinto, Lowery said, 'There's more reason than that for checking the junk yard. Let's work backwards from all the Nazis seeming to split or withdraw at about the same time. Those I'm interested in are the Schleissers, Duke and Clory. We'll assume there has to be a reason for their actions. And the reason has to be a crime. Why else run and booze uncharacteristically? The important word is uncharacteristically. Now, we've had no crime reported here that can tie in with the Nazis, have we?'

'I checked twice, on your instructions, going back to Wednesday. The computer shows one car theft and two highway accidents in a ten-mile radius.'

'Then we assume it's a crime not yet discovered, not yet reported. A crime of some magnitude, befitting Nazis who are violent men. We assume homicide.'

256

'Shit, Harold, you'll forgive me if I think you're overworking your *assumer*.'

Lowery went on. 'So we're talking murder. And what could lead to a murder which would involve the Bethills Nazis? What previous crime do we assume the Schleissers and their friends are involved in?'

'Warren Gross,' Manguson said, voice beginning to change, to lose some of its cynical edge.

'Yes. *I'm* here because of Warren Gross. Why shouldn't someone else have been here because of him? I interviewed Gross's mother and grandmother. My men interviewed an uncle and two male cousins. The father came in from Denver for the funeral. And Warren was a member of the JDL, not exactly your lie-down-and-walk-all-over-us type of organization.'

Manguson glanced away from the misty windshield. 'You think someone came up here to avenge Gross?'

'It's a possibility; even a reasonable assumption. And continuing to work on reasonable assumptions, and backwards from the Nazis' uncharacteristic actions, we have someone coming here late Wednesday or early Thursday to avenge Warren Gross, and being killed – the as yet undiscovered crime which led to the exodus of our Nazis.'

'And since you think they got rid of one vehicle in the junk yard, they might have gotten rid of another – the car driven by the person wanting to avenge Gross?'

'Right, though we don't have even the minimal information we had about the truck used on Fairfax. We don't have anything except the fact that Duke Eiser worked for Cross on Wednesday . . .'

'And called in Thursday morning,' Manguson interrupted, 'to say he was taking a week off for Christmas. Old Cross wasn't exactly shocked since he knows Duke's drinking habits, which can bust loose around the holidays, but he *was* surprised because Duke always gave him good notice before.' He nodded to himself. 'Uncharacteristic.'

'That's it. We're going to look in the compacter and

around the yard. For whatever the Good Lord throws our way.'

Manguson turned off the two-lane highway and onto the dirt road running around to the back of the junk yard.

'If there was a killing,' Lowery said, 'there was also a body. And if they thought to compact the body along with the car . . .?'

'You thinking of bloodstains? With all this rain?'

'Scraps of flesh, bone, clothing. Bodies have a way of refusing to be completely disposed of. The LA County Homicide files will attest to that.'

Manguson pulled up to the back gate. He opened the car door and smiled. 'Hey, another way to go, Harold!'

His smile disappeared when he tried to remove the wraparound chain from the gate posts. 'Old Cross pulled a switch on me. He put a padlock on this gate.'

'Or Duke did.'

'Yeah. Won't do him any good though. This outer fence is full of holes.'

They found one almost big enough to crawl through, some twenty feet further along to their right, not far from the pile of auto parts behind which Cross's dog had been eating its kill. Lowery held both his flashlight and Manguson's while the patrolman pulled at the frayed wire, enlarging the hole. At that point it began to rain again, and Manguson said, 'I miss the drought!'

Lowery thought he heard something respond from inside the yard. 'I hate to remind a cat lover of an unpleasant scene, but do you know what the Jim Croce song says about being meaner than a junk yard dog? I think I just heard Fido in there.'

'You're kidding,' Manguson said, freezing.

Then they both heard it, and out from behind a mountain of junk came the part-boxer part-lion (or so it seemed to Lowery), a massive shadow lunging towards them.

Manguson jerked backward, digging for his gun. 'This time the bastard gets it!'

Lowery aimed and illuminated both flashlights, saying, 'Fire into the ground.'

By which time the dog had stopped, a few feet away from the hole in the fence. It blinked in the beams of light, then crouched, drawing itself together as if about to spring. It kept growling, not barking, and Lowery saw the reason. A dog's mouth has to open to bark, and this dog's mouth was once again holding a bloody something.

'That's a foot,' Manguson whispered, gun out and aimed at the dog. 'That's an ever-loving mother-fucking human foot!'

Lowery agreed. A foot with a shoe attached. Or a half-boot, out of which projected eight or ten inches of nearly cleaned bone. 'Don,' he said quietly, 'we have to get him to lead us to the rest of his meal. If you fire your gun, he'll run and not necessarily to the body. So put it away.'

'What?' Manguson whispered. 'And have him try *us* for the next meal?'

'He's stopped growling. Just wait him out. This is our unreported crime.' And he marvelled that his assumptions, his guesses, his deductions in support of an unreasonable refusal to accept defeat, might be about to pay off.

The dog's growls ceased. They stood on one side of the fence and the dog crouched on the other. After a while the dog no longer crouched but simply lay. And began chewing over his foot and bone.

'Christ,' Manguson muttered. He belched softly.

'Don't look directly at it,' Lowery said, but his own eyes seemed riveted to that gruesome meal. He began talking to the dog in a soft, affectionate voice.

'Hey, puppy. Good dog. You got more yum-yums?'

'Lord,' Manguson groaned.

'C'mon, doggy,' Lowery said, and took a small step forward.

The dog, whose eyes had lifted as Lowery spoke, now raised his entire head and growled.

'Nice boy. We'll go have yum-yums.' He made his voice light and playful. 'C'mon now. Yum-yums!' He stooped, turned sideways, began easing through the fence.

The dog rose and sidled away, growling half-heartedly. Lowery came all the way through and spoke in the same light, playful tone. 'C'mon, Donny. We're going to the yum-yums. Nice and easy. And if you talk, make it as if to a child.'

The dog dropped the foot and loped off. Lowery quickly aimed the flashlights, arms extended as if holding two shish-kebab skewers, and hurried after the shape escaping into the darkness.

'Move it, Donny,' he sang sweetly. 'Keep watching the mutt in case I lose him.'

Manguson said, 'Yes, all right, he dropped the footsie,' and Lowery had to choke back sudden laughter.

The dog was moving fast now, and disappeared behind a huge pile of junk. Much like the one he'd last lunched behind, Lowery thought, and hurried after him, praying he hadn't gotten away. Or circled back to get the foot and then to take off.

Which would mean no body and no foot and a hell of a job digging up this place with no guarantees of finding anything.

'Better get the footsie,' Lowery sang. 'Get it now, Donny, or we might have nothing.'

'Jesus Christ Almighty,' Manguson sang back, and his footsteps withdrew.

Lowery came around the pile of junk, aiming the flashlights. Rain was running down into his eyes and neck, but he hardly noticed. Because there at the end of the twin tunnels of light was a pit extending under the outer edge of the junk pile. And the dog was tugging at something, dragging something out of that pit it had dug.

'Another footsie,' Manguson sang softly behind him. 'With a legsie attached.'

'Put a shot near him,' Lowery snapped.

The dog looked at him, growling at the change of tone, going into a crouch again.

Until Manguson fired his service revolver into the ground. Simultaneous with the explosion and barrel-flash, the dog leaped straight up into the air. He landed ass to the officers and running.

Lowery went to the pit. The dog had dug quite a way in to get at the body, then pulled it to the opening and gnawed off the left foot and leg from the knee. Lowery put down the flashlights and steeled himself to reach in and grasp the remaining foot.

Manguson came around to the other side. Between them, they dragged the body out.

It lay in the rain, earth turning to mud and running off the face, which was revealed as a middle-aged black male's. Lowery pointed at the stained and punctured area in the left front of the victim's jacket.

'And look at the throat, Harold. Either wound could be the cause of death. Knife, you think?'

Lowery didn't know, and at this point didn't much care. He had his unreported crime.

After Manguson left to call the CHP from Cross's office, Lowery found the victim's wallet in his breast pocket, complete with a thick sheaf of bills, a driver's licence, and three major credit cards. In a small flap compartment were a half-dozen business cards which listed the Theodore Brown of the licence as *Teddy Bear Brown, Restaurateur of Thomasine's* with a Studio City address.

Brown must have driven here a day or two ago from Los Angeles. The body was in full rigor, but not yet into obvious decomposition, though there was just a hint of that sickening sweetness.

Manguson returned. 'Help is on the way. Let's get over to the compacter.'

Lowery nodded, murmuring, 'In a minute,' thinking it was no longer important to find evidence of a compacted vehicle. What he now had to find was a connection between Teddy Brown and Warren Gross, which would lead to a connection between them and the Bethills Nazis.

'Congratulations, Harold,' Manguson said, patting his shoulder.

'Yeah, you too,' Lowery answered. But his feeling of triumph was gone.

Those Nazis had killed two men, one a Jew, the other a black, which was according to their preference. He knew it, Manguson knew it, and he might soon be able to convince some brass here and back home. But he hadn't made an arrest yet, and couldn't see how he was going to unless someone cracked.

He decided to stay on in Bethills well into next week. Longer, if he could get Captain Gensen to approve.

Even if he had to return to LA, he'd be back. Carl and Horst Schleisser and their friends had to come home eventually. He'd be waiting for them.

They'd had an excellent dinner and a marvellous bottle of wine. They'd left Rita's car parked on the street near Alberto's, after David tipped the attendant and reclaimed her key. Then he'd driven up to Mulholland in hopes of a break in the misty, drizzly weather that would allow them to see the Valley lights. Instead, it had begun pouring.

'Nine o'clock and all's well,' he said, laughing, feeling that even rain was beautiful tonight. Because with no view, all they could do was look at each other. All they could do was kiss, touch, grow impatient for lovemaking.

As before, her embrace was sudden and powerful, a clutching almost painful in its intensity. *Actually* painful where her long fingers dug into his sides. And her kiss, starting as a response to his own gentle brushing of the lips, increased in pressure until she was leaning over him and pressing his head back.

Again he laughed, saying, 'Easy does it,' but pushed her away because her violence did disturb him a little.

She withdrew immediately, dropping her head, saying, 'Oh!'

'Just joking,' he muttered, and started the engine, anxious to get home where they could relax and talk and *ease* into lovemaking. He had to defuse her, somehow . . . and then wondered at his thought. *Defuse.* You did that to a bomb.

He drove slick, winding Mulholland carefully, windshield wipers barely handling the continuing downpour. 'Can you believe this weather?' he asked, wanting to get the conversation going again. Not that it had gone all that well in Alberto's. She'd been very quiet tonight, that *electricity* she gave off even more evident than on their first date.

She murmured, 'Usual rainy season,' and looked out of her window.

'You haven't been here as long as I have. There was a time the rainy season consisted of two drizzles and a low-hanging fog. That was during the drought. But even before, I don't remember it being this consistently wet for this long a period of time. Day after day, with barely a break. Week after week. Three or four years running now. Maybe the weather pattern is changing . . .'

He heard himself babbling on. He was full of tension – of electricity – himself, and he hadn't been, despite his worry for Teddy, when they'd met at the restaurant.

It wasn't Teddy worrying him now; it was Rita. Rita and himself. Because he was losing the anticipation of bed. He was beginning to feel a certain dread. Not what he'd felt with Vanessa, which was simply the knowledge that he didn't want to make love. But a growing fear, an actual distaste.

He had to stop his mind from running on this way! He would ruin a good thing. A *marvellous* thing, judging by their first meeting.

Yet even then . . .

He put his hand on Rita's thigh, feeling the thick

263

hardness, the deep muscle. 'You can crack ribs with those legs,' he said, and smiled.

She finally faced him and smiled back, but weakly.

'We're both a little nervous,' he said, and moved his hand upward, almost to the joining.

He was gratified to hear her breath quicken, to hear her gasp his name when he pressed his fingers into the heated bulge.

They went right from the garage to the bedroom. They undressed, helping each other, and he refused to think of tension and Teddy and anything but Rita. And, perversely, an image of Vanessa nude in high heels, prancing about, laughing at his excitement, flashed through his mind.

'I could use a shower,' he said.

She was on her knees, removing his shorts. His penis was turgid, and when she touched it, he began to feel what he'd expected to feel.

'Shower with me,' he said, though he wanted a few minutes alone, time to clear his mind, to eliminate distress and confusion.

'My hair . . . you go ahead. I'll wait for you.'

She was still in panties and brassière. He hesitated, feeling that once he grasped that hard, swelling bottom, kissed those big, pendulant breasts, his problem would be solved.

Looking up she saw his eyes, read his look, and pressed a soft kiss to his glans.

'Yes,' he murmured, and put both hands on her head.

She took him in her mouth, and he bent over and released the brassière clips on her back. He kept saying, 'Yes, yes,' wanting to go on this way to orgasm.

But since that would leave *her* unsatisfied, he drew her up and they stumbled on the bed and fell there. She said, 'I knew you were the one. I knew it. I knew it!' She rubbed her breasts in his face and hugged him and somehow he was on his back again and her hands were pinning his shoulders again and he began to feel claustrophobic panic.

He fought it with a laugh. 'I do want that shower, so it can be perfect.'

'All right.' But she seemed to have trouble releasing him, and he had trouble restraining himself from *throwing* her away, using fists if necessary!

He said, 'Back in a few minutes,' and fled to the bathroom, where he locked the door and called himself all kinds of idiot! Before he could turn on the shower, he heard the phone ringing. He immediately thought of Teddy, but didn't want to go back into the bedroom.

Whoever it was could wait. He had to calm himself, bring order to his mind so as to save this relationship. He couldn't understand his reaction to a little kinky sex play – because that's all it was with her dominance and near-violence – when he had always welcomed games with Vanessa.

Perhaps he hadn't solved as much as he'd thought he had with the action in Bethills.

The phone stopped ringing. He turned on the water and got into a hot shower. He scrubbed and lathered and began to relax. Five or ten minutes of this and he'd be ready for boots and whips!

Vanessa hung up and stood beside the phone, swaying a little because she'd been taking two Quaaludes a day since Wednesday morning when Teddy had called to ask for Dave. Like he had in the old days when she and Dave would get caught with their pants down, caught by love and lust, and end up in her bed with the day shot for anything but more love and lust, and people calling to find out where he was and when he'd be back. Her Dave who was with someone else, she was sure of it, because when she'd cleared her head enough to call the office, Carrie had said he'd left on 'a short vacation, maybe back Friday, but hey, I thought you'd be . . .' Then Carrie had stopped and Vanessa had known Dave was with someone else on one of the little vacations they used to take together; the Palm Springs, Vegas, La Costa, Puerto Vallarta, Acapulco vacations.

She was crying and picked up the phone and called his home again. It was Friday and Carrie had said he might be back on Friday and please God let him be back because she couldn't live with the Impossible Secret any longer, not without help, and who to turn to but the man with whom she'd eaten the hundred pounds of salt? No time left to eat it with anyone else. All over for Vanessa because she had stopped fighting and felt or imagined the weakness, and felt or imagined the lumps growing under her arms, and seen or imagined the change in her stool, blood maybe.

The phone rang and rang and she was going to hang up again and go out somewhere, find people to talk to, when the ringing stopped. 'Oh Dave, bunny,' she wept. 'Oh darling.' The line clicked. He had hung up. Her mind was shocked, and momentarily cleared by shock. She couldn't believe it. Even without love, her Dave didn't do such things.

Unless he was with a woman. Unless there was no way he could talk to someone weeping and calling him darling.

She was fully dressed; just had to get her raincoat. She could take the twisting canyon short-cut and be at Del Flora in twenty minutes, maybe fifteen. Maybe ten if she said, 'Screw the rain and cliffs,' said, 'O death where is thy sting?'

But in the car she knew where death's sting was, no matter what her mother's Bible-reading claimed. 'O grave where is thy victory?' she said, speeding through the rain, hearing a horn blow to her left, thinking she may have passed a red light and not being able to stop, though she knew where the grave's victory was. It was in bringing darkness without light and sleep without waking, and she didn't believe what her mother believed about Life Everlasting and Love Everlasting, because God had given her the Impossible Secret and what was loving about that?

Dave had been love everlasting. Dave was hers and she would prove it. She would lay the Impossible Secret on him no matter who was there; stand at his door and shout it out and see if he could allow her to carry it alone and die alone. And if he really cared nothing, actually turned her away, she would know at last that human love like God's Love and Life Everlasting was a fairy tale, something to make the dark go away.

She saw the big Vineland sign and turned off Ventura into the hills and giggled as the old Jag sedan skidded and ended up facing back towards Ventura. It stalled and more horns blew and a woman was facing her in a big new car, glaring and blowing her horn and moving her lips. Vanessa got the Jag started and opened the window and leaned out into the rain. 'God bless you, darling,' she called, and the woman stopped blowing her horn and moving her lips. Vanessa got going in the right direction, and laughed, and said, 'A soft answer turneth away wrath, right Mom?'

A moment later, on another right turn, she skidded again and almost went into a Volkswagon Rabbit with a man and woman and little girl wearing a round funny hat. The little girl laughed at the jolt with which her father stopped the car, but the father and mother stared white-faced at Vanessa.

Vanessa was suddenly crying, saying, 'Sorry, sorry,' because she didn't want to hurt anyone and it was Christmas and there *had* to be a loving God and Life Everlasting because otherwise what point would there be to having mothers and fathers and little girls at Christmas?

She drove on, more carefully despite the Quaalude fog. She heard a voice and tried to turn off the radio and it wasn't on. The voice was hers. She was saying, 'Our Father who art in heaven.' She was reciting the Lord's Prayer, as she had when she was a little girl with a funny hat and her parents smiling and helping when she forgot a word. 'Hallowed be Thy name, Thy kingdom come . . .'

Immediately after the phone stopped ringing, Rita

heard the shower start. She lay in bed and tried to remain confident that this evening was the beginning of a new life.

But *why* was he in the shower? Why wasn't he here with her? Why did she feel growing despair? He had been excited, he had stiffened and wanted her, *so why was he in the shower*!

The phone began ringing again, bringing her up into a sitting position, staring at the night-table and the sleek brown Trimline. She meant to have Bell install one for her. It had push-buttons and took up much less room and David had three of them around his house . . . *and it kept ringing*.

She wanted to lift it and examine those buttons. She slid across the bed so as to be able to pick it up the moment it stopped ringing.

The shower was going full blast. The phone had rung six times and was beginning the seventh when she reached over and picked it up to see the underside of the curved instrument.

The weeping woman's voice said, 'Oh Dave, bunny. Oh darling,' and Rita hung up and slid back to the other side of the bed. She closed her eyes and told herself a man like David, a movie producer, would necessarily know and experience many women. But they were all from before he'd met her.

She had to remember that: they were all from before he'd met her, and that was only about a week ago. They'd spent a grand total of five or six hours together. They were almost strangers and she had no right to expect him to cut himself off from other women.

'Oh Dave, bunny, oh darling.' The intimacy of that weeping message tore at her. The betrayal of her feelings, her hopes brought a pounding pulse to her head. She fought back tears and whispered, 'Daddy, don't do it.'

She got up. She walked into the darkened hallway and then to the kitchen which he'd lighted on their way from the garage. She was going to get a drink of water, splash some into her eyes, regain control of herself. But she didn't go to the sink; she went to two drawers beside the sink.

The first drawer held silverware. The second held many knives, big and little: bread and carving and steak knives. The steak knives, set into a handsome board, had carved-wood handles and about four inches of Solingen-stamped steel curving slightly upward to sharp points. The very best for David Howars: clothes, restaurants, utensils, and women.

She took a knife and hurried back to the bedroom. Her purse stood on the dresser and she dropped the knife inside, and immediately felt better. If he threatened her with fists or betrayal or rejection – any of the beastly ways men destroyed women – she would protect herself.

The shower was still running. She wanted to kick that door! Wanted to break it in! Instead, she went back to bed and lay down, looking across the large room at the dresser and her purse. She was protected now. She was ready. She would not be abused.

The shower finally stopped. His voice called, 'Be there in a minute, hon!' and he sounded right again, loving again. He came out, towelling his hair, smiling. 'As the old commercial goes, "Thanks, I needed that." ' Then he jumped into bed, grabbing her and kissing her breasts.

The purse was forgotten and the weeping woman forgotten and the fire rose in Rita Goran and she wanted this man as she hadn't wanted anyone since Daddy.

Which made her pause, though David never noticed. Which made her blink and stare at the ceiling and ache in a terrible way.

But only for a moment.

David felt terrific! She was still violent in her hugging, her kissing, but then she grew still and he was able to bend over her, caressing, examining, probing. And God he wanted her now!

269

Wanted a *woman* now, to be more honest. Because he knew it wasn't Rita Goran alone who could give him pleasure. The period of malaise, of loss of appetite for everything but food, was finally over. He would love Vanessa too. There might even be others, an occasional fling, though he had never been high on promiscuity, on swinging.

His soul was no longer sick; just as when he'd been married and begun failing Arlene, then solved it by clearing up a career problem. Now he had cleared up an even deeper problem; a hate problem.

Rita was staring up at a point beyond his face, lying very still. He liked a little more involvement than *this*, and whispered her name as he began parting her legs.

She seemed to awaken, saying 'Oh Daddy,' which was a phrase as dated as Daddy-Oh, but then again she was almost of his generation.

She was coming at him in her aggressive, powerful way again. At first he tried to persist in his own style; then saw it would end in conflict and made up his mind to accept it, to lie back and enjoy it.

She crouched over him, biting his nipples and kissing his belly and working her lips down to his genitals, then took his rigid penis in a grip that had him moaning. She looked down into his face and said, 'Love me,' and he gasped, feeling he could give *any* woman love now.

She was mounting him in that sudden and violent manner. Was plunging him into her, her face twisted, her eyes closed against him as if it were an act of fury, of vengeance for some terrible crime.

A rape, yes, with her hands pinning him down and her fingers digging into his shoulders and her bottom pounding his thighs as she *used* him, worked towards milking him of strength and joy and love.

He was going to come – helplessly, angrily, but inevitably – as she humped him, eyes closed and mouth snarling, riding his penis from glans to base, panting her Oh-Daddy or Daddy-Oh. And it was as if he weren't

270

there. It was as if he were a vibrator, a dildo with which she was achieving her fantasies.

Then her right hand left his shoulder and clamped around his throat.

His approaching orgasm was aborted by the swift return of claustrophobic-type panic, followed by rage, and he said, 'Let go!' But she was beyond hearing now. She was open-mouthed and shut-eyed and into her own orgasm now. Her powerful hand squeezed his throat and he couldn't breathe and couldn't shout. He could only slap her face, as hard as possible from that awkward position.

It cracked like a shot. Her head rocked to the left, her eyes flew open and the imprint of his hand showed white against the red flush of her cheek.

He tore her fingers from his throat. 'You were choking me!' He heaved himself up, his penis already limp, and threw her off to the side. He went around the bed to the bathroom, washed quickly and returned to the bedroom. He was still trembling with rage.

'What the hell's wrong with you! Passion is one thing, but don't you know you were actually strangling me?'

She was on her stomach, face in the pillow, making whimpering sounds.

He went to the closet. He dressed in slacks, sports shirt and loafers, giving her time to turn over, to face him and talk to him.

She didn't turn over.

His anger was gone; he began to feel pity. There was something wrong with Rita Goran. This hadn't been a funky sex game, but an unconscious assault. That electricity, that tension, was illness.

'Did I hurt you?' he asked, touching her shoulder.

He heard a muffled response which he took for, 'No.'

'You really scared the hell out of me.' He laughed a little, losing the immediacy of that stranglehold. 'I think we should talk about it. Have other men reacted the way I did?'

She lifted her head a bit. 'My purse,' she mumbled.

271

He saw it on the dresser . . . and the door chimes sounded. 'I'll get rid of whoever that is,' he said, rising, annoyed at the interruption. 'It's only nine thirty. Plenty of time for a drink and talk.' He took the shiny black purse from the dresser and tossed it onto the bed.

When he left the room, she was pushing herself up from the pillow.

He didn't bother with the peep-hole at the front door, calling, 'Who is it?' with more than a little irritation in his voice. People just didn't show up at your home without an invitation, or at least a preceding phone call.

'Me, bun,' Vanessa's voice said.

He froze.

'It's important, Dave, bunny. It's my life.'

High melodrama, and Vanessa had always been in the very opposite camp.

He opened the door. She wore a raincoat, open, and nothing on her head. Her hair was limp and streaming and her face coursed by rivulets.

He stared at her, not recognizing in this haggard, unsteady woman the saucy, self-sufficient sex-pot he'd known so many years. Then he stepped aside. 'I've got a guest,' he said. 'Let's go in the kitchen.' He began leading the way.

When he glanced back, however, she was well along the hall to the bedroom, running, swaying, obviously half-bombed, and this too wasn't like her.

He started to run after her, calling, 'Wait!'

When he entered the bedroom, Vanessa was standing just inside the door, staring at Rita. Rita, who was in underwear and shoes, clutched her purse and stared back.

Vanessa turned and bumped into Dave. He grabbed her as she almost fell. She said, 'I'm sorry. But I have to talk to you.' She went around him and left the room.

He waved an arm. 'Sorry seems to be the key word tonight. We're all sorry, right?' He tried a smile. No smile from Rita Goran. She held the purse against her breast and stared. 'She won't stay long,' he muttered, and left.

He came into the kitchen, where Vanessa was sitting at the table, wearing a dish towel over her head as a babushka. He smiled, beginning to see behind the drowned-kitten look to the beautiful woman he'd cared for, if not loved. She looked up, and it wasn't rain water on her cheeks, it was tears.

'I've got leukaemia,' she said, voice trembling. 'Hodgkin's disease. I've had it for a year, maybe more. I'm afraid, Dave, bunny. I don't want to be alone with it.'

He sat down, stunned. 'A year!' And she'd never let on.

They looked at each other. After a while he took her hands from her lap and held them.

She said, 'I'll go home now. Call me when you get the chance. Tell your friend I'm sorry.'

He said, 'Have you been drinking, smoking pot?'

'Quaaludes.'

'Christ, Vanessa, that's not part of any chemotherapy!'

'I don't think I'll need them any more, if you call.'

'Of course I will.' He heard footsteps in the hall and went out of the kitchen. Rita was taking her raincoat from the closet. 'She's ill,' he murmured. 'I don't want to send her out in this rain.'

'You don't have to,' Rita Goran said, voice high and very tight. 'I'm leaving now.'

'I'll just tell her to wait. We can have a drink at Alberto's.' He began to reach into the closet for his own coat. 'We really should talk . . .'

'I don't want to talk and I don't want to drink!' Her voice had exploded in a shout; her face was twisting violently about the mouth.

As he muttered the key word, 'Sorry,' she raised her purse and hugged it to her. Her voice quieted, as did her expression. 'Please call me a cab. I'll wait in the bedroom.' Her mouth twisted briefly. 'Unless you and your friend want to use it.'

'The bedroom's fine,' he said, thinking he was well rid of this one.

She walked away.

He went to the kitchen, where Vanessa looked at him with her streaming eyes. He used the counter phone to call for a cab, then sat down with her. He took her hands again, kissed them, told her he'd missed her.

Her eyes stopped streaming. She smiled a little.

He began asking questions, aching for his long-time lover, his long-time friend. Whatever she had lacked for him, whatever he had lacked for her, the friendship part had been very real.

And with his war finally over, it was real again.

The cab came at ten, which was a half-hour from the time David's slut had arrived. For a night like this, it was average, but for Rita the wait had been endless. Not only did she want to leave this place of rejection and humiliation, but she wanted to leave before he spoke to her again, tempting her to impose the punishment he so richly deserved.

He'd struck her! He'd tossed her aside in the middle of the act of love! He'd left her for the drunken slut! He'd done more to hurt her than any man since Daddy and Will.

If not for the slut arriving, he would have died for the first two abominations. If not for the slut remaining, he would not only have died but died *slowly*!

Though of course she had to remember Lieutenant Stone and Detective Lowery and that young officer, Placer, and the car with the tilted headlight that might have been following her. She remembered reading how the police changed what they called 'tails' in the middle of an operation, which would explain the tilted-head-light car disappearing on Doheny. And there *had* been another car, that Datsun, which had turned with her onto the street where Alberto's was located.

When David entered the bedroom to say the cab was here, he also tried to hand her some money. She walked

274

past him with eyes averted. He looked terribly evil to her now. She remembered all the things she'd read about movie people and their loose morals. Then remembered a publication Will had subscribed to from the Liberty Lobby; also a number of pamphlets he'd bought through their ads which dealt with Jews.

Anti-Christ. Alien-Minded. Responsible for the Crucifixion of Jesus, the Russian Revolution and both World Wars. Manipulating the government and the media . . . and Christian businesses, Will claimed, when his own business began to fail.

After his death she'd thrown it all out and cancelled his subscription, thinking it was tripe. But now she realized the Liberty Lobby was right. Jews *were* the anti-Christ, *did* manipulate Americans.

Which was why the police were watching her! David had ordered them to!

She wished she had those articles to throw in his face, would have loved to have said something about them. But she just kept walking, out the open door and through the rain to where the cab waited. He called, 'Goodbye,' mocking her, she felt, and her hatred was so intense she almost burst into tears at not being able to act on it.

Then, mercifully, they were driving away, and she could push him from her mind as she looked out at the drenched and foggy canyon roads.

Sometime later the driver, who was young, slight and hirsute with moustache and beard, said in a bantering way, 'You have some hot-blooded young dude jealous of where you go?'

She didn't like that, sensing an insult involving her age. 'Just take me to Alberto's.'

'Yeah, sure, the man gave me directions and all.' She saw that he was looking into the rear-view mirror, and that intense light from that mirror was illuminating his eyes. 'I just meant that someone's been behind us since we came out of Del Flora and he's stuck even though I took a short cut on some flakey roads, and even

275

though I wanted to see for myself and doubled back once. So I figure the odds are we're being followed.'

She turned and looked through the back window. Headlights came around a curve and flashed for a moment before the cab went into another curve. 'You think so?' she muttered, heart sinking.

'Yeah. Want me to go to the sheriff's station?'

'Oh no,' she said, straightening in her seat. 'My son sometimes . . . no problem at all.'

The driver nodded and said no more.

Rita sat huddled in the right corner, the handbag in her lap, opening and closing the clasp. The pounding pulse was back in her head. Her mouth was dry and she took out a stick of chlorophyl gum and chewed it.

She tried to think, and couldn't. The pounding grew heavier and her fear grew with it. She turned and looked back, seeing headlights. 'Is it a Mercedes?' she asked, hoping against hope.

'I think it's one of those Jap sports cars.'

So now she knew. The police had changed 'tails' and she was still being followed. They would never stop until they put her in jail and then into the gas chamber.

She opened and closed the purse. She whispered, 'Daddy,' and he wasn't here to help and no one was here to help and David Howars was an evil Jew who had destroyed her last chance and had talked to the police, and they wouldn't listen to her and wouldn't understand that she had acted only in self-defence.

She couldn't allow David Howars to destroy her. She opened the purse and put her hand inside and grasped the steak knife.

She would fight the Evil.

Tony Stone sat in the dark on the corner of Del Flora and Nichols Canyon and smoked half a pack of cigarettes and listened to all six tapes he carried in his glove compartment. Three hours wasn't long for a surveillance, but he'd been a spoiled lieutenant for years now, and today he'd put in a full shift. Besides, this was a boring, nothing stake-out; an old broad shacking with a date. Or maybe not even that, since a Jaguar had parked on the street near the house and another woman had entered.

But he was committed to waiting for Goran to emerge, even if it took till morning, which he rather doubted since her car was parked on a main thoroughfare with daytime restrictions.

When the cab had pulled into Del Flora, he'd gotten out and walked part of the way up the little cul-de-sac, staying in the shadows on the opposite side of the street from where Goran's date lived. He'd seen the cab enter that driveway and Goran hurry out to it. The date had been in the doorway, not knowing how lucky he was to have survived.

Stone had run back to his car, and when the cab emerged from the cul-de-sac he was ready.

Not a good area in which to tail, especially with the wise-guy cabby doing a number on him with a little double-back around some connecting roads. Stone figured he'd been made and wondered who had spotted him first, Goran or the cabby. She was a tough one all right.

He dropped back, deciding that if she was going somewhere before picking up her car, he would have to cede her the privacy. He would go directly to the Toyota and stake it out until she arrived; then follow her home whether or not she'd made him. The worst that could happen was that she would sweat it, lose some of her cool.

And tomorrow night there would be a new man on the surveillance.

Actually, he should be using three or more, but he didn't have the manpower or clearance. So he himself would have to pick it up again, driving one of the official wrecks.

He came down Nichols, no longer seeing the cab. He hit Sunset and took La Cienega to Melrose and Alberto's. It was ten twenty and the streets had emptied considerably, but he didn't let it bother him, didn't hunt for secluded hiding places. He parked right out in the open, on the east corner this time instead of the west, on the same side of the street as the Toyota, which meant he would have to watch it in his rear-view and side-view. Might throw her off a little, his being in front of her, because how the hell much could a schoolteacher know about police methods anyway?

Of course, if he was right, she was a schoolteacher who had butchered a whole classful of guys!

The cab driver said, 'I think your son gave up, or maybe we weren't being followed in the first place.'

'But you said something about doubling back?'

'Well, he could have been using our tail-lights as a guide, letting us lead him through the rain and fog. It was real thick up there.'

She began to feel a little better. 'Let's make sure,' she said as they reached Fairfax Avenue, moving south towards Melrose. 'Park for a few minutes.'

'Fine with me. The meter keeps running.'

He wanted to chat, but she asked him to please keep looking for the Datsun. 'Or for any other car that might have taken over from the Datsun.' At which he said, 'Lady, that's no son,' and pulled away from the curb.

Not that it made much difference. They came towards Alberto's from the east, and facing them near the corner was a Datsun Z with someone behind the wheel. The cab driver looked at it but said nothing, continuing on to the white sedan in mid block.

He U-turned, stopping directly behind her car. She paid him what was on the meter plus a dollar. He said, 'Thanks, good luck,' and waited anxiously for her to get out.

The moment she closed the door, he U-turned again and sped away.

So she was on a dark street with rain falling steadily and her head pounding and the person who was harrassing her, persecuting her on David Howars' instructions (that article on Jews said they exerted undue control over government) sitting smugly in the Datsun with his back to her, thinking he had 'tailed' her and tricked her and was oh so clever!

Well, she could be clever too! She entered her car and started up and drove slowly forward, tapping her brake, which he couldn't know since it was her rear lights which were flashing red. He would only see her car bucking.

She turned off the ignition and of course the car stalled. She was in the middle of the street, perhaps thirty-five feet from where the head faced forward in that Datsun; the male head filled with plans to destroy her.

She started and bucked forward again. This time when she cut the ignition, she kept rolling, turning the wheels towards the curb, parking with the rear sticking out into the street as she came to jarring halt. Now she was about ten feet from the Datsun. Now she would prove who was fit for survival, she or the *men*!

She got out, walked to the front of her car, and looked helplessly at the hood. She turned and looked up the street to the west where no one could be seen entering or leaving Alberto's. She turned to the east and looked past the Datsun to the intersection and an occasional car, but no one walking in the rain. And no phone booth in sight, so what was a poor woman to do?

She held her purse in both hands and began to walk east, looking around quickly, nervously, as if frightened by being alone at night in this city so plagued by murders; as if unsure of where to seek help. She brushed raindrops from her eyes and came abreast of the Datsun, where the male head was bent low and turned away from her.

She smiled to herself. She said, 'Thank heavens!' and stepped into the street and came around the back to the driver's window, where the male head had now mysteriously turned in the opposite direction, still away from her. It could have been funny if it hadn't been so utterly evil, so dangerously calculated to destroy her.

She tapped on the nearly closed window. 'Sir, excuse me!'

The head turned; the man sat up straight; she recognized Lieutenant Stone through the rain-spattered glass. Which explained his pained smile as he rolled the window down half-way. 'Hi,' he said.

'Well, hello! And they say you can never find a policeman when you need one!' She laughed, and the pulse pounded in her head. 'I broke down right behind you.'

'I saw,' he said, and opened the door. 'If I can't start it, I'll call the Auto Club.'

But he would never do that. He would never trick and harass and torment her again. He was half out of his car, his torso clear of the door frame, bending low as people do when they emerge from cars. And she simply thrust David Howars' fine steak knife into his neck, trying to stay clear of the anticipated jet of blood.

As he screamed and plunged forward, she drew it out and thrust it in again. And as he fell onto his side in the gutter, an arm waving at her, a hand clutching at her, gurgling and beating his shoes against the car, she bent and hacked two more times at the front, at the jugular. He gave a convulsive kick and went still. The rain continued to fall and the streets ran wet and she couldn't tell blood from water.

A car passed, tyres hissing through a puddle. She wiped the bloody blade on the Lieutenant's hound's-tooth jacket; then, holding the blade with the lapel, brought a fold around to wipe the fine wood handle. She left him in the street and returned to her car. And smiled at herself for worrying about fingerprints when she was taking the knife with her; when she would use it again tonight. Smiled at herself for worrying about *anything* when they were bound to know who had done it to him and Vincent Rossa and the others.

Of course, they still couldn't prove it. If she went

home right now, they might not be able to do anything at all to her.

But she didn't care to go home. Her head still pounded. Because the one who had done so many evil things was in his rich home with his drunken slut, laughing at her.

She started the Toyota. She would return to David Howars' house. No point in being afraid of anything any more. She would punish them both. And – small, unbidden thought pushing through the growing thunder in her brain, the growing madness – might still remain free, might still survive, if she did as she always did about fingerprints and being seen.

She giggled – a childish sound – thinking it was almost Christmas and what a present this would be, finishing the last of the betrayers, then going home! Perhaps even to her real home: to New York and her son and his wife and their newly-born child. And Roger would have forgotten his suspicions about her killing his father and she would live with them, an adored mother and mother-in-law and grandmother, freed at last of the search for love.

She pulled away from the curb and drove quickly, despite the pouring rain, wanting to be done with the Evil so as to begin her journey towards that marvellous dream.

Vanessa slept, lips parted, full bosom rising and falling heavily. She'd been asleep at the kitchen table when David had returned after seeing Rita to the cab. He'd lifted her out of the chair and talked her into partial wakefulness, but the powerful Quaaludes had her in their grip and he'd had to half-drag, half-carry her to the bedroom. Where he'd removed her raincoat, pulled off her shoes, and put her under the covers.

He'd stood looking down at the pale, delicate face framed by heavy brownish-red hair; the beautiful face which had changed around the eyes where her travail showed clearly, where the threat of death had created new shadows, pouches, folds. Delicacy was turning to fragility, and he'd wondered how much time she had left.

He'd kissed her cheek, felt pain for her, felt angry and helpless.

Now it was a quarter to eleven and he sat in the kitchen, sipping a brandy, planning the day they would spend together. The LA County Art Museum had a new exhibit . . .

The phone rang, causing him to start. He moved quickly to the counter, catching it before the second ring, not wanting it to disturb Vanessa.

The unfamiliar male voice said, 'Mr Howars?'

'Yes.'

'Have you watched the news tonight?'

'No. Who is this?'

'Ricco Malafortuna, Teddy's partner. I called my home and the maid gave me your number.'

He recognized tension in the man's voice. 'What's wrong?'

'Teddy was found buried in a junk yard near a town called Bethills. I got him some information about a truck used by Nazis on Fairfax Avenue which was stolen in Bethills. You know anything about that?'

'Yes,' David whispered. No one left to call him Du-vid'l. 'Thank you. I'll take care of it.'

'Wait a minute. You'll take care of what? You know who did it? You know why? Talk to me, man!'

'Those Nazis,' David said, wanting to cry.

'What the hell was he doing with Nazis?'

'Trying to help me.' He hung up. He got his coat and went to the guest room for the case with the guns. It also held the air pistol, rat poison, hypodermics, pills, electrical urinal weapon and other nonsense he wouldn't need because he was no longer interested in perfect crimes, escape plans. He was interested only in the guns and extra ammunition, which he jammed into his raincoat pockets. Interested only in finding the Schleisser home where the *Times* said the meetings took place and where he would walk in and kill everyone there. *Everyone!*

The phone rang. He went back to the kitchen and lifted it off the cradle. Malafortuna's voice said, 'Hello? Listen, I can help you!'

He put it down on the counter and went to the garage.

No one could help him.

Rita Goran had tears in her eyes as she approached the top of Nichols Canyon and Woodrow Wilson, where she came to the required full stop. They were tears of joy, brought about by her visualizing the reunion with Roger. She dried them with a tissue; then adjusted the windshield wipers to high. It was difficult enough to see without tears, the rain once again coming down in sheets. If it kept up much longer, the floods and slides would begin.

Headlights suddenly appeared in front of her, on the opposite side of Woodrow Wilson, coming from the direction of the three cul-de-sacs, one of which was her destination. The car never even paused at the full stop, swinging out in a climbing turn towards Mulholland. As it crossed before her lights, she recognized David's Mercedes.

Without hesitation she turned after him. The Evil had to be eradicated. The final punishment – actually an extension of self-defence, of survival – dealt out before she could go home to Roger. And if anyone was with him in the Mercedes, or waiting for him at his destination, well, survival dictated there be no witnesses.

He was turning onto Mulholland, not pausing for the fullstop there either, driving dangerously fast for this kind of weather.

She crouched over the wheel, biting her lip, determined to keep pace no matter what the risk.

An eternity later – actually less than ten minutes – it became easier as they entered onto the Hollywood Freeway North, which soon merged into 5. He increased his speed to seventy miles per hour, and she moaned softly as she forced herself to match it.

There was very little traffic so she stayed in the same lane as he and back about half a city street, though she didn't think there was much chance of his noticing her. Darkness and the weather prevented her from seeing inside his car, and he had even less chance of seeing inside hers, looking back through his mirrors.

Still, the strain of maintaining that high speed on these streaming roads was beginning to tire her. She hoped he would turn off and stop soon.

Ricco Malafortuna had paced around his study a while after Howars had taken his phone off the hook. Goddam amateurs! Howars and Teddy – who was experienced enough to have known better – had gotten themselves mixed up with those Nazi creeps, and it had cost Teddy.

And cost *him*, Ricco thought. Without Teddy Bear, there would be no Thomasine Two. And even the well-established Thomasine's would suffer, might even go under. Which would be laid at Ricco's door.

'God*dam!*' he said, spitting out pieces of cigar. He felt sick, disgusted, and it was more than just business, more than pure self-interest. It was anger – building quickly, needing an outlet – at the people with the dumb uniforms and dumber emblems, who were part of what he most feared and hated: violence for insane reasons, in this case racial. Hell, he wasn't all that fond of Hebes himself, and except for Teddy he didn't have close contact with a single black. But *kill* them for that?

He got a fresh cigar and lit it, calming himself. He picked up the phone. He didn't like to disturb the big man this late, but it was an emergency and he punched out the number.

'Yes?'

'Hope I'm not disturbing you, Joseph.'

'Not at all, Ricco. What's up?'

'Teddy Brown of Thomasine's is dead.'

'I know. I watched the ten o'clock news.'

'I'd like to do something about it.'

'What can you do about it? He was dug out of a hole. Too late for intensive care.' He chuckled heavily.

Ricco produced an answering chuckle. 'You might have read an article in the *Times* last week about Nazis in the San Joaquin Valley. A friend of Teddy's says they did it.'

'So?'

'The friend is an amateur. He might try to do something and he might not. Either way he won't get us any satisfaction.'

'We need satisfaction?'

'Teddy was our man. He was part of the Organization.'

'He was a spook. He got himself killed for spook reasons. I don't consider him a part of the Organization.'

Ricco grunted away from the phone. Running into that flat, heavy voice was like running into a brick wall. 'Joseph, I'll pick up the tab for a hit. On the senior Nazi, the father, the one responsible. It's important to me.'

'That's a joke.'

Ricco grew silent. The big man's voice had changed over the course of this conversation from friendly to irritated.

Irritated wasn't good. And it continued with: 'A hit here is stupid, for no profit.'

'Well, I can see your point, Joseph. But . . .' He had to say it. 'We don't always hit for profit. There's friendship and honour. There's vengeance.'

'For a *spook*? I think you need a vacation, Ricco. I think you're a little crazy.'

Ricco grew instantly sane, courtesy of sudden terror. He laughed. 'You're probably right, Joseph. I thought I'd give it a try. I liked him, for a spade.'

'That's your business. But my business is *business*.' He chuckled, pleased with himself. 'Right?'

Ricco said, 'Right!' and, 'That's damned good, Joseph.'

'Somebody must've said it before me,' the big man said, voice friendly again. 'You straightened out now, Ricco?'

Ricco chuckled. 'Sure. Just a hot-blooded guinea blowing off some steam.'

'Save your hot blood for paisans.' The line clicked.

Someone *had* said it before Joseph. Calvin Coolidge; 'The business of America is business.' Joseph was an ignorant, fat, heavy-handed, insensitive clown!

And thinking of him like that would get Ricco Malafortuna and family sent to Lima to run a drug drop.

He would have a case of Asti Spumante sent to Joseph first thing tomorrow, and along with it a little note apologizing for his 'hot Italian temper'.

His cigar was chewed through. He put it in the ashtray as Senta knocked and said, 'Want to see the eleven o'clock news?'

'No. Call me for Carson.'

He would compose the note to Joseph. Everything would be all right. He would remember the Godfather movies, the other Mafia movies and TV shows, the ones with honour and loyalty and courage.

He wouldn't allow himself to think he worked for animals.

TEN: *Saturday, 22 December*

At five thirty, despite having his window wide open, allowing rain and cold air to hit his face, and despite reducing his speed to fifty miles an hour, David felt he was going to smash up at any moment. Unlike his last trip to Bethills, he had started very late after a long emotional day. There was no way he could continue now, though he had only a half-hour to go. And even if he reached Bethills, he'd have to get some sleep.

He'd stopped for gas in Bakersfield and dozed off as the attendant filled his tank. The man said, 'I seen it before. Then we get a call for a tow truck and there's a hell of a wreck. Better stop.'

He'd ignored him, but he couldn't any longer. Livingston was up ahead, and he pulled off at the first motel sign, following a service road around in a half-circle and coming to a small, single-barracks affair with a neon sign over the office reading: *Hideaway Arms*. He considered going on to a recognizable name, like Holiday Inn or Howard Johnsons, but his exhaustion was overwhelming and he parked between the only two cars nosing the barracks.

As he got out, he noticed a lighted brace of phone booths to the left of the office, and reached back into the car for his pen and pad in the door pocket; then walked stiff-legged through what was now a very fine rain. He stretched and groaned and felt the weight of the two pistols and box of fifty centre-fire cartridges in his pockets. Enough to kill every Nazi in Bethills, but not enough to bring back his one and only friend. Nor to ease the burden of pain and guilt he felt at his friend's death, which one radio newscaster had characterized as, 'Shot several times, buried in a junk yard, and partially eaten by dogs'.

He entered the first booth and found a battered white-pages directory. He turned to the S's and ran down the page with his recessed ballpoint. And was surprised when he found it: *Schleisser, Adolph, NRP, 122 Field Road South, Bethills*, followed by a number.

He punched the top of the pen, circled the name, and copied the information onto his pad. He didn't expect to use the phone number, not even to check if anyone was home, because that might create suspicion, give some warning.

He finished, and his mind clouded, and he stumbled from the booth to the office. A bell over the door jangled. After a moment, a heavy woman in a brown bathrobe came through a back door. He signed a card, paid twelve dollars, and accepted a key; then went back out into the mist to the fifth door from the office.

The room was small and painted a gangrenous yellow, but the bed was clean and he was in it within moments. Then he dragged himself out of it to get the raincoat from his pile of clothing; to bundle it and its weaponry under the covers with him.

After which he passed out.

Rita was sure the torture was deliberate; one more thing for which he had to pay. He kept driving; driving for what seemed forever!

He had stopped once for gas and she'd passed him and pulled onto the shoulder under some heavy-leafed trees, shutting her lights. They had covered about two hundred miles at that point, and while her Toyota had been filled earlier in the evening and probably got twice the gas mileage his Mercedes did, she was worried about how much further she could go without filling up. Also, even with the overcast and the rain, it was getting lighter.

As they approached Livingston, her gas gauge showed slightly more than a quarter-tank. That and her terrible weariness made her sob dryly, 'Evil, evil!', hating him, desperate to end this agony.

At that point his directional signal flashed a right turn and he left the freeway. She said, 'Thank God!', and dropped further back.

As she exited, he made the hairpin turn onto a service road running parallel to 99, heading back south. She increased her speed, afraid she would lose him.

She needn't have worried. A few moments later the Mercedes' distinctive tail-lights flashed red as he slowed and turned into a small motel's parking area. She drove a little beyond the entrance and cut her lights and ignition. She saw him go to the phone booth, and a moment later into the office.

She caught herself dozing, and jerked awake. She saw him walk to a door and enter a room. But she wasn't sure just which room; hadn't been able to count doors from here. About a quarter of the way from the office, but that wasn't specific enough. She couldn't knock on doors, waiting for him to answer so she could put the knife into his chest or throat. She would be seen, remembered, prevented from going home to Roger.

Nor could she get a room and sleep as he was doing. She had to be able to watch, to see him leave. Had to follow him until he stopped and she could catch him alone.

What she could do now was fill up with gas at a station they'd passed a short distance back. Then she would return here, where she could see him emerge, but where he wouldn't pass her on his way back to the freeway. She would nap in the car; with one eye open, as the cliché went.

She was about to U-turn when she thought of something: despite the time he'd spent in the phone booth, she hadn't seen him actually using the phone. Maybe he'd been searching for a number. Maybe his destination.

She smiled. People said 'bookish' as if it were an insult; as if it implied a person wasn't prepared for the realities of life. But her reading had given her some good pointers in the past. Now she took her purse, left the car and walked quickly to the phone booths. Entering the one nearest the office, she saw that a directory was open, and her eyes were drawn to a name circled in ink. She took a pen from her purse, used the back of a gum wrapper to write on, and returned to the Toyota. She drove towards the gas station, though she was no longer worried about running out of gas. Local phone books didn't list towns very far away, so her quarter tank would do nicely.

That's if he had actually circled that name. That's if he was actually going there.

Perhaps she should call Adolf Schleisser and say, 'David is on the way,' and learn from the response whether he was expected?

Carl drove up to the ranch at 6.00 a.m. and pulled around facing the road, ready for a quick departure. He didn't know how Father would react to his disobeying the stay-away-until-New-Year's instructions, but Carl hadn't been able to stand another hour of this goddam 'vacation'!

Rose stirred beside him. He didn't wake her. They'd begun fighting again. He wanted his children, his normality, his father's respect once again. And more than anything, he wanted to change Father's mind about making Horst Führer of the NRP.

He heard a sound he remembered from the firing range Father had built in the far north field, before it had been planted; the sound of a shell being jacked into the chamber of an automatic pistol. He looked out his rain-spattered, fogged side-window. Father stood on the porch in baggy work pants and old lumber jacket, his Walther aimed at the LTD.

Carl quickly lowered the window. 'Father! It's me! Don't you recognize the car?'

'Who's in there with you?' Father asked, and he sounded awful and he looked even worse.

'Just Rose.'

Father didn't lower the gun. 'Get out and leave the door open.'

Rose was awake. 'What's going on?'

Carl murmured, 'I don't know. He's acting crazy.'

'Stop whispering!' Father shouted. 'Anyone else in there is going to get a bullet!'

'Father! Rose is in here! My wife!'

Father was coming down the steps. 'Stand aside,' he said, but he sounded calmer because Rose had got out of the other door and was staring over the top of the car.

Carl backed a few steps towards the hood. Father leaned in, the gun going before him. Suddenly he straightened and looked at the road leading up to the house. 'I hear a car coming.'

Carl heard nothing. He said so. Rose said so too. Father tilted his head, listening, then said, 'What're you doing back so soon? You want that Jew cop questioning you?'

'It doesn't bother me any more,' Carl said. 'I'm fine now, Father. We had enough vacation.'

'I said to stay . . .'

'He's fine now,' Rose interrupted. 'What's been happening here, Father?'

'Get in the house!'

The flush moved up her face, and Carl quickly said, 'Make some breakfast, honey. We'll be right in.'

She nodded tersely and walked around the car to the house. As she passed Father, she gave him a quick look. Father said, 'Stop staring! You haven't the faintest idea of how a Nazi woman is supposed to act! Carl should beat you good!'

291

She went up on the porch and into the house, slamming the door hard enough to waken everyone inside.

'That one is a bitch,' Father said, looking past Carl at the entry road. 'You sure you don't hear a car?'

Carl shook his head. 'I heard about Horst's speech.' He was going to work around to saying, 'But he's not sincere,' and so on; had been practising to himself all during the drive from San Diego.

He didn't get the chance. Father said, 'Don't mention his name again! I got a call Thursday. He wouldn't say where he was; just that he wasn't coming back.' He ran a hand over his greying stubble, and Carl saw the heavy tremor.

'I honoured him,' Father said, and now his voice too was trembling. 'All of us honoured him. His speech was good, yes, but words are cheap. The Führer followed words with action. Even unto the final action, death rather than dishonour. But Horst . . .' He spat. 'The first sign of trouble and the dirty Jew-lover runs!'

He was looking at the road again. 'I hear them,' he muttered. 'Come on.' He took Carl's arm and began walking. 'We're together in this, Carl. You killed a Jew and I killed a nigger, and in Germany we would have been given medals, but not here.'

'Killed a nigger?'

They went all the way down to the mailbox. There were no people, no sounds except the cries of birds in the heavy fog.

'Really killed one?'

Father nodded. 'At Clory's. Last Wednesday after the meeting . . .'

When he finished, Carl's heart was pounding and he was sweating around the face, just as when the Los Angeles detective had been here. Just as then, he was full of fear.

He had killed without planning to. But his father had deliberately shot a man down, nigger or not, and as he said, this wasn't Nazi Germany and he could get the gas chamber.

Carl was sorry he'd come home. Yet his father was looking at him and he had to comfort him, had to prove he could come through for him. 'Anyone could have put the body in Cross's . . .' Then he looked at the Walther still in his father's hand. 'But what are you doing with that gun? If they find a bullet in the nigger, they can match it to the gun!' He wanted to add, 'And you call me *dummkopf!*'

Father stared down at the Walther. 'You're right. I haven't been able to think since I heard they found the body last night. I keep waiting for them to come here, and they don't come.'

'Lucky for you they didn't!' He began to pull his father across the blacktop road to the fields. 'We've got to bury it! Right now!'

Ten minutes later the gun was deep under a vine and Carl's fingers were raw and filthy, earth jammed under every nail. He led his father back up the driveway, anxious to wash away the signs of that hasty burial. And comforted him at the same time. 'The police not coming is a good sign, Father. If they had anything pointing to you, they'd have been here like a shot.' But he felt they would come anyway, maybe that Los Angeles detective again, who might be a Jew and might never give up.

His father said, 'Clory, Duke, all of them left. Of course, it's a natural time to take vacations, the holiday season. But I was alone. I had to hide my feelings from your mother and the girls. Can't tell a woman a thing like this. They kept wanting to go to Merced to see Santa Claus and buy more decorations and more presents, and I couldn't leave the house. Just couldn't.'

He suddenly threw his arm around Carl's shoulder and hugged him fiercely. 'I think I went a little crazy. But now you're here, Carl. I was wrong about you – you're still my strong right arm, my tower of strength. Horst isn't a Schleisser, isn't your brother or my son. Not any more. It's the two of us, Carl, like it used to

293

be. The two of us sharing the NRP and the ranch. Sharing everything!'

Carl was still sweating, still full of dread over that inevitable visit from the police. But he was also smiling to himself, triumphant over his brother the Führer who would never get another dime from the grapes; who had made his brother the *dummkopf* a hell of a lot richer than he'd ever thought to be. And when Father died, it would all be his – the ranch and the NRP; the money and the leadership and the respect.

But most important of all, Horst would never again be able to take from Carl his father's love.

Lowery slept late because he'd gone to bed late. It had taken until 3.00 a.m. to get things straight with the Highway Patrol. 'Matters of jurisdiction,' as Don Manguson's lieutenant had put it.

Right. Couldn't be helped. But it was crap and he much preferred the loose way he'd worked with the young patrolman. Now he was on notice that every move he made was to be cleared with the CHP. Now he was in the grip of red tape and it was going to be very hard to make a quick, instinctive move.

Like the move he'd wanted to make last night at about eleven: come down on the Schleisser home with several cars of officers. Pressurize the Nazis and watch for a crack in someone's composure. Jump on that someone and widen the crack to a damaging statement, then a confession. Not forgetting, of course, to repeat the Miranda warning loudly, clearly and as often as necessary: 'You have the right to remain silent. Anything you say can be used against you . . . You have the right to talk to a lawyer . . .' To be certain no Nazi murderer walked away after conviction because his lawyer found that particular loophole. And to use the grim words as another way of breaking the Schleissers' cool; of helping them to crack.

But every idea he'd come up with had been shot down. The old man who owned the junk yard, Cross, felt certain 'Duke wouldn't come into the yard after hours,' this despite Manguson's showing everyone how easily he and Lowery had come into the yard. 'And anyway,' Cross insisted sleepily, 'he's on vacation. That Nazi business is just play-acting.'

So no APB to pick up Duke Eiser. And the local newsman, a feeder for the Associated Press, warned at eight not to mention Eiser or Nazis 'or any names at this time', and warned at 1.00 a.m. that 'nothing has changed and better remember it if you ever want another story'. Hard-nosed protection of the individual, and the American Civil Liberties Union would have approved.

Lowery didn't. Lowery was a police officer and police officers were drowning in a sea of murders and constitutional protection of the murderers. Admittedly, he said, there was no way to tie Harv Clory or the Schleissers directly to the body. But, he argued, there were the time-tested methods of deductive reasoning, circumstantial evidence, connective probability. Also to be applied to the suspects were opportunity, ability and (with some luck on the autopsy and/or location of the murder site) ballistics.

Disagreeing when he finally arrived on the scene was the jockey-sized local DA, Andrew Molineux, who was annoyed at being rousted from his bed, especially since he was on vacation until after New Year's.

'Not one hard piece of evidence,' Molineux said, confirming Lowery's suspicion that all brass everywhere used the same few expressions to torment all investigators everywhere. 'Not a single fingerprint. Not a single bullet or fragment of bullet. Not a single witness. *Nothing* at this stage. So we *do* nothing at this stage. We wait until an autopsy, an investigation of various possible murder sites . . .' he'd glanced at CHP Lieutenant Ahearn, as massive as Molineux was diminuitive, who had shrugged, '. . . a witness, brings forth evidence on which to base action.'

Lowery groaned. Lowery pleaded: just authorize a

quick swoop-down on the Schleisser home, the centre of Nazi activity in this area, and see what could be found. A gun that had been recently fired. A nervous Nazi. A woman who'd been told too much and was about to grow hysterical. Mr Carl Schleisser ready to crack wide open.

District Attorney Molineux and Highway Patrol Lieutenant Ahearn said they would take it up with their superiors, would bring it under advisement, would certainly be able to get approval for 'a standard police inquiry which might turn up what you want'.

In a pig's ass! That standard police inquiry would take place in a day or two, after everyone at CHP, the DA's office, the coroner's office, his own superiors at Parker Centre, his own assistant DA assigned to the case, and who the hell knew who else, had mulled it over and given their astute judgements. Which would add up to: *No Hard Evidence.* And the passage of that day or two would give the Nazis time to set up their stories, their alibis; pull themselves together.

He had wondered what Tony Stone would do in his place. It was on his mind when he fell into an uneasy sleep, and it helped awaken him a little after noon of another grey, rainy day. Without leaving the warm bed for the chill room, he reached to the nightstand and the phone. He called Stone's home first. When there was no answer, he called the Santa Monica North Station, where young Placer's brief, sombre statement brought him bolt upright.

'Jesus, no! Who was he on?' Then, 'Yeah, take this number; keep me informed.' He hung up, feeling sick. You knew it went with the territory, but a middle-aged lady schoolteacher?

It could have been someone else; some junkie thinking to take a guy in a car on a dark street. But Rita Goran wasn't home and the longer she stayed away the more it looked like the middle-aged lady schoolteacher was everything Stone had thought she was, a middle-aged lady monster.

That and the American Nazis and the weather made this a morning Harold Lowery would just as soon have skipped.

But he had to get back to DA Molineux and CHP Lieutenant Ahearn and find out if they'd been able to goose the coroner's office into doing its job on 'this most inconvenient weekend', to quote Molineux.

First, however, he called his SIT at the West Los Angeles Station and spoke to Detective Two Clawson, who gave him the first positive news he'd had in what seemed like years. 'That piece of metal you found in the compacter. We got a call from the FBI who got a call from GM. It's definitely from a Chevy Series Sixty truck.'

Okay. Small potatoes. But another brick in the jailhouse he was building around the Nazis. Certainly something to strengthen his own conviction that they were involved in two killings.

But after speaking to Ahearn and Molineux, after learning that 'this most inconvenient weekend' was going to go by without clearance for 'interrogation of anyone but Duke Eiser, if he appears', and that the coroner would perform his autopsy 'sometime Monday', Lowery pulled the covers over his head and shut out the whole fucking town of Bethills!

Stone wouldn't have waited until the autopsy report, he was sure of it. Stone would have begun the interrogation, begun the tricks like the ones he had tried on Rita Goran – the smoking and the obvious searching – begun the surveillance and free-time tailing, all without bothering anyone higher up.

Of course, a lieutenant *was* higher up, could go a ways further than a detective two, and Stone had been on his own turf . . .

Lowery decided he was beginning to give himself excuses, beginning to adjust to the situation like a man limping to accommodate a splinter in the sole. Instead of yanking that splinter out.

He had to yank it out. Had to learn once and for all

if that nagging feeling that the Schleissers were ready to be taken was true.

He could go there right now, but, inconvenient pre-Christmas weekend or not, they might reach someone to complain to. And no Don Manguson to help forestall this; no local cop to press the right buttons, because Manguson couldn't buck a direct order from his superiors.

But tonight. He could catch the bastards relaxed and with no easy telephone access to officials who were at home, not offices; at dinners and churches and parties, celebrating a King of Love, and even if reached, not overly inclined to interrupt that celebration for these dogs of hate. Tonight he would choose his time and put them under surveillance. He would get one of them out alone somehow, to be shocked and frightened into helping solve both killings.

'So help me!' he said, speaking not only to himself but to the man so much on his mind tonight, his friend Tony Stone.

David saw the white car again when he turned onto Eucalyptus Road in Bethills. It was seven thirty and normal winter nightfall was intensified by that lingering, on-again-off-again rain, but he could tell the car was light-coloured when they passed under a glaring, crime-preventer street light. And knew it was white because he'd seen it earlier, after leaving the motel in Livingston, when he'd stopped at a restaurant in a shopping centre.

The small white car had drawn his attention by pausing, going on, pausing again, and finally U-turning to return past the shopping centre entrance. He'd thought then that the shape behind the wheel was a woman's. He'd also caught himself thinking that Rita Goran had a small, light-coloured car.

He hadn't seen Rita's car when they'd met at the Beverly Hills Hotel, and had only glimpsed it far down the street when he'd tipped the parking attendant at

Alberto's to give her the key and leave it there. But he recalled her saying she owned a white Datsun.

He'd forgotten the white car after leaving the restaurant, because why in the world would Rita Goran be in Livingston? Especially tonight when he was in Livingston? It had given him a chuckle, that paranoid mind of his, and he'd had little enough to chuckle about.

He'd slept from 6.00 a.m. until almost 5.00 p.m., an incredible eleven hours. A record for him, at least since those Army furloughs and long parties and even longer catch-up sleeps.

But unlike those earlier sleeps, this one hadn't been uninterrupted. Fragmentary dreams flawed it. Thoughts close to the surface of consciousness disturbed it. Not about anti-Semitic women on trains, and not about Nazis, but about sick people, dying people. One dying woman.

He'd awakened no less than five times: twice for the bathroom; the other times because Vanessa was worrying his mind, gnawing at his determination. He knew he had no choice in avenging Teddy; knew if he didn't, it would haunt him the rest of his life, making the woman on the train seem mild by comparison.

As for Vanessa (he'd told himself that fifth and last awakening), she was finished. Almost no one recovered from Hodgkin's disease.

Still, many lived on for years, good years, with chemotherapy.

And a handful – yes, he'd read of them – after what was called remission, recovered fully. Vanessa had said her doctor believed she could be one of those. But doctors would bend the truth to boost a patient's spirits. The odds were that she would die.

Die alone, if he wasn't there.

And he wouldn't be there. He could see no way to kill and escape unpunished. He was using two guns registered to him. He was driving a car registered to him. There were no escape stratagems for what he was going to do.

299

Old J. W. Colfert would have disapproved. Old J.W. would have suggested, at the least, the time-honoured Molotov cocktail. *Boom*, and the Schleissers and their loved ones would burn as his mother's and father's loved ones had burned, including any children in that house, as his parents' child-relatives had been incinerated. Equitable, correct?

But he hadn't quite been able to justify that to himself, just as he hadn't when dealing with the boy in the dream. Teddy had been shot down and he would pay back in like coin, shooting the Schleissers down.

Perhaps he should attack Clory's diner as that was the only address Teddy had? Unless that *Times* article had sent him to the Schleisser home . . .

Round and round, and he hadn't been able to get back to sleep and wanted to desperately so as to escape all thought. Wanted to sleep the day away because darkness was needed for crouching at lighted windows and being able to see targets clearly and firing at them until the odds were right for walking in and finishing them face to face.

It was a mad plan, he'd known, and he wasn't really mad enough for it, and yet had to do it. Vengeance is mine, saith the Lord, but He did nothing to avenge His people and He did nothing to avenge Teddy.

He'd finally hit on a way to sleep without dreams and thoughts. He'd found several sheets of motel stationery in the dresser and written, 'In my own hand, a final addition to my last Will and Testament, in which I leave fifty thousand dollars to Miss Vanessa Brooks.' He'd added that this was to be free of all claims by his family, and was his dying wish. After which he'd put it in the breast pocket of his raincoat, buttoning the flap over it, and fallen into a dreamless sleep.

Now he was driving down Eucalyptus Road towards Clory's diner, wondering if that was where the battle would be. It depended on who was there. It depended on who wasn't there – passers-by; innocents.

He watched his rear-view. He couldn't be sure any

longer if the white compact was there. Headlights were there, but he'd stopped watching for a while and headlights were much alike.

He decided he was fighting growing fear with anything he could find. He had spent eleven hours in bed and two hours in a restaurant and was going to spend time fooling around at Clory's when there was only one logical place for the assault, only one place he should go. He was thinking of Vanessa and cars following him and Clory's and anything but 122 Field Road South.

He slowed and used his directionals, because the lights behind him had nothing to do with David Howars and no one knew why he was here and what he was going to do. He turned in at the big sign and small diner.

Two old vehicles were parked up against the building; a shabby panel truck and an even shabbier Dodge sedan. He got out and walked up the steps and stopped at the door. No music. No loud voices.

He went inside to find two men who were perfect matches to the vehicles outside. The man behind the counter was old – at least he looked old, with sunken cheeks and grimy pallor and a surprisingly thick head of grey-streaked hair.

The man on the stool across from him, now turning to look at David, could have been his twin at first glance. Second glance revealed it was only in that shabby, derelict impression that they were alike. This one was heavier and didn't have as much hair. He quickly drained what looked like an inch of water from his glass, and the counterman moved his own glass out of sight.

David smiled. 'Little celebration never hurt anyone. Clory or the Schleissers around?'

The counterman said, 'Nossir. Not expected neither.'

'I've been invited to a special meeting.' He made himself look cautious. 'You know, NRP.'

'I'm just a replacement. Clory's gone till New Year's. Want something to eat?'

301

'I'll have it at Adolf's. 122 Field Road South, right?'

The counterman shrugged. 'Got me. I know where it's at, but I never knowed the address.'

'Refresh my memory. I was always driven there by . . .'

The counter man gave him the directions before he could finish speaking, anxious, no doubt, to get back to his 'water'.

When David came outside, he looked for the white car, didn't see it, and accused himself of continuing to play delaying games. 'Over the top, Duvid'l,' he said and got back into the Mercedes.

As he pulled onto the road, he suddenly had to urinate.

But he'd gone to the bathroom back at the restaurant in Livingston. This wasn't need, it was fear. The weight in his pockets made him want to piss. The road disappearing under his headlights made him want to piss, and so badly that he had to stop and do it at the side of the road.

When he finished and turned to his car, he saw headlights back towards Eucalyptus. Standing still. As he was.

More paranoia? Further attempts to take his mind off the way? Or was someone actually following him?

What difference did it make? If it was a Nazi, he would arrive in time to die with the others.

If it was anyone else – the mad Miss Goran who wasn't mad enough to follow him for three hundred miles – still no difference. She couldn't stop him.

If it was Malafortuna or one of his associates, they would want to help, and he would be finished before they could.

Back in his car, he floored the accelerator, racing along the unlighted rain-swept country road.

But then the skies really opened and pounded the Mercedes' metal roof and he slowed. He would have to walk in this downpour, stand in this downpour, try to aim and kill in this downpour. Perhaps he should park and wait?

The rain was a friend. The rain would keep the Nazis indoors, to be targeted in their lighted lair.

And those headlights behind him were nothing and he would *not* allow thoughts of Vanessa or rain or anything else to drain him of rage and hate and purpose!

He was gasping now, as if running instead of driving. He heard himself; heard the sounds of a man fighting for his life.

Up ahead a verticle row of small red circles danced in air. They turned out to be a line of reflectors fastened to a post, marking the entrance to a climbing dirt road. When he angled his headlights partly up it, he saw a parcel-sized black mailbox with a large red swastika on the side, and on the door the number 122.

He backed to the road and looked in his rear-view mirror. No headlights.

He drove another twenty or so feet and pulled to the right side, against a hill, the same hill, he supposed, on which the Schleisser home stood. He manoeuvered back and forth, getting as far off the road as he could. For safety's sake.

'For *stalling's* sake!' he snapped, and shut lights and ignition and got out, determined not to waste another minute. Because with each minute wasted, his nerve was also wasting.

He kept his eyes on the ground as he walked, so as not to see lights in the distance; so as not to see anything but the image he had created of Teddy lying in a hole in that junk yard, 'partially eaten by dogs'.

The dirt road was a driveway, not more than fifty feet long. But his head was drenched by the time he reached the circle and saw the house on his right. The Schleisser house. His target. Where the war would recommence.

He should have taken a hat. Or bought one in that shopping centre in Livingston. Or did he have his old golf cap in the Mercedes' trunk?

303

He was stopped again. He was wasting minutes again.

Or *savouring* minutes, a part of him cried. Savouring what few minutes might be left of his life.

He moved to the right, hugging the trees and brush which came right up to the side of the house, to a window around the corner from the porch. But it was the porch that had the brightly lit windows, while the side window gave only a faint glow, a night-light or light from the other rooms.

He came to a stop, torn with indecision.

That side window was safe to look into.

Those porch windows would commit him to firing and entering, and ending not only the Nazis' lives but his own.

His own had never seemed so sweet, and he told himself he would check out that side window, would see what he could from there, and steel himself and then mount the porch.

'You *will!*' he whispered, water trickling into his mouth, and it was salty and he knew he was being drenched from inside as well as out.

He went to the side window, crouching beneath the sill. He had yet to put his hands into his pockets where the revolvers were, the full-sized Colt Trooper in the right, the five-shot Smith and Wesson in the left.

Another form of resistance to taking action, this avoidance of his weapons. He should have had a pistol in his hand the moment he started up the driveway.

He was very tired of the war within himself now, and straightened at the window, wiping water from his eyes, drawing the Colt with his right hand. He looked into a darkened room with a lighted rectangle of doorway at the end. In this rectangle stood a very big man in what looked like part of a storm-trooper's uniform – the boots and pants. Instead of the brown shirt and Sam Browne belt, he wore a red Santa Claus jacket and was laughing as he fiddled with a hook-on beard.

The children asleep or somewhere else. The father trying on his costume for Christmas Eve.

The father was a Nazi father, and Nazi fathers had been good fathers after they'd finished work at Buchenwald and gone home to wash death from their hands. They had played with their children, become Santa Claus to their children, after murdering Anne Frank and the little boy in knickers with his hands in the air that a Nazi had photographed on his way to a death camp. After murdering the hundreds of thousands of Jewish children.

He turned to walk to the porch, free finally of doubt and fear and inner arguments. *And bumped into someone!*

He choked off a shout and darted to the left, into the shadows of the house, feeling something burn his right shoulder. And saw Rita Goran coming after him with a knife and couldn't believe it or understand it, but reacted against it by lashing out with his left hand, clubbing her in the face.

She fell, sitting down in the mud, and said, 'Evil, hitting me and rejecting me and leaving me for the drunken slut.'

He gasped for air, heart thudding, shaking his head, unable to say a word.

'You made the police follow me,' she said. 'You're the Anti-Christ Zionist and we all know what that means. You're the enemy who makes everything go wrong.' She began to cry, and began to clamber to her feet, the knife still in her hand. 'Why are you so evil?'

She was lifting the knife again, so he stooped and punched her again. And stumbled away, back towards the road, sickened, overwhelmed by her madness, her words. (Did everyone on earth hate Jews?) Overwhelmed, too, by seeing in her what someone else might have seen in him: the intense and revolting need to *kill*.

He asked himself, 'Who is she?', and didn't care; cared only to get away from here. To feel sane again.

Carl had thought it would be all right. The police hadn't come, and he and Father had drunk schnapps after putting the girls to sleep because they'd been on the go since 6.00 a.m. when he and Rose had arrived. Carl had tried on his Santa Claus outfit, and except for Father drinking more than anyone could remember, it was a good evening.

There was one other thing: Father had been hearing cars and people all day and when it got dark he kept looking out from the porch, kept going into the side room, even the back bedroom where the girls were sleeping. 'I hear them,' he'd kept saying.

Then he'd seemed to settle down, and Mom had heated up strudel and Father had eaten even more than Carl and Carl could eat strudel for the *Guinness Book of Records*! So when Father said he heard 'them' again, Carl tried to get him to laugh at the Santa Claus outfit.

But Father was going around to all the windows. And suddenly, from the side room, he said, 'I told you!', and ran to the kitchen closet where he'd put his old Remington ·30 pump-action rifle. He'd been fiddling with it since they'd buried the Walther, cleaning and oiling and loading it. Now he ran out of the house and into the rain with it.

Mom said, 'God, what's wrong with him?'

Carl said it was the schnapps and he would soon see no one was there. But then he heard him shouting and thought he heard another voice answering. He stood up from the table, the good feeling gone, fear taking its place.

If the police had come. If they'd found evidence; anything linking Father to the nigger's death. If it came out about Fairfax.

'Go and see what's happening,' his mother said.

Carl wished Rose were here. Rose would know what to do. But she had quarrelled with Father and left to see a movie in town. She'd been gone almost three hours . . .

'It's *Rose* out there!' Carl said laughing. 'I thought I heard a woman's voice.' He strolled out onto the porch. And saw Father with his back to the house, arms holding a woman around from behind, struggling with her.

Thinking it was Rose, Carl yelled, 'Let her alone, Father!' At the same moment, the woman screamed wildly, jerking like a brahmin bull. Startled, Father let her go.

That's when Carl realized the LTD wasn't here, so she couldn't be Rose. The next instant she whirled on Father, hand upraised. She had a knife, and Father said, 'Wait!', and the hand with the knife struck his chest. Father gave a high-pitched shriek, and Carl said, 'Oh God!', and stood there, frozen.

The woman was hacking away with the knife, screaming, 'Anti-Christ!' and Father had stumbled over his rifle lying on the ground behind him and was falling straight back, one hand up to stop the knife which didn't stop hacking.

The car came up the driveway, but it wasn't the LTD. The tall man jumped out and ran to the woman, who was bent over Father now, still stabbing, still screaming about Anti-Christ.

Carl couldn't make himself move until the tall man threw the woman to the ground. Then he ran to his father, who lay still, his mouth gaping, water and blood mixing on his broad chest. The gaping mouth belched air, the lips moved, the eyes blinked in the rain. His father seemed surprised. 'I only asked . . . I wanted to know . . . my property . . .' The belch came again, louder, and his father seemed to empty.

'Papa,' Carl whispered, using the forbidden childhood term.

The tall man shouted at him to phone for an ambulance.

Carl obeyed, running back to the house and phoning and not answering his mother's frenzied questions. She left. He stood there, wondering what it all meant.

The tall man finally came into the kitchen with the

woman. That's when Carl recognized the Los Angeles detective and began to understand.

The woman was saying the Anti-Christ Evil had run away and that Father had attacked her on his orders. She giggled. 'They all look so surprised.' Then her face got mad and she shouted, 'Except David! Find him! Or I can't go home to Roger!' She acted crazy, but Carl wasn't fooled. He understood it all now.

The woman had come to avenge Warren Gross or the nigger.

More would come when they found out Carl wasn't dead too.

And the police had been watching the house, just like Father thought, which was how the detective had gotten here so fast.

But not fast enough because Mom was screaming outside, 'Adolf! Adolf, don't leave me!'

The detective was changing the woman's cuffs from in front of her to behind her back, and said, 'Go out to your mother, dammit!'

Carl went. But he stopped a few feet away. His mother was holding his father in her arms, rocking back and forth, screaming his name. Because his father was dead.

He turned and walked back to the house. He shivered uncontrollably and took the schnapps and drank from the bottle. The detective – Lowery, he now remembered – was on the phone. He hung up and looked at the woman who sat at the table, head hanging, mumbling to herself. Lowery said, 'Miss Goran, tell me again why you came here. Who is the Anti-Christ Evil?'

She kept mumbling and Carl couldn't understand and neither could Lowery, though he bent close.

Then Lowery straightened and looked at Carl, a hard look, and Carl was afraid.

'You killed Teddy Brown,' Lowery said.

'No! I was away! A motel in San Diego! I can prove it!'

'Nothing you or your Nazi witnesses say is going to

308

be believed. Not as long as Warren Gross's death . . .' He paused. 'Accidental death, more or less. Not until it's resolved.'

'Accidental death?' Carl asked, shaking and drinking from the bottle. 'You give me your word?'

'The law will give you what it must. Which is that you didn't plan the assault. That it was the result of a fracas, so the charge should be second degree. I'd like to put you in the gas chamber, but the law will probably let you go in about a year. If you help the law.'

'Your word?' Carl asked, shaking and drinking and unable to meet those cold eyes. Blue, but maybe still Jew eyes that would like to destroy him as Father had been destroyed.

Lowery turned away from him, back to the phone. 'I'm getting a warrant for your arrest on a charge of murder.'

'Not murder! I hit the Jew . . . the boy, because he was trying to jump into the front of the truck with my brother.' He drank again and said, 'My brother Horst. I think he's in San Francisco. He was in Clory's when my father shot the nigg— the black man.'

Lowery took out a little card and read him his rights, just like on television, and he drank and listened to Mom screaming outside and didn't allow himself to think that his father was dead.

The woman who had killed his father put her head down on the table. He said, 'Ask her why she did it. Ask her if they're coming for me.'

'If they are, you'll be safe in jail.'

Carl nodded and finished the schnapps and sat down across from the woman, who was sleeping with her head in the strudel crumbs. He said, 'My brother Horst told Clory and my father where to bury the black.' He laughed a little and said, '*Heil* Horst,' and laughed some more, that half-bottle of schnapps getting to him.

The detective asked him questions and he told him everything – about Harv getting Duke to steal the truck and hide it at Cross's, where it stayed until the Fairfax

309

demonstration; and how it happened that the JDL Jew got killed, and how Duke got rid of the truck in the compacter and later did the same with the black's Cadillac.

By then other police were there and he saw that baby-faced trooper and said, 'Hey, Manguson,' and Manguson said, 'Tell us about the black guy, from the beginning, Carl.' So Carl told him what Father had said and where the gun was and it wasn't betraying anyone because Father had done it and Father was dead.

By then the kitchen was full of people and there were flashing lights outside and sirens coming and sirens going. He saw Rose. She was taking the girls out and they were all crying. He waved and said, 'They can't get me now, don't worry. Home by next Christmas.'

Lowery said, 'Maybe,' and walked away. Carl got scared and shouted, 'You promised!' A small man who said he was 'District Attorney Molineux' asked him to go over everything from the beginning, and he'd already done that and wanted to rest on the table like the woman who'd stabbed Father and who was now gone.

They read him his rights and he said, 'Jesus, I've heard it a dozen times!', and laid his head on the table. Someone yanked it back up by the hair and he had to tell his story again.

Suddenly he was outside being pushed into the back of a car with a heavy grille between front and back, and the driver was Manguson. His hands were cuffed behind him, painfully, and he couldn't get comfortable and said, 'Hey, fellers, don't go acting like *Jews*!'

The one who'd pushed him in was sitting down beside him. It was Lowery. He smiled and said, 'But I am a Jew, old buddy,' and slammed the door. 'Take us home, Don, you lucky devil. All the way to LA, and a day off afterwards. Who's the plainclothes bringing Goran?'

Manguson answered and they began to talk about things to do in LA.

Carl wanted to talk about Fairfax and how it wasn't his fault, but when he tried Manguson said, 'Shut your mouth! Your lawyer has to listen to that crap, not us!'

Carl realized that the Jews had got to him and nodded bitterly. But then he reminded himself of what Father thought about the defeat of the liberals and the new conservative-Christian consensus and how it all was beginning to swing their way. And he smiled and fell asleep.

The rain slackened as David drove onto the freeway. He was calm now, though still a little sick in the stomach. About Rita Goran. About ever having gotten involved with her.

But then he realized he'd been lucky to have dated her, to have triggered her madness, her hatred. If she had not shown up a few moments ago with her knife and strange anti-Semitism, he would have gone on to that porch; he would have killed the Nazi in the Santa Claus jacket and perhaps others in that house.

But seeing Rita's murderous insanity, he had suddenly seen himself. Because what was he doing there but what she was doing there? Ranting and raging and ready to kill. And it was *vile* and he'd fled from it!

Vengeance would have to be the Lord's, and he begged Teddy's forgiveness and hoped the police or Mr Malafortuna did the job for him.

He turned his mind from Teddy. It was still too painful a subject to be laid to rest with thoughts, with words. It would have to be handled as he had handled his father's early and unexpected death – not too well, with grief and guilt catching him at odd hours over a period of years.

He put on the radio and found an FM classical music station and said a little prayer of thanks for being alive to enjoy Mozart. And was home by 2.10 a.m.

He'd slept so much the night before that, while he was stiff and grimy, he wasn't at all tired. He took off raincoat, jacket and shirt, cut through on the left shoulder by the mad Miss Goran's knife but barely scratching his skin. He got a soft sweater-jacket from the front-hall closet and went to the kitchen and the refrigerator for something to eat. Mrs Gomez had made one of her great *pollo chino* casseroles, an original recipe, her own strange concept of how the Chinese prepared chicken. And absolutely delicious.

Someone else had obviously thought so too, because a third was missing.

He turned towards the hallway and the master bedroom. He had left Vanessa there on Friday night and it was now Sunday morning. Quaaludes or not, he hardly expected her to still be there.

She was, but not quite as he'd left her. Her hair was freshly washed, set, curled at the bottoms. Her scent was Chanel Number 5 from the supply he gave her each birthday. She wore black lace at the shoulders and bosom, and if he was correct that particular nightgown ended at mid-thigh.

As he looked at her, feeling the old affection, the old urge, she opened her eyes. 'Where've you been, bun?'

He said he would tell her tomorrow, or the next day; whenever they got away to Palm Springs or La Costa or Vegas; to wherever it wasn't raining.

She beamed. He showered in record time and got into bed and kissed her. He wanted to discuss her health, what had to be done, but she was healthy enough in one way and he never got the chance.

312

ELEVEN: *Tuesday, 25 December*

Lowery was apprehensive, coming up in the elevator with a gaunt man on crutches, walking down the hall into the hospital smells, the odour of pain. And the pitiful little Christmas tree on the nurses' counter did nothing to change this. 'I've hated these places,' he whispered to Maria, 'ever since I had my tonsils out.'

She laughed quietly and hugged his arm. 'This is a celebration, Harold. This is a gift from God.'

He guessed she was right. And when they entered the room in Cedar Sinai's intensive-care wing and he saw Tony Stone's eyes jump to him and jump all over his girl, he laughed too. 'Hey,' he said. 'On Saturday I was told you were almost gone. How come you didn't go?'

The slender, black-haired girl sitting beside him said, 'He's too curious about Rita Goran to go. If you fill him in, maybe then we'll get rid of him.'

Tony Stone was half-sitting up against his adjustable bed. He had a tube in his arm, and a thicker one entering the mass of bandages around his throat that Lowery preferred not to look at. He moved his right hand, and Lowery realized he was using a pad and pencil.

The girl said, 'I'm Debbie. He wants you to tell him why Goran was in that town.'

'Bethills,' Lowery said, and introduced Maria. He drew the only other chair in the room up to the bed on the side across from Debbie, and used it himself. He looked down at the pad.

313

'Who she following?' Stone wrote.

'Man named David Howars. I visited him Sunday morning and had him at the station yesterday. I still don't know why he was at the Schleisser house. The son, Carl, didn't see him and says no one else did either. Howars says he was a friend of Teddy Brown's and went a little crazy and wanted to face the Nazis. How he guessed they were involved in Brown's death I don't know. But he committed no crime. Rita Goran says he's the Anti-Christ or the devil or something. Really crackers, that lady.'

'Howars lives Nichols?' Stone wrote.

Lowery said, 'Right. Was he her date on Friday night?'

Stone wrote, 'Yes. Lucky alive.' He tore off the sheet. 'How many Goran confess?'

'Four with names. Another whose name she can't remember. And her husband back in New York. Maybe her father too, though as I said she's really psychotic right now, being held in LA County Hospital's psychiatric wing. They think she might come back a bit towards normal in time, though I doubt it'll be enough to stand trial.'

Stone's eyes showed anguish.

Lowery said, 'Well, at least she's locked away.'

Stone wrote, 'Nuts freed when not nuts.'

Lowery shook his head. 'Can't see it, Lieutenant. Not a mass murderer.'

Stone wrote, 'Yes!' and underlined it. 'Happened before!' He tore off the sheet. '*Must* go to trial!' He suddenly dropped the pencil and closed his eyes.

Debbie grabbed the bell cord. 'I think our visit's over.'

Lowery rose. 'You stay.' He wanted to say something more to the Lieutenant, who should have been happy to be alive. But Stone's eyes remained closed and he made wet gulping sounds deep in his throat.

Lowery and Maria went to the door. A stocky, greying nurse hurried in. Lowery waited as she bent over

Tony, checking his tubes and bandages, murmuring to him. When she walked out, he followed. 'How is he?'

'Doing well,' she replied mechanically. Then, seeing the look on his face, added, 'Really a remarkable survival, considering the loss of blood and tissue damage. But he gets emotional rather easily. Common enough among victims of violent crime. It takes a very long time to get over being assaulted. That's why no television, no newspapers.'

Lowery hadn't thought of the lieutenant as a 'victim of violent crime', someone who had 'been assaulted'. Cops didn't consider themselves victims, but rather soldiers who might be killed or wounded in action. Still, reviewing the scene in Stone's room, thinking of the growing number of police casualties, he realized 'victim' was the correct term.

He grew sombre, preoccupied, as they walked to his car, failing to respond to Maria's reminders of the great news – his promotion to detective three and coming opportunity to take the exam for lieutenant. Until she nuzzled his cheek and squeezed his butt and whispered she had a sure-fire cure for depression. 'If you'll let me drive. To a real fun-house. A wild place where we can do things together we've never done before. This is definitely the time for it, honey.'

He sat beside her, his excitement climbing, wondering which of the X-rated motels she had chosen.

She took him to a grey, wet, crowded Disneyland. She made him laugh and forget the mad city and the victims and his career among them.

But later that night, he remembered the Nazis, knew he could never forget the Nazis. Because he was the Lone Litvak.

Las Vegas was strangely different on Christmas Day. The major showrooms were, as the Vegas expression went, 'dark' and the custom was down to a minimum. The casinos, operating at about half staff, continued to take money from the many hopeful and pay it out to the few cynical, though there were less of both.

The weather was superb, a mild, dry sixty-eight degrees when David and Vanessa arrived at noon, and that's what they had come for. They'd been held up by a visit from a Detective Lowery on Sunday, and the same detective had asked David to 'drop in at the station for a brief run-through of your story on Monday'. Then he'd finally seemed satisfied and the vacation was on.

Not that David blamed him for doubting the reasons he'd given for going to the Schleisser home, though they were basically the truth. And while he'd sweated a bit on Sunday because of Horst Schleisser and the thought that he might pay for that Nazi's life with his own, he'd been freed of fear last night while watching the eleven o'clock news.

Horst Schleisser was alive and well in Bethills where, to quote the voice accompanying the filmed story, 'he arrived to attend his father's funeral and to co-operate with police who are continuing to investigate the Warren Gross and Teddy Brown killings.'

Alive but obviously not happy, as he stood grimly aside from his mother and a group of others identified as 'members and supporters of the late Adolf Schleisser's neo-Nazi NR party'. Stood alone except for a buxom girl who looked even grimmer than he did.

This morning's *Times* had run the same story, with the additional details that newspapers provided over television. One of those details was that Horst Schleisser was not yet charged and might never be, since he was going to provide the state with 'necessary evidence to support his brother's confession'. Also, 'The younger Schleisser, who will run the family grape ranch from Merced, has been provided police protection. Threats have been received against his life and the life of his fiancée, Miss Janet Koen, who is of the Jewish faith, another contradiction in this drama full of contradictions.'

The story then proceeded to 'the murders allegedly committed by Rita Goran of Santa Monica, whose presence at the Schleisser home is still a mystery. A local reporter stated she insisted she was following "an evil lover" identified only as "David" at present.'

The 'evil lover' was certain he would be further identified in time, but it was of no consequence. Rita Goran was in a mental hospital and Horst Schleisser hadn't died and J. W. Colfert was not only a lousy writer, he was a screw-up murderer.

Using a new movie as pretext, David had talked to an electrician acquaintance this morning before flying out of LAX, and learned that Colfert's method could well have worked, 'if the subject were properly grounded. Which depends on lots of things, like the soles of his shoes, the condition of the floor, how much juice jumps from that screen up the urine. Which also depends on lots of things, like the insulation over the raw wire covering the connection to the grille, what kind of metal the grille is, the wire itself . . .'

So David had been lucky old J.W. hadn't gone into those weaknesses, and that he himself hadn't made provisions to correct them and ended by actually killing Horst Schleisser. Who seemed to have been the very poorest choice as object of Jewish vengeance.

At six, David and Vanessa drove in their rented car to a small Presbyterian church on the outskirts of town. An ad in the local paper had read *Open to all*, and the place was jammed.

David thought the sermon moderately intelligent, the people properly worshipful, and Vanessa touchingly hopeful about her own future in the eyes of God 'Who I believe in at Christmas and not much at any other time, is that wrong, bun?'

He said it was a lot more than he felt.

Not that he wasn't a Jew. At least he'd resolved *that* in these past few weeks. But a social rather than a religious Jew. Perhaps even a genetic Jew, which was an irony, what he and so many others had fought to reject all their lives, yet in keeping with what Teddy had said that night at Canter's.

'. . . you've got to become a Jew . . . *some* kind, so you can get back to living with Christmas and shiksas and a few Nazi nuts . . . so your insides can simmer down.'

It was eleven when they returned to their suite, dinner and a little blackjack behind them, and his insides were nicely simmered down. Vanessa stirred them up again, in the good way. Afterwards, he fell asleep wondering if the dream would come now that he knew he hadn't killed his enemy.

It didn't, but he still woke up sweating and straining, Vanessa shaking his arm. 'Bun? That dream again?'

'No. Little upset stomach.'

She asked if he wanted her to go down to the lobby for some Bromo. He said certainly not, she needed her rest, the staging operation that would start her towards full recovery was coming up . . .

He stopped because far from comforting her he had brought fear to her eyes.

Then she nodded, held out her arms, hugged him. 'Yes, yes, you're right.'

He didn't enjoy being hugged now. Not by her.

He said, 'Get some sleep,' and went to the sitting room, closing the door behind him. He turned on the television and tried to forget the dream. And couldn't, as he had never been able to forget the old nightmare.

He'd been in a room with two other people: Vanessa and a pleasant young man, who were sitting together on a couch. David couldn't see himself at first, but Vanessa would smile at him, would wave a hand in his direction, and the young man also gave him an occasional smile.

Then the young man grew embarrassed; tried to stop Vanessa from speaking. And while David hadn't been able to hear her words up to this point, he began to hear them now.

'Don't feel upset for David. He's a wonderful man,

my bunny. I'll always love him, but . . .' She pointed at him. '*Look*.'

David tried to laugh away sudden anguish; tried to talk.

His laughter was a hacking cough; his voice so weak it couldn't be heard.

Vanessa said, 'He wants me to be happy. He knows I'll never leave him. But just *look* at him.'

The young man looked. David managed a palsied wave. Then Vanessa put her hand in the young man's lap and his manhood jumped up and their clothes dropped away.

David finally saw himself across the room, a shabby old man in a rocking chair, watching, nodding helplessly, because she was right. It was understandable and natural and no one was to blame.

He shut the television and went to the window. Las Vegas wasn't much of a view town. 'Carny lights and hookers,' as Teddy once said.

He missed his friend. He wondered what advice Teddy would have given about this new dream; about encroaching age and death.

Probably to ignore it, as he had done, especially with women.

He turned to the bedroom. He woke Vanessa with kisses, caresses. When she realized what was happening, she said, 'Hey, a bonus!'

Exactly. What he had left; what she had left. A bonus.

319